P9-CEB-027

GHOST
MEDICINE

GHOST
MEDICINE

ANDREW SMITH

Feiwel and Friends

New York

A Feiwel and Friends Book
An Imprint of Macmillan

Library of Congress Cataloging-in-Publication Data

Smith, Andrew (Andrew Anselmo),
Ghost medicine / by Andrew Smith.—1st ed.
p. cm.
Summary: Still mourning the recent death of his mother, seventeen-year-old Troy Stotts relates the events of the previous year when he and his two closest friends try to retaliate against the sheriff's son, who has been bullying them for years.
ISBN: 978-0-312-37557-7
[1. Coming of age—Fiction. 2. Death—Fiction. 3. Friendship—Fiction. 4. Ranch life—West (U.S.)—Fiction. 5. West (U.S.)—Fiction.] I. Title.
PZ7.S64257Gh 2008
[Fic]—dc22
2008007109

Feiwel and Friends logo designed by Filomena Tuosto

First Edition: 2008

10 9 8 7 6 5 4 3

www.feiwelandfriends.com

For Jocelyn,
Trevin,
and Chiara,
with all my love

PROLOGUE:
THREE POINTS

I can see myself lying in the dirt, on my back, on a warm, starry night, with my feet up on those rocks, ringing a swirling and noisy fire, listening, laughing, seeing the sparks that corkscrew, spinning above me into the black like dying stars, fading, disappearing, becoming something else; my hat back on my head so I can just see my friends from the corners of my eyes. I can feel the warmth of the dirt in my hair, smell the smoke, hear the horses' hooves as they move restlessly in the humid summer dark. And I can close my eyes and see the conjuring, electrified, and vaporous shapes of the granite mountains, those two fingers; parting the wind, luring the thunder in that time of year.

I never really figured out why those boys had to die. But everything starts somewhere else, and keeps going forever after you can't see it, can't see anything, anymore. I believe there's some reason beneath it all; but I'm going to stop trying to figure out those reasons because I've never been right, or lucky, one time yet. At least I can tell the truth, as well as I can remember it, about how I gave up all those pieces of myself and watched while the same thing happened to them, too. Because I can still close my eyes and feel the wet of the rain that summer, smell the horses, the blood, the river on the mountain that called three boys up, and remember how three boys died, too. And that was a terrible and frightening thing, but it was what we wanted. *I know this is what I want.* I can still hear myself saying that.

I will look back at all of the things that happened to me this past summer and I will always wonder where they came from, and will never guess where they'll go; but the more I think about that time, the more certain I've become that somehow things started in the middle, on that day after the celebration, and then bloomed out in every direction possible, away from the center, and collided with us all.

That was the day when Tommy Buller, Gabriel Benavidez, and I went swimming in our underwear in the lake and Chase Rutledge stole our clothes, just trying to be mean and nothing else, I guess. But, of course, we wouldn't let it go at just a prank.

I have tried to make sense of it as best I can; to look for the healing, the signs, the medicine in those scattered events — the running away, coming home, Tom's fight, and those amazing and beautiful wild horses that belonged to no one, but were harbored by the woman who lived on the other side of that broken fence.

And I can't help but wonder, sometimes, what might have happened if we hadn't shot Chase Rutledge.

That was the day when everything kind of blew up on us.

+ + +

But if I'm going to tell the whole truth, I guess I better start at the beginning.

ONE

Sixteen is too young to lose your mother, people kept telling me. She died in June, before the summer came.

· · ·

I had planned to wake up earlier, at 3, so my father would, hopefully, be sleeping. But when I looked at the clock and saw 3, I told myself ten more minutes would be okay, and then ten more, and then it was 4:15 and I knew I had to hurry.

I got dressed and put on my shoes and grabbed my hat. The rest of the stuff was already packed up by Reno's saddle in the tack room. I paused outside the back door and caught the screen in my gloved hand so it wouldn't slam behind me.

It was still dark. I pushed the gap in my gloves between the fingers down to tighten them to my hands. I turned up the collar on my coat; it was probably about 40 degrees. An owl called from out in the trees somewhere. There was no moon and

I had to get to Reno's stall by memory because I couldn't see the ground at my feet yet. He was excited, and made those surprised and excited horse noises like he was chuckling about a joke we were playing on someone; but the barn was far enough from the house that even if my dad were awake and had his window open, he probably wouldn't hear us.

It was almost beautiful how badly I messed things up that morning. I had planned to go south and stop at the Foreman's house and get Tommy up to come with me, but by the time I got Reno saddled, the sky was turning pale blue in the east. There'd be people up around Three Points now, so I couldn't go that way.

The night before I went to the kitchen table where the yellow legal pad kept a kind of stratified archaeological record of my family, its curling top pages rolled back over the binding to reveal the most recent evidence of life. I folded them all back over.

Dad, I fed Mom dinner and she ate a lot. She looks really good today. See you tomorrow —Love, Troy

And through and through the blue-lined pages, some in pencil, some in marker, some from him, most from me, some torn out, some just torn in half. And some, the farthest back, were in her writing, too, and I brushed my fingers across the words and felt the marks she'd left on the paper.

Dad: I'm taking Reno to camp out for a few days. You can call the Bullers' and see if Tommy is going, too. I'm going that way. Don't worry about me. I'll be back soon.

I wasn't planning on going away forever. I wasn't running away from home. I was just taking my horse out on a morning in June and I brought enough stuff with me in case I didn't come back right away.

I headed away from home north into the dark woods that covered the foothills on our upper property; past the apple orchard, Reno walking eagerly in the direction of the massive mountains above us.

Now we were alone and that was that. The moving was a lot easier than the starting.

I like how in June the day can change by 50 degrees or more; how it gets colder and colder just before sunrise; how the first light trickles like a bright fog through the trees; and how things sound and smell within that light.

By midmorning I was already sweating. I got down from my tall bay horse and took off my coat and gloves. I took a drink from my canteen and filled it again in the cold rushing water. We had been following the creek, then the river, up into the mountains. We stayed close to the water where we could, but here and there the huge slabs of granite it spilled over made it impossible to follow anything but its sound. There were big falls here, emptying into clear green pools. The pools kept plenty of trout, and I could deal with that. I had killed and cleaned other animals for food before, but I wasn't going to do that unless I really had to. I had my .22 rifle with me, but I'd always rather fish.

I wouldn't even have to do that for a while. I had some cans of tuna, some pork and beans, a small plastic box of hard-boiled eggs, some crackers, and some candy bars.

I took off my hat, a black Stetson with a flattened brim, and set it down atop a rock by where Reno was sucking at the stream. It had been a Christmas gift, too big, from my mom and dad, when I was twelve and came with its brim curled tight like some kind of carnival souvenir hat. I burned my fingers working that brim over a boiling and hissing teakettle to get it where it would sit flatter. Even at twelve, I'd never wear such a hat, pointed like a TV prop. And I never wore cowboy boots, either. I wore tennis shoes in summer, and waterproof hikers in the wet and snowy months of winter. The only music I'd ever listen to on purpose was bluegrass, avoiding the stuff that was too religious, just because I liked the instruments used in it. My pants were all 501s, and I liked them loose on my waist so we always bought them big. But I didn't wear a belt, even though Gabriel's sister, Luz, gave me a nice one for my sixteenth birthday that I just kept sitting out in my room, on display like some sort of trophy, because of how beautiful I thought Luz was, and how I felt about her. And I only wore a collared shirt for school or if we went somewhere, so I was pretty much always in T-shirts, and they were pretty much always too big and dirty from something.

you disappear in those clothes that big, Troy.

While Reno drank and rested, I climbed up the rocks along the side of the falls, which dropped about twenty feet to the pool below. From here I could look down the mountain like I was standing on a church steeple. Where the trees widened out along the rocky course of the river, it looked like a picture I had seen taken from the top of St. Peter's. In the distance I could see the break in the trees, and a thin blue slice of the lake. It was after noon when I found this place. I thought it was a good place to spend the night.

I tied a rope corral between the trees after I had unsaddled Reno.

I found a flat, soft spot of ground under a thick redwood and put my pack down against it. I spread the light sleeping bag out and brought some round rocks back from the edge of the river to build a ring for my fireplace. I walked back and forth, out and in, gathering a stack of wood and pinecones. I washed my hands in the cold rush of the water and sat down on my sleeping bag cross-legged and opened my pack. I took out what food I would eat for dinner and slung the cord-tied pillowcase of food over the branch of a redwood. The sun was already down, but that was just because of the height of the granite fingers jutting up from the mountains. The sky would still have a few good hours of light in it, but the air was already cooling, so I started a fire and ate.

It was less than a day's ride, but I had never been up this high before. I looked up through the treetops, getting darker and darker against the pale sky, at those huge smooth stone fingers. From a distance — the other side of the lake — they looked like the two fingers on a saint in one of those medieval paintings.

Reno snorted.

"I hear you. I'm right here."

I took my shoes off and made a pillow with the soft part of my pack, if there was such a part. Once I stretched out and realized I would be able to sleep in this spot, I sat back up and put some more wood on the fire. My .22 was folded in my coat alongside the open zipper of my sleeping bag.

"I'm going to sleep now so be quiet."

Reno made his laugh.

* * *

I found myself dreaming.

you disappear in those clothes that big, Troy.

We were in my old room in the house we lived in, in Guadalupe, before we moved up to the lake. I must have been four years old, but in the dream I was me, sixteen. My mom was sitting on the white chair between my bed and the door. The room seemed too small, but I think it was because I was sixteen, in my old room.

The house was laid out differently, too. My mother was looking out the window, and I was standing in front of it looking at her. But the window in my dream was really narrow and tall like the window of a church, not like the one in my house, the one we'd sit by, sometimes. I didn't look out the window, but I knew there was a dog-ear cedar fence right on the other side, and another house just beyond.

I had a brother who died in an accident. I was so small; I don't really remember him anymore, although he finds his way into my dreams. His name, unspoken, Will, was always in my head, always a question about how much his passing hurt her, made her so quiet, pushed us away from that house where I was so small.

When I sat down with her by the window, Will was between us.

My brother looked beautiful, just like he was really there,

and not a memory of a ten-year-old boy who had died so many years ago.

you're a cool kid, Troy.

I'm not trying to disappear, Will. I like these clothes. I don't want to be here.

And I was crying and it felt just like I was crying; and I was thinking, *Am I crying while I'm sleeping?* I didn't know.

She was patting the seat, wanting me to sit next to her like I always did when I was small and she wasn't sick. But then I was sitting on the edge of her bed where I was taking care of her when she was dying, and she wouldn't eat; and I was looking out the narrow pointed window from there, over the top of the graying fence, at the house, too close, on the other side.

Then I was running. I loved to run. If our school had more than sixty-five kids in the thirteen grades, we could have a track team like they did in Holmes, and I'd have been on it. I was running across a bridge, water rushing far below. A big brown dog was chasing me, biting my legs. I lifted her up as she kept biting at me, raised her over the railing of the bridge.

I want to wake up, Mom.

you disappear

I was swallowed in black, so dark I could feel it like trying to breathe in warm, thick water. Then I heard a voice, low and menacing, saying over and over, "The angel is sleeping in the woods."

I saw Gabriel Benavidez, sleeping under a tall tree. Everything was gray and dim, but I could see the glint of the little gold crucifix he always wore, burning like an ember in the fog. It was raining, but he did not move at all. And I called out, "Gabey! Gabey!"

the angel is sleeping in the woods.

✦ ✦ ✦

I felt my face when I woke up. I wasn't crying. But in my chest it felt like I had been. I had only slept for a few minutes, but my heart was pounding like I had just run a mile. I tried to close my eyes, but they kept opening and staring, just staring.

I kept looking around, to see if someone was there, watching.

We left.

We went up the mountain.

I was so tired. I took my shoes off and tied them over Reno's saddle horn. I folded my legs back over Reno and crossed my feet to the top of his hips. I hugged my arms around his neck as he kept moving forward at a slow walk. I closed my eyes, and slept on my horse's back.

he could come down to San Diego and spend the summer with us and his cousins.

My father's sister talked, after the funeral, as though I was a foreign visitor who couldn't speak English. The food was all laid out in neat little circles on long tables. Flowers were brought in after the ceremony. Guests went from plate to plate, from arrangement to arrangement, reading the cards, no doubt measuring their own generosity against others'.

And I was sitting between Luz and her brother then.

let's go outside and get our horses.

do you want to?

I don't think he wants you to come with us, Troy.

Gabe was pointing to my father. And in that dream Luz and I were standing in a zoo, looking into the cages, all empty. Only one cage held horses, but it was so full, the horses tried to push their heads out through the bars.

I know what to get you for your next birthday, Troy. A belt. Either that or you're going to have to start eating dinner at my house more often.

I loved being at her house, even if I was afraid of her mother and her father, and why did he give me that horse?

aren't you going to eat, Troy? You disappear in clothes that big.

Then I was looking out that tall, cold window again. Past rows of graying dog-ear cedar fences that turned into headstones, growing into the gables of barns, then mountains rising up. Transforming again, the rocks became two fingers of an illuminated Christ, holding a cigarette that glowed orange and exploded into the galloping fire that leapt along the ridgetops of the dark rolling hills outside the car window as my parents drove home from the hospital the night my brother died; and me, feeling like we couldn't just drive home and leave him there, like we had forgotten something and needed to turn around and get it. I was only four years old then, but the thing I remember most about that night was seeing those flames, the orange slashes of fire, zigzagging like a rattlesnake, like Tommy's crooked smile. It was all I could see in that horrible silence, the blackness of the hills against the dimmer blackness of the sky, and the pulsing, racing fire that ran toward our house, pushed by the warm, dry winds of autumn. And the orange fire became the galloping horses: Reno, riderless, in front; Luz on her paint, Doats; and Gabriel on his silver buckskin, Dusty; and Tom on the angry and arthritic Arrow, trying to keep up, laughing wildly as the hills fell away, crumbling beneath them.

the angel is sleeping in the woods.

     ✦   ✦   ✦

I jerked my hands up, to brace myself for some kind of collision. I saw stars in a black sky. I was flat on my back, lying in tall grass, shoeless. My head ached. I felt for my hat, gone. I pulled my hand back from my hair. It smelled of blood. Reno stood beside me, his nose down in the grass by my head, sniffing at me.

    And I stared up at the sky, remembering the time I'd fallen from Reno as Tommy, Gabriel, and Luz watched.

damn, Stotts. Whoever taught you to ride a horse?

I don't think I learned so much about riding as falling off from this one.

are you hurt, Troy?

no.

he's too big. I think he's too big for you, Troy. I'm going to make my daddy trade you for another one.

no, Luz, don't. I'm okay.

And she was picking up my hat, brushing it off. She knelt beside me and combed my hair back over my eyebrow with her fingers, cooling my skin, healing me. I thought it was the most perfect moment I had ever lived, and I felt Tom and Gabe's envy on me.

I'm okay, Luz. Look, he wants me to get back on.

Stottsy, that look means he's not tired of trying to kill you is all.

And Gabe laughed.

How long had I slept, or been knocked out? I was sweating on my back where I had been lying. I sat up, and pulled my knees into my chest. I stood, feebly.

I could see the blackness of the treetops cutting a jagged border around a dim sky. The sun was already rising in the east. I leaned against Reno, brushing off the bottoms of my socks, one at a time, and putting my shoes on. I wondered if I had had enough, if I should head down the mountain now and go back home.

Reno blew air through his lips.

"I'm okay, bud." I uncapped my canteen and poured a little

water on my hair. I wiped it with my bare hand. Not too much blood, not much of a cut, but a good-sized lump.

"Where's my hat?" Reno nudged my chest with his nose as if trying to answer me.

"I'll tell you what. When I find it, if it's right side up, we'll go home. If it's upside down, we'll keep going up."

It was about ten feet away. Upside down.

I ate my last candy bar, giving the final bite to Reno. I wasn't tired anymore, and although my head stung a bit when I replaced my hat, I was feeling pretty good as we set off following the ridgeline as it rose to the north. Reno was eager to ride, as well.

We rode higher into the mountains until it was nearly noon, stopping once in a while to take a drink or to allow Reno to graze a bit as I just stared and thought. We had followed the stream as much as possible, and as it forked smaller and smaller, kept along those feeder streams coming from the east.

Ahead I could see the line where the trees stopped, giving way to the paleness of granite and snow on the higher peaks. Where the upper ridge split and opened up to the mountaintops there was a nice-sized pond, brilliant green, surrounded by what looked like maybe the last stand of pine forest.

This was far enough, I thought.

you ran how far?

sixteen miles, I guess.

damn, Stottsy. I wouldn't even like to drive sixteen miles without the air conditioner on and a Coke between my legs.

what'd you do that for, Troy?

I don't know, I didn't start out thinking about how far I'd go and before I knew it I was coming into Holmes on that dirt road. And then it was either turn around and come back, or just keep going and never come back. But you know, I don't particularly like Holmes.

are you tired?

I feel good.

good enough to do it again?

yep.

you're crazy.

❖   ❖   ❖

We rode around the entire shore of the pond. It had a rock bottom, and the water was clear and cold. In the afternoon sun, dropping at an angle, I could see fish sitting still, then jerking into deeper water when Reno's hooves clapped down.

At the rounded north end of the pond, there was a crooked old log cabin set back under the dark and low pines, half-dug into a mounding of earth and rock shards so that it was hardly noticeable. It had a flat log roof, which had accumulated so much dirt and debris over the years that small trees and brush and wild purple irises grew on it. A black metal stovepipe jutted up out of the right side. It had a square doorway with no door, and one four-paned window with clouded, cracked glass.

I knew that lumbermen had built cabins a hundred years ago or so on the lower slopes, when the redwood forests were being cleared. Occasionally, signs of these old cabins would make themselves obvious along with the rusted cables and machinery that had been used before the lumber companies had to stop the clearing. This had to have been the cabin of a hunter, or maybe a hermit, but it looked sound enough. And empty, too.

"Do me a favor. Don't run off, okay?" I said to Reno as I got down from the saddle.

The cabin was maybe ten feet deep, and the window allowed for enough light that I could see everything in it. The roof sagged in some spots, but even with my hat on I could stand up straight. There was an old four-leg woodstove at the end away from the window. Like the cabin itself, it was missing its door, but the pipe looked functional. Near the stove was a bed, partially carved from the log wall and made complete with dried redwood planking. The floor was dirt, but had accumulated an eclectic macadam of bottle tops, flattened cans, rocks, broken glass, and shell casings from guns of all sizes.

A wood Coke crate was nailed to the wall, its empty square bottle cubbies having at one time served to help organize the person who put it there. A table by the window was covered with dust and pine needles, empty, unlabeled jars, one plate, two forks, and two yellow and rusted paperback books: *The Idiot*, and *Jude the Obscure*. Thumbing through them, I decided that

I'd read the Hardy book if I stayed on long enough or got bored, because the first pages of *The Idiot* had been torn out, probably to get the stove started.

I went out and took the saddle and pack down from Reno. At this side of the cabin, an old galvanized tub was half-dug into the hillside, where a slow trickle of spring water kept it constantly overflowing. Reno drank from it.

I climbed up the hill to the back of the cabin's roof and cautiously walked out onto it. The stovepipe had a crude cap made from a porous and corroded coffee can. I pulled it up and looked down the pipe to see if it was clear. A bird's nest came up with the coffee can as I lifted it. It had long since been abandoned, and there was still half a small blue paper-thin eggshell in it, a rusted drop of dried blood on its inner surface.

I could see light at the bottom of the pipe, so I knew I could probably get a fire going without worrying about not waking up in the morning.

I spread my sleeping bag out on the plank bed. I cleared off the table and put the books on top of the Coke crate on the wall. I arranged my pack and food bag on the table and went outside to gather dead wood for the stove. The moon was rising behind the trees across the pond. Reno rested patiently in the temporary corral I roped on the side of the cabin. I was suddenly very hungry and very sleepy.

I got a fire going in the belly of the stove, without having to resort to book pages as kindling. I opened a can of pork and beans and put it on the surface of the stove. When my food was warmed, I sat up on the bed and ate. Looking out the doorway of the cabin, I could see the white moon, frozen like a dripping comet in the still surface of the pond. Even now, remembering it, this was about as perfect a place as I had ever seen.

✦ ✦ ✦

Reno woke me in the morning with his usual wake-up-and-feed-me call, that laughing and untiring sound that horses make to let you know they're ready even if you're not. I slipped my feet into my shoes and went out into the bright, clear daylight. Reno was still in his pen, patiently waiting for me as though to say he approved of our new home. I untied the rope and let him go free and he ran out toward the pond, kicking his back legs like he was shaking something unpleasant off of them.

By noon I had already caught three nice-sized trout and left them tied on a rope stringer at the edge of the pond. I wasn't hungry, and would save the fish for later. I walked back to the cabin, where Reno was slurping up water from the steel trough.

"Time to do a little cleaning up, bud. I smell more like you than you do."

I always brought the same standard supplies with me when I camped out for more than a day with Tommy and Gabriel: one extra change of clothes, and a bar of soap and toothbrush, which I kept inside an old metal Boy Scout mess kit. I washed my dirty set of clothes with the bar soap in the pond, and hung them out to dry on the windowsill of the cabin. I brushed my teeth and bathed in the cold water at the edge of the pond. I dressed in my only dry clothes, still dirty and bloodstained from my fall. I'd wash that set of clothes tomorrow. Then I sat out under a tree with my canteen and some Oreos I'd brought, and began reading the Hardy book. That would please my dad;

I knew I'd have to read it in twelfth grade, if I survived the eleventh, and with the way things had been going for me this past week, and knowing I'd have to deal with people like Chase Rutledge back at school, that was a gamble anyway.

I know now that when I rode up the mountain alone that time, I was telling myself I was mad at my father, and I just didn't want to look at him for a while. But it was all so confusing, too. I hadn't spoken to him for days, since the fight we'd gotten into the night my mother died, and I was so frustrated at how he could just go on and not show that things bothered or hurt him, even if they did. And if that was what being a man meant, I guess I didn't see the point at all.

He was always like that. I knew he grew up here with Mr. Benavidez, and that when they were boys they were best friends. But when he grew up and moved away that time to start work as a teacher, they just stopped talking to each other. And when we came back here after my brother died, my dad and Mr. Benavidez treated each other so politely, like they were members of the same stamp club or something. Maybe Mr. Benavidez was afraid because he didn't know what to say to a friend who'd lost a son, but both of those men just seemed to me like they never wanted to show how things really affected them, and it always made me wonder about the cost of growing up.

And I wondered why I couldn't see my father's grief. Or why he wouldn't show it to me.

After a couple hours, the wind had picked up and big black thunderheads began rising behind the crest of the mountain. There'd be a storm coming in soon, so I penned Reno back into the rope corral and quickly set to cleaning my fish with my Dawson knife at the pond's edge. By the time I had finished, the first explosion of thunder rolled down the mountain, and a flash of lightning electrified the air from the other side of the pond.

Reno chuckled nervously from his corral as I ran to the doorway, and the first big gobs of raindrops began splattering down. Rain poured, bringing with it that honey-thick smell of summer thunderstorms, and the sky dimmed to twilight in an instant. I sat in the cabin as the rain bucketed down, eating the fish I cooked on the stove, and reading as long as the light held.

I read all day and just let the time slip by. I enjoyed reading, even if it was stories about people like Jude Fawley who just can't hold on to anything good around them.

I was already at chapter thirteen, where Jude arrives in Christminster. The language was strange and a little difficult, and I had to stop several times to admire the drama of the lightning strikes through the amber haze of the four-paned window.

The roof was fairly sound, leaking only around the stovepipe, allowing trickling drips to fall, sizzling on the iron stovetop. My eyes grew blurred with the reading.

Reno never troubled about storms. In fact, it had always been a chore to get him into the barn in bad weather. When it rained or snowed, Reno would just stand there motionless, getting drenched or accumulating white frosting, depending on the weather. I had this big tom turkey, mean and white, about forty pounds, and I could always tell when a storm was approaching in winter because before any rain or snow would fall, the turkey would get up on Reno's back as though he were riding my horse. I hated that bird. Any chance he got, he'd be after me with his claws, jumping and scratching like a fighting rooster.

Thanksgiving's coming soon, Troy.

not soon enough for me, Dad, but I don't want to have to do it.

then he's just going to keep getting bigger and meaner.

The house we lived in had sat empty for years before we moved in. It was my grandfather's place, but I never knew him. My father sometimes talked about how he never really liked the farm, and moved away when he went to school and became a teacher, but it was my mom who made him come back, and he would get quiet and angry every time she'd bring some new animals home. He'd pretty much given up, but he did tell me, "They're going to all starve to death if you don't feed them, Troy, because I refuse to do it even once."

The rain stopped just before sundown.

✦ ✦ ✦

In the morning Reno was eager to move. He stamped his hoof down and scooted it back like he was strong enough to set the world spinning away beneath him. I had put the clothes I had washed the day before by the stove and although they were still damp, I changed into them. Feeling clean and awake, I washed my other clothes and set them out on the windowsill. I put a last piece of fish inside my mess kit, packed my book and rifle, and then I saddled Reno and headed him north to the edge of the tree line.

We rode fast, Reno, always so energetic in the morning, wanting to break out into a full run where the ground was spongy from the thunderstorm. As the trees got sparser, crookeder, rubbed bare by the wind all on the same side as though a herd of goats that could only face a single direction browsed through, I looked up to a drift of snow and made out what my eyes had always allowed to blend in with the white: the wreckage, nearly intact, wing and fuselage, of an airplane.

Even if I had wanted to I could not get up to that plane; it was too high and the rocky, snowy terrain around it called for mountaineering equipment to negotiate a path. So, laying broken there like a fallen statue of a dying angel, a giant dead bird, a crucifix, it could stay there, keeping its story to itself.

When I rode away from it, I felt suddenly heavy. It reminded me of everything I had left my father's house to try to forget.

TWO

After the first week, I stopped counting the days.

I settled into the routine of fishing, looking for berries and firewood in the forest, finishing that book about Jude Fawley's miserable life, and taking Reno out for occasional runs, every day growing more and more comfortable with my quiet life in the cabin, where I never had to talk to anyone, never had to think about anyone, even if I still couldn't stop myself from doing it.

Most mornings I woke to the sound of two nesting hawks calling at each other from opposite sides of the pond. I could make out the shape of the plane from just beyond the west shore of the pond, and from time to time I would look up at it, half expecting it to be gone when I did.

I had started reading *The Idiot* at page 78, and by page 200 was still trying to figure out who all the characters were and why they kept changing their names every other sentence. I'd have to ask my dad about that sometime. I was sitting on a rock, fishing line in the water and book open, facedown, to hold my place beside me, when Reno snorted, smelling the air, curling his lip back and baring his teeth. A rider was coming from out of the trees, down the lower ridge from where I had come all those days before, no doubt coming toward the smoke spiraling up from the cabin's stovepipe chimney.

It was Luz Benavidez riding her black-and-white paint, Doats.

I'd been in love with her ever since I could remember, but I never said anything to her to make her think so. We'd seen each other nearly every day since we were kids. I always believed there was a wildness that Luz loved; something I would never have, someone that I could never be. And I wasn't good enough, or handsome enough for her, anyway. I bit the inside of my mouth so many times when I was around her just to make it hurt so I wouldn't have to think about her. But it never really worked, and I'd come home some days after school and throw myself down on my bed, frustrated that she never noticed me and that she always treated me just like she treated her younger brother, Gabriel.

And we were such close friends that I was afraid I'd ruin it by telling her I loved her. Sometimes, it was hard enough for me just to say hello to that girl, anyway.

I watched her as she rode along the shore of the pond, confident, sitting straight. I didn't realize until then how much I had missed my friends. And she looked beautiful, her hair, gold and brown, tied back in two braids wrapped around her head and tucked up into her hat, her pale green eyes shining and visible even at a distance. She was looking right at me and smiling.

She jumped down from Doats and hugged me tight.

"Are you okay?"

"I guess so."

"Well, if you wanted to disappear, you could have done a better job. I've only been out since this morning and I came straight up here." And then she exhaled a sigh. "Look at you— you look so skinny, Troy."

I guess I did, too. But I hadn't really thought much about eating since I'd left. Now I suddenly wanted to tell her about everything that had happened to me and why I had come here. Luz. Every summer her skin got browner while her hair lightened. There were some strands of pure blond running through it, and there was just a little sweat pasting some of the fine strands down to the back of her smooth, soft neck. Her eyes were like her brother's, serious and calm, wondering and wide.

"Well, I've pretty much been living off fish and berries."

"That'll turn you into a bear, Troy Stotts. A real skinny one."

I pulled at a belt loop to hitch my pants a little higher, knowing she was scowling at how my Levi's dropped below my waist.

"I'm sorry, Luz." I felt like I disappointed her, again. "Anyway, I found this cabin and kind of made it home for a while."

"Your home is down there on the lake. Your father is about sick with worrying over you now. Everyone's been looking for you. Even the sheriff."

Chase Rutledge's dad. Looking for me. I knew he couldn't have been trying too hard. Everyone knew about Clayton Rutledge, just nobody ever said it.

"Well, you can tell him I'm okay. Do you want to see this place?"

23

"Are you really okay?"

"I said it."

"You say a lot of things," she sighed. "But you never even tell your best friends what's really bugging you."

I knew that.

I thought about Tommy and Gabe. When we were kids, we'd promised each other to be friends for life. And I suddenly felt like I betrayed them in some way by running off.

Reno liked Doats, who was older and a little indifferent to my horse. His real name was Wild Oats, but Gabe and Luz came up with the shorter call name since Gabe couldn't say it when he was little. "Anyway, I've brought some real food with me if you can fit any of it in you."

"I could try."

I showed her how I had set up the cabin. We walked the horses up the shore of the pond, me showing Luz how I had been surviving by fishing. I didn't tell her what I wanted to, about how I needed to come here, about how I felt seeing her; it just stuck in my throat, formed, but unspoken. Mostly I listened, as Luz told me about the little things from home: how Tom Buller and Gabriel were doing, that her father and Tom's dad had gone to Wyoming for a horse auction, and that her mother didn't know that she had come looking for me.

And I could tell that she thought she would find me, too. She had brought ham sandwiches and chocolate cake from home. She also brought along some carrots for the horses.

We ate at the table in the cabin in the late afternoon. I slid it across the floor so we could both sit on the wood bed. I wanted to look at her, but I just looked at the food she unpacked. I felt my face turning red, felt her looking right at me, sitting so close

I could feel the static between us, needles from invisible electric magnets.

"When are you coming back, Troy?"

"I haven't thought about that yet."

"I'm going to tell your dad you're okay and that you're coming back."

Her hand brushed against my leg as she adjusted herself on that bed. I hoped that it was too dim for her to notice I was sweating.

"You can if you want to." I rubbed at my neck, remembering the fight I'd had with him, like it was a dream; and my indignant fingers dumbly trying to testify, to offer some evidence of what he had done.

I took another bite of sandwich, trying to show her I didn't want to talk about this. I could tell that hurt her feelings, so I talked.

"You know, when my grandfather died we moved up here because this was his home, where my dad grew up. With your dad. At my mom's funeral, everyone was talking about me going away and stuff, to live somewhere they think is normal or something. But I don't want to leave this place. And my dad and me, we're not liking each other right now for a bunch of reasons I don't want to say. Maybe I should've talked to him about it, but I was mad. I was mad at everyone, especially him because I thought he wasn't there when my mom was dying. And I know I was being stupid and selfish but I guess I thought I was suffering more than anyone else, like I was some kind of saint or something. I was stupid and I could see that. And I didn't even cry or say anything at her funeral 'cause I was just so mad. And I needed to just get away to try to get my head back. But I don't know if it worked out because I honestly feel more lost and messed up now than ever. And he has every right to be mad at me, too. But I'm not running away, because running away means that you know where you *should* be, and that's the biggest thing I need to figure out, I guess, but I just kept messing things up worse and worse. Then, when I left, I thought to go by Tommy's and get him but I messed up and slept too late and headed up this way instead, by myself. Then I fell asleep on Reno and fell off and busted my head open."

"Well okay, you said it. Thank you, Troy. What a mess!" She laughed, looking across at me. But I saw her eyes were wet. "I remember when you first got that horse and how Tommy told you Reno wasn't going to ever get tired of trying to kill you."

I remembered that day. "I think he *is* tired of it, but that doesn't mean he'll ever quit it."

"Your dad's not mad, Troy. He's waiting for you to come home."

"I know. Probly."

She brought coffee, too. I usually don't drink it, but it tasted real good after our meal. We boiled it on the stovetop and shared the one cup she had brought along. I sat on the floor, she sat on the bed behind me. We watched the fire in the belly of the stove.

"Troy, I wanted to say something to you."

I didn't say anything, I just waited and stared at the fire. I took a sip of coffee and set the cup down on the dirt floor beside me.

"Troy, we've been friends since we were four years old. I loved your mom, too. And I just wanted to tell you I'm really sorry. I can't imagine how much it hurts. But you've got to come back home, Troy. You can't stay up here by yourself like this."

And now I could tell she was crying.

I pulled my knees up to my face and closed my eyes. I felt her hand on my shoulder and then she reached down and grabbed my hand. And then I cried, too, which made me mad at myself. I wanted so bad to stop feeling like that and then it would just keep coming back and I hated that.

"Things'll be better, Troy."

"I don't know."

Because I didn't know if things ever got better, or worse, than they had always been. Days would just plod along and happen whether you were ready for them or not. And no matter how disappointed or how elated life might make you, it was always going to just keep happening, pouring over you in a neutral, lukewarm flow. Like spit, I guess. I yawned. My eyes were watery, my hand sweaty and warm where our fingers intertwined.

We both fell to sleep like that, me sitting on the floor and Luz lying down behind me and holding my hand.

look, it floats. You stay in it. You float, too. See you at the bottom of the falls, then it's Gabey's turn.

you disappear in that water, Troy. Don't go under the water.

Tommy and Gabe running down the shore toward the flats before the lake. The white foamy water, stinging like shards of ice suspended in its roiling flow, tightening my chest, making my T-shirt and jeans shrink to my skin, shrinking to my bones, closing around my face like a pillow being pressed down.

Troy, Troy

how do you like the hat, son?

it's too curled up. I'm going to fix it. And I'm taking off that band with the feather in it. A real Stetson. I love it. Thanks, Dad. You're the best.

And the cold, painful water now swallowing me up, keeping my eyes open, seeing white and gray like staring dumbly into a fluorescent light. I was looking through the window from the outside now, looking in; my mother sitting on the white chair; quiet, like always, my brother beside her.

Then I'm on the chair, sinking in, deeper and deeper. The water is covering me up.

✦ ✦ ✦

When I opened my eyes, it was dark. The embers of the fire glowed orange inside the stove. I was lying on the floor, curled up, my head pillowed on my aching and numb arm. Luz was covered in my sleeping bag, sleeping on her side on the plank bed, one arm hanging down, fingertips just touching my shoulder.

She shouldn't have been there. I knew she was going to get into trouble at home, but I didn't want to wake her. I looked at her, sleeping, and thought how lucky I was to be here alone with her. I wished I could go back home, that it would be like it was, sitting by the fire pit with Tommy and Gabriel, dizzy, laughing in the smoke and warm nighttime. I sat there on the dirt floor and watched her sleep, watching with envy the rise and fall of the cover over her body.

I made myself go outside and saddle Reno. He was in the rope pen next to Doats. Doats followed us as I took Reno out around the other side of the pond for a run in the early morning quiet as the dark sky gave way to the pale color of slate, which in turn softened to a cottony blue.

She was awake when we came back.

"I thought you stole my horse." She was coming out the doorway as we rode up.

"I couldn't stop him from following."

"There's coffee."

"You make coffee for horse thieves?"

She frowned, which made me a little uncomfortable.

I got down from Reno as Luz tended to her paint. I could see her saddle and bag were all packed up, ready to go. I picked up her saddle and walked over to where Doats was drinking at the steel trough.

"I didn't mean for you to get into any trouble, Luz. I'm really sorry."

"It's a good thing my dad's out of state. I've got a long enough ride back to figure out what to tell my mom."

"I wouldn't think there's that many miles in between here and home." I cinched Doats' saddle in place.

"How can you do that, Troy?" And then I could tell she was mad. "I know you think that life can be funny. Sometimes you say really funny things that make us all laugh. But that mouth of yours is always straight and sad. When am I ever going to see you smile at things instead of just make fun of 'em?"

I'd never really thought about it before, but I was suddenly aware of my straight-mouthed face. But I don't think I felt sad, really, at least not at that moment. I just sometimes felt like I was in some kind of audience, watching myself do things between moments of distraction.

And then before I knew it, Luz whirled toward me and grabbed the back of my neck in both of her hands and kissed me straight on my straight lips. Then she was up on Doats, giving out a "hyaw!" and they were off toward the trees, heading down the mountain.

I guess I always knew that eventually one of us would break down and do that, and so many times I'd pictured myself getting slapped afterwards.

I let out a "who-eee," loud enough for her to hear as she rode off. I stood there, watching her go; openmouthed, chest pounding, smiling big.

I went into the cabin and gulped down the coffee she had left in her tin cup, kind of wondering what side she had drank from, trying to keep that feel of her lips on mine. I just sat there on the edge of that plank bed, looking at the stove, not blinking. I felt a little tired and dizzy. I could smell her hair there, like strawberries and tea where she had laid her head down on my sleeping bag and it reminded me of all those times we had gone to the Benavidezes' when I was small; Gabe running around the house barefoot, constant trickle of snot from his nose at three years old, her trying to get me to play dollhouse or with her toy horses, the sounds of our moms' voices through the halls, laughing about things we would never know.

I called out the doorway: "You want to go home, Reno?"
And Reno, of course, answered back in his own language that
I understand, but can't put into words.

I started gathering up my belongings and I repacked them a
little less carefully than I had organized them when I left home
that morning weeks ago.

THREE

I wondered which way I would have gone if Luz hadn't come looking for me; if I stayed up there, waiting for something.

✦   ✦   ✦

My father just waited; he always did that. His patience and quiet ways made most people think he was aloof, that he didn't care about anything. And it frustrated me, too, to watch him expect things to be predictable, and then try to act unsurprised when what he expected never happened. But I knew things about my father I didn't have to say; all boys know those things about their dads.

After Will left us, my father stopped talking more than a few words every day, and I thought of him as some kind of professor who was quietly measuring the experiment of our lives with emotionless eyes. And I could tell he wanted to say things, too, but he held them in and I tried to be good and strong like his older boy. And I wanted to tell him things, too, but after my mom died, when it was just us left alone, I couldn't bring myself to do it, even if I kept telling myself I had to.

As Reno and I made our way down through the trees, I listened to the rush of the river.

I remembered Tommy and Gabriel coming to my house, kidnapping me on my sixteenth birthday, and how my father had insisted I go with my friends as my mother lay sleeping in the room where she would die. And I didn't want to go; I didn't want to do anything, but my dad told me to go, and Tommy and Gabe practically dragged me out before I could even get my shirt on. That was when we took out the kayak Tommy found and went over the falls. I lost my shoes and nearly drowned; and I remembered them taking me to the Foreman's house afterwards, the smell of the cake Luz had baked for me there, and me, completely stripped naked out of my freezing clothes, shivering and wrapped in nothing but a hole-pocked towel, as Luz laughed and insisted on taking a picture of me at their surprise party.

And that night, when I came back home, dressed in Tommy's clothes, my dad didn't say anything; didn't ask where we went, or why I was wearing Tom Buller's things, even though I knew he noticed, was measuring the changes in me, quietly, at his distance.

+   +   +

Once we had come down into the foothills and passed through the break in the old white plank fence surrounding the apple orchard, Reno began moving purposefully, knowing exactly where and when he would stop. The apples weren't nearly in yet, but some of them were big enough that Reno spent a few minutes at one of the branches, hanging bent with red-green fruit, before turning away and resuming his quickened pace toward the familiarity of his barn.

It was late afternoon now, the long shadows of mountain, hill, and treetops painting over our white barn with its loose-boarded sides, the broad open breezeway turned at an angle against winter winds. Reno's stall was positioned along a row of others off to one side, the henhouse on the other, all of it contained by a big pipe-and-wire fence. Our three goats stood in front of the breezeway, eating at a fresh flake of hay that must have been dropped there by my father. Hens scratched and squatted in the dirt, cooling their feathers after the long hot day.

I stepped down from Reno and opened the pipe gate to his stall. He went in, chuckling, willingly, on his own. I threw his reins over the top rail and removed his saddle and pad, soaked with sweat, and threw them onto the pipe rail, as well. I looked for the little nail in the wall to make sure his brush still hung there as I freed him from that halter.

"Are you hungry, Reno?"

Those were probably the words he recognized most, and he threw his head up and down, nodding and neighing, smelling the alfalfa there.

"I'll brush you down when I get you some food."

I latched the gate behind me and then walked down the breezeway to the small hay room where we stored the feed. I could hear Reno stamping at the bottom rail with his front foot, trying to knock it open, as though he were afraid I'd walk off for good and not feed him first.

"Troy? Troy?"

I heard my father calling me from out by Reno's stall.

He was standing back at the end of the breezeway when I turned out of the hay room, blue-flowered alfalfa sprinkling down from my cradling arm.

"I'm here, Dad."

He moved through the hallway straight to me and grabbed me by the shoulders. And then he hugged me hard, pressing the flake of hay into my chest. I think he was crying.

He knocked my hat back off of my head and put his fingers in my hair. He kissed my ear and said, "Oh my God, Troy, don't you know how much I love you, son?"

Do you know who my favorite boy in the whole world is?

I am.

Do you know how much I love you?

Forever and ever.

We used to play that game when I was four. Every day. Every day until maybe I got too old, or maybe he thought I just forgot the answers. But even when I was four, I knew he was afraid, and that he was trying to hold on to me because he couldn't hold on to the son who was born first.

"I'm sorry, Dad. I love you. I'm sorry."

Then he held me back and looked at me, all the way down to my dirty tennis shoes.

"She used to always say you were disappearing. Look at you, boy, you look like you've lost twenty pounds that you can't spare." And he pulled the waist of my 501s out from my side. They opened a gap out about four inches from my body.

"You look like you haven't been eating regular either, Dad."

"Why don't we do something about that, Troy?"

I looked at all the hay scattering down my front, into my pants, pockets, and the sides of my shoes. "I'll bet Reno's wanting us to remember he was out there for all that time, too."

"Do you think you've got enough for him?"

"I'm wearing enough for all the Benavidez horses." I thought about my mouth. Straight. "And I better go easy on him right now, anyway, or he might get sick."

My dad didn't know horses.

He put his hand on my right shoulder and we walked like that out to Reno's stall. I tossed the flake into his feeder and he went right to it. I brushed him down as he ate.

"You've got yourself a good one there, son."

"Yeah. I know."

"But I'm surprised he stands still for being brushed by a kid who smells as bad as you do."

I looked at my dad. Straight mouth, too. I never had noticed that before. "I guess I could use a shower and a change before I eat."

"I won't stop you."

The shower steam was fogging up the mirror. I took my shirt off and dropped it on the counter by the sink, small black circles staining the shoulder from the time I landed on my head after falling asleep on Reno. I realized I hadn't really looked at myself since before she died. I was way too skinny. And I seemed kind of old, too. I wondered what I looked like to Luz.

The mirror fogged up and I looked like my father. I stared,

glassy-eyed at a reflection in which I saw him for the first time; this was my father's face. Then I wiped away the steam droplets and stared straight into the eyes of my mother. I rubbed the itch from my eyes and got into the shower.

We sat down at the kitchen table across from each other, he just looking at me for the longest time. The yellow pad was gone, replaced by a new, unused one. We ate a dinner of eggs and bacon. He had poured me a glass of milk, even though he knew I couldn't stand milk. I drank it anyway.

"I missed you a lot, son. It made me crazy there for a while. But I knew — hoped, you'd come back."

"So did I." And then I asked: "Luz didn't come by earlier today?"

"Yeah. She did. So I knew you were okay."

"Thanks for the dinner, Dad. This is about the best-tasting food I've ever had in my life." And he watched me as I took a difficult swallow of milk. I was trying to make him feel good, even if I knew I couldn't.

"Where'd you go for all that time? What did you do?"

I told him that I went up onto the mountain. I left some parts of it out, for whatever reasons, but I did describe the cabin to him, and the nice pond where I fished for trout nearly every day.

"I'm jealous, Troy. I wish I could do that. Maybe someday we can go up there together and live like that for a while by ourselves."

"We need to get you on a horse, first."

And my dad laughed. He mostly felt about horses the way I felt about milk. But I drank it for him, so I figured he could find a way to tolerate a horse, too.

"I read a couple books, too, Dad. But I've got some questions about one of 'em. . . ."

+   +   +

The morning after I came back I called the Benavidez house to see if Gabe was around. Of course, I was hoping Gabe wouldn't answer the phone, but that would still have been better than talking to Mrs. Benavidez. As I listened to the phone ring, I played through all the things I'd say depending on which person answered.

Luz answered the phone. And even though I wanted that to happen most of all, I realized I didn't have a clue as to what to say to her.

"Hi. I got back last night."

"Hi, Troy."

"I was going to come by and see Gabey this morning if you're all not busy or something."

"Do you want to talk to him?"

"No." And then I felt really stupid. "You could just tell him, if it's okay."

"Okay."

I panicked, thinking she was about to hang up.

"Luz, you're not in trouble, are you?"

"No. I'll tell you later."

"Oh. 'Cause Luz," I gulped, "I'll be leaving in about ten minutes and coming in through your west gate on Reno. Okay?"

"I'll see you later, Troy."

So I knew she would be there.

The west gate to the Benavidez ranch was huge, made from three straight redwood poles, the lintel pole ornately carved with the family name. They had been on this land for more than a hundred years and raised the finest cutting horses and thoroughbreds that could be found anywhere. On both sides of the gate, along the outside of the fence rail, sat benches made from wagon wheels. Luz was sitting there when I rode up.

She was dressed in her usual manner: tight jeans and gray Justin boots (she and Tommy Buller always wore Justins), a loose and untucked shirt unbuttoned at the top, hair down, and hatless.

"You clean up pretty nice, Troy Stotts."

I got down from Reno. "Once or twice a year," I said, and as I sat down beside Luz I pulled my hat down straight over my eyebrows, low, the way I liked it.

"Is your dad okay?"

"Yeah, he was pretty happy to see me come home. And I feel a lot better about things now, too. I really want to thank you, Luz, for coming up there to look for me," I said, and I held her hand, "and for being such a good friend, too. I hope you didn't get in too much trouble with your mom."

"She hasn't even said anything about it yet. After you called, she told me to ask you to come for dinner tonight."

"Dinner? By myself?"

"No, Troy, the rest of us plan on eating, too. I'll tell her yes. And Gabey's real excited about seeing you, too. I had to sneak out just now so he wouldn't follow me down here. But will you please take that hat off?"

Luz took my hat and set it down on the bench beside me. My dirty-straw–colored hair fell down across my eyes and she combed it back with her left hand. "I like your hair long like this, Troy. Don't cut it all off again."

I couldn't stand it anymore so I kissed her on the cheek, and then she turned and I kissed her mouth; and I know my mouth wasn't so straight after that. I exhaled, relieved that I had finally made a crossing to the girl.

"Yeah. I can come back for dinner."

"We'll send someone to pick you up at five, so you don't ride that poor horse to death," she said, and looked right at me, smiling, "and so you don't smell like horse sweat at the dinner table."

"Troy Stotts! Troy!" It was Gabriel, running down the road from the house toward us. Gabe was like a brother to me, and I wanted to see him, but my heart kind of sank with the thought that he had seen me kissing his sister.

"Oh God. I'm sorry, Luz."

"Don't worry about Gabey. I'll handle him."

*   *   *

I waited and waited. It was 5:15, and no one had shown up in our drive yet. I was sweating in my collared shirt, standing there by the door. I wasn't going to wear my hat, either. My hair was kind of hanging down over my left eye.

"Think it's about time for a haircut?"

"No."

"You look like you're going on a date or something, son." My dad was sitting in the living room under the big front window, legs crossed, reading. We and the Bullers were the only people I had ever known who didn't have TV sets. Over the years, I had gotten used to it, but I still liked watching it on rainy days over at Gabe's.

I sighed. "Oh."

"Well? Are you?"

I sat down next to my dad.

"Kind of."

"I like her, too, Troy."

I sighed again.

"I just wish I could get moving 'cause I kind of feel sick inside."

"Relax. I could take you down there —"

"No."

Finally I heard the clanking of the F-150, kicking up dust and rattling down the drive. I turned and looked past my father and saw Tommy Buller driving up. I knew my dad was about to say something again about how he didn't really like me riding with Tom, even though the Benavidezes sent him out plenty of times, so I hurried for the door.

"I'll be back," I said, wanting to let him know I'd come home this time.

And as I opened the door and moved out into the dusty front yard, my dad called out after me, "Troy! Have fun!"

I opened the rusty door and looked across the cracking bench seat at Tom Buller, who smiled wide enough so I could just see a bit of the tobacco in his lip. He held out his right hand to grab mine and half pull me up into the cab of the truck. Even though he was seventeen, we were in the same grade, but Tom Buller always liked to keep his own schedule when it came to things like school.

"Welcome back, Stottsy. We were all afraid you and that horse had left us for good." And he smiled as he jammed the grinding column shift down into drive.

"You look a little prettied up for having dinner with Gabe and his family," Tom said, obviously digging for something.

I didn't say anything as he U-turned the truck around in front of the house. I rolled the window down and looked out like I didn't even hear what Tom had just said to me. I could see my dad watching us through the window as we pulled away.

Tom got this wicked coyotelike look on his face, the look he got whenever he was trying to do something funny-mean, like when he got me to take the kayak over the falls.

"Hey, Stotts, want some beer?" And he grabbed an open beer can wedged upright against the dash in the open, dirty ashtray. I knew he was joking, that this was his spit can.

"Oh man, I could sure use a cold beer right now," I said, and I took the can from his hand and put it right up to my lips and tipped it, but just a little, and pretended to swallow.

"Thanks, Tommy. That was just what I needed."

Tom burst out laughing.

"Oh man, Stotts, you're crazy. You scare me."

But I held the can out, offering. "You want some, too?"

Tom crawled the truck slowly down my drive and then hit the gas hard when we were out of sight of my house, spinning the back tires and causing a slight fishtail as we headed around the lake and south toward the Benavidez ranch.

"You staying for dinner?" I asked.

"Naw." Tommy spit smoothly. "I already ate."

Of course I knew the Bullers wouldn't be eating dinner at their boss' table, but I asked it anyway. Arturo Benavidez made a fortune raising and selling his horses all over the country, and he respected the Bullers enough to let them live in his Foreman's house, but they were just workers to him, and he never crossed that line of socialization. So I felt a little stupid and embarrassed that a friend I admired as much as Tommy Buller might think he was a little less privileged than I.

"Well, where you been, Stotts?"

"I don't know, Tom. I'll tell you about it sometime."

"Okay."

*   *   *

Luz Benavidez wore a dress at dinner, so I was happy I got myself what I'd considered dressed up by putting on a shirt. It was a red dress, tied behind her neck so you could see her shoulders and upper back, tight at her waist, and falling just below her knees. Her hair was tied back, too, which made her shoulders and back even more noticeable. She was about the most beautiful girl I had ever seen. The Benavidez house smelled so good, and I was so hungry, but how could I eat at the table with Luz Benavidez looking like that and not miss my mouth, fumbling with a fork and knife?

Her father and Carl Buller had flown back from Wyoming that afternoon, and when he saw me come in Mr. Benavidez, smelling like soap and cigars, shook my hand hard enough to break bones. And that house seemed so big and vacant to me; it echoed like a cave as I nervously found my seat at their table. So it was just Luz, Gabe, their parents, and me.

Fernanda Benavidez did all the cooking for her family, every day. She didn't need to, though; they employed dozens of people at the ranch, all told. She was from Italy, and had a thick accent and a deep, loud, carrying voice that was kind of intimidating because she always sounded mad, even though she rarely was.

It was one thing to have my dad cook bacon and eggs for

me, but eating at the Benavidez house was like a feast at the finest restaurant. It was too quiet, though, and I had to force myself to keep my eyes down as I nervously worked on a plate-sized steak.

"It's good to have you here, Troy," Mr. Benavidez said. "How is your father?"

"He's good, thank you. We're doing a lot better."

"You need to eat more, Troy. Look at you." Mrs. Benavidez scowled. Did all moms say things like that? I don't know, but I do know everyone picked up on the fact that it made me a little sad to hear anyone's mother saying so; it made it hard to keep eating. So I took a drink of water. Gabe cleared his throat. But his mom was staring right at me, looking mad. I couldn't ever figure her out. Luz could talk about my straight-mouthing all she wanted, but Fernanda Benavidez had a mouth that always turned down at the edges, even when she smiled.

"He's a fast runner," Gabe protested. "Runners don't eat a lot. Give him a break, Mom."

Mr. Benavidez glanced disapprovingly at his son. It made me feel even more uncomfortable. Gabriel never seemed to measure up to his father's expectations.

"This is an excellent dinner, Mrs. Benavidez." And I cleared my throat and drank again. "Thank you."

I wanted Luz to say something. I caught her looking my way from across the table, but she just looked down at her food. Something was wrong; I could tell.

"You're going into the eleventh grade now, Troy?" Mr. Benavidez asked, but I know he knew the answer because I was in every grade with Luz since kindergarten.

"Yes. And my dad's getting me some AP tests this fall."

"Is your father going to come back to teaching?"

My father had taken the last half of the school year off from teaching high school.

"He's planning on it."

"The board will be happy to hear that."

The board of the school consisted of Mr. Benavidez; the sheriff, Clayton Rutledge; and one other parent.

"School's a long time off," Gabriel said. "Let's talk about something happy."

"Did you get any horses up in Wyoming, Mr. Benavidez?" I asked.

That energized him. "Oh! I've never seen such ugly horses. And for so much money. What a waste of time! Even Carl said he'd rather be caught riding a burro."

I couldn't eat everything they gave me, and I was a little embarrassed. When we were finished with dinner, Mr. Benavidez sent Luz in with her mother to make coffee and told Gabriel to go get him a brandy. Then he told me, "Let's go out on the terrace, Troy."

I'd have just as soon taken a bath in honey and gone out on that terrace alone with a bear, but there was nothing I could do.

I felt pretty sick as he opened the glass-and-wood doors leading off the dining room. "Come on, it's nice outside." And he smiled at me.

The terrace was a planked wooden deck, finely furnished, above the ground floor of the house. It was wide and long, with an intricately carved rail around its edge. Potted jasmine grew at perfectly spaced intervals along it. I walked to the railing and took in the broad view of the huge Benavidez holdings, which stretched into the distance, farther than I could see in the moonlight. Art Benavidez followed behind me.

"Do you think one day you'll be a teacher, also?"

"Only if I can't do what I really want."

"And what's that?"

"Well," I said, and swallowed, "I'd like to write books. And I'd like to own this ranch."

He laughed. "You'd have to change your name."

"Or carve some pretty big redwoods to make some new gates."

His smile was a relief, but it was short-lived.

Gabriel opened the door and came out, carrying a fishbowl-sized glass with about two inches of amber-colored liquid in it.

"Gabriel," Benavidez said, "will you please excuse us for a few minutes. Troy and I are talking about something important. Go help your mother and sister."

If I were wearing a necktie, I would have hung myself off that balcony right then and there. So I guess there *are* times when dressing up pays off. Gabriel looked disappointed and slammed the glass door as he left.

"Your father and I have known each other since we were boys," Benavidez said. "And except for those years when he was away at college, your family, like mine, has been here on the shores of this lake for a very long time.

"Your father's father was a farmer. You probably don't remember him, but he was a good man. He would have been proud to see you, Troy; I know this. We had the ranch on this side of the water, your family farmed on the other. But we were always great friends, despite our differences." He took a drink. "Do you know the difference between farmers and ranchers?"

Of course I had to stop myself from saying something smart-alecky, like I usually do when I'm nervous or terrified. And so Mr. Benavidez took a drink and went on:

"At the end of the day, at the end of each year, a farmer always totals up what he has lost. But a rancher always counts what he *has*. This is how I think and how your father thinks, too. It was how we were raised, and even though we think differently, we are still great friends." He drank again. "So how do you count things?"

I thought I knew the answer, but said, "I don't know."

And I never thought coffee could take so long to brew.

"I will talk to your father. I would like you to start working here, beginning Monday morning, at six o'clock. You're old enough. I will pay you three hundred per week, like I pay Tom Buller."

I was shocked. Nothing could be better than working on that ranch with all those incredible horses. Nothing.

"I'll be here."

Benavidez drank again. He moved closer to me, leaning on the railing, looking straight at me.

"I talked to Luz this afternoon. Her mother was very upset about her not coming home the other night. Very upset. I could tell you that I will not allow you two to ever see each other again, but I don't think that would be very smart. Luz is growing up, she would find another boy — who?

"My daughter has never lied to me. I am happy for your father that she found you there and brought you back home. Things

47

could have been very different otherwise. But I am telling you, Troy, that what happened the other night must never happen again or I will send her away and you will not see each other. Ever."

And I looked him right in the eyes then, and I was serious when I said, "I'm sorry. We . . ." and I stopped myself from saying what I knew he already heard from Luz.

"I like you, Troy," he said. "Very much. That's why we're having this talk right now. That's why I'm offering you a job. But I am keeping an eye on you now. And my daughter. And I need you to respect that; and to respect Luz as well."

He turned back to the house and waved at the door. They were all three looking at us through the glass. "Look, here they are with the coffee."

I must have looked like a ghost.

I was so scared of that man I felt like throwing up. If it weren't for the railing, my knees would have probably given out. I don't know if I said three words for the rest of the night, but when the coffee was finished, Benavidez told Gabriel to call Tommy to take me home.

"Can Gabe and I ride along?" Luz said.

I wanted to tell her no, but Mrs. Benavidez said, "You both can go with Troy. That would be nice." She looked real mad, too, like she always did, even if she wasn't.

I felt Benavidez' eyes on me.

*   *   *

"Stop the truck now, Tom," I said once we had gotten out of sight of the house and through the west gate.

Luz and Gabe were sitting in the bed.

"What?"

48

"Stop the truck. I'm gonna walk home. I want to."

Tom stopped the truck right in the middle of the dirt and gravel road.

"You're not walking home, Stotts," he said grimly.

I opened the door and got out. Tom got out of the driver's door, saying "What're you doing?"

"Why're we stopping?" Gabe asked, sitting with his back to the cab, arm slung over the side.

I started walking down the road, disappearing out of the sideways cones of headlight into the darkness.

"Troy!" Luz called out. "Tommy! You're not going to let him walk home by himself!"

I heard the truck start up, the grinding sound of its tires rolling slowly up behind me, could see the lights brightening my path, stretching a long black distortion of me out ahead, then shining white-hot on my back.

"Come on! Get in, Stotts. What's wrong with you?"

I stopped walking and went back toward the truck. I stopped at the side of the bed. "Get up front, Gabey. I need to talk to your sister."

"Let's all just ride back here," Gabe said.

"How nice," Tom said, sarcastically.

"Gabe. Please?"

"Oh."

Gabe got in the cab and I jumped up next to Luz. I sat down right next to her.

"We can go now," I said, and patted the back window twice.

Tommy pulled the truck forward into the night. Luz and I sat there, talking about her father, talking about our arrangement, and holding hands.

"He's just trying to scare you and at the same time let you know that he likes you," she said. "It could be a lot worse. And he's giving you a job, too."

"To keep an eye on me."

"He has a lot of faith in you, Troy. You're like a part of our family."

I wanted to kiss her so bad just then, too. And that made me feel madder, so I just looked at my feet.

It was about 10 when we got back to my house. I could see my dad inside, through that big window, moving from the kitchen into the living room. Tommy turned the truck off and I let go of Luz's hand.

"Hey, Troy," Gabe said, getting out of the truck, "I want to take Tommy back there to Reno's stall so he can take a look at that chip in his hoof."

"Thanks, Gabey."

Tom Buller was a pretty decent farrier. Gabriel Benavidez was a real slick liar. And even though he was playing a game with me about wanting to sit back there with us, he must have known that I was going to kiss his sister again before I'd go home.

They all three sat up in the cab after Tommy's ranting about Reno's hooves being all square and fine when he and Gabe got back from the barn. They drove off down our dusty drive and I let myself into the house.

◆　◆　◆

After that night, Luz and I talked on the phone every day. Tommy and Gabriel teased me that I was always checking in with her, that I had to get her permission to spend time with my friends; but I took their teasing, because I knew they were wrong, that there was something much bigger pulling Luz and me together, and neither one of us could do anything about it, even if we'd wanted to.

+ + +

"How'd it go?"

My dad was sitting on the couch, arms out along the backrest, stretched to both sides. He was wearing a white T-shirt and had his reading glasses on.

"Really good," I said. "They asked about you. We had steaks. And Mr. Benavidez wants me to go to work for him starting Monday, if that's okay with you."

I always called Luz's father "mister." And ever since he was a kid, my dad called him Arturo, even though most people around Three Points whitewashed the name to Art.

"Wow. Really? That'd be great," he said. "He'll work you hard, though. I don't think you even weigh as much as a bale of hay."

"I can lift 'em. It'll be okay. Good night, Dad."

And he just quietly watched as I disappeared into my room.

FOUR

om Buller didn't need much of an excuse to get into a fight with Chase Rutledge the night after I started work at the ranch, and Chase seemed more than willing to give the little it would take. I'd brought Reno with me so Tom could trim his hooves, and as we were riding past the church we saw Chase, leaning there in the dark on a shovel. We knew he was doing something he shouldn't.

Tom said, "What're you looking at?" to Chase.

And Chase just smirked and said, "The teacher's boy and the son of a drunk." He was smoking a cigarette and he flicked it off the back of his middle fingernail, launching it like some small orange comet that sprayed off sparks when it bounced from Arrow's neck, which made Tom's horse recoil as though he had been whipped.

Tommy inhaled and looked over at me, and then he just about flew off Arrow's back down to the dirt road, tossing that shovel back out of Chase's grasp to go scooting noisily along the ground and send our two horses nervously rearing into the dark, and me, slipping down from Reno's saddle to land on my elbows and butt in the dust.

And from my resting place there in the dirt, I first wondered if I had broken my arm, and then watched in awe as that gangly Tom took on the much-bigger kid. I never saw anyone who could fight like Tommy Buller, all knees and elbows inside the flailing reach of the taller boy, crushing into ribs and legs as Chase crumpled down to the road.

Then Tommy flipped him over, had his legs bent back, crossed in a V as he straddled them like he was roping a runaway calf, and grabbed Chase's greasy hair, pressing his bloodied face hard into the dirt.

"This bastard's got a gun in his pants!"

I got up to my knees, then feet, and brushed the bits of gravel from my bleeding elbows as Tommy pulled a small wood-gripped black revolver from Chase's back pocket.

"Here, Stotts." And he tossed the gun back to clatter down at my feet while I flinched an attempt to catch it. And I didn't know what he expected me to do with it, either, so I just popped the wheel and spilled out the five .22 caliber rounds into the dirt and then threw the gun as far as I could into the trees across the street from the darkened church. Then I saw Jack Crutchfield running off, away from the church, down the street where I had thrown Chase's gun. Even in the dark, I knew it was Jack because no one else around looked as overfed or ran as slow. Chase and Jack did just about everything together. They were punks who got away with whatever they felt like and we hated each other.

"Okay. I'm done, Rutledge." Tommy panted and pushed

Chase's face hard into the dirt. Chase just kind of moaned and gasped. "I'm gonna get off you now. I don't think you want any more, but if you do I got plenty left."

Tommy got up and straightened out his shirt and jeans. There wasn't a mark on him. Chase struggled up to his hands and knees, head hanging low, and spit a blob of blood as a rope of red snot wormed down from his nose.

I gathered the horses' reins and walked them over to pick up our hats where they'd fallen in the dust on the road.

As I handed my friend his hat, keeping an eye on the still-kneeling and wheezing Chase Rutledge, Tommy said, "Damn, Stotts! What happened to you?"

"I fell off Reno."

"Damn!" Tommy laughed at me, his black eyes squinting and shining even in the dark, and he pulled his little round can of chewing tobacco from his back pocket.

"Well, if you hadn't've thrown that shovel . . ." I offered as an excuse for my horsemanship.

"That was fun," he said, and then spit back in Chase's direction.

Chase had gotten to his feet, limping away from us as though he were headed back to his house, and was holding the wadded end of his shirt up over his mouth and nose, so he sounded a little muffled and weak when he said, "One of these days I'm gonna kill you, Buller."

And Tommy just grinned and spit and said, "Well, bring some friends and I guess it'll be a fairer fight then."

I think I admired Tommy Buller more than anyone else in my life at times like that. I wanted to be like him, the way he always seemed so fearless and could smile at the worst times and barely get winded in a fistfight.

The evening was summer-warm. I was only wearing a dirty T-shirt and my Levi's. Tom's shirttail hung out behind him, but other than that, he looked like he could have come straight from church. I brushed the dirt out of my hair and pulled my hat on tight and Tommy just laughed and spit, looking at me, and said, "Damn!"

And I could only say, "Well, you shouldn't've thrown that shovel!" as we got up on our horses and rode off toward my house on the north side of the lake.

Eventually, we found out that the lock had been busted on the community donations box and that a statue of Saint Francis had been overturned, so it wasn't too much of a stretch for us to blame it on Jack and Chase, even though we both kept quiet about it, knowing how far Deputy Rutledge tended to go to make sure his son and his friend never suffered the consequences to what his father called their "mischief."

Tommy wiped his hand over his face. "Did he hit me?" He looked at his palm.

"He never even touched you once. If there's blood on you, it's his."

Tommy stopped Arrow there in the road.

"Get down, Stotts."

"What?" I circled Reno back around to face him.

"Get down."

He was standing there in the road, looking at me that way he did, squinty-eyed and grinning like he was playing a joke on me and I had no choice beyond cooperation.

I knew better than to argue with Tommy Buller because he could get an idea — or a plan — in his head, and that would be it. There was no way of harnessing that energy once he got charged up. And he even said "get down" one more time to me as I was slinging my leg up and over the saddle.

"Okay. What's up, Tommy?"

Tom Buller's mouth stretched back in his tight-lipped coyote grin.

"Punch me in the face, Stotts."

I sighed and my shoulders slumped and I started to turn back to get on my horse. "Hell, Tom."

"Come on, Stotts. Punch me." Tom grabbed my shoulder to pull me back around. "No one's gonna believe I beat the hell out of Chase Rutledge if I don't at least have a black eye to prove it."

"No one'll ever beat the *hell* out of that boy."

And Tommy put his chin right up to my face and smiled. "Come on, Stottsy. Just once."

I exhaled deeply and then propped his chin up between the thumb and index finger of my left hand. "Well, okay."

I made a fist with my right hand and cocked it back, low by my hip. Then Tommy snapped his chin back out of my hand and we both started laughing.

"Damn, Stotts!" he yelled. "You're crazy! You were really gonna hit me!"

Then he spit and held out his fist and I punched it once and said, "Well, you shouldn't've thrown that shovel."

"And when are *you* gonna learn to stay on that horse of yours?"

We both laughed and I pulled up the waist of my jeans and we climbed back up onto our horses.

56

"Where'd you learn to fight like that anyway?"

"Losing at least a hundred times, I guess."

And I thought, *That's a lot of times to not give up and try something else.*

"Thanks for the trim on Reno, Tommy."

"No sweat, Stotts. Stop feeding him so much alfalfa." Then he spit off into the darkness. "We're still going to the fire pit tomorrow night, right?"

"Yeah." I looked over at him, but Tommy had those narrow eyes fixed on the road ahead, still smiling.

I asked, "Do you think he would really do it? Chase, I mean?"

Tommy spit again. "He's too much of a coward."

"That's what I mean, Tom."

Tom Buller didn't say anything to that.

"I saw Jack running off when you were beating on Chase," I said.

Tommy laughed, "You saw Crutchfield *running?*"

"And what do you think he was doing with that shovel, anyway?"

"Planting roses, probly. Or waiting for me to come along and throw it at your horse so I could laugh at you for falling off him."

I never believed I knew very much about horses; I still don't now. There's more to them than I can guess. But I do know that there are some horses you can just look at and tell they don't like anything about you. Chase Rutledge was like that, at least toward me, even if I never really did know the reasons I gave him.

"What kind of gun was that, anyway?"

"Loaded," I said. "A twenty-two. I threw it across the road. Probly shouldn't've, though."

"Yeah."

+   +   +

The next afternoon I rode out to our fire pit on the other side of the lake just as the sun was stretching the shadows of those tall trees on that part of Benavidez land. I knew Tom and Gabriel would be there, stoking the fire high, already laughing, already telling their stories.

I like the color of the sun at dusk, when it cuts down away in the west, turning the air a kind of amber like the whole world is seen through the smoke of Tom and Gabriel's fire. I like the way the fading light sucks all the lingering heat from the day at that time of year. It was the time of day you'd see deer, which meant quickness. Everything meant something in the woods — I had read as much in a book on Indian medicine. Deer were quickness medicine. Coyotes meant someone was going to play a trick on you. Hawks were messengers. Snake medicine means change. I always knew Tommy Buller had strong snake medicine in him, even though he played the coyote most of the time, because he could always shrug things off so easily and be new again, just like a snake shedding its skin. It was all reasonable enough to me. Well, as reasonable as any other explanation I ever heard for why things happen or how things fit into this world. I told my friends about it, too, and the saying made it seem unarguable to me.

I said it to Tom and Gabe, and they got serious enough to stop laughing and consider it.

"And bears mean strength," I added. "If you dream about 'em. Or if you see 'em at the right moment."

"Everything's some kind of sign, I guess," Gabe reasoned.

Tommy leaned forward and spit a long brown splash of tobacco, sizzling, into the fire. We watched him as he threw a pinecone into it, making it flare like an illusion in a magic show.

And then he got that joking, black-eyed coyote look in his eyes and kind of winked at Gabriel and said, "Yeah. And pinecone is dumbass medicine."

And we all laughed at that.

Gabriel played to Tommy's teasing and fixed his serious eyes on me. "And my sister is . . ."

Then they both looked at me, thinking I would finish it.

"I don't know."

We stared into the fire for a long time after that, each, I'm sure, thinking about what I really would have said if I were telling the truth.

"What about horses?"

And I said, "Horses. They're all different. Some are smart, some are stupid. Some are good, some are bad. Some of 'em you just can't ever like. And some of 'em you like right away and you understand 'em, and there's no telling why."

Tommy yawned and stretched his long legs out against the rocks in front of us. "I like your Reno. He's a good one."

"Everyone likes him."

"You never said why Benavidez gave him to you."

"'Cause I don't really know."

And then Gabe smiled, but you could never tell with that smile of his what he was meaning because he was usually so serious. Or maybe scared. "I do."

I could tell he was waiting for me or Tommy to just beg him to talk, but we just stared straight into the fire, my eyes getting heavy and watery from the smoke and light. And we sat like that, silently, for the longest time before Tommy put his head all the way back on that old saddle in the ground, like he was about to go to sleep. Then I gave out and took my hat off and just rested my head straight back in the dirt.

"Okay, I'll tell you what I think," Gabe said.

We were flat on our backs, staring up at the sky, the stars, the rising smoke, feet toward the fire.

"Get ready, Stottsy, he's thinking now, too. This'll be really good."

"He's the kind of horse anyone would want. But the kind of person who'd pay for him would be the wrong person for the horse. So my father made a bargain with the horse. The horse chose you and in exchange, he made him promise that one day he'll take you far away from Benavidez land."

And I guess I took Gabe's bait. "All right. Why?"

"Tom, I think you were right about the pinecone medicine."

"True, Gabey. True."

+ + +

I thought I could feel myself getting smaller. It was an easy enough thing to feel, lying there on my back in the dirt, looking up at the endlessness of the night and listening to my friends pick away at me because they knew more about me than I thought I would ever show them.

FIVE

When I got to the Foreman's house in the morning, Carl Buller was standing with his right foot up on the trailer hitch, resting an elbow on his knee and smoking a cigarette. Tommy was coming out the screen door, pulling a T-shirt over his head as he switched his hat from hand to hand.

I had been working at the ranch for about a week, and nobody bothered me with questions about where I had gone when I ran off, or what I had done, so I was willing to let it go that way. I knew what it was that caused their distance, too, because I saw how their faces slightly changed when they were around their own parents. And what does a kid say to his friend whose mom just died, anyway? Either way, I let it go because all I wanted to do was get rid of that ghost in my head.

I saw it every day after Will died; she, just looking at me like I was something so fragile and temporary, and me, afraid of scaring her into thinking I might leave her, too. So I made it become a sort of enormous rock I was always pushing uphill, or trying to; trying to make her not afraid anymore, but it was really me who was afraid, unwittingly playing this zero-sum game that she, in vanishing away from me, instead, ended up winning. I tell myself now that I had time to say everything to her that needed to be said; and I heard more from her than probably anyone else in her life. And I always knew what she was thinking, what she was really afraid of.

We would sit, every day, for an hour or more before my father came home, and we talked. She would ask about school and how I was getting along, and I would tell her about my friends and what they'd said at the fire pit, how Tommy never stopped playing his tricks on us, and she'd laugh sometimes. And I always knew she was listening to me, but I could see that look she had. She hurt about the boy who died. And I sometimes found myself getting angry or feeling cheated by how careful, for her, I had become, and I hated that about myself but I put up with it anyway.

٭ ٭ ٭

Working at the Benavidez ranch wasn't much like work, not like the kinds of chores your dad will put you on that you never want to start. And even though the days could be tiring and I'd come home so sore and dirty, working alongside Tom Buller always made me feel healed and alive.

"Hey, Stotts."

"Tom."

"We got to trailer up the horses. We're going to have some fun stuff to do today. Help me get Arrow out here."

"You boys are gonna need ropes," Carl said.

I yawned and stretched, following Tom around the house to

Arrow's wood-rail stall, where they kept him during summers. "What're we supposed to be doing?"

"CB's gotta fix the fence at the southwest range. Some of the calves are loose out there on that crazy goat woman's land. She keeps saying we cut the fences down and kill her goats."

Tom always called his dad CB.

"Do you?"

"We cut the fence down once in a while, but we always put it back up in time. I don't know who the hell'd want to be killing her goats, though. Might be a cat. Might be she's just crazy anyway. I know she hasn't taken a bath in all the years we've worked on this ranch."

"And how do you know that?"

"Just wait and you'll know, too, if we see her out there today."

Tommy and I rode in the bed, alongside the spools of barbed wire and clattering tools Carl had hastily thrown in before we left. Tommy pulled his hat down to his nose, as though he would actually be able to sleep in the jostling bed of that rusty and noisy truck.

✦ ✦ ✦

As far as I knew, nobody around could say what her last name was. We just always called her Rose or the Goat Woman; everyone knew who you were talking about. She had lived there for longer than most people could remember, on about twenty acres that were pretty much surrounded by Benavidez land or U.S. Forest Service property. She lived in a house made from one of those aluminum half-pipe airplane hangars. She had a well, but no electricity. I really don't know how she survived there.

There were at least two dozen strays that had gotten through the break in the fence and onto her property. Tommy and I spent most of the morning herding them back onto the Benavidez ranch. A couple wanderers had gotten pretty far onto the Goat Woman's property; they would take the longest to get back.

"The thing to remember," Tommy said, "is to not get too mad when you realize how completely stupid cows are, and that the last stragglers are probably going to make you just want to give up and shoot 'em."

As the day heated up, Tommy and I rode farther into the oak-forested hills on Rose's land. Carl stayed behind, pulling fence wire, using the truck to stretch it tight.

"You think Reno could jump the fence with you on him?"

"No doubt," I said. "I'll show you when we get back."

"Especially if CB's done fixing it. I hope he leaves a hole till I get Arrow back over."

"I'd like to see you jump him."

"If I tried to jump him, he'd take me down from this saddle, slap me around a bit, get on my back, and say, 'Now you jump the damn fence, boy.'"

"And I bet you would."

While we rode, looking for the last of the strays, Tommy pulled out his can of chew and put a new wad of dip into his mouth.

We saw her shiny house as we came over the rise of a small hill. There were about thirty goats of various sizes and colors, some hornless, some flop-eared, wandering around it; many lying down, bent-kneed, in whatever shade was available. A couple of our cows were drinking from a long steel trough fed by the windmill pump on her well, on the opposite side of the corrugated half-pipe house; and there were dozens of horses. The horses looked wild, and I had never seen a herd like this before. Tommy told me that when Rose moved up here, people said she had a couple horses and then over the years she had picked up a few more and just let them go on her land.

You could tell none of them was even gentled, much less saddle-broke, but it was a beautiful sight, all those horses — paints, sorrels, roans, old and young, none gelded, just having the run of the place. I stopped Reno at the top of the hill, under a shady oak, and just admired it all in awe.

"Is that the craziest thing you ever saw?" Tommy said.

"I don't know what it is. It almost makes me feel jealous."

"Don't get all romantic on me, Stotts. 'Cause between cows, goats, and wild horses, I'd be hard-pressed to tell you which is dumber. Let's go get those cows so we can call it a day."

Tom spit. I pushed my hat down tight and we rode toward the house.

The structure bled rust where the bolts held the skin down to its inner ribs. The door was on the flattened end, in the shade now, and there were two small windows with awnings over them, poking out off the curved sidewalls, and another beside the door. A rusted-out '53 Chevrolet pickup sat on its naked wheel hubs in the dirt at the far end, windows down. A loose, tumbled stack of stove-length oak was piled beside it, some spilling from its bed. Beside the wood was a pile of green-glassed wine jugs, the big kind with screw-off metal tops and finger holes alongside their necks. Some were broken, some intact, most had their labels peeling away like dried leaves. As we rode up, the goats turned their heads in our direction, bleating their pathetic hellos or their beggings.

As we rode past the front of the house to where the cows were, the door opened and Rose came out, propping a shotgun diagonally against the front wall while she looked at Tom and me.

"Sorry to intrude," I said. "We're just rounding up our cows and we'll be right out of here."

I heard Tommy mocking me, under his breath so the woman couldn't hear.

"Sorry to intrude? Sorry to intrude? Jeez, Stotts, she's not the Queen of England."

I guess I sounded pretty stupid.

Rose looked to be about seventy years old. Her hair was gray and clumpy; you could tell she cut it herself because it fell to an uneven line above her shoulders. She was short and heavy and wore a dirty flowered sundress that went past her knees. Her legs were either bruised or grimy, maybe both, and she was barefoot except for fraying, thinly strapped sandals. Her eyes squinted out at us from a face that looked like one of those dolls made from a dried apple.

"You boys," she said, "you tell your daddy to stop cutting the fence line and killing my goats. There's plenty for your Benavidez cows to eat on your own damn side of the fence."

"He's not our dad," I said. "We just work for him."

"I guess he can't find any full-growed cowboys what don't wear tennis shoes and T-shirts, then. How old are you boys, anyway?"

"I'm sixteen," I said.

"Old enough," Tom said at the same time.

"That's just children," she said. She grabbed the gun by its barrel and put it just inside the jamb of the door. "You can get your cows and go. But since they've been here on my land all this time, I'm going to ask you boys if I could get you to move some of that cordwood into my house for me."

Tom began angling Arrow toward the calves. "We really got to go."

"Hell. It's not like I want the whole pile moved."

"We can help," I offered.

And then Tom said, just low enough that only I could hear him, "Crud." He spit. "If it's not too much of an intrusion."

We carried the wood in armloads to the inside of her house and stacked it next to her stove. It was like a cave in there. The floor was dirt, her belongings were strewn down the length of the building, and where there was enough light to see up to the support of the structure, I could see huge spiderwebs.

"You boys want some milk or something?"

It had to be goat's milk. Unrefrigerated.

"No thanks."

Tom spit on her floor. She didn't even notice.

"You seen all my horses? I just started with the two. Then I picked up two more from some folk squatting on forest land when they were forced out. That's it. Ha! They just kept foaling. I never did nothing to care for 'em, but they sure are nice.

"You. Tennis Shoes. You got a real big and pretty horse."

"Thanks," I said. "You think that's enough?" And I brushed off my arms.

"It was enough a few stacks ago, but I wasn't going to stop you."

Tom was looking up at the pitch-black ceiling of the curved house.

"You got some real nice-looking horses out there, too," I said.

"I think we better get going," Tom said, edging toward the door.

"I used to have cats, too. Lots of 'em, but they all got ate. I had a twenty-four-pound cat. Biggest cat I ever seen. He never got ate, though. One time he even got bit by a rattler and that didn't kill him, neither. He just swolled up as big as a couch. Ha! I swear I thought to make a chair out of him if he died, but he didn't. You know what happened to that old twenty-four-pound cat? See those spiderwebs? Summers I get the black widows in here big enough to cook and eat like crabmeat. You know what happened? Well, he liked the smell of some old perfumey bug spray I got and he just got into that can and drank it. The whole can! Just like that. Ha! Wouldn't you know it? Bug spray! And I even seen him eat a newborn kid, one time, like it was nothing."

"If Stotts ever gets bit, he'd probly make a decent hat rack." Then Tommy spit again and I knew Rose saw him do it.

"But that was a big cat. Ha!" she continued. "Everyone said that who saw him. Big enough to set on."

I thought she was funny. Tom was about halfway to the door. The thought of those spiders hanging upside down over my head was weighing on my mind a little.

"I had to dig a big hole to bury that twenty-four-pound cat in."

Tommy said, "How do you know he weighed twenty-four pounds?" Then he spit out the open door and followed it out.

"Thank you, boy," Rose said. "Now, mind you tell those ranch hands to quit cutting the fence down and to leave my goats alone."

"I don't think anyone's messing with your goats, ma'am," I said. "At least no one's ever told me anything about it. And we're fixing the fence right now, which is why we're kind of in a hurry, 'cause we don't want to get stuck this side of it."

Rose followed me out into the bright, hot day. Tommy had one foot in his stirrup, about to launch himself up onto Arrow.

"You. Boy. You, black-haired boy with the boots on."

He was up on Arrow now, and looked down at her.

"You chewing tobacco?"

Tom spit to answer.

"It's been a real long time since I had any tobacco. Could you spare me some?"

Tom looked at me and kind of rolled his eyes. I was smiling, though. He pulled the can out of his back pocket and put a fresh wad into his mouth.

"Here." He handed her the can.

Rose opened the can, smelled the tobacco, and messily put some into the side of her cheek. "I knew you boys was nice boys when I saw you come up. That's why I didn't shoot you."

"Thanks for that," Tom said as I got up onto Reno.

"And you. Tennis Shoes. You come back some time and catch one of my horses and I'll let you keep 'em."

"You mean that?"

"The both of you can," Rose said, and spit, every bit as nicely and professionally as I had ever seen Tommy spit. She held the can up for Tommy, but he waved it away and Rose smiled and kept the tobacco.

We had the last of the strays back to the fence line. One more post had to be strung and Carl would be finished, too.

"Tommy, if she was about a hundred years younger, I think you'd be in love with that tobacco-chewing woman."

"Yeah, Stotts. And I'd have to fight you to get her 'cause of her horses."

"You boys finished yet?" Carl called out.

"This is the last of 'em," his son said.

SIX

The next day when Gabe, Tom, and I went shooting
started out innocently enough, I guess.

We met at the Foreman's house at 6, while the air of the
morning held that dry summer coolness that promised scorch-
ing heat by noon. Carl was backing the old Ford F-150 into the
hitch of a horse trailer when Gabe and I rode up.

"You want to give me a hand here, Troy?" he said. "Tom's just
getting his butt out of bed. He'll be out in a minute."

I lowered the hitch onto the receiver after Carl Buller
stopped the pickup. Then he got out and came around to help
with the rest of the hook-ups. He smelled like cigarettes and
coffee and alcohol. And although there was never a time I can
recall not seeing him drunk or on his way to it, Carl was one of
those drinkers who still managed to get out of bed early every
day and get his work done. I suppose he had his reasons. Tom's
mother ran away from them when he was just a baby. I talked

once or twice about mothers with Tom Buller, and it was probably the only thing we ever talked about that made him uncomfortable and quiet. I understood now what kept my friend from mouthing certain words, and I never for a moment believed I knew anyone in my life who was stronger or more admirable.

"Moving some horses today, Carl?"

"Benavidez bought a real pretty Walker for his wife. I'm going to go pick her up out past Leona this morning."

I finished closing the bolt on the chain on my side of the hitch and wiped the rust from my hands onto the leg of my blue jeans.

"CB, I'm gonna use the reloader when we come back today." Tom came out of the house, pushing his stringy black hair back with his right hand and then placing his hat down on his head to hold it there. "Gabe, can you come in here and help me grab some stuff?"

"If you're hungry, Gabriel, you boys can take whatever I got in the kitchen."

"Thanks, Carl," Gabriel said, and vanished behind the dark, slamming screen door.

Carl lit a cigarette and leaned against the gate of the Ford, looking at me. Then he looked over at Reno.

"Where you boys going to be shooting today?"

"Tom says we're going to ride down to that big south field 'cause that little hill with the cross on it's a good enough backstop and there's no cows down there now."

"Just make sure you don't let that Gabey blow his own head off. Benavidez wouldn't look kindly on me if that were to happen."

"I don't exactly think he'd want to immediately adopt me, either," I said, and Carl looked at me, smiling and wincing in the bitterness of his filterless smoke.

"Is Tom's horse around back?"

"You could get him. Take care." And then he yelled to the shut screen door, "'Bye, son!"

I could hear Tom and Gabe both shouting their good-byes from within the house as I walked around back to the wood-fenced stall where Arrow stayed during the warm-weather months. From the front of the house came the rattling clatter of the truck and trailer driving off toward the west.

Tom and Gabe came out the back door as I was cinching Arrow's saddle.

"Hey thanks, Stotts." I don't think he ever called me Troy unless he was talking about me to someone else. "You got your gun?"

"Yeah. It's on Reno."

Tom slung his saddlebag over Arrow and hooked it onto the saddle. He reached into his right back pocket, permanently branded with a faded moon-shaped stress mark where he carried a constant supply of smokeless tobacco and pulled out a black-and-green can of Kodiak. He took the can, label side up with the head of a bear on it, between the thumb and middle finger of his right hand and whipped it down four times, each shake making a cap-gun pop as his index finger snapped against the lid.

He pried the cap from the can and extracted a small wad of the wet black-brown dip and jammed it down into the lower right corner of his lip. He wiped his fingers off on the butt of his jeans.

"That's nasty stuff," Gabriel said.

Tom held the can out in his left palm, the lid still off. "Want some, Gabe? Stotts?"

I don't know why, but I wanted to try that stuff so bad; all those times being with Tommy and watching him doing it. So I don't know why, but I just said, "Okay."

And Gabe said, "No way!"

And Tommy laughed and said, "No way, Stottsy!"

But I took the can from Tom and, feeling like an expert from having watched him do it so many times, cornered a wad between my thumb and finger and only spilled a little bit before I got it down between my lips and teeth.

"The trick is" — and Tommy spit a big wet string down at his feet — "don't swallow it, or they say it'll make you sick, but that's never happened to me. And know when to shut up and just smile. That's one of the hidden benefits. It makes people shut up." And he spit again before saying, "So let's go!"

Well, first of all it smelled pretty good, I thought. And it didn't taste bad, either, although it was powerfully minty and it kind of burned in my mouth. But then in about twenty seconds, as we were walking Arrow around toward the other horses, I all-of-a-sudden had to grab on to one of his stirrups just to make sure I wouldn't fall down. Everything suddenly seemed far away, including Tommy's laughter and his voice echoing dimly, "Pretty good buzz, huh, Stottsy?"

"Oh yeah." And I spit, but not with the same seasoned and classy experience as a Tom Buller. I got it on my shoe.

Gabriel watched me, in shock and disgust, his mouth open and curled down.

And to think I'd actually seen Tommy Buller drive a car

with this stuff in his mouth and not veer off into the lake. At least I knew I could count on Reno to navigate me safely.

We rode slowly south toward the field the Benavidez cattle pastured in during late spring, now picked fairly clean; the grass dried straw-blond. I disposed of my chew and washed out my mouth and spit. Then I took a long drink of water from my canteen. I was still undecided as to whether or not I liked it enough to try it again. Tommy kept his in for a long time, and could carry on conversations naturally so that you'd hardly notice he was chewing. Sometimes, because of the way he'd punctuate his speech with spitting, you'd swear he had it in his mouth even when he didn't.

"Give me your money," Tom said, holding out his hand. We each gave him five dollars. It was our way of gambling on our shooting skills, although I believed at the outset that they'd both be better off just handing their money over to me and saving their bullets.

Tommy had brought along an assortment of targets: empty beer cans and plastic milk jugs. We never used bottles or glass for targets on Benavidez land. And none of our horses was gun-shy, but as Tommy set up the targets atop rocks or downed trees on the hillside, I tied the three of them up in the shade of a big mushroom-shaped oak about a hundred yards away.

I walked back to our makeshift range, carrying a brick of five hundred rounds and my old Winchester bolt-action .22. My dad gave me the rifle when I was ten, and it was already about forty years old at that time. But it was real easy to take care of, and it shot with extreme accuracy.

Tom brought out his .40-caliber handgun, the magazine ejected and the slide latched back so we could all see it was unloaded. He reloaded his own ammo because bullets for that thing were expensive, while .22 rounds were practically free.

Gabriel didn't have his own gun. I doubted his parents knew he was with us. I had taken him shooting before, though, and he was a fair shot with my .22, even though he seemed afraid of guns. But I think Gabriel was more afraid of admitting he was scared to me and Tom than he was of shooting. Of course, living where we did meant that people pretty much had to have guns. I guess, for boys, having a gun was about the same as having a bicycle if we had lived in the suburbs. And Benavidez did try to push the issue on him, but I knew Gabriel had such an aversion to guns and the thought of hurting things, even though he'd tag along with me and Tom no matter what we wanted to do.

"Okay," Tommy said, "ten shots at ten targets. After you shoot, you go up and set 'em up again. First one to twenty-five wins the cash. Who wants to go first?"

"Not me," Gabe said, to no one's surprise.

"You set 'em up. Go ahead, Tom."

Tom pushed ten of the stubby rounds into the magazine and slid it, with a click, up into the handle of his gun. He pressed down on the catch and released the slide forward. He raised the gun with both hands and cocked his head back slightly. "Okay, I'm going across left to right."

I was watching Tommy and the target arrangement, but when he pulled off the first round, I could see Gabriel jerk, startled, out of the corner of my eye. Maybe I did, too. Even out here in the open field, that gun of Tom's was painfully loud.

He missed the first shot.

"Why don't you just give me the cash now?"

"You'll get a chance with that peashooter, Stotts."

He cleanly hit the next seven in a row, but missed the last two targets.

"I'm up. Let's see how you did." And we all walked up the hill to replace the targets and count up the score.

It really was kind of unfair, my using a rifle against Tommy's handgun, but he didn't complain, so after I hit all ten targets in my first round I offered, "Let's trade guns for round two, okay?"

"Fair enough," Tom said.

"Can I try your gun?" Gabe asked Tommy, who widened his eyes and said, "Sure, if you really want to."

We walked back down to our shooting place and Tommy handed Gabe an empty magazine and a box of reloads.

"Just push in ten of 'em like you seen me do," Tom instructed. Tom pulled the slide back on the .40 and latched it, then handed it to Gabe, who inserted the magazine.

"Okay, now. When you release the slide, there'll be one in the chamber, so be careful 'cause it won't stop shooting till it's empty. Aim it just like a rifle, only your arm's the stock." And Tom spit down at his boots.

We both stood back, behind Gabriel, watching him take aim at the first target. He pulled the trigger, and a good five seconds before we realized it, all of these things happened at once: The first target, a beer can, spun up in the air, whirling like a propeller blade and disappearing into the brush behind it. As the gun kicked back in Gabriel's hand he said, "Ow!" and pulled his hand in toward his chest. Gabriel let go of the gun and it flipped over the back of his hand. When the gun hit the ground, it discharged a second time, this time sending a bullet cutting through the air just between Tommy and me. We were standing just about eighteen inches apart.

I looked at Tommy, slack jawed, examining him up and down to see if there was any blood. I'm sure Tommy was looking for the same thing on me. Neither of us said anything, we just stared at each other, each thinking, I'm certain, about how unlucky we almost were.

"I hit it!" Gabe was joyous. Then he realized what had happened with the gun, no longer in his startled hand.

"You know, Gabey," Tom began, "we always promised to be lifelong friends, but I wasn't planning on me being barely seventeen when that came to an end."

"I can't exactly say sixteen is an old man, either," I said, "so why don't you just stick to the .22, bud?"

Tommy carefully picked the gun out from the weeds at Gabe's feet. "You didn't by any chance bring a couple baseballs with you, Gabey?" Tommy asked. "You'd take us for sure."

Gabriel could throw a baseball faster and straighter than anyone I'd ever seen.

We all laughed. I know Gabe felt horrible, and things didn't get any better for him when Tommy added, "And by the way, you only have eight shots left, Gabey."

"No fair!" Gabe said, but, after almost killing us, there was no way we'd let his protest amount to anything.

Gabe ended up scoring five on the first round. I'm sure his nerves got the better of him, because I'd seen him do better with my rifle plenty of times. Tommy's handgun was a little heavy and difficult for me to aim, and as I hefted it, I kind of got a sense that it was hungry to get a person.

Despite using the pistol, I took nine targets in my second

round, so it looked to all of us that I'd be the winner again today.

"It's not over yet, Stotts," Tommy said. "Let's count 'em up."

And we all went up to reset the targets. That first beer can was getting the worst of it; its top was nearly shorn off. Once again it had been knocked behind the log on which it had rested, into the cover of dried grass.

"There it is," Tommy said, and stepped over the log while Gabe and I looked along our range at the other fallen targets.

That's when Tom Buller kneeled down right on top of one of the biggest rattlesnakes I'd ever seen.

The thing I hate most about rattlers is how whenever you're looking for one, walking with that feeling that it's around and trying to be careful to see it before it sees you, you never see one. And then one day you're walking along, minding your own business, thinking about something that bothers you, admiring the beautiful day, thinking about a girl, and next thing you know you're calling yourself every variation of stupid for nearly stepping right on one.

Tom let out a stifled scream and jumped back, but it was too late. The big snake whipped back around and bit Tommy through his pants, just below his right knee.

"Dammit!" And Tommy grabbed at his leg tightly with both hands and rolled onto his side.

The snake, fat and black, slid off through the grass, down the length of our target range. I chased after it. Our guns were left behind, resting at the spot where we'd been firing from, but I found a branch from an oak tree and began clubbing the snake. I hit it squarely in the center of its back and it suddenly bent, stiffly, at a right angle, and turned back toward me. His back was broken, he would die for sure, but not soon enough. I drove his head down into the ground with the end of the branch and his body wriggled and twisted in protest. I stepped down on his head with my left foot and pulled the Dawson from my back pocket, opening it with the thumb of my right hand. The snake twisted violently as I cut the head clean from the body, and then, as blood vomited in thick purple clots from the wound, the decapitated rattler crawled off a few more feet into the weeds.

I stepped on the headless snake at the tail end and cut the rattle off. As I cut, the body still twisted and coiled and tried to crawl away from me. Gabriel was in shock, frozen, staring down at Tommy, afraid to move.

Sometimes I wanted to take hold of Gabriel and shake him so hard. I can't really blame him for having no confidence, because I know he understood his father believed Luz was so much better and smarter and that Gabriel could never be man enough to run that ranch. But at times I still angrily hoped that my friend could snap out of his runt-of-the-litter complex, at least when he was with Tom and me; especially when we needed him.

I still had the open Dawson in my hand, the rattle in my left.

Tom was lying on his left side, rocking, clutching his right knee, and moaning.

And I didn't know whether I should laugh or cry, or just kick him for being so reckless, but I heard myself saying out loud, "I can't get mad at Tom Buller for being Tom Buller." Then I spit and wished I had some more of that tobacco.

"You'll be okay, bud. Here." I knelt beside him and stuffed the rattle down into Tom's hip pocket.

Gabe still hadn't moved.

"I'm going to need some help, Gabe," I said and he took the few careful steps over the log toward us.

"Sorry, Tommy, we're going to need to see how bad it got you. If it's bleeding and deep or just in the skin," I said and then began cutting up the side seam of his jeans from the bottom. "Pull that boot off, Gabe."

Gabriel pulled Tommy's boot away and I cut his pants up just past the knee.

"It burns so bad!" Tommy said. "Oh God, I'm going to puke."

"What're we going to do?" Gabe asked, his voice cracking.

"Listen, it's going to be okay. Just do what I tell you, Gabe. You're not the one who's bit."

"Man, it feels like your horse is standing on my leg. It hurts really, really bad, Troy."

That's when I knew he was in bad shape. He used my first name. I saw the little pink holes where the rattler had bitten into Tom's leg, and it was striking to me how insignificant they seemed compared to the amount of pain Tom appeared to be in.

"Yeah, you're bit. But it's just under the skin so it's not too bad."

"Yes it is, Stotts."

"Are you going to have to suck the poison out?" Gabriel asked.

"No. That's not what you do." I couldn't believe Gabriel had lived up here all his life and didn't know what to do for a rattlesnake bite. Everyone knew, I thought. But I did find my-self remembering about what to do from reading it in a book.

"I'm going to get that chew, Tom," I said, and winced as I put my fingers into his mouth and pulled out his wad of tobacco. "You don't want that in your mouth right now. Here." I pressed the chewing tobacco down over the bite marks.

"My mouth tastes really bad, Stotts. What did you have on your hand?"

"Nothing. That's the poison. It'll do that to you. Come on." And I grabbed his right arm away from his leg and put it around the back of my neck.

"Gabe, you got to help me walk him down to the shade by the horses," I said. "We're going to sit him up against the tree. You keep him sitting up and keep him cool. Put water on his head and give him some to drink if he'll take it. I'm going to ride Reno out to the Foreman's house and call for help. Got it?"

"I can do that," Gabriel said.

We got Tommy seated against the tree. He was yellow and sweaty and his mouth just hung open like there was something in it you couldn't see. I grabbed the three canteens we had with us and tossed them down on the ground by Gabriel.

"Don't tie it off, either," I said. "I'll get help. They'll probly send a helicopter."

And then I wiped back Tommy's hair from his clammy fore-head. "You're going to be okay, bud. You're tougher than any twenty-four-pound house cat."

"But will I ever dance again, Doc?"

"Don't worry, Tommy," I said, "Christy McCracken's already got the tickets for the end-of-school dance."

I heard Gabriel laugh nervously behind me. I wondered if

he was picturing those two all over each other at the dance back in May.

"If I wasn't about to throw up all over myself, I'd slug you for that."

I got up onto Reno's saddle.

"Stotts," Tommy said to me, his open mouth slurring the words slightly, staring down at his knee, which was swelling now, "for once in your life, ride him hard and don't fall off."

I held on to Reno, tight and low against his neck. I let him go. I had never ridden him this fast before, I had always struggled with holding him back because he was so big and strong for someone my size.

Do you like him? Because I know he likes you very much, and sometimes these things just happen with horses.

He's a great horse, Mr. Benavidez.

He's for you, Troy. Take him home.

What? Why?

I was only thirteen years old, and sitting on Reno was like being stopped at the top of a Ferris wheel. He was so big, and his front feet were dancing like he wanted to bolt from a starting gate. Mr. Benavidez was holding him steady and when he saw I had my tennis shoes in the stirrups and had pushed my black Stetson down across my eyebrows, tight, he let go.

He's mine?

I'm sure he is.

Thank you, Mr. Benavidez.

You are welcome, Troy.

✦ ✦ ✦

I looked up at the mountains, their granite fingers. Sweat, salty, stinging, blurred my eyes. I looked up to that cross-shaped airplane, where it would be if I could see through those rocks.

He'll be okay, he'll be okay.

Reno pushed so hard and I stayed on him, holding the reins loose and steering him with my face and shoulders, pressed against his thick pumping neck. I felt like Tommy Buller, a real rider. I wished he could see us cutting across the south field toward his house.

I called for rescue at the Foreman's house. Carl hadn't come back yet, and, as usual, the doors had been left standing open. Then I phoned the Benavidez house, and Luz, worried, rode out to meet me on my way back to the south field. The helicopter was already landing by then.

Tommy spent four days in the hospital, and after he got out he never walked entirely straight again. Part of the danger of living where we did, up in the mountains, was that in an emergency you had to handle things yourself or wait for help and hope for the best. A lot of the kids we went to school with didn't like the fact that it was thirty miles to the nearest movie theater, but there were no such things as stoplights up here either, and Tom and I liked that just fine. So his knee never recovered entirely from the rattlesnake bite, but Tom Buller never complained about it, either.

✦   ✦   ✦

We knew Tommy wasn't supposed to get on a horse so soon, but he just waited until Carl wasn't paying too much attention, which wasn't much of a wait, and rode out to meet us at the fire pit the day after he got home from the hospital.

"You should see what it did to my leg," Tommy said. "It turned so black and puffy, I looked like something you'd find floating facedown after a flood. It's still so purple, I don't know if it will ever look right."

"Let me see," Gabriel said.

Tommy pulled his jeans' leg up slowly over the top of his boot past his knee. The wound looked horrible. The flesh was separated and brilliant red where the doctors had to cut the dead tissue away, stitched together with thick black fibers. It looked so painful, but Tommy just smiled and poked at the edges with his finger.

"Are you gonna be okay, Tom?" I asked.

"It feels like my knee's never going to work right again," Tommy said, slightly bouncing as he pushed his pants back over his boot. "But you gotta see this."

He lifted his shirt up past his bony ribs and pulled the waist of his jeans down as the smoke from our fire curled around his pale body like the hand of some giant ghost. Gabe and I saw the tattoo of the rattlesnake on his right hip. It was small and black, with diamonds on its back, looking like it was crawling along his belly toward his heart.

"Did it hurt?" I asked.

"Not as much as getting bit," Tommy said, "but it hurt pretty good. It still hurts a little."

"That's a good one," Gabe said.

"You should've gotten one of a forty caliber, too," I said.

"I would've, but the guy couldn't draw it."

Tom was lying, grinning. We knew he had drawn it himself. He could draw anything.

"Oh shut up," Gabriel said.

"When did you do it?" I asked.

"Last night. I went to Holmes."

I leaned in to Tommy and looked closely at the inked figure on his skin. It was so black where the ink had gone in, it almost looked like velvet, but the flesh around the clean edge of the snake was pink and swollen. I held my finger just above the tattoo, and I could feel the heat from Tommy's side, and then I touched him.

"Ow!" Tommy yelped suddenly, and I nearly jumped out of my shoes.

Then Tom and Gabe started to laugh wildly, and I swatted Tom's hat from his head, feeling foolish for being startled so badly.

"Why'd you do that, anyway?"

"What? Scare you?" Tommy asked.

"No." I pointed at his hip. "Why'd you get that?"

"I don't know," Tommy said. "I guess it's kind of a warning to me. Maybe it's a warning to the other snakes out there. So it'll keep 'em away."

"Or maybe it will attract 'em," I said. Then I looked right at Tommy, could see him watching me, the small pulses of our fire reflecting in his eyes. "I was scared about the whole thing, Tom. You know?"

"I know," Tommy said. "And thanks, Stotts."

Tommy just smiled that bent-up confident grin he always wore, looking down in admiration at the black snake crawling across his belly and then he let his shirt fall back down to cover it.

SEVEN

You sure are one scrawny little cowboy, Tennis Shoes."

"Everyone says that. I can't help it."

"I guess as long as you're sitting in a saddle your pants'll stay up anyways."

I went back to Rose's by myself a few days later. I brought her some tobacco and a little brown kitten I'd picked up in front of the market in Holmes. I told her it was named To-bacco. I had gotten Carl Buller to buy me a jug of that wine I saw outside her place. He thought it was for me. I didn't say anything. I watched Rose open it. We were sitting outside her front door on two folding chairs I had dragged out from inside the place. Reno was standing, drinking at the trough.

"Those bottles out there. It's not 'cause I liked the stuff, par-ticularly. Winery people gave it to me. Ha! Winery people. Looking at my land. Wanting to put grapevines on it. So I told 'em not to come up here if they didn't bring some wine next time. So you know what they did? They delivered twenty cases.

And I never had any idea to sell to 'em anyway. I told 'em if you planted grapes here in this ground, they'd come out tastin' like cows and horses. Ha! You want some, boy?"

"I'm too young."

"There's no laws on my land."

"My name's Troy. Troy Stotts."

"That's a strong name for a boy. And the other one, your brother — the one with black hair that wears them boots?"

"Tom. He's not my brother. He's still not walking right from that snake bite."

"Snake? Ha! He got bit? Did he swell up?"

"Well, he turned colors. That's for sure."

"Did I ever tell you about that twenty-four-pound cat I had?"

"Yes."

"Well, every time I go into town, they never have no cats, so thank you, Troy Stotts, 'cause this one'll be a good one."

"Did you walk all the way to town?"

"I got a station wagon out there. But it's no good, really. I got a lawyer who takes care of my money and pays my land taxes for me, that's why I went. You got a girl?"

"Yes." I thought about Luz. I had never said such a thing out loud, and wondered if the saying made it true.

"She pretty?"

"Yes. She's smart, too."

"Then you better be careful. What's her name?"

"Luz."

Rose smiled. She patted my knee softly with a wrinkled hand. "Don't mind the things you give up. We all do it."

"What?"

"What you have to give up to go and make her yours. Don't mind it. But don't forget it, neither."

I didn't know what she was talking about, so I just pretended like I did, kept my mouth closed, and nodded.

Rose patted my knee again and said, "You'll be okay, Tennis Shoes. I can tell that."

"You said me and Tom could come back and get some horses."

"I knew you liked 'em. I could see it right away. Of course you can get yourselves horses. I said it, didn't I? I don't ride 'em. I hardly even get 'em any feed but once in a while."

"We'll bring some hay next time."

"Will you move some more wood in then?"

"I'll do it right now."

"Thanks for the cat, boy. I don't think this one'll get that big, though."

"You got a big black mare out there that looks pregnant. She's real pretty. And she looks mean, but I like that sometimes in a horse. As long as she's not crazy mean, you know? 'Cause if she's not crazy mean then she'll be mine, and no one else's. You know that about horses?"

"Sounds like you want more than a couple horses for you boys."

"I would."

"Will you bring more tobacco?"

+ + +

I never liked the sheriff's son, Chase Rutledge. He was eighteen and had just graduated from school, so Tom, Gabe, and I had spent enough years dealing with his torments, name-calling, and otherwise just unlikable attitude. More than anything else, I think it was just a natural resentment Chase felt toward us and our friendship, something that he never had with the selfish and shallow punks who called themselves his friends. Growing up, he mostly left Tommy alone, though; most likely because Tom Buller had a reputation for being a real fighter, and Chase knew well enough about that.

So I kind of cringed when I rode Reno to Papa's store one night after work to buy some tobacco for Rose and saw Chase's best friend, Jack Crutchfield, standing alone on the deck outside the front door. And Jack, fat and mean, knew I was there but he didn't even look at me when I walked past him.

Inside I saw Chase, tall and dirty, the boy who rarely seemed to shower or put on anything clean. He was standing at the counter, arguing with George Hess, who refused to sell him whiskey.

Chase just stared at me, and I looked away, pulling my hat down straighter.

And when George handed me the tins of tobacco I'd asked for, I could almost feel the heat coming from Chase as he got madder.

"You'll sell that kid tobacco, but you won't sell me a bottle?" Chase whined, scratching the greasy hair under his baseball cap.

I cleared my throat, looked down, and waited for George to make my change.

"Tobacco's one thing," George said, "but whiskey's out of the question, Chase. What would your dad say? And besides, I know this isn't for Troy. He doesn't chew. It's gotta be for Tommy or someone else. Isn't that right, Troy?"

I stuttered, "Uh, yeah."

George handed me my change and, turning away from Chase, I wadded it up and stuffed it with the tobacco into my back pocket. As I opened the door, I could hear Chase pleading, "Come on, George."

And George Hess said, "I told you no, Chase. Now just get on home."

Chase Rutledge slammed his hand down on the counter and followed me out.

I could tell Chase was wanting to make some kind of a scene, so I quickly began untying Reno's lead from the post in front of the store.

"Stotts."

"What, Chase?"

Jack stood, breathing hard through his nose, right behind the sheriff's son.

Chase looked both ways across the dark street. There was nobody else around. I knew he was looking to see if Tommy was with me.

"Go in there and ask George to sell you a bottle of whiskey."

I took a deep breath.

Jack grunted. "Ask him, Troy."

"He won't sell it to me, Chase," I said.

"I bet he will. He thinks you're a good boy."

Chase moved closer. I could smell him. I held Reno's lead in my hand, feeling trapped.

"Do it, Stotts," Chase said, close enough that I could feel the heat of his breath.

"Forget it, Chase."

"Think you can stand up to me without Tommy Buller around?"

I looked right at him. "Yeah. I do."

Then Chase Rutledge said, "You're a pussy, Troy." And before I could do anything about it, he balled up a fist and punched me in the gut. I doubled over and fell onto my hands and knees, still holding Reno's lead and jerking my horse forward. I must have stayed down there for more than a minute, trying to get my breath back, because when I cleared my head and straightened up, Chase and Jack were gone.

I heard them laughing somewhere out in the dark.

I never said anything to Tom or Gabriel about that night. I wanted to forget about it. But I was nagged by the feeling that I had to get even.

*　*　*

Every morning always began the same way at my house: feeding Reno, cleaning his stall while keeping an eye out for the turkey, feeding the goats, throwing scratch to the hens and cleaning their nest boxes, gathering any eggs laid during the night, although they tended to lay most in the afternoons. I liked the routine well enough, and I always loved mornings at my home most of all, the color of the sky, and the smell of the air. My dad told me that he always resented having to do the chores when he was a boy, but when we moved back after my brother died, I just naturally started doing them even though at first I was too small. At first, I think my dad wanted to forget everything about boyhood in general, and my mom hurt so bad that she just needed to try to find some cure, somehow, for the ghost of her older boy, so even at four years old I knew enough to leave them alone, especially in the morning, and I'd wake and find myself outside, breathing that air, seeing the colors of the stretched and slanted sun, trying to find something to do that would become my routine. But the morning after I brought Rose the kitten was when things began to take a turn away from those routine days that just happen and then are forgotten.

I could smell the coffee waiting for me in the kitchen. I had grown to appreciate coffee in the mornings, ever since the day Luz came up to that cabin and we had shared some. I'd drink some coffee, do my morning chores, and, while I was out, Dad would get some breakfast for me.

I slipped my feet into my loose shoes, put on a clean T-shirt and my hat, and went outside.

I swear Reno could hear me getting dressed because every morning as I put on shoes he began his usual chorus of feed-me calls from out in the barn. That morning, on top of his bellowing, I could tell he was running around inside his enclosure.

I stepped down the three wooden steps, the middle one a bit wobbly, onto the cool ground. In the hay room, I flaked off some alfalfa for Reno and the goats. I grabbed two small orange buckets and scooped some scratch into one and some sweetened four-way grain into the other.

You know how sometimes you can be so caught up in the hypnosis of a routine that the whole world could be on fire in the corner of your eye and you wouldn't really notice it until a burning tree fell on your head? Well, that's kind of how things worked out that summer morning, because something was terribly wrong, right in front of me, but I might just as well have been blind.

So it wasn't until after I had dropped some hay onto the ground for the goats, put Reno's in his feeder and fended off his usual barrage of nose pushes and nudging until I gave up the grain, and tossed some scratch out onto the dusty ground in front of the henhouse, while looking out for that mean tom turkey of mine, that I noticed the large trail of blood like some gruesome treasure path leading out to the edge of the enclosure to a thick little stand of pines where a narrow creek flowed most of the year. I remember thinking, *Oh. Blood.* And it looked ridiculous, too, like spilled paint or clown's makeup, but I knew it was blood, it couldn't have possibly been anything else.

I first looked at Reno, at his legs and belly; but he looked fine. I walked toward the blood, got about halfway across the pen, and then my eyes followed the trail out toward the trees. Right on the other side of the pipe fencing, still and motionless, was a mountain lion. She was staring at me, her mouth open, panting noiselessly. Her muzzle and face were wet with blood, but it looked black, not like the candy-colored red streaming across the ground in front of me. Just below the bottom rail of the pipe corral, half-in, half-out of our enclosure, was the carcass of one of our small black goats.

The lion just watched me, as if to say: "Well, what are you going to do about it?" I looked down, but there was nothing to throw at her. I took my hat off, but I wasn't about to throw that. It wouldn't have gone far enough, anyway. So I flailed my hat around and began yelling, "Get out of here!"

Reno startled a little and trotted over to my side as I continued waving and yelling.

The lion took up the little goat in her jaws, pulled it backwards a few feet out of the enclosure, then disappeared into the darkness of the trees. I could hear her dragging the carcass, stepping heavily, snapping small twigs. Then she was just gone.

I heard the *whack!-whack-whack* of the screen door back at the house, then the sound of my father tramping across my worn path, following my footprints to where I stood, Reno beside me, staring down at the crazy redness in the corral. I wasn't scared, but my heart was thumping heavily, and I could feel the surge of caffeine and adrenaline pushing small pindrops of sweat out of my temples.

My dad came up to the enclosure, undid the catch on the gate. "Were you screaming?"

"A huge mountain lion got one of the goats. That little black stupid one."

Calling a goat stupid is like calling water wet.

But you didn't mean that about those wild horses, too, did you, Tommy?

Well, they're not so dumb, I guess.

You wanna come back here with me and get us a couple of 'em?

She said we could.

Bring her some more tobacco. And Tommy? I'd take 'em all if she'd let us.

I showed my dad where I had seen the cat carrying off its kill. We climbed between the rails and followed the blood trail back into the trees. There was no mark on the ground here, so following the lion was difficult, and both of us realized we didn't want to get too close to her anyway.

"I guess we should call Fish and Game."

"Dad, by the time that guy gets out here it'll be April. I'm calling Carl Buller and see what he says we should do. They've probly had lions before on the Benavidez."

"You could call him. But I don't think it'll come back here anyway. Look how long we've lived here and never even seen one."

We went back inside and had more coffee. I was nervous about leaving Reno out there, but I couldn't believe a cat would think of bothering him. We penned up the other two goats inside the barn and sealed shut the henhouse. My dad got on the phone to the Fish and Game Department, and had to call the opposite end of the state just to get the number of our local agent, and then he had to leave a recorded message for him anyway. I went back to my room and got my .22 from the closet and propped it, along with a box of loose ammo, beside the kitchen door.

"I wouldn't shoot a lion with a .22, Troy, unless you're sure you can outrun her."

"Let me use that thirty-ought-six then."

"I say we just wait a while. She's not coming back for anything else here."

But my dad was wrong.

✦   ✦   ✦

It rained the next afternoon. The stain of blood disappeared.

She rode out to see me. I was working alone that day. I had driven the F-150 out into the pasture to drop off some dry bales of alfalfa to the horses after the rain. I saw her riding out on Doats, wondering how she could get away, unnoticed, from her parents' watching.

We sat on the open tailgate of the truck, swinging our feet in the air over the edge, leaning back against the hay, hooks hanging like floppy ears from the bale's upturned corners. I put my arm around her shoulder and we hooked our ankles together and swung those legs, like one, up and down off the gate. And we sat there like that as the horses gathered around the feeder, sticking their noses through the metal poles that supported the hay as they ate, occasionally looking up, ears perked, and sniffing at us. I can't imagine there was anywhere better either of us could be.

And she kissed my cheek, so softly. We sat there, watching the horses, looking at the sky, smelling the smell of the land.

"Isn't this about the most beautiful place in the world, Troy?"

I took my hat off and put it on her head.

"I wouldn't pick anywhere else over it."

She picked up a piece of straw and tickled the bottom of my chin with it, and we sat there for the longest time, not saying anything, just watching.

"What do you want, Troy?"

"You mean more than *this*?" I asked. And I know I should have been choking on nervousness, but I felt so relaxed beside her.

"Yes."

"Nothing could be better than this, Luz."

She brushed the straw through the hair over my ear.

"How about you?" I said.

Luz cleared her throat and put her hand on my knee.

"My dad says that one day this whole ranch is going to be mine," she said. "He says that I'd be the only woman who could ever keep it running."

"I bet that's true."

I lay my head back farther in the hay and stretched my leg out straight and held it there, so I could see the shape of her ankle where it rested over my foot.

"Is that what you would want?" I asked.

"I love it here," she said. And she said it slowly, so my heart nearly jumped out of my mouth because I thought she was about to say something else. Something about me, that I wanted to hear, but it scared me just the same.

My throat was still tight. "Does Gabey know that?"

"No."

"Oh."

I lowered my leg and began swinging our feet from the edge of the gate again.

"He doesn't want this place, anyway," Luz said.

"He doesn't?"

"No. He only wants our dad to think he'd be good enough to do it."

"He is good enough," I said.

"I know."

+ + +

By Friday of that week, the lion had taken another of our goats, and the Fish and Game officer hadn't called us back. Carl said we should track the cat and kill it ourselves, and I was starting to feel more and more like doing that, too. So when I got home that day, nervous because I had to leave Reno behind in the morning to drive with Tommy into Holmes, the first thing I did was to go out to the barn and check on my horse. It started raining softly.

And there was the cat. I saw her right away, but her coloring blended right in with the bare dirt in the grayness of the afternoon drizzle. She was in the middle of the enclosure, hunched over my big tom turkey, biting its neck as it offered up a feeble and fading flutter of protest. And even though I was kind of happy to see that mean turkey finally meet his match and then some, I was mad at the thought of this cat coming back to take whatever she wanted from us. So I grabbed a big rake propped up against Reno's stall, and I threw it like a spear. It tumbled in the air, landing so its handle struck right across the lion's shoulders.

The cat shrunk down, alarmed, and without looking back at me leapt through the bars of the corral and vanished. The turkey lay in the mud, a big mound of bloodied white feathers, wheezing a bubbling spray of blood from its nearly severed neck.

And Reno just stood there in the mud, getting rained on, watching the whole thing impassively, the way that horses do.

"A couple months early for Thanksgiving," I said, straight-mouthed, as I looked down at the bird's remains.

I put Reno and all the other animals inside the barn and closed it up. I picked up the turkey by its horny, muddy feet, its purpled head lolling limply beneath its huge carcass, wings splayed out like filthy fans. It was heavy, about forty-five pounds, and in good enough condition that I wondered whether my father would ask me to pluck it and clean it.

I put the turkey on top of a big plastic trash bag and left it in the mudroom off the back porch and waited for my father to come home.

I called Tommy.

"We've got to get that mountain lion. I just hit her with a rake. She killed our turkey."

"Hit her with a rake? Jeez, Stotts, you're a caveman!"

"We could go out tonight, but it's gonna get dark in about an hour and I don't want to be out there in the dark, you know? Can you see if we can get out of work tomorrow and you and Gabey meet me up here early in the morning?"

"CB'll cover for us. Sounds like fun."

"Bring your gun."

"As long as you keep Gabey away from it."

"And Tom? We're not saying nothing to my dad, okay?"

"Even if one of us gets killed, bud."

"So we'll have to leave before he's up. Meet me at the bridge at five."

"Happy Saturday, Stottsy."

My dad told me to clean and gut the turkey. Then, he said, he'd cook it. I didn't really mind being assigned this duty, and I half expected it. But I'd never done it before, and now, looking back, I don't think I'll ever do it again.

"How?" I asked him.

"Well, you know what a turkey looks like when you buy it in the store. Make it look like that," he said, smiling. And that was about the extent of his instructions. But he stayed and watched me while I worked at it, and I never asked him for help and he never told me I was doing anything wrong. He just watched me and smiled.

After I took off the head, which wasn't too hard since the lion had gotten it most of the way free, I had to deal with all those feathers. I'd seen my mother put a bird in boiling water to do this, but we didn't have any pots big enough for this thing. So I worked for over an hour, plucking it in the sink and pouring boiling water from the teakettle onto it as I went. This made the bird give off a smell like a boiled barnyard.

Once I had it plucked, it looked reasonably good. I took the feet off at the knee joints and opened up the body cavity. Then the powerful stink of that tom turkey came oozing out, smelling like cigar smoke mixed with furniture polish and cheap perfume. That about nearly made me gag. That, and the texture of the guts, the popping little air sacs in the lungs, which looked like pale pink caviar, and my father standing quietly behind me, watching me, blood spilling down the yellowing porcelain of the sink basin, me reaching into the cavity up to my elbows and holding my breath all the while. I had taken my shirt off because I didn't want any of the blood and guts on it, and I was splattered all over my chest and belly.

"Man, I bet most third-graders don't have this many guts in 'em." I squinted my eyes, my mouth was turned down in sour disgust.

My dad laughed.

Then I went to clean out the crop, full of gritty, chewed-up food, looking like a pale and warm kind of oatmeal, which added another depth to the overall stench. When I was finished, I washed the bird off. I held out my arms, away from my body, fingers pointed up like a surgeon, like those mountains. But I did it.

"There. You can cook him now. I'll be in the shower for the rest of the night."

And I left my dad standing in the kitchen.

Even under the running water of the shower I could smell that turkey. What I had always remembered and associated with holidays and family reunions was now somehow transformed into something else, mature and unpleasant. I put on clean clothes, but that smell was everywhere in the house.

It was raining steadily now. I walked through the living room, stopping and bending down by our woodstove to breathe in a cleansing smell of burning oak.

My dad was sitting at the kitchen table, waiting for me.

"Feel better?"

"Yeah."

"Smells good, doesn't it?"

"Smells. That's for sure."

"I don't think it'll be ready before midnight, though."

"I don't think I can eat right now, Dad. I think I'm going to bed."

And I didn't eat turkey again until the following year.

✦   ✦   ✦

I woke up at 4 the next morning. The house smelled like turkey. It was still raining, but lightly and sporadically. I pulled my jeans on over the long johns I slept in, but even then they weren't going to stay up. After not eating the night before, I felt like I was shrinking. I pulled a T-shirt on over my thermal, and then a sweatshirt over those.

It was lucky that my dad had stayed up so late cooking that turkey, because I knew he wouldn't wake if I made myself some coffee before I left. While it was brewing, I stuffed the inside pockets of my coat with candy bars and cookies, a couple pieces of bread. I sighed as I pulled my pants up, tried to stick out my belly, but I couldn't get it out far enough to snug up the waist on my pants much at all.

I poured a cup of coffee, black. I blew on it and sucked in a small sip. It tasted like turkey broth. I almost spit it out. I poured the rest of my cup back into the pot and left it for my dad. I quietly cursed that stupid bird for ruining my appetite for just about everything. I hoped he suffered while he was lying there in that mud. I hoped he could feel himself being cooked.

My rifle was still resting beside the door. I dumped the box of bullets into my coat pocket. I wished I could've taken my dad's deer rifle, but that was impossible now. I'd be okay, I thought.

I walked out into the dark rain.

The air smelled good, cool and clean. I kept my head angled down, watching my feet push up little swells of water as I stepped, silently measuring the amount of time it would take until water began dropping down in front of me from the brim of my hat.

The "bridge" wasn't really a bridge at all. It was really just a big concrete pipe that had been placed in the creek running from behind our property. Before my father put it there, we would have to drive through the creek bed to get to or away from my house, and sometimes that would mean getting blocked in or out during the winter and having to cross by wading, which was never fun when the creek ran fast, muddy, and cold. As I walked there, I watched my breath form clouds out of my mouth, occasionally ducking my mouth into the upturned collar of my denim coat to warm my face.

Tommy and Gabe were sitting in the truck, waiting. I was glad they were early because it told me they wanted to be there, too. They both got out at the same time, Tommy moving mechanically from behind the wheel. His leg had stiffened up quite a bit after the rattlesnake bite, more so in the mornings, but Tom rarely complained. And any time he got close to griping about it, Gabriel and I reminded him that we had let him keep the fifteen dollars the day he got bit. Tom willingly pretended he didn't remember, although he could remember almost getting shot by Gabe.

"Damn, Stotts, that's all you brought?" Tommy asked, pointing a thumb at my rifle, then spit a splash of tobacco onto the rain-puddled ground. "You could've at least brought your rake!"

"I couldn't get my dad's deer gun," I apologized.

"Well, if you shoot her, you better kill her, 'cause I don't want to be there if she gets pissed at you."

"I don't think she was too happy about the rake anyway."

"Do you think it's a female?" Gabe asked.

"She could be pregnant," I said.

"Why's that?"

"Jeez, Gabey. Don't you know why females get pregnant?" Tommy said, and we all laughed.

Then Gabe punched Tom's arm. "Shut up."

"She's obviously thinking she's settling in," I said. "I don't want her to clean us out. Or start looking at Reno. Or me."

"So why doesn't your dad just go out and bag her?" Gabe asked.

"Fish and Game's not doing anything, but he wants to give them time to deal with it because it's the law." I know my friends thought my dad, so boring and teacherlike, never took risks and always followed rules. My nose was running and I wiped the sleeve of my coat across it. "I think we should follow the creek up. Tommy, you can go on one side and me and Gabey'll go on the other since he doesn't have a gun."

"Yeah, and he probably tastes better, too. He kind of smelled like bacon this morning when he came and woke me up," Tommy lied, grinning, trying to scare Gabriel.

Bacon. Meat. I could feel my stomach rising in my throat, the pepper and vinegar taste of vomit burning in the back of my nose.

"Shut up," Gabe said. Then he smelled his hands.

"Anyway, I think she's got a place where she's staying in that dark stand of pines right in back of our corral, so that's where we really want to be careful."

Tommy pulled his pistol from his coat pocket and cocked it to chamber a round. I loaded my rifle's single-shot breech.

"Okay, then, let's go." Tommy held out a fist, sideways. Gabe and I hammered down on it with ours.

And Tommy walked right across the creek, sloshing water up to the knees of his jeans. When he got to the other side we all began following the creek up behind our house.

◆ ◆ ◆

I told Tom and Gabe about my dad making me gut that turkey. Gabe groaned and said it sounded "sick," but Tommy just held his fingers over his mouth and gave me a dirty look because I was talking too loud. I didn't say anything after that, but I did give him a dirty look back, and we made our way deeper into the darkness of the quiet woods.

I felt different that morning, like something had been

emptied out of me. But it wasn't an emptiness from not eating, it was something more. As I lifted my soggy feet over the slick rocks and brush on the forest floor, I thought about how Rose told me I'd be giving things up; and I believed that what she said was beginning to make sense.

I played at being grown-up when I was a kid, but it was something I could always snap right out of. I guess all boys want to be grown-up when they're little. So as we walked along, I glanced over at Tommy and back at Gabe from time to time and tried to picture them from my earliest memories, just to see if they looked different, too, in some way from the boys I knew. And Gabe said, "What?" when he caught me looking at him, but I just turned my head away and said, "Nothing." Tom wiped his sleeve across his nose.

And if I closed my eyes, I could almost see Luz and me sitting beside each other in that truckload of hay.

My friends and I went out there to kill something, and I couldn't help myself considering the weight of that, feeling a bit excited, looking back at Gabriel, seeing him bite at his lip, while Tommy just slogged along through the mud and moss across the creek from us, as quiet as if he weren't even there.

EIGHT

I gotta pee," Gabriel whispered, and turned toward a tree.

I looked across the creek and saw Tom's silhouette moving stiffly from black trunk to black trunk; like a ghost, or like the way, sometimes, you can see a big owl flying at night, blacker than the sky itself and not even making the slightest noise.

We were trying to be as quiet as we could now. We had moved past my house, beyond where I had seen the cat vanish those two times.

Tom didn't notice we had stopped. He kept following the edge of the creek, sometimes ducking under branches or broken saplings, then out of my sight and into the dark. It was still raining, but most of it was getting held up in the treetops, so I was only feeling an occasional drop or two. When I closed my eyes, the sound of the erratic dripping was like a slow fire.

"Are you done yet? Tommy's way up ahead."

Gabe didn't say anything. He was still turned away from me, hands down. I heard something move in the trees near where Gabe had been peeing.

"I heard that," I whispered.

"Do you think that's it?" Gabe said, almost inaudibly, as he fumbled with his fly.

"Shhh." I raised my rifle, pointing it past Gabriel's ear.

"What am I gonna do, Troy?"

"Get behind me, but don't make noise."

"Aw hell! I peed on my leg."

We stood there for what seemed like twenty minutes, Gabe behind me, both of us breathing with our mouths open, just listening to what we could — the creek, rain, birds now and then. The sun was starting to gray the sky.

Something moved.

I saw the cat. She was only about ten feet away, just looking at us with that dispassionate stare, unafraid.

"Do you see her?"

"Oh my God," Gabe whispered, his mouth about an inch from my ear. "Troy. Let her go."

It was like an optical illusion. She was right there, enormous, plainly visible. But her coloring and markings made her almost transparent among the tree trunks and dirt and decay on the forest floor.

"I'm going to shoot her," I said, so low I almost couldn't hear it myself.

"Don't!" Gabe hissed. "Please, Troy. Let her just go away. Please."

"I can't, Gabey."

I lined the sight of my rifle. I pointed at the side of her shoulder. There was a bit of a branch in the way; I couldn't tell if it was a tree or part of her. I aimed right into her eye.

"We can't just stand here till she goes away. I'm going to kill her."

I don't mind saying that I was scared. I watched my sight shaking on, then off target. I breathed in deep, exhaled, tried to loosen my shoulders, my grip on the trigger.

On target.

As I fired, Gabriel pushed the gun away. I could hear the bullet striking tree limbs, cutting so far away, so fast.

"What the hell, Gabey!"

I pulled the bolt back, the shell arced noiselessly, glinting a dull brass streak over my shoulder. I could see the pink of the cat's tongue in her open mouth, jerking back and forth with her panting like some kind of bouncing toy. Her amber eyes, brassy like the bullet shell, were fixed right on Gabriel as he crouched down by my side and whimpered, "Don't, Troy. Please!"

I jammed my hand down into my pocket and fumbled for another bullet. Without taking my eyes from the lion, I slid the bullet into its seat and bolted the rifle again.

"Damn you, Gabey. You touch me again and I'm gonna shoot *you*."

I heard him breathing; staccato, like he was crying.

I raised the rifle again. The cat was hunching down, lowering herself under a fallen black and rain-slick sapling, still watching Gabriel, coming toward us. Her head came out from beneath the small tree. I fired.

"Got her!"

Right in the eye; I was sure of it.

She howled quickly, a sound that I could only have imagined before. I could smell her, now just paces away. She leapt straight up into the air and flipped over backwards, hind legs tucked up to her belly like an acrobat. She landed with a soft thud, back on her feet.

I pulled the bolt back quickly, the spent shell ejecting and bouncing off Gabriel's raised arm. I reached down into my coat pocket and nervously tried to push another bullet into the breech, but it went in crooked. I couldn't get it in the gun.

"Troy!" Gabe spun around and bolted off, through the trees toward the creek. I could hear him running, crashing, splashing away.

The cat was standing on all fours. It shook its head several times, slinging blood, like she was shaking off a bad dream.

She was coming at me.

I pulled the crooked bullet out of the breech to try to straighten its seating. I dropped it, felt it hit my boot and bounce away. I grabbed another from my pocket, brought it up to the open rifle.

She was hardly bleeding, stepping slowly through the damp underbrush as though nothing were wrong. Did I miss? She shook her head back and forth like she was saying, "No. You shouldn't have done that."

Getting closer.

I got it loaded. I raised my rifle and fired before I even had my eye on the notch of the sight.

I missed badly. I thought about running, but decided to hit her with my rifle if I had to. I didn't think I'd get another chance to load, and my hands were shaking too much anyway.

Then that roar. That familiar roar of Tommy's .40 caliber,

pulling shots off, and in between the explosions, the sound of the shells ejecting, whizzing past me, hitting trees. *Bam! Bam! Bam! Bam!*

The cat collapsed, deflated.

"You okay, Stotts?"

I exhaled. That was all I could do.

"You are insane, man. Just insane." Tom put his hand on my shoulder. "Gabey! Gabey! We got it! Gabey!"

Gabe was across the creek.

I realized I had dropped my rifle. I picked it up. I could hear Gabriel slogging back across the water, breathing hard.

I sat down right where I was. I felt the wet of the ground soak through my pants.

"Thanks, Tom. I owe you five dollars."

"I'll take it."

Tom dangled a fist in front of me. Numbly, I punched his knuckles.

Gabe looked white and sick. He dropped an open hand to help me to my feet. I didn't look at him.

"Troy. You're sitting in piss."

"Thanks, Gabey. Thanks." I dropped my head down between my knees and just sat like that, not saying anything, for what must have been at least five minutes.

Gabriel started to cry.

"I'm sorry, Troy."

"Stotts? What happened?"

I kept my head down. "Nothing. You didn't do anything, Gabey."

I put my hand up for him, but Tommy pulled me up. Gabe

had his face buried in his arm and was leaning into a tree, shuddering as he cried quietly.

"What's wrong with him?" Tommy said.

"Nothing."

I should have known better than to ask Tom Buller to bring him along that day. I knew how Gabriel was, how he was so scared of everything, a rabbit in a world of wolves. He was always falling apart under the least pressure; like he almost did the day Tommy was bitten by the snake, but I had known that boy since he was a baby and I loved him almost as much as I loved his sister.

I put my arm on Gabriel's shoulder and lowered my face right next to his ear. I whispered, "It's okay, Gabey. It's okay. I didn't mean to —"

"Troy!" He was crying hard and had to wait a bit before he could say anything. "I'm sorry I made you mad at me. I didn't want you to do it." He had to breathe a few times before he could go on. "I just wanted her to go away. It's not her fault."

"I know, Gabey. I know."

"Jeez, you guys!" Tommy said, and I heard him spit. "That thing was about two seconds away from having you, Stotts."

I felt so bad for Gabe. I guess I almost started to cry a bit then, too, looking at that beautiful animal lying there in the dirt, wanting Gabriel to be bigger than he was. I heard Tommy stepping over the sapling and then I took Gabriel away from that tree, with my arm tight on his shoulder and we turned around and saw what Tommy and I had done.

The lion was slumped down, lying on her side, head curled under her shoulder.

I heard Tommy click the hammer down on his pistol.

"Well, boys, let's have a closer look at that kill."

The lion was huge, thick, and heavy. I was the first to touch her, amazed at the texture and depth of her fur. Her eyes were like yellowed glass, fixed open. I had hit her in the eye socket, but it seemed like such a trivial wound, like the bullet had just smoothly passed beneath her eyelid. Blood ran down the side of her muzzle like tears. We grabbed her feet to roll her over straight. The feet were as big around as my opened hands. I pushed her pads in to reveal her black, sharp claws.

You could tell she was moving good when Tommy shot her. None of the bullet holes matched up in a straight line from one side to the other, as each bullet found its way in and out of her. She gave off very little blood from these wounds.

We were all sad. I could feel it. Looking at that cat, I couldn't help but wonder what she had been thinking, where that thinking part of her was at that moment. And I pictured my mother, the last time I saw her, eyes open and quiet, the same as the cat's, with an expression that looked like she'd run headfirst into something she thought she could break and then just didn't care about anymore.

Gabe's face was streaked with his tears and he wiped at his nose with the slick sleeve of his jacket.

And she was so beautiful and impressive, lying so still there in the wetness of the forest.

"I'm sorry, cat," I said. "We had to do it."

Then I heard Gabe crying again, swallowing hard. I looked at Tommy and knew he was upset, too. He just didn't have that gleam in his eyes, and when he saw me watching him, he turned away and spit at the ground. With all the reckless ease that

Tom Buller absorbed the bad things that happened to him, he could still get so pained when he saw an animal or one of his friends suffering, and that was one of the things I liked most about him. Neither one of us was going to give Gabey a hard time about the crying. I didn't need to say that to Tom Buller, and he didn't need to say it to me, either.

Tom crouched down beside me, kneeling at the cat. We both touched her side. Tommy put a finger to one of the bullet holes, dipping it past his fingernail into the blood. He made a line with the blood above his nose, right in the middle of his forehead, and then he tasted the blood from his finger.

He swallowed and straightened the look on his face. "Okay, pinecone, what kind of medicine is this one?"

I breathed out, watching a sort of fog form between me and the lion, mixing with the fading heat from her body. I knew. I remembered.

"Ghost medicine." I swallowed, a lump in my throat.

I took the middle two fingers of my right hand and wiped at the blood on the lion's face. Then I made two lines down over my own right eye, starting above the eyebrow, ending at my cheek.

"I'm sorry, cat."

Ghost medicine. I could feel it, too.

Then Tommy said, "What's it do?"

"You know how you can look right at 'em and not see 'em? The cats, I mean. How they move so quiet? They're like ghosts."

The rain was crackling its fire sound through the trees. A wind blew through the tops, saying, "Ssshhhhhhhh."

"It makes you like that. Like a ghost. So people can look right at you, but not see you if you don't want them to."

I put my fingers in the blood again and marked across my other eye. I closed my eyes. And then I tasted the blood, too.

"And it does something else, too." When I took my hand from my mouth I could taste how that blood was still living. "It makes the other ghosts leave you alone. It's everything you could ever want."

"Damn, Stotts," Tommy said, and looked at the red smear on his fingertip. "You joining the tribe, Gabey?"

Gabe didn't say anything. He was breathing hard, still kind of crying. He dropped to one knee beside us. He put a thumb to one of the side wounds, like he was being fingerprinted for arrest, and, expressionless, smeared a slash of blood across his cheek.

"There's no way I'm tasting it," he said, and wiped his thumb on his pants. "You guys are sick."

"I got her with that first shot. See it? I knew I did. She would've died."

"Yeah. Of old age. Or maybe she would've choked to death trying to swallow your skinny carcass in one bite," Tommy said. "Anyway, we could get in lots of trouble for this. It's against the law, you know. So maybe we should just get the hell out of here."

I couldn't do that now.

"Let's go back to the truck and get a shovel so we can bury her," I said.

And we all three, painted and worn, made our way back along the creek to that little bridge. And along the way we talked about Tommy's difficult horse, that Goat Woman and her twenty-four-pound cat and the horses we'd be getting from her soon, and Gabriel's older sister. And then Tommy grinning and pretending that he couldn't see me and Gabe anymore because we had disappeared.

And as we walked through the woods, wet past our knees, Tommy waved his hands in the air, smiling and acting like he was trying to feel where his invisible friends had gone.

NINE

We knew better than to even knock on her door without first gathering up a couple armloads of stovewood.

The inside of that round steel house saved up all the colds from a year of nights. Maybe it wasn't so much the temperature as the thought of those black widows dangling up there. Rose was bundled in what looked like at least six layers of sweaters, the outermost pink, and stretched to the limit of its buttons' holding strength.

"Sit down, boys," she said, pointing us toward her two folding chairs and the oak half-barrel that doubled as a table and a third seat. We dumped the wood down on the dirt floor by the stove.

"We got some stuff for you. Food, too," I said. "We'll be right back."

And we went out to get the supplies we'd brought.

"You better believe I do," Tommy said when Rose asked him if he had any tobacco.

As soon as we sat down, that brown kitten pounced on my lap, but I pushed it down. Tom spit at it and it howled and kicked its back legs up and disappeared in the dark end of Rose's home.

"He's a real mean cat," Rose said. "That's good out here 'cause he might live a long time that way. Anyways, I don't use bug spray no more."

And then Rose spit at the side of the woodstove, making a hissing sizzle. "You boys come for your horses, then? Well, you better get out there and catch 'em. It's not gonna be too easy, you know."

"It'll be easy enough," Tommy said, and spit on the floor.

"Are you sure it's gonna be okay if we take one for each of us?" I guess I still couldn't believe she was just letting us take some horses for nothing.

"Sometimes people'll just give you something, Tennis Shoes, without expecting nothing in return," she said, and pushed the tobacco down deeper in her front lip with her tongue. "Is that so hard for you to reckon with?"

"Sometimes everything is too hard for that boy to reckon with, Miss Rose," Tommy said. "But we're working on him. Let me just get him up on that horse of his and he'll stop asking you to say no to him."

Rose pushed herself away from the stove and turned to face me.

"Well, get up. I want to see you cowboys catch those horses."

Tommy reached out his right hand and pulled me to my feet. I almost never took my hat off inside Rose's house, but not just because I was afraid of the spiders, it was that I felt like Rose's place was somewhere you just didn't need to take it off and it wouldn't matter. I pushed my hat down straight as we walked out the door into the bright sunlight. Tommy snapped at his can of tobacco and held it out to me.

"Want some?"

"Okay."

Rose laughed behind me as I dipped my fingers into the can. "Ha! Look what he's doin' to that boy now! Ha!"

I told Tom, "Last time I did this, you got bit by a snake."

+ + +

We didn't get any horses that day from Rose. I could hear her belly-laughing as we took off after them, Reno trying to cut right into them and Arrow lagging back on the outside. Tom and me leaning forward over the saddle horns, swinging ropes to move the ones we had our eyes on, trying to cut them out. The black mare that I admired looked like she would be foaling soon, and I didn't want to scare her too bad, but she was smart and stayed away from us by hiding among the other horses. Tom was after a real tall reddish-roan stallion that looked to be about two years old, and maybe seventeen hands already. And he was the one in charge, I could tell, because where he went the rest of those horses followed along, younger colts trailing in the back. There was no way Arrow would get Tommy anywhere near that mean boy.

We weren't used to riding like that, either. Reno was so tall and Arrow's legs were so stiff, and cutting wild horses from a nervous herd was a lot harder than they always made it look in the movies, where no one would ever get dirty or make a mistake, or have his horse going one way when he was leaning the other.

Tommy was the first to fall off. He landed on his elbow and was bleeding pretty good, but got right up and brushed himself off, cussing at Arrow, and went back for another try.

I laughed at him when he fell, and then immediately fell off myself when Reno took a sharp turn to his left and I flipped, facefirst, over his shoulders. I landed on my chin, got dirt in my mouth, and a cut over my eyebrow. But it was still fun. I came up spitting dirt, and my tobacco with it. I wiped the blood away with the back of my gloved hand and replaced my hat as Tom rode up to me.

"Want some more?" he asked, holding out his can of tobacco.

I spit out some more dirt. "Yeah."

"Is it me, Stotts, or are these the spookiest horses you ever saw? And fastest."

"I can only get close to the ugly ones."

"I guess they like your looks."

"Well, that big roan of yours is going to have to get shot before you lay a hand on him."

"With a bazooka."

"Twice."

I looked down and noticed one of my shoes had come off and was about ten feet away in a patch of weeds. I limped over and got it, jamming my dirt-crusted socked foot back into it without untying. I tossed Tom his tobacco, and he snapped it down and took some more for himself. "What do you say we try again another day, Stottsy?"

"I was just waiting for you to say so. Let's go tell Rose we'll try again after we're healed up. And clean."

Rose was waiting outside her house when we rode up. That

small brown cat saw us and took off into the brush, running like it was on fire. The sun was getting low and the afternoon was cooling.

"Ha! You two cowboys look like you run into a pack of Indians."

"Might've," Tom said, and spit.

"We're hoping if you don't mind if we come back another day and try again," I said.

"Mind? Mind? It's you the ones who should mind doing it again. Ha!" Then she turned toward her door. "Well, get down now and I'll give you something to drink before you go home. Of course I don't mind you boys coming back to get your horses. I gave 'em to you." And she opened the door.

Tommy looked at me. I shrugged my shoulders, then, painfully and slowly, we got down from our horses.

Rose was opening up one of those big green jugs of wine when we came in.

"You boys just drink a glass of this and you'll feel a lot better."

"Okay with me," Tom said.

So we sat there around the light of her stove in our usual places, Tommy looking out for that cat, and she gave us each a big glass of yellow-looking wine.

That wine tasted horrible at first, but it kind of changed flavors as I drank more and more of it out of the glass. And she was right, it did make the hurting stop; and it made me feel real warm inside, too. Tommy finished his first and Rose offered him more, but I said no, 'cause we had to go before it got dark. We got up, a little rubber-legged, but I felt more like riding my horse right then than I had in a long time. At that moment,

Tom wouldn't have even had to ask me twice to go out there and try to catch that roan and the black mare again, too. We thanked Rose and told her we'd be back soon; then we left.

"Man, I got to pee really bad," I said.

"Me, too. Let's go over there in those trees. I guess it would be pretty rude to take a piss right here next to her house."

"Rude? Jeez, Buller, she's not the Queen of England."

And then we both laughed, really hard.

The sun was down and the sky was pale slate by the time we rode away from that steel house. Along the way, I noticed that Tommy was getting Arrow to move pretty good and confident, despite the lameness in his front legs.

"You look like hell, Stotts."

"You've probly rode with uglier. I'm not cut bad, anyhow, it just bled a lot," I said. "It doesn't hurt."

"I bet it doesn't right now."

"When do you want to come back?"

"Tomorrow. And I'm bringing her some bug spray for that new cat of hers."

"Then you won't have nothing to spit at in there."

"I bet you're not much bigger than that cat, Stottsy."

"Do you think she knows we don't know what we're doing?"

"It's a fair guess." He spit and wiped his mouth on the back of his hand.

"We could put up a pipe corral on the other side of the fence when we catch 'em," I said. "Benavidez wouldn't mind. We could tame 'em there."

"We're never gonna catch 'em," Tommy said.

He lifted his hat and scratched his fingers through his black hair.

"I am."

"You got some kind of strategy?"

"I'm gonna try to be nicer to 'em, I think."

Tommy burst out laughing. "Damn, Stotts, that's a good one. You know what I believe?"

I leaned forward in my saddle. Tommy had to be drunk, I thought. He never told me what he believed, not one time in my life.

"What?"

"Wild horses don't even know what sugar is."

And we laughed and slid sideways and slumped over in our saddles along the trail to the ranch as darkness fell, all the way back to that little chute we had cut in the fence.

"Watch this, Tommy. I'm jumping it."

"I guess you still have plenty more blood left in your head, then."

And I snapped Reno's reins a little and gave him a kick and we circled around once and went right for that barbed wire fence and I pulled him up, staying low and forward on him, and he glided right over the top of that fence like it wasn't even there.

TEN

I believe that things happen for a reason, but I do not believe, like most people I know, that those reasons are conscious and directed. There might be a God, but if there is, I know He is not benevolent; He is, at best, ambivalent to all of the things set in motion in this world. So things do not happen by coincidence, and everything that is, is really a collision of paths. And so luck, which I also do not believe in in the way that most people do, is merely a chain of certain reckless collisions.

I believe all things happen for a reason, then ripple like the surface of a pond once a rock has been skipped. And I believe in the medicine, the signals. Tom Buller had the snake medicine that brought change, the shedding of the skin, that ability to just crawl out of the past and be new. Nothing seemed to matter or leave a mark on him. That summer, we all had the ghost medicine that made us vanish and fade in ways we never thought, never saw. Anyway, it was what we wanted. And I guess that's how all boys die.

I spent a lot of days after that season of the ghost medicine, as I remember it all now, wondering how I ended up banging and scraping into so many troubles in such a short time, through such a young life.

✦　✦　✦

I remember sneaking to her house to meet her, the night after Chase Rutledge punched me; I can almost hear the faintness of our whispers, feel the warmth of her breath at my ear.

"Luz?"

She looked over at me. Her feet were bare; she didn't want her father to hear her stealing through his home to meet a boy outside his front door. She stood on the second step, just tall enough there to look directly at my eyes.

I took my hat off and held it at my side. I know she could see the sweat pasting my hair to my ears and neck. I should have been home, in bed. But I couldn't sleep for thinking about getting punched by Chase, and considering all those things I should have done and didn't; so I came to see her, my throat knotted tight, determined to say to her what I knew I had to.

"You're the most important person there is to me. We've been together since almost as long as I can remember and you're my best friend. I know we're supposed to be together for a long time. Don't ever go. I don't know what I'd do if he sent you away."

"Did he tell you that?"

"Yes."

We were so close. I could feel the heat of our breathing mixing together, clothing us, connecting.

"Don't listen to him."

"I have to. I'm scared of him."

"He's scared of you."

* * *

And I remember Tom Buller, standing in a pen at the ranch next to one of Benavidez' breeding stallions, about to touch the horse's nose, standing carefully beside him; and the stallion took a bite at his hand. We both knew how the worker Ramiro lost a finger to a stallion like that one; and then Tommy just went crazy on that horse, punching him right on the neck so hard it sounded like hitting a watermelon with a baseball bat and he flailed his arms and screamed and the horse leapt up and tried kicking at Tommy. And Tom just breathed right then, all calm, no more than two seconds later, and began talking sweet and soft to that stallion and walking up real slow with that same hand held out to his nose. And he told me, "I'm scared of him, but he's terrified of me. So we'll just learn to play brave around each other and see who quits first. Till he learns that I'm more important. Now you watch, Stotts. I bet this stallion never so much as pretends to nibble at me again." And then he stroked the horse's nose and walked away from him just like that. And that horse never bit again.

Tom Buller was the best with horses I ever saw or will see.

* * *

"It's cold in here," I said.

It was the day after we tried chasing Rose's wild horses. We drove the truck out there after work.

"I know," Rose said. "I just didn't feel like getting out of bed today."

Tom spit, and then looked at me.

"I'll get that stove lit," he said.

"Thank you, boys."

"Here." Tommy handed her three new cans of tobacco. "If you didn't get out of bed, I bet you're missing this."

Rose struggled with opening a can and then Tommy just took it from her, having gotten the stove lit, and made a circle around the wrapper with the edge of a fingernail. Then he swatted it down a few times and gave it back to her.

"You boys are too nice to me."

"One of us is," Tom said.

I sighed. "Well, this isn't good, Rose. What were you gonna do if we didn't come by? Just stay there in bed?"

"Haven't you ever had a day when you just didn't want to get out of bed?"

"I haven't had any other kind," I said.

"Will again in the morning," Tom added.

"Well, when you lived as long as me, you get to do it sometimes, that's all. Ha!"

I opened a can of soup and put it on top of the stove.

"You need to eat something," I said.

"Never thought I'd hear Troy Stotts saying that to anyone," Tommy said, then spit.

"Eating in front of others is bad luck," Rose said.

"We wouldn't want that."

"Well, I guess we could break it if you boys'd have a glass of wine with me. Ha!"

"I'll pour it," Tommy said. "It'll warm us up for that ride home."

I brought the can of soup over to Rose's bed. Tommy

brought her the wine and then we both sat down by the stove and drank ours. It warmed me up right away and Tommy quickly refilled all our glasses before I could suggest leaving after the first, but I didn't protest.

"How old is your girl?"

"Sixteen."

"Sixteen? Ha! When I was sixteen I was married!"

"He practically is, too."

I shot a look at Tom, and he spit again.

Tommy went on, ignoring me, "He doesn't do anything without calling her first, just so she knows where he is all the time."

"But then I was a widow when I was eighteen and I went off to work making clothes for the movies and I never got married after that. Ha! Never wanted to, neither."

"You never had any kids?" I said.

Rose looked at me, then out the window. I could see the light of the fire from the stove in her eyes. She looked tired and sad.

"Never had no one," she said. "But I have you two fine cowboys now. Ha!"

"You don't want us," Tom said. "Believe me."

She smiled at Tommy and drained her glass, then went back to spooning the soup from that opened can.

"Tell me about your folks."

"I only have a dad, he's a schoolteacher. My mom died in June."

I never said it aloud before. It stuck in my throat. I felt naked.

"Oh, that's terrible. I'm sorry, Troy."

"So am I."

That was the only time I remember her calling me Troy. Then she turned to Tommy, sitting there in that cave of a steel house.

"Well, how about your folks then, Tom?"

That was the only time she ever called him Tom, too.

And I saw Tommy lose his smile for just a moment. He turned his face and pretended to look at the floor, just like he did when we stood over that cat we'd killed.

"I only live with my dad, too. My mom ran out on us when I was too small to remember."

"Aww . . . boys shouldn't have it like that. And you still both growed up perfect anyway. And beautiful handsome, too. You're both so lucky."

She stood up, a little wobbly, and moved over to where I was sitting across from the stove. Then she lifted my hat and kissed me right on top of the head. I looked at Tommy. I could feel myself turning red. And then she walked over to Tommy and he just about recoiled in terror.

"Take your hat off, so I can kiss you, too."

"I don't smell good."

"Ha!"

And he was really embarrassed, too, when she kissed him.

"You smell like chewing tobacco and horses. If they ever put that in a bottle, I'd drink it."

"They do bottle it. It's called bug poison."

"Ha!"

She sat back down and folded her hands on her lap.

"I knew that about you, Tennis Shoes. I could tell the first time I saw you that you were extra sad about something. I could see it in your eyes. But this one — he's always the happy one, isn't he? You want to always have friends like that, so if you're ever starving to death or freezing in the cold, you know he's gonna just say, 'It ain't that bad.'"

And we finished a third glass before I could make Tommy agree to leave, but I knew he had to pee by then so getting him out of the house was pretty easy.

"She didn't look very good," I said.

"Damn, Stotts. If she ever did we weren't born yet. Our dads weren't born yet."

I laughed.

"You know what I mean."

"This time I do. I guess."

Tommy cleared his throat. "Stotts? I never said it, but I'm sorry about your mom."

"Okay." I watched as Tommy raised a crumpled can to his mouth and spit, but he kept his eyes straight ahead, watching the road rushing beneath us. I remembered how Tommy was just "that skinny boy who doesn't have a mom" when he and his father moved to Three Points so Carl could take the job with Mr. Benavidez. Tommy was eleven. He was the first kid I knew who didn't have a mother.

I said, "I'm sorry about yours, too."

And Tommy got real serious, like I'd never seen him.

"Your mom got taken away," he said. "Mine ran."

I looked out at the land, dimming, running past my eyes in the twilight.

"I got mad about it," I said. "You get mad?"

"Nope." Tom Buller looked over at me, showing the beginnings of that grin of his. "If the things that happened to me never did, I wouldn't be sitting here right now. Want some tobacco?"

"Yeah."

ELEVEN

The morning Chase stole that Ford truck right from out front of the Foreman's house had a lot to do with all the trouble we kept causing for each other.

It was a Monday morning, and I had been working at the Benavidez ranch pretty much every day. It was just before sunup. I was riding Reno up to the Bullers' place when I saw what happened.

The day before, Carl and Tommy had delivered a young gelding to a ranch about a half-day's drive away. I guess when they got back that night Carl was so tired he just left the truck with the trailer still hitched to it about halfway on the dirt road leading toward the main house through the Benavidez property. It was one of those things that's so unusual and unexpected that you *do* see it, not like rattlesnakes and mountain lions that just blend into the scenery. As the Foreman's house came into view, I saw Chase Rutledge walk right up to the driver's side door on that truck, get in, start it up, and drive away, trailer and all. And not just *drive away*; he sped off so fast the trailer fluttered behind like the tail of a tadpole.

There was a part of me that didn't want to say positively that it was Chase that stole the truck that morning, because it was too dark and I was too far away to see his face. But I knew it was Chase because of the way he walked and his baseball cap.

And I also know now that Chase Rutledge did what he did to us because I saw him that morning.

"Haw, Reno!" I nudged Reno with my heels and he took off running toward the Foreman's house. Just as we got up to the front porch, Carl came out the door, buttoning a shirt over his T-shirt.

"What the hell?"

"I just saw Chase Rutledge take the truck!" I said.

The lights turned on inside the house and Tommy came out onto the porch.

"Jeez, it's cold!" He was barefoot. "What's all the noise, Stotts?"

"Chase took the truck. Chase just peeled out with the truck and trailer and all."

"Well, let's go get him," Tommy said, and went back inside to get the rest of his clothes on.

"Well, why in hell would Chase Rutledge take the truck from right here in front of the house?" Carl said.

I didn't want to tell him that it wasn't *actually* in front of his house. "We should call his dad."

Carl looked at me, then out at the road as he fumbled for a cigarette. His hand was shaking a little.

"You're going to have to tell him what you saw, Troy. You sure it was Chase?"

I looked at him as he lit the cigarette.

"Maybe you'd better go on up to the main house and check with Art first. Maybe he knows what this is about. Anyways, you could always give Clayton a call from there. Better to be sure first before you go waking up the sheriff and telling him his son's just stolen a truck."

I really didn't want to call Sheriff Rutledge, but I was mad enough at Chase that it didn't seem to matter much.

"I better tell Mr. Benavidez, first then," I said.

"Hold on, Troy. You want Tom to come with you?"

"Tell him I'll be right back after I straighten this thing out. He can saddle up Arrow in the meantime 'cause we might have to ride in to the sheriff's."

The sun was just coming up when I got Reno tied to the hitching post in front of the Benavidez house. Mrs. Benavidez opened the door when I knocked. I knew I wouldn't be waking anyone up; the Benavidez family always had breakfast together before the ranch work began.

"Well, Troy, good morning," she said with her displeased-sounding voice, a slight, choppy accent underneath it.

"I'm sorry to be banging on your door so early," I said, "but it's real important that I speak to Mr. Benavidez. I think some-one just stole Carl's truck."

"Why don't you come in, Troy. We were just about to have breakfast. I'll have Luz set another place. Arturo's in the kitchen."

I took my hat off and went inside. Mr. Benavidez always shook my hand when he saw me; hard, too, like he was trying to tell me something. Gabriel was sitting at the kitchen table, drinking milk. Luz made eye contact with me for just a second as she got up to fix a place for me. I hadn't seen her in a few days, had only heard her voice on the phone, and I guess I kind of missed her because I just watched her move through that kitchen like some kind of spirit. But the presence of Mr. Benavidez reminded me that I was there for another reason, even if I wasn't in a hurry to get to it.

Mrs. Benavidez poured me a cup of coffee.

"Hey, Troy," Gabriel said as I sat down.

Mr. Benavidez cleared his throat, impatiently.

"I'm sorry, Mr. Benavidez, but I just think I saw Chase Rutledge steal that truck Carl Buller drives for you. The truck and the trailer. So I came by to see if you gave him permission to do that before I go and call his father."

"Chase Rutledge?" Luz said.

The coffee was burning hot; I almost spit it out. I guess my face was half-frozen from the ride down here.

"Well, it was dark, but I'm positive it was Chase I saw take the truck."

"No," Mr. Benavidez said, "I don't know anything about that. What did Carl say?"

"He told me to come check with you and then call the sheriff."

Mrs. Benavidez was heaping food on my plate.

"Give him lots of meat, Mom," Gabe said, a mean smile on his face.

"Give him lots of everything," Luz added, and I could tell she was looking to see if I was wearing that belt she had given me, which, of course, I wasn't. And the fact that my T-shirt was untucked and I was wearing a denim jacket still didn't hide the fact very well, either.

"Thanks, Gabey," I said. I looked at the plate his mother set before me. "Thank you, Mrs. Benavidez."

"I guess we should call Clayton," Mr. Benavidez said.

"As much as I don't want to do it, I better make that call," I said, "'cause I was the only one who saw him do it."

I wasn't too surprised that Mr. Benavidez showed so little concern for what had happened. It wasn't like Chase could get too far driving a truck and trailer everyone knew belonged to Mr. Benavidez, anyway.

"You might as well finish your breakfast first," Mr. Benavidez said. "You know Clayton Rutledge's not going to be ready to deal with a problem this early in the morning."

And I was relieved and grateful to be able to spend at least a few more minutes there at that table.

"I don't like that boy," Luz said.

I looked at her and said, "Neither do I. Never."

"I wonder what he's thinking — taking that truck?" Gabe said.

"I don't know," I said. "But it's probly some stupid prank he's pulling to look tough in front of his friends. I hope he causes a lot of trouble for his dad over this."

"I doubt he will," Gabe said.

I thought Gabriel was more than likely right about that. All his life Chase was getting into trouble, but never suffering the consequences. If anything around town ever was missing, broken, or set fire to and Chase didn't do it, he probably knew who did.

Then the phone rang and Mr. Benavidez left us there.

"When you're done working for the day, I'll ride with you back home," Luz said.

Mrs. Benavidez looked up from her breakfast to see what I'd say.

"I'd like that."

Mrs. Benavidez sipped her coffee. "Gabriel can go, too."

"Maybe I don't want to," Gabe said.

I knew he was just trying to make his mom mad; I could tell by his smirk. Normally, he'd never say no to a ride out to my house. Mrs. Benavidez just exhaled through her nose and looked at the three of us.

"I'll be doing some grooming and clean-up work with Tommy, so I shouldn't be too late unless this truck thing becomes a big deal."

Then Mr. Benavidez came back into the kitchen, looking grim.

"Thanks for breakfast, Mrs. Benavidez," I said, standing up, "I'm real full."

She eyed a measuring glance at what was left on my plate and scowled.

"I think you should get on the phone to Clayton now," Mr. Benavidez said. "There's more to it than just the truck and trailer. Carl just called. He left five thousand dollars cash in the glove box from selling that gelding yesterday."

+ + +

"Deputy Rutledge? This is Troy Stotts." I always sounded stupid on the phone. I got nervous talking to people I didn't really know. And all the Benavidez family were just standing there watching me, like I was a singer onstage.

"Stotts? The teacher's boy? The one missing last month?"

"Yes, sir."

"It's barely seven o'clock in the morning, boy. Is something wrong?"

"Yes, sir. I was riding in to work this morning at the Benavidez ranch and I saw someone taking that F one-fifty the Bullers drive for Mr. Benavidez. It had a horse trailer hitched to it, as well."

"You work at the Benavidez ranch? Aren't you kind of small? How old are you anyway?"

"Sixteen. Yes sir, I work here. I'm calling from the Benavidez house right now."

"What do you do for 'em?"

"Well, Deputy Rutledge, I was just calling 'cause I saw someone steal that truck."

"Maybe someone's just borrowing it from Carl. Are you sure?"

"Yes. I saw it. I talked to Carl and Mr. Benavidez about it and no one had their okay to take that truck."

"Where did you see this?"

"In front of Carl's house. This morning, maybe at five-thirty."

"In front of the Foreman's house? What were you doing out there at five-thirty?"

I breathed hard into the mouthpiece. This was the most I'd ever said to Clayton Rutledge in my entire life. Maybe I woke him up too early.

"I was going to work."

"At the ranch? All right, then. I guess I'll have to come out there and we'll get this thing figured out. I'm sure there's nothing to it. You just go on and do your work, son, and I'll get out to Bullers' place later this morning. I bet we'll find the truck before then, anyway, knowing Carl."

My heart was pounding hard; I was sweating a little. Maybe it was from that strong black coffee. Then I said it.

"Mr. Rutledge, I think it was Chase I saw taking the truck. And there was lots of money inside, too."

"Chase? He's been over at Jack Crutchfield's since yesterday getting a motorcycle. Are you sure it was my boy?" But I heard the tone in his voice change, too, and I knew he wasn't just irritated over my waking him up.

"Well, it was dark still."

"Let's just work on one problem at a time, boy. I'll be out at the Buller house in a bit."

And he hung up.

And then he never showed up all morning, either. Tommy and I worked in the main stables all that time until just after noon, and when we had finished for the day we rode back to his house. Still no truck. No sheriff. Carl was sitting out on the front porch, smoking. He looked sick. He had been drinking.

"Rutledge hasn't been out?" Tommy asked.

"Hell." And he exhaled a cloud of smoke.

"Do you think I should call him again?"

Carl shook his head and leaned back in his chair. "He's a real piece of work, that sheriff. Acting like he's really got a job to do around here. Hell."

Gabe and Luz must have checked for us at the stables, because they both came riding up from the direction of the main house as we sat there just looking at Carl and each other, wondering what we should do about this.

"Well, CB, we're all riding Stotts home. So if he does show up, you can tell him where to find 'em if he needs to. Come on, Stotts. Let's go."

Tommy sounded disgusted with his father. He pulled Arrow's head around and I followed on Reno to meet up with Luz and our chaperone.

It was another one of those perfect times; like Luz softly combing my hair back with her fingers when I got thrown from Reno, or sitting in the hay-filled truck bed with her at evening, watching everything and nothing at the same time. When I look back at that summer and the years before it, those times I can remember most clearly: the colors, sounds, smells — riding alongside with these three friends I had grown up with: Tommy on that cranky horse of his, Gabe on his Dusty, who I know wanted to ride harder than Gabey ever would, Luz on her painted Doats; riding in that late afternoon when the sun had teased at warmth and then receded away behind the coolness of the stretching shadows making their way across the dirt road around the shore of the lake north toward my home.

I yawned big.

"Are you tired?" Luz said, and jokingly, "Tommy, you and Carl aren't working him too much, are you?"

"Work?" Tommy said. "Do you *work*, Stotts?"

"At the Benavidez ranch, sir."

"You're pretty scrawny to work at that ranch, aren't you?" Tommy said. Of course, I had told him about my phone call that morning.

"What time do you get to work?" Gabe said, playing along.

"Five-thirty."

"What were you doing at the Benavidez ranch at five-thirty?" Tommy said.

"Going to work."

"Where do you work?" Luz asked.

I sighed and yawned again.

"Fall asleep on us, Troy, and we'll sling you over the saddle like we killed you," Gabe said.

"I'm not about to ever fall asleep on Reno again," I said, remembering that knot on my head. "You wanna race Dusty up to that tree there? You can say go."

And before I was done saying it, Gabe and Dusty took off and got a clean three lengths on us before I even touched my heels to Reno. I could have waited longer, but Reno wouldn't. As soon as he realized a race was on, he was right out, leaving the others behind in our dust. It helped wake me up, but of course Reno overtook Dusty and sailed past the tree well ahead. Gabe lost his hat just before the finish line. I swung Reno around as he and Dusty caught up to us.

"You better pick that thing up before it makes the ground dirty," I said.

Reno was backpedaling and wheeling his hooves, eager to run again. Gabe got down from Dusty and walked back to get his hat.

"Dang, that horse of yours is a runner," he said. He brushed his hat off and replaced it on his head, his hair slicked back. He must have combed it before Mrs. Benavidez dispatched him to keep his eye on me. On us.

"Okay, showoffs, if you didn't want us to ride with you, you shoulda told us to stay home!" Tom called out from the road behind us. We rode back to catch them up.

"Damn, Stotts, I was bettin' with Luz how far you'd get before you fell off."

Luz rode up next to me and leaned over close. "He said you're getting to be a damn good rider."

I wanted to kiss her real bad. I looked at Tom and Gabe, then back at Luz. "And what did you say?"

"I told him if you did fall off, I'd kiss you."

"You shoulda told me before I took off," I said, straight-mouthed.

We rode together, four horses abreast up that dirt road to the tree that had been our finish line, listening to the *clop-clop* of the horses' hooves against the ground. Then we heard that rattling Ford truck coming straight down the road toward us.

"I don't believe this," Tommy said.

The truck braked and shifted sideways in the road, with nowhere to go; its path blocked completely by our four horses. And Chase Rutledge was driving.

Tommy was first down from his horse, followed by me and then, finally Gabe. Luz stayed back on Doats, who kept the other horses steady in their places. Tommy went to the driver's door and opened it. Chase just sat there, blankly staring straight ahead through the windshield, looking at Luz and the horses. He was wearing that greasy, blackened sheriff's baseball cap, hands resting on top of the steering wheel.

"What the hell are you doing, Chase?" Tom said.

I could tell Chase was careful with what he said to Tom Buller; and how he said it, too.

"I was just using the truck and trailer to move Jack's motorcycle over to my house," he said. "I asked your dad and he said okay."

"That's a lie," I said. "Carl never said you could take it. I called your dad this morning after I saw you steal it."

"I didn't steal anything," he insisted.

"I tell you what, Stotts. We already called the sheriff on him.

What do you say we just go ahead and make a citizen's arrest? I got some zip ties in my saddlebag. I say we just cuff him up and leave him here and let his daddy come get him," Tom said, getting closer and closer to the side of Chase's face.

Chase didn't say anything. He just stared at Luz. He clenched his fist, and I know Tommy noticed it, too, so I didn't say anything. Chase couldn't be stupid enough to fight, I thought, because he'd not only have to deal with Tom, but with me, Gabe, and probably Luz, too.

"Yeah, let's tie him up, Tommy," Gabe said.

"I think that sounds like a good idea," Tommy said. "We could tie him up and then *not* call his daddy. Just leave him here."

I could tell Chase was getting mad and scared. But I knew Tommy wasn't serious about tying him up, either.

"Look. Here's what you're going to do, Chase," I said. "You're going to take this truck on back to the Foreman's house and you're going to park it back where you got it. Then you're going to walk home to see your dad. And we better not ever see you anywhere around Benavidez ranch again."

Chase didn't say anything to me, but just looking at him sitting there, stubborn, in that truck made me madder and madder. So I added, "Or next time we're gonna mess you up."

"What do you mean by that, Stotts?" Chase said.

And Tommy said, "It's a good way to get yourself shot."

Tom slammed the door shut and spit. Chase looked at him, then me, then fixed his stare straight ahead.

"And Chase," I said. "Slow it down."

The three of us got back up on our horses and moved them to the side of the road to let the truck through. Chase didn't look at us as he drove past, slowly, until he wound out of our sight.

"You didn't say nothin' about the money," Gabe said.

"Probly better to wait and see after he gets the truck back," Tommy said. "Anyways, we all know it was Chase now."

"Maybe you should turn around," I said to Tommy. "You could give Carl a hand."

He knew what I meant. He pulled Arrow's head around and was facing back the way we had come. "Anyone want to ride along? Gabey?"

Gabe looked at me, then Luz. "Mom would kill me. You know that. Then Dad would spit on my corpse."

"Why don't you both go on back with him?" I said.

"You don't want to ride home alone," Luz said.

"It's how I got here. I'll see you in the morning, Tom."

"See you, Stotts."

And I rode off toward home, my heart pounding from standing up to Chase, and regretting that I hadn't fallen from my horse.

TWELVE

When I was near the drainpipe we called "the bridge," I heard a car coming up behind me. It was the sheriff's black-and-white Ford Bronco. His headlights were on, but not the flashers on top. I pulled Reno over, hoping Clayton Rutledge would just drive past us, but he lowered the passenger-side window and stopped right alongside.

"Troy Stotts?"

"Yes."

"Why don't you get on down from that horse, son. I'd like to talk to you."

I could hear him crunch on the parking brake, and he got out of his side of the car, leaving it idling, parked a little diagonally in the dirt road like he was doing something important and dangerous, with the headlights still on. I got down from Reno, put my hands into the pockets of my jacket, and walked around to where he was standing, by the front of his car in the light.

"That's a real big horse you got there, son. How big is he?"

"He's a lot bigger than me, I know that."

"I bet you paid a good bit for him, too."

"Less than you'd think," I said. I looked down at my feet.

"So what is it you do there at the ranch?"

"Whatever the bosses tell me to do."

Then Clayton Rutledge got a little closer to me. He put his right hand on the hood of the vibrating car and tilted his face down at an angle. I could smell his breath, hot and moist, and he hadn't shaved today. But I knew he at least took the time to eat a few good meals, judging by the taut balloon of flab that hung over a belt that I couldn't picture how — or why — he'd ever put it on, unless it was just to hold that gun of his, a big Smith & Wesson .357. His voice raised in pitch and volume a little. I could tell he was uncomfortable, but also trying to scare me.

"So you say you saw Chase stealing that truck Carl Buller drives?"

"I did."

"Did he break into it?"

"No, sir."

"Did he have the keys?"

"They were left in it, I guess."

He exhaled a big gust of humid, foul breath into my face. "Look. Chase didn't steal nothing. He just used the truck to get a motorcycle he bought from Jack Crutchfield. He told me he found the truck abandoned quite a ways from that Foreman's house with the keys still in it. So he decided to bring it back and he used it to move this bike on the way. He said he had permission."

"Not from anyone who could've given it."

"He was just borrowing the truck. Carl Buller told him it was okay."

"Not before he took it, he didn't."

"Well, you know Carl." And I understood what he meant by that.

I was just looking past him, sometimes glancing back at Reno. The sheriff was getting mad, I could tell.

"Look, Troy. My son's a good boy. He just graduated high school. He's been a lifeguard over at the pool at Holmes. He doesn't get into trouble. He's a good kid."

"Well, so am I, but I never stole a truck before."

Then he pushed me, just enough to snap me back a little, with his left hand straight-arming my shoulder.

"Okay, smart ass. I'll tell you how it is, then. I'm two years away from retirement. Two years. This is a good job, patrolling from home, and I don't want to get sent anywhere else in this county. I'm done with that. We do things different here, you should know that — you lived here longer than me. It's not like the big city. People leave their doors open and their keys in their cars. I tell 'em not to. And out here you just gotta take care of things for yourself. And for me, that means I just gotta solve problems for everyone. I'm going to retire soon and I don't need any trouble here. My son's a good boy, he was just using the truck to move that dirt bike and now he's brought it back, so it's all good now. Fact is, you don't really know *what* you saw this morning."

I know he was just trying to get me to doubt what I knew I saw.

"Was the money still there, too?"

"What money?"

"There was five thousand dollars in cash in the glove compartment Carl put there from selling a horse for Mr. Benavidez yesterday."

"I'll look into that. If it was there this morning, it's still there now. But you know Carl Buller."

"Yeah. I do."

"And did you tell Chase that you'd kill him if you ever saw him back on Benavidez land?"

"Yes." I didn't even think to lie. I said it because I hated his son.

Clayton shook his head. "You know, I could throw you in jail right now for saying that. You know that's against the law?"

I waited. Then I said, matter-of-factly, "Well, if you're not going to arrest a car thief, I guess you're not going to put me in jail for just shooting off my mouth, either."

I just wasn't thinking. I wasn't trying to make Clayton mad, it just happened.

And then, with the hand that was resting on the hood of the car, he hit me right across the face. I tried to duck, but he caught my nose with his thick fingers and as I spun away I could already feel the blood running out, warm and thick and smelling like metal.

✦ ✦ ✦

Clayton Rutledge handed me one of those blue paper towels from a service station. I was sitting on the side of the road, Reno was smelling my head, which was between my knees. Blood was flowing down the front of my shirt, onto my pants, onto my jacket. My eyes were blurred.

"Here. Clean yourself up, boy."

Then he went back to the car. I heard him open the door.

"You just better know that next time you go accusing anyone around here of anything, you better get your story straight first, boy. Or let the real police handle it. You just be glad I'm not handcuffing you and hauling your butt in right now, 'cause I could do that."

Then the door slammed shut and he pulled out. I kept my head down as he drove away. I was crying. It didn't hurt so bad; I was just mad and a little scared, too.

Things'll be better, Troy.

I don't know.

Don't cry, Troy. Don't cry anymore, son. Things'll be better now. She was tired. Too tired. She fought hard for a long time and we did the best we could and she got to be here until the end. That's all she wanted, so don't cry, son. It's you and me now. We have each other and we'll be okay. I promise. I just hate to see you cry, Troy. It hurts me worse than anything.

I guess it'll stop when it stops.

My dad wasn't home when I got back, and I was relieved about that. I got some clean clothes on and washed up. Then I called Tommy and asked him if it would be okay if I spent the night over at his house and if he could come get me. I didn't say anything else, I just hung up, sure that Tom knew something was wrong and he'd get here as soon as he could.

Then I started to write my dad a note on that yellow pad in the kitchen when I heard him opening the door. He must have gone pretty far because he had bags from a grocery store in his arms. He came into the kitchen and put the bags down by the sink, then looked at me with wide, surprised eyes.

"Oh my God, Troy. What happened to you?"

"Reno rode me right into a tree. It was dark and I wasn't paying attention."

My dad grabbed my head with both of his hands and looked right into my eyes.

"Your eyes look terrible. Are you okay, son?"

"Yeah. I just had a real bad bloody nose. You know how that messes up your eyes."

"Looks like you've got two black ones, son."

"I know. I'm an idiot." And I caught myself because I felt like I was about to start crying. "I put all my bloody clothes in the wash."

"I swear that horse is going to kill you one of these days."

Stottsy, that look means he's not tired of trying to kill you is all.

"Or die trying." And then I kind of laughed, which, I'm sure, tipped my dad that something was not right.

"You *sure* you're okay, Troy? There anything wrong?"

"Really, Dad. I'm okay. And Dad, Tom Buller's coming to get me so I can spend the night there. We got a lot of early work to do tomorrow, if that's okay."

"You're working too much, I think." And he went to the freezer and opened it. "Let's get some ice on that nose. It's probably broken."

"Dad. I'm not working too much. I love it there."

And he came back from the sink with a towel bundled around some ice cubes. I sat down on the couch with that ice pack on my face and waited for the sound of the Ford pickup signaling Tommy's arrival. It came in a few minutes and I said good night to my father and left.

+   +   +

"He took the money," Tom said as soon as I opened the door.

"I know it." Then the dome light's shine fell on my face.

"Jeez, Stotts, what the hell happened to you?"

"Clayton Rutledge punched me for smarting off." I took a deep, quavering breath to calm down.

"Troy Stotts smarting off? No way, man. Who'd believe it?"

I smiled and it hurt.

"What did your dad say?" he asked.

"I didn't tell him. I told him Reno treed me. What did your dad say about the money?"

"He went to Benavidez and told him he'd quit if he wanted him to, but Benavidez wouldn't have it. He said Rutledge explained it to Benavidez and it was all cleared up. So CB got pretty messed up. He's out cold now."

"Take me to the main house, Tommy. I'll walk back to your place after I see the man."

We drove away from my house in silence, the headlights cutting narrowed triangles of light into the blackness of the night, the graveled road skimming below them, dull and gray like the surface of the moon.

"What're we going to do, Tommy?"

"I don't think there's anything we *can* do," he said.

"He said he was going to arrest *me*," I said.

"That would be too much work," Tom explained. "I think Clayton Rutledge's worked more in the last twelve hours than he has all year."

It was after 8 when Tommy dropped me off outside the main house. I knocked, quietly, because of the hour. I waited and then knocked again. Luz opened the door. She gasped when she saw me, then came outside and closed the door behind her.

"Oh Troy! What happened?"

"Clayton Rutledge."

"Oh no!" And she grabbed my head and lightly touched around my nose and eyes with her cool fingers, so soft. I would have taken twice the beating to have her touch me like that again. I closed my eyes because I felt like I was going to cry. "I'm so sorry, Troy. We can't let him get away with it. You need to see my father."

"That's why I'm here. But I can't go in yet, give me a minute."

So we sat down on the steps, looking out at the night. We didn't talk; she had her arm around me and my head was down between my knees the way I was sitting after Clayton hit me; and we just stayed like that for the longest time, me feeling miserable and wonderful at the same time, feeling the warmth of Luz Benavidez next to me.

"Okay. I can go in now."

We stood up and kissed once before she opened the door.

And then I whispered, "But Luz, I don't want everyone looking at me and asking questions. I'm really tired and worn out. I just want to see him alone."

"Go upstairs and wait in his office. I'll get him."

I was scared sitting in that office, just waiting. And then I heard his footsteps coming up the stairs and I wished I hadn't come at all. I stood up when the door opened, holding my hat in front of me with both my hands, like a shield. Mr. Benavidez stopped and stared when he saw me. I stuck out my hand.

"Hello, sir," I said.

He took my hand. Not so hard this time.

"Troy. What happened?"

And then I told him the whole story. He stood there, in front of the door as if to block my escape, listening and nodding his head occasionally.

"This is outrageous, son," he said. "In the morning I'm going to call the county sheriff and see if there's something that can be done about Deputy Rutledge's behavior. Has your father seen this?"

"I was scared. I told him I had an accident," I said. "That I fell off Reno."

"Pretty soon everyone is going to think I gave you a bad horse," Mr. Benavidez said and smiled a little. "But I want you to know that Clayton did come by here to explain what happened with the truck. And I have to tell you that his son's story and yours do not agree. So it is your word against his, and in this town that means you will lose."

"But what about the money?"

"That's another matter. Carl has made mistakes before, although none quite so expensive. Clayton explained that anyone could have taken the money. Even Carl, although I know this is not true. So I don't know what I'll do about that, other than forget about it and try to make it up by selling two horses tomorrow. You see, this is how ranchers think. And Clayton said that there is little that can be done officially. Now as for your injury . . ."

"And you're just going to take it like that?" I said. I wasn't so scared of Mr. Benavidez as I was mad at his putting up with Clayton Rutledge and his son, but I tried my hardest to not sound disrespectful after what he'd just said about Tom Buller's dad.

"The sheriff says there is really nothing that can be done. He said if charges were pressed, they would also be pressed against you. So it's better left alone. Things will work out, I'm sure."

"I'm sure." I felt myself almost choking. I wanted to cuss so bad, and that's something I never did.

"I'll make that call in the morning."

"Thank you." And I moved past him toward the door. "Good night."

Luz was waiting in the hall. I know she could see the disappointment in my swollen eyes as I walked past her to the staircase.

"Good night, Luz," I said, and left that big house.

+   +   +

Tommy was waiting for me on the walkway to the main house, by the side of the dirt road. He had a heavy brown jacket on, collar turned up so it almost touched the brim of his hat.

"Been waiting long?"

"Just got here, Stotts," he said. "Here." And he pulled a tall can of beer from each of his pockets. "Thought you might like one."

"I might."

We popped open those beers and they sprayed us a little, after being jostled in Tommy's pockets. I took a long swig. It tasted bad, but felt cool and tingly and calming as it went down. A wind was blowing steady from the northwest, so we walked with our heads down and hats pulled low, sometimes tipping back to drink.

"You don't have to tell me that Benavidez doesn't really care about the money and stuff, 'cause I figured it would be like that."

"He said he was going to call the sheriff in the morning," I said.

"Yeah, but he won't really try to do anything," Tom said. "Because they're like kings, Benavidez and Rutledge. And they're totally in control of their own share of just about everything you see around here. Neither one of them wants to go to war with the other 'cause there's too much to lose. So I could've told you that."

"I'm quitting."

"No you're not, Stottsy. I won't let you do that."

"Well, what am I supposed to do?"

"I don't know. Let's get in and have some more beer. I don't think CB'll be awake till Wednesday, anyway."

We took our dusty shoes off on the porch and went into the Foreman's house. I could hear Carl snoring from a back bedroom. We threw our coats and hats on the long wooden bench inside the front door, like we always do. I followed Tommy into the kitchen.

"You hungry?" Tom asked.

"Yeah."

"Well, I hope you know how to fix food, 'cause so am I."

"Let's see if there's anything that just needs opening," I said.

We sat on the couch in the living room and ate pretzels and bologna sandwiches, talking while we drank beer. I fell right to sleep on that couch before I finished my second beer. Tommy threw a blanket over me and left me there.

The angel is sleeping in the woods.

No. I don't really know about you, Stottsy. You're scary smart.

We were sitting around the fire: me, Gabey, Tommy, and my dad was there, too. I remember Gabey was dressed all in white. Dad was smoking a cigarette. I looked into the flames and there were flames on the hills, streaking up to the mountains, circling the bottom of those two granite fingers, gray-white against the starlit sky. I was holding my Dawson folder, but I knew somehow I had broken it; the blade wouldn't open. I felt blood in my hand.

And my father waved his arm through the tongues of the lapping fire at Tommy. Snakes crawled out of the tops of Tommy's boots and he just kept brushing them off his legs, laughing, as more and more came out.

And then my father picked up Gabey, all small and bundled up like a sack of ice cubes, and he dropped him into the fire. Tommy and I got up and looked down into the fire, which was sucking down into the earth as though it had been turned upside down. I reached in after Gabey, bent forward at the waist, plunging my arms down into the fire, but it had become foaming icy water and all I could see was the swirling foam in front of my eyes and I know I stopped breathing, too, and I *knew* I was dreaming, but I screamed anyway.

Gabe. Gabe!

It was light. I heard Tommy running down the hallway from his bedroom. I was soaked in sweat.

"Stottsy, you okay? I heard you screaming for Gabe or something."

"Oh man," I said and touched my eyes, then jerked my hand back at the shock of pain from the bridge of my nose.

"I had a really bad dream. I must've got hit pretty hard yesterday."

"Naw. I think that baloney was rotten."

I sat up on the couch and yawned. "I can make some coffee if you got it."

I tossed the blanket aside and went with Tom into the kitchen. They had one of those coffee pots that cooks on a stove, like you'd use for camping. It took us a while to find the coffee can, but we finally did, and I managed to put it all together.

"So?" Tommy said. "What was that scary dream about?"

"I don't know. It was too weird. I was trying to pull Gabe out of a fire but it was sucking me in."

"I'm not going to say it, Stotts. You know. What you think I'll say."

"Yeah. I'm crazy."

The coffee was starting to boil. Tommy stretched and rubbed his eyes.

"So are we going to work today even if CB doesn't get out of bed?"

I took a breath. I wanted desperately to forget about the day and night before, the dream that woke me.

"I want to," I said.

THIRTEEN

The fires came early that year, the summer my mom died.

The winter before had carried so much rain and snow on its gray shoulders, then the summer of the mountain lion, the ghost medicine that promised to make us vanish, to cure our ghosts, brought so much growth in the underbrush; and that growth, in turn, withered and dried under the heat of a particularly fierce July.

Tommy and I were out by the fence line, at the temporary corrals we had built for those horses we'd finally gotten from Rose. They were tame and calm now, and we were happy for that. The big roan had gotten to the point where he would smell Tommy, and Tom was touching him just about every day, so he was close to being ready for the halter. He looked to be about three years old, so we figured he hadn't been wild for so long that there was nothing we could do with him, and he wasn't too old to geld, either.

"It just hurts to think about," Tommy said.

"You wouldn't want to keep him if you didn't geld him," I said.

"It's the thought of it, I guess."

"He's had his way enough, though. I'm sure it's his foal mine's carrying," I said. "It kind of makes you wonder, huh, when you see a horse like him, though. I mean, look at his legs, how fine they are. And look at how big he is. He could easily kill you, he practically did that time we finally got a rope on him. But now he lets you get in there with him and he smells up against you and he even lets you touch him."

"I want to get on him."

"He's going to let you do that, too. And he doesn't have to, you know that, 'cause you know he could just as easy kill you. But he's going to *let* you do all this to him, and it's no humiliation to him. It's a bargain."

"Man, you're weird about horses. I think that Reno's messed up your head."

"By landing me on it too many times, I bet."

That mare of mine was doing well, too. I had her on the halter and could take her out on walks, ponying with Reno. But like horses can be sometimes, he was jealous of her, and I saw that. Sometimes she followed us off the halter. And she was getting real big and wide, like she was getting ready to foal. I named her Ghost Medicine, for the lion we took that day. Tommy named that stallion Duke.

Duke could be pretty mean, so we separated the corral with pipe down the middle, running right over the big trough we kept filled by hauling water out of one of Benavidez' water trucks. The horses were standing along the rail, head to tail, flicking each others' faces with their tails, in the shade of one of those big umbrella-shaped oaks, when I noticed a column of pale smoke off in the woods, a few miles to the south of us.

"There's a fire over there," I said, pointing.

Tommy squinted his black eyes at the smoke. "It looks like it's probly down by the highway, maybe three or four miles."

"Think we should go back in and tell 'em at the ranch?"

"Let's watch it a while. Could just be the Forest Service burning something on purpose."

So we watched the smoke, sitting there with our legs inside the corral and our arms draped over the top rail. When I first saw it, the smoke was translucent and sand-colored. A few minutes later, it thickened up to a solid white; and then finally it began mushrooming up in big round pillows of dark gray and black; thick and ominous. It wasn't good. And it was heading north, towards the Benavidez ranch, and us.

"It's gonna be a bad one," I said.

"What do you say we do, Stotts?"

We fixed our stares at the distant smoke, over the tops of the trees.

"We gotta go tell Rose 'cause she might have to get out. If it gets bad we might try to run some of her horses this way."

"Okay. What about these two, then?"

"Well, if it gets bad then we'll have to let 'em out. If they're smart enough they'll head for the lake. It's not that far."

"I could go get the trailer."

"Yours isn't going in no trailer today," I said.

"Okay. Let's get over to Rose's."

I jumped Reno over the fence and opened the chute gate for Tom and Arrow. The smoke was nearly filling all the southern sky now and our shadows fell dim on the ground; the daylight had gone orange. I heard the rumble of the propellers of the first water-dropping plane overhead.

I saw Rose's windmill over the rise of the hill before her house. It was turning, facing south. The wind, hot and dry, was picking up. Rose was standing out in front of her house, hands on her hips, wearing that dirty flowered dress of hers, staring up at the smoke like she was mad at it. The sky was nearly gone now, and smoke was low to the ground. The air stunk of burning brush and tree.

"Ha! My two young cowboys are back to see the fire," she said. "Well, I been here for the last fire, more than twenty years ago. But a steel house don't burn!"

"I bet it makes a good oven, though," Tom said.

She had an old Ford Falcon station wagon with fake wood paneling on the sides, all faded and flaking away. She drove it a few times each year to pick up supplies and visit her lawyer, so I knew it could run if she needed it.

"Do you need us to help you get anything loaded into your car?" I asked. The problem, I knew, was that the easement through Benavidez land that gave her access to the highway was south, toward the fire.

"I'm not going anywhere just yet," she said. "But I guess I'd take that cat."

"It looks pretty bad," I said. Ashes were falling from the sky, soft like snowflakes. Some were black and curled. Some were smoking. Our shadows were gone, but it was still afternoon.

Tom got down from Arrow and handed his reins to me.

"I'm going to get some stuff out of the house for her in case she decides to go."

I tied both of the horses up at the post by the goat trough. Tommy was already coming out the front door carrying two jugs of wine.

"I got her tobacco in my pockets. This is all she'd want anyway."

"Ha! You got some tobacco? See, you boys is good ones," Rose said.

"Did you see that cat in there?" I asked.

Tom kept walking around the side of the house to the station wagon. "If I did, I wouldn't say."

I went into her house and turned toward the back wall. I walked right into a thick, sticky spider's web. I felt my stomach rise up and I took my hat off and shook it, certain there would be a big black widow on it somewhere. I gave a quick look toward Rose's "living room" — the seats around her stove. No cat. That was good enough for me.

"I can't find him in there," I said as I came out the door.

But Tom was holding Rose's little brown cat, its paws straight up on the front of his shoulder like he was aiming to use Tommy's face as a scratching post. I grimaced, still feeling spiderwebs on me.

"What's wrong with you?" Tom asked.

"Nothing. Put him in her car and let's see if we can move some of those horses over."

We left Rose there, standing by the Falcon with an open jug of wine, which she was drinking straight from the mouth, arm chicken-winged under the weight of the green bottle like it was moonshine. I'm glad she didn't offer any, because Tom Buller would have taken it, and that meant I would, too, and then we'd burn to death for sure. I guess she knew we were determined to try to move some of the horses over to the safer ground near the lake, so she just smiled and watched us, that cat with its paws up on the metal-trimmed steering wheel of the station wagon like it was getting ready to go even if Rose wasn't.

"You're going to have to go pretty soon, Rose," I said.

"You just take care of yourself, Tennis Shoes. Ha! I've lived a long time by not being in a hurry."

Tom and I rode out toward the foothills and trees at the western end of Rose's land. We could see those horses right away, circling around one another nervously, older foals sandwiched between mares, colts mimicking the stallions who'd raise their heads up and sniff the air. They were jittery, and the sky was angry and orange-brown like it was the end of the world.

"You hold 'em on this side," I said to Tom and then Reno and I cut around the herd, between the horses and the trees, Reno running fast and straight like he knew more about what we were going to do than I did.

We started to nudge the horses forward from the back of the pack, yearlings, colts, and fillies, all were scared of a horse carrying a rider. Then the whole herd started to move and I saw Tom and Arrow across their undulating backs, pushing them north and letting me cut them east from my side. It was a beautiful thing, and it made me feel proud to see my friend across that small sea of horses, knowing what we would do without saying anything to me, just spitting his tobacco and calling out "Haw!" like that laugh of Rose's, to get them moving the right way.

It was like riding through a dream. The light was all but gone now and smoke and dust hung low against the ground. I was sure the fire would be right on us soon.

We headed the horses over the rise down towards Rose's steel house, scattering nervous and bleating goats as we did. The Ford Falcon was gone, and I was relieved that Rose had decided to go away, at least for now. I caught sight of Tom looking over at me as we ran the horses by. He had noticed it, too.

Once in a while, one or two of the horses would cut away and either Reno or Arrow would widen out their path to lead them back in, so when we got to the fence line we hadn't lost a single horse that I could see. I sprinted Reno up ahead of the pack now so I could get down and open that chute gate we had cut into the fence. Then I got back on Reno and helped Tommy get the leaders through the gate.

There must have been as many as fifty horses, and I knew our holding corral wouldn't be big enough, especially if some of them started to push against the rails or try to jump them, so once we had gotten them through the chute I jumped Reno over the fence and came around to set them all loose on Benavidez land without setting free the two horses Tom and I had been working on. There was nothing else we could do for Rose's herd; we had to hope they would be able to get away from the fire and the Benavidez ranch had enough running room for them, as well as the safety of the lake.

I opened the gate and swung it back, riding on the middle rail and watching all those horses run, thundering past me and Reno, and off toward the north. I looked back at Tom, on the other side of the fence at the chute gate, and I could barely see him through the fog of smoke. He waved his hat at me.

"We did it, Stotts."

"We better get out of here quick, Tom. It's coming this way."

Through the smoky haze I could see an eruption of orange flames pulsing from the canopy of one of the oaks on Rose's land.

*   *   *

The fire burned for three days. That first night was the worst; we all thought we'd have to leave. I always associated those nighttime brush fires, the orange lines twisting and writhing like snakes on the hills, with dying; and I thought about those horses we set loose, and all the burning. I stayed at Tom's house throughout those days, just moping quietly beside him as we worked; I had told my dad that they'd need me at the ranch in case we had to move out some of the stock, and that was the truth.

"Okay with me if you don't want to talk, Stotts."

I looked over at Tommy. We rode out to the main pasture fence the morning after the fire started, watching the Benavidez stock, and keeping our eyes on the walls of tumbling smoke that rose in great orange pillows across the sun. Ashes peppered our hat brims, and we both had bandanas tied across our faces to block out the stink, but it didn't help much.

It was such a terrible thing, but it was impossible to ignore.

"'Cause I'm worried, too," he continued. "So if you want me to shut up, I will, but it's pretty hard for me to be out here with you and not talk about anything. You want me to shut up?"

"No."

Tommy spit.

"Then tell me."

"Tell you what?"

"Tell me about it, Stotts."

Tommy nudged Arrow right beside Reno so we were practically touching. I just kept my eyes on the smoke. I was so tired. I hadn't slept, couldn't stop my head all night long from picturing things that had been.

I remembered my mother.

You disappear in those clothes that big, Troy.

She had driven me to the dance at the community center, that first high school dance in ninth grade in September, before she got so sick. I sat in the car, afraid to go out, watching as Chase Rutledge, laughing, walked past us toward the doors, a girl drunkly swinging along at his arm.

I want to look different, Mom. I wish I was good-looking. I'm the smallest boy here.

I see all the other boys going in there, Troy. You're the handsomest one here.

I sighed and looked out the window.

Who are you going to dance with?

No one. I don't even know any girls.

Luz is coming.

Okay, then. Luz.

I bet you that the others will ask you to dance with them, you'll see.

I pulled my hat down over my eyes and opened the door. She was watching me, then, looking at me like I was about to break.

Relax, Troy. Have a good time. Luz wants to dance with you. She told us a week ago.

You shouldn't've said anything to her about it a week ago. I'll see you.

I closed the door.

+ + +

"You won't tell anyone?" I asked.

"You're talking to me, Stotts," Tommy said, and pulled the bandana down to his chin so I could see he was looking right at me, that he wasn't smiling.

Tommy lifted the bandana back across his nose. "Man, that stinks. Sure doesn't have the same smell as our fire, does it, Stotts?"

"I'm just hurting, Tom."

"I know."

I sighed. "Nothing's right."

Tommy spit.

"Lots of things are. You know that."

"When we watched those flames on the hills last night, it made me remember a lot of things I try not to think about," I said. "When I was four, when my brother died, we drove home from the hospital at night and everything was on fire. It was so quiet in that car. The only thing I heard was the sound of the road, and my mother and father in the front seat crying and not saying anything or looking at each other. And all I could see out the window was black, and these crazy zigzags of flames all around on the hills. It looked like we were driving into hell, and I kept thinking, *Where's my brother? We can't just drive away and leave him there.* I try not to think about it. I try not to think about my mom and him, but sometimes I can't stop it. I'm sorry."

Tommy looked at me, and then up at the smoke clouds I was watching.

"I'm sorry, too, Stotts," he said. "How'd he die?"

"We were doing something we weren't supposed to do. We were playing on the roof. He fell off and broke his neck."

Tommy spit again.

"I played on roofs before. Don't all boys do that?"

My eyes burned. I rubbed them.

"I never told anyone that, Tom."

"No one'll ever hear it from me, Stotts."

He held out his fist, and I punched it.

✦   ✦   ✦

When the fire had burned itself out, the damage was great. It even came onto Benavidez land, but never got near any of the stock or buildings on the property. Two of the locals who lived near Three Points lost their homes, and so our annual '49ers Day celebration had to be postponed for a week. And on the third day, Tommy and I rode out to see if we could find where the horses went, and to check on Rose.

The horses all looked fine. They were scattered around the old south pastureland where we had gone shooting with Gabriel. We found them all, even Ghost Medicine and Duke.

I took a drink from my canteen as Tommy dipped into his tobacco. Everything still smelled like burned paper.

"There's some real good horses in this group," Tommy said. "I guess I didn't notice 'em all before."

"Look at that tall sorrel there. Look at her legs," I said. "That's a real nice-looking horse."

"I like that one," Tommy said and pointed to a big chestnut bay with black legs and a big white face. "Kinda looks like a young Arrow, don't he?"

We just sat there looking at those horses for a while, then Tommy said, "So what're we gonna do about 'em, now? I bet it was just luck we got 'em over here so easy without one of us breakin' a leg or something."

"We need to check on Rose before we can move 'em," I said. "We don't even know if the fence got burned down or not."

"Let's go see." And then he spit. "Want some?"

"I'll wait."

Where we had built the holding and training corrals there was no sign that a fire had burned through, but right from the fence line we could see the blackened ground and burned trees on Rose's land. And as we rode farther in toward her house, the burning looked worse and worse.

"It got her place for sure," Tom said. "Now we'll see how that steel house made out."

I couldn't help but feel sad for Rose, sad for this land.

Isn't this about the most beautiful place in the world, Troy?

As we got closer to that rise before her house, I saw a little black, charred mound. I rode up to it and saw it was a burned goat, just kneeling down like goats do when the wind blows too hard; dead and stiff and peaceful like one of those castings from Pompeii. I looked over at Tom.

"Well, I told you there's not much stupider than a goat," he said.

"I know."

There was no rust and no shine left on that big steel house of Rose's. All around it was burned away. The pile of oak firewood around the Chevy pickup was still smoking and smoldering, and the shell of the truck looked thinner, a blackened eggshell surrounding nothing, ready to crumble and implode if one of us touched it. The house itself was black with thick soot, but all around it on the ground there was an eerie kind of bloom of gray on the earth where the house had given off heat and continued to bake the ground.

"Rose? Rose?" I shouted as we came up to the house.

There was no answer, just the rusty, creaking sound of that steel windmill pumping water from the ground, its black fan blades spinning dumbly, water trickling from the cistern's overflow into that trough of ash-blackened water. There were no goats around to drink it anyway.

We got down from our horses.

"Rose?" I called out at the door, still shut, just as we had left it four days ago.

"That car's not here," Tom said. "That's a good sign. She's okay, Stotts."

I grabbed the doorknob and immediately jerked my hand back.

"It's hot."

I pulled the bottom of my T-shirt out to insulate my palm and tried again, wiping black grime all over my shirt. I pushed the door in. The house reeked of smoke, and I could hear crackling sounds inside like you'd hear in the belly of a stove that's burned for days and days.

"I bet that got rid of those spiders," I said.

"Don't go in, Stotts. Look." Tommy pointed to the little four-pane window looking out from the side of the door. The glass was melted, the lower panes ballooning out a little, the two on top shattered.

"Poor old woman."

"It won't be nothing for us to clean this place out for her, Stotts. There wasn't hardly nothin' in it anyway and now she can get a clean start. We'll bring her what she needs and fix it up. It'll be okay."

I wiped my eyes with my black hand, smearing my face.

"I wonder where she is," I said.

"Somewhere where she can drink wine and spit her tobacco, probly."

FOURTEEN

I don't know the origins of Three Points' annual '49ers Day celebration; I guess that it had something to do with some fools back in history thinking they could pan enough gold from the rivers here to keep food in their bellies. Tom Buller and my dad both believed it was just an excuse for people to get together and drink and gamble and act foolish. So the real truth is probably somewhere between those two explanations.

It was always held on the first weekend in August, but that's when the big fire broke out. Rose still hadn't come back to her steel house, although Tommy and Carl and I had managed to get all her horses back onto her property, which wasn't half-burned. I was disappointed that it had to be postponed for a week following that wildfire because now that I was sixteen I was finally old enough to compete in the only thing about the day that ever held my attention: the Three Points Biathlon. Some people came from as far away as Colorado or Wyoming to compete in the biathlon, which combined trail riding and target shooting. Riders were started in staggered runs, beginning in the early morning just after the parade, and had to get their horses over a four-mile course that had three checkpoints where each rider would have five shots at five targets. One checkpoint involved shooting from horseback, one required standing, and one required prone firing. Every target missed added one extra minute to a rider's overall time, and every rider had to use the rifles supplied by the event organizers. There were judges at every checkpoint, and this year my father would be at one of them.

So with all that running through my head, and knowing that Tommy and Gabe and I were going to camp out at the fire pit that night, needless to say I was up well before sunrise on that Saturday morning.

I pulled on a pair of 501s and went out to the kitchen and poured myself a glass of orange juice. It was still hot in our house, and I wasn't wearing any shirt, just standing there in the light of the open refrigerator drinking my juice. My dad came in and turned on the overhead lights.

"Good morning, son. Sleep good?"

"Morning, Dad. Un-uh. Too nervous, I guess."

"Hey, why don't you wear that belt Luz gave you for good luck?" My dad pulled up on one of the empty belt hoops on my jeans. I know I'd gotten taller in the last few months, just not any thicker.

"I don't need any luck," I said.

"Well, then, do you want some eggs?"

I started to say no, but then I told him yes because I knew it would make my dad happy to make breakfast for me and I figured that I could always just leave them anyway, since I knew I was too jittery to eat. "I'll go get Reno up while you fix 'em."

I stopped just inside the screen door, my hands ready to push, looking out, away from my father. "Dad?" I said, and I could feel him looking at me. "I'm going into eleventh grade now and so next year might be our last summer together if I end up going away to school."

"Yes?"

"Well, the reason I'm saying this is that mare Ghost I got is a real good horse with a real good head, too. She's going to be a good riding horse once I'm done with her and when I do, I want to give her to you so next summer you and me can take that trip up to that cabin like you said you wanted to do. I've been thinking about that for a long time but just didn't have the guts to ask you till now. So will you do it?"

My dad never liked horses.

"I swear I will, Troy," he said, and put his hand on my shoulder. "I promise we'll do it."

I made sure Reno looked especially good that day. He was clean and combed and his mane hung perfectly straight and even. The saddle and all my gear were soaped and shined, too, and Reno felt the excitement of the morning. Every '49ers Day began with a parade, which was always led by the numbered riders competing in the biathlon, with the Holmes School band, a Forest Service fire truck, and a few other local entries following. The parade was always announced by the sheriff over the PA system on his car, and immediately after, the biathlon's first rider would get sent out.

Of course I didn't eat more than a couple bites of my breakfast, but my dad didn't seem too bothered by that. I was just about to make an excuse for not wanting to finish when Tommy drove up with the trailer to take me and Reno to the start.

I ran back to my room and put a T-shirt on, then grabbed my hat and headed for the front door.

"I'm going, Dad."

"I'll see you up there, son. Good luck," he called out from in the kitchen.

"I don't need it," I said as I shut the door behind me.

I pulled Reno around the side of the house where Tommy waited. As I got him up into the trailer, he shook his head back and forth, trying to say he'd rather run. That was good, I thought.

Tom and I closed up the trailer and climbed into the cab.

"Ready for the big shootout, Stotts?" Tommy said as he started the engine.

"Thanks for coming to get us. It would be a lot of riding, even for Reno. You and Gabe all set for later?"

"I'm going to drive Arrow and Dusty up to the fire pit, if that's okay with you. So we'll just all meet there after the barbecue."

"That's okay. It's not too far. It'll be fun."

"Yeah. I don't think Gabe's even really got permission from his dad to come along, but that's his problem, 'cause he's coming anyway."

"Sounds like you're kidnapping him."

Tommy, grinning, steered with his knee and opened up his can of tobacco.

"Want some?"

"Not now. I feel sick, kind of."

"You'll shoot and ride the hell out of that thing, don't worry," Tom said, and I felt better just hearing my friend talk like that. "CB and Ramiro are taking off this morning to flatbed some hay down that easement road to throw out for those horses. I gave him a can of chew for Rose in case she's back yet and I told him to tell her we'll come out on Monday and see her."

"That's really nice of them. Tell your dad thanks if I don't see him."

"It's not that nice. He's taking it out of our wages anyway."

"Just so he's not charging us feed store prices."

"Feed store prices plus hourly for him and Ramiro." Then he spit into his ever-present, half-filled cup. And I laughed. I knew he was joking, and I knew that Carl would probably end up not charging us anything for that hay, even though I believed it was a fair thing to do.

Tom looked at me. "Where's your bandana?"

"What?"

"You should have a bandana or something when you ride in one of these things. You never know. You might need to wipe the sweat off your hands or your eyes or keep the dust out of your face. You could even get cut. You need one."

"I didn't think about that."

"Well, here." Tommy tilted over to one side and pulled a pressed and folded red bandana from his back pocket.

"Is it used?"

"That would make it even luckier." Then he spit again.

I tied the bandana around my neck like an outlaw in one of those old westerns. "I don't need any extra luck. Thanks, Tom."

"You just win, Stotts. We're all going to be betting on you."

"That makes me feel even worse, then."

There was always a lot of money being bet on the biathlon. Everyone knew it was illegal, even the sheriff, but it was just like a regular horse race and, of course, Clay Rutledge gambled on it just as much as anyone else. And everyone said he took his own cut from it, too. Bettors could put money to win, place, or show on any one of the numbered riders in the event and the betting tickets were sold right over the counter at Papa's store. Most people thought the money from the biathlon was the only thing that kept Papa's open for business from one year to the next.

There were at least fifteen riders already there at the check-in when Tommy and I got to Three Points. Most of them I had never seen before, but there were a few hands from the Benavidez ranch who said hi to me, and I saw Chase Rutledge and that leopard Appaloosa of his there, too, which didn't do anything good for my nervous stomach.

"I feel like I'm gonna throw up," I whispered to Tom as we went to the sign-in table.

"Aim that way," he said, pointing a thumb like a hitchhiker toward Chase.

Then I saw the Benavidez family there by the table, all smiling at me like I was some kind of hero. Gabriel came up to me, snaking through the crowd gathered around the table filling out forms and paying entry fees.

"Hey, Troy. You look like a bank robber," Gabe said.

"Don't say that too loud, I think Rutledge still wants to put me in jail," I said. "You coming tonight?"

"Sure thing."

"Troy!" Mr. Benavidez smiled and reached out a hand. This

time he squeezed real hard and slapped my shoulder, too, with a stinging left swat. "Let me pay your entry fee. You can be sponsored by the Benavidez ranch."

"No offense, Mr. Benavidez." I felt myself turning a little red. "But no thanks. I wouldn't know what to do with this fifty dollars I got in my pocket otherwise, and I've been ready to do this since my birthday."

"You're quite a young man, Troy," he said, and then he started to say something else but Luz cut him off.

"Hi, Troy. Are you feeling good?"

She was looking at my pants sagging over the tops of my tennis shoes, so I know what she was thinking.

"I can't wear a belt when I ride. It hurts. Sorry, Luz," I said, looking down. "And I feel horrible. I think I'm sick or something."

My hand was shaking and I could hardly write legibly when I filled out the entry forms at that table. To make things worse, they were all looking over my shoulder as I wrote.

I paid my fee and drew a Popsicle stick from inside a big upturned hat. I drew number seven and was handed a printed bib and four safety pins to attach to my shirt.

"Number seven, Dad, number seven," Gabe said, indicating which number to place money on over at the small store. Maybe I was dreaming, but I heard a couple other people saying "number seven" from within the crowd.

"All riders should report to parade lineup," the sheriff was announcing from his loudspeaker.

"I should go get my horse," I said.

I saw Mr. Benavidez grab his wife's arm and turn back toward Papa's, Gabe following. Somewhere back in the crowd I saw my father, could read his lips as he was talking to another spectator. He was saying, "Number seven."

I felt as dizzy as the first time I chewed that tobacco with Tommy, and I followed my friend back to that old Ford truck, where Reno was tied outside the trailer, numbly aware that I was barely holding that bib number in my hand and Luz was following along.

"Here," she said, "give me those," when she saw that I couldn't get the first safety pin open with my sweaty hand. She took the bib and pins from me and I wiped my hand up on that bandana around my neck.

"Don't scream too loud if I stick you, Troy," she said and she pressed the bib up to my chest and opened the first pin. Then she slid her other hand up inside my shirt and I felt her cool, smooth arm slide up my belly and chest and my knees nearly buckled underneath me.

Tommy must have known what was happening because I felt his hands bracing my shoulders from behind me.

"Easy there, Stottsy. You're not resting on us yet."

And me standing there, barely, wishing there were a dozen more pins to hold that number seven to my chest. After she closed the fourth pin, she turned her hand around and pressed her palm on my breast.

"Your heart is beating so hard," she said.

"I know."

She rubbed her palm down my belly softly and then she pulled my shirt down straight and smoothed out the number by rubbing it down on my chest. Then she pulled that red bandana around so the knot was behind my neck.

"There," she said. "You're the handsomest rider in the bunch by far." And then she looked over at Tommy and back at me and said, "Good luck, Troy."

And then she leaned forward and kissed me softly on the cheek.

"Oh, he says he doesn't need any," Tommy said.

I didn't say anything, but I heard Mr. Benavidez calling for Luz from somewhere far away. She whirled around and disappeared into the swirling and buzzing crowd.

As fast as I could, I ran behind the trailer and bent forward with my hands on my knees and threw up all over the tire.

"That's probly a good thing, Stottsy," Tom Buller said, standing right behind me, next to my horse. "That's probly a real good thing."

And then I heard him spit.

They began playing the national anthem. I was late to line up. The parade was starting, and we were supposed to be in numbered order.

"Come on, Stotts. Get up on your horse before it's too late."

I moved over to Reno's left side and got my foot up in the stirrup. I stood there for a second and then I wiped my face off with that bandana.

"Now *that's* lucky," Tom said, pointing at the smear on his bandana.

"I feel good now."

"Good. 'Cause I'm going down there to see George at the store and I'm gonna put a week's pay on number seven."

"Please don't, Tommy."

"Don't worry, Stottsy," he said. "I'm betting you all three ways. There's no way I can lose."

And then Tom Buller slapped my leg as I got up on my horse and turned away toward Papa's. Then he called back over his shoulder, "I know you don't need it, so I won't say it."

I rode Reno to the lineup and found my place near the front. There were thirty-two of us, so I figured the staggered start would take almost three hours and if we were lucky, the last riders would be in by noon. Last year's winner got to wear number one; he was an older rider from Holmes who had grown up most of his life in Texas. He was real good, and won the event the last three years running. I saw Chase off behind me wearing number nineteen.

The flags in front of us started to march and all the riders fell in behind them, riding single file because the deputy was going to announce each of our names over the speakers. I heard the Holmes school band begin playing behind us.

I saw Luz and her family standing along the parade route, smiling and waving to people they knew. I looked right at Luz and saw her staring at me, too. She smiled, and I thought about her saying I was the handsomest rider and it made me feel real strong; and I tipped my hat at her and smiled back. I wondered if she still saw me as straight-mouthed.

And I saw my father there in the crowd, too. As I watched him, I saw people come up to him and shake his hand or hug him and pat him on the back. I knew what they were asking him — if he was okay, if I was, if we needed anything. I was glad I didn't have to hear it.

I looked for Rose, too, knowing that she would never come to Three Points just to see this parade. I looked anyway.

Then when I came up to the black-and-white Ford Bronco,

I saw Clayton Rutledge sitting by his open window on a tall barstool, holding a wrinkled bundle of papers, his microphone held up to the side of his mouth as he announced the riders.

He looked at me and said, "And no, folks, we haven't made an exception to allow babies to compete this year. Riding up wearing number seven is young Troy Stotts, who believe it or not is really sixteen years old."

I heard some people in the crowd laugh.

"And that fine-looking horse he's riding is a Benavidez cutting horse named Rita."

He's not a cutting horse.

I could have slapped him with a hay hook right then and there. I looked over at Luz, and then I heard Gabriel yell out, "That's his own horse he's on and his name is Reno and he's a thoroughbred!"

I clenched a fist at Gabe and shook it.

"Thanks, Gabey."

And I looked at him and he mouthed, silently, but real big so I could read his lips, "He's an idiot."

Tommy came up behind them and I heard him yell out, "Go get 'em, young Troy and Rita!"

And then I put my head down because that made me laugh hard.

After the parade, we all gathered at the starting line for the biathlon. Since I was number seven, I had half an hour after the start for me to check Reno's saddle and make sure we were both ready for the race. Any longer than that would have worn me down, so I was happy with my place. Number four was about to be sent, with five on deck. I'd have to move over to my spot soon.

Tommy was squatting down, checking Reno's feet.

"He looks real good. Where's your dad?"

"He's gonna be at the number two range. Standing. That's the hardest one, I think."

"Did you see the rifles?"

"Number five," an announcer called, meaning five was about to be sent, with six on deck.

"They're real good. Marlin biathlon rifles. They cost a lot. Really dialed in."

"You get a thousand bucks if you win."

I put a tennis shoe in Reno's stirrup and lifted myself up onto him. I arranged the reins back and straightened my bandana. Then I leaned over and whispered in Reno's ear, saying, "Do good, boy."

"That's a lot of money."

"Number six."

"Tommy?" I started to walk Reno over to the on-deck area. Tommy grabbed my knee hard. I was going to tell him that I'd kick him if he ever called my horse "Rita" again; 'cause I know how he's got that coyote in him. "Thanks for the bandana."

"You already said that." And then he spit and held up his fist, and I punched it hard so I knew it hurt him, because it made me wince, too. And then he slapped Reno on the butt and said, "Stotts, remember . . . turn invisible and pass them all."

The first mile of the course was steep uphill. I had an advantage there because of Reno's strength and my size. So when I came into the first set of targets, I felt calmer and more confident than I had since I woke up.

The first station involved shooting from horseback, which can be a tricky thing if you are on the wrong animal for it. A lot of the riders put plugs in their horses' ears. But Reno knew how to hold steady, so I could prop an elbow on one knee to steady the sights. Every station was judged, too. Judges kept track of riders and their scores, and they kept stopwatches so they could give credit time if there were ever two riders showing up at the same set of targets. The targets were small iron knock-down circles, about the size of a half-dollar, set off no closer than fifty feet at any station. Each rider had five shots at five targets, and then had to reload the rifle for the next rider before leaving.

I took a long time making my shots at the first station because I was afraid of missing. I took them all down and I heard the judge say "I'll be damned!" when I did. He probably had money on someone who'd already come through, I thought. I put the five shots in the rifle's clip and handed it down to the judge and said "Thank you" before riding off on the second mile leg.

On that second leg, I passed rider number six, a woman from Holmes who looked to be about thirty-five; I'm really not good at guessing ages. I could tell she was pretty mad as Reno and I brushed past her.

It was getting hot, and I was sweating in the saddle. Reno was sweating, too, breathing hard, but loving the speed of the racing toward the next station. I untied the bandana and wiped my eyes and hands, then I tied it on to the saddle horn as we came into sight of the second station, where my dad was judging. And there he was, stopwatch hanging from a cord around his neck, a blue Dodgers baseball cap on his head, looking as out of place there as if he had been wearing a shirt and tie.

"Did you pass six?"

"Way back there," I said. "I got 'em all at one."

I got down from Reno, feeling cooler from the air hitting the sweat on my jeans. My dad handed me the rifle and said, "All right, number seven. Five targets from a standing position. Only one rider's got 'em all so far, son."

Standing was hard because after riding two miles, you tend to be shaky and, with no rest for your elbow, shooters have a tendency to pull their shots. I tried to relax my shoulders.

"Dad, you remember what we talked about this morning?" I said. "I plan on holding you to that promise, you know. I'm going to get you on that horse."

He had a kind of disappointed look on his face, but he smiled a little. Tried to, anyway.

"You don't have to worry about that, son. I'm proud you asked me. But you better make that horse you got extra nice. Now you better start shooting before six comes in."

"I think the first snow'll come before six gets here."

And then I took all five at station two, as well. I reloaded and gave the gun back to my father.

"Thanks, Dad."

"Tom Buller told me to say he owes you five bucks if you get all five," my dad said.

"He could afford it if I get 'em all at the next one."

I smiled, pulled my hat down straight, and Reno and I were off on the third leg.

The third leg was mostly downhill and through the trees, in part following the shore of that river that nearly killed me on my sixteenth birthday. Reno and I took it fast and I could hear the five shots of the rider in front of me as we neared the last set of targets. Number five was barely out of there when we rode up.

Clayton Rutledge was judging the third station.

I knew he'd be there, but I kind of felt my guts shrink when I saw him standing with his clipboard, his eyes staring at me like they had that night he stopped me on my way home.

"Well, well, it's the Stotts boy," he said. "You already been through the first two? How many'd you get?"

I got down from Reno. Clayton made no move to hand me the rifle.

"I got 'em all."

"That's pretty lucky shooting for a boy your size, I'd say." Then he held up the rifle and turned it over in his hands. The barrel pointed right at my belly as he checked it. "Let's just see if that number five got it reloaded."

He carefully removed the magazine from the rifle and squinted as he counted the bullets it held. I knew what he was doing, and I began to get a little mad but I wasn't going to say anything to him this time.

"I hope you worked out your head, boy. Chase and me don't hold no hard feelings about that mistake you made."

I exhaled a big breath and held out my hand to get that gun. "These five are lying flat, right?"

"Five targets from a prone position. That means laying on your stomach, boy."

He handed me the gun and I flattened out on the ground.

"The wind's coming up," he said. "You might need to adjust for that. 'Cause that first one on the left is a bit cockeyed. I seen two riders in a row miss that same one today, but I thought it was the wind. Maybe when I reset 'em I'll turn it this way a bit more."

And he just kept talking like that as I tried to take aim.

I missed my first shot. I put my face down in my hand.

"You missed!" he said. "Let's see ... number seven. One penalty. You are number seven, right, boy?"

"Sheriff Rutledge, could you please stop talking?" My voice was shaking as I said it. He didn't say anything, but I could hear his footsteps as he walked up alongside my legs and then stood right beside my left hip, casting his large shadow over me.

"I'm sorry, boy. Go ahead and finish up."

I could feel him looking at me, spilling his big black shadow on me. I re-aimed the rifle, but I missed again.

Rutledge cleared his throat. I could hear the sound of his pencil scraping the page where he tallied the misses. Two minutes. I was so mad at myself I could have howled. Clayton didn't say anything then. I took the next three targets one after the other.

"Now don't forget to reload," he said.

My hands were shaking, he could see that. I had to somehow try to make up two minutes on the rest of the riders in that last mile, figuring there'd be at least a few who'd get all fifteen. I quickly reloaded the rifle, felt like throwing it, but handed it over to the deputy.

"I didn't think a kid your size would take fifteen of fifteen, but you did dang good, boy."

I didn't say anything. I leapt up onto Reno and dug my heels in and we were off toward the finish at a full gallop.

That last mile came down by the bridge and the flats. I kept my head low alongside Reno's pumping neck, holding the reins loose and letting him run as fast as he could, just hoping I wouldn't slip and fall. We caught and passed number five and I even saw four cross the finish line by Papa's store about thirty seconds in front of me, so missed shots or not, I knew we'd post a fast time. I just never should have missed those shots, the easiest ones in the race.

And I saw them all there, cheering as I came to the finish line: Tommy, Luz, Gabriel, and his parents, but I wouldn't look at them as I crossed because I felt so bad I think I would have started to cry.

There was a makeshift livery for the horses behind Papa's and I went straight there with Reno. I took off his bridle and saddle and threw it over the top rail of the corral piping. I started brushing him down.

"You did real good, Reno. I'm sorry I messed up."

Tommy and Gabe squeezed through the rails of the corral. They looked overjoyed.

"You were awesome!" Gabe said.

"I missed two."

"You?" Tommy couldn't believe it, either. "You missed *two*? Did you see your time?"

"I'm sick about it, Tom. It was at that Deputy Rutledge's station. He was *trying* to make me miss."

"Even with two penalty minutes, you're still in first place by a long shot," Gabe said.

I looked at my two friends. "I am?"

"I have a good feeling about this," Tom said.

"It's 'cause of Reno, that's all," I said. "But there's a lot of riders still coming around."

Then I saw Luz resting her arms on the rails of the corral,

watching us. She smiled at me, and I shook my head and looked down. I walked over to where my saddle was sitting and untied the bandana and wiped off my face and neck with it, then I tied it back around the saddle horn.

"I didn't do good, Luz."

"What do you mean? You're in first place right now."

"Yeah. But I could've put it away. I missed two easy shots."

"You did good enough," she said. "I'm so proud of you. Are you hungry?"

They were starting the barbecue out on the street now.

"Yes." But I wasn't.

We all sat together in the shade by the side of Papa's, away from the gas pumps. I kept that number seven pinned to my chest the whole day. While we ate and talked, me keeping an eye on the riders coming in behind me, George Hess, who owned the store, poured beer after beer from a row of gleaming steel kegs in washtubs of ice lining the street in front of Papa's.

When the last of the riders had come in, my finishing time was only good enough for second place, beaten by fifteen seconds. What made it even worse was that it was Chase Rutledge who had come in first to claim the thousand-dollar prize. I got five hundred for second. I guess there was lots of money bet and lost because that Texan who had won the biathlon for three straight years came in tenth overall.

I was disappointed I had let all those people who bet on me down, but when Tommy showed me the fistful of cash he had won for betting me three ways, I felt a little better.

"It would've been a lot more if you won, though, but you'll get 'em back next year."

"Next year I want you to be riding that big boy, too."

"First and second, Stotts."

"We could do that."

I found my dad, laughing and drinking a beer with Mr. Benavidez. I asked him to hold on to all that cash for me since Tommy, Gabe, and I would be leaving for the fire pit before evening.

"You had an excellent ride, Troy," Mr. Benavidez said, and shook my hand.

"Thank you. I could've done better, though." I cleared my throat and continued, "Me and Tom are going on a campout tonight, so we'll be back in at the ranch Monday morning if that's okay, sir. My dad said it was."

"That's fine, Troy. Have a good time."

I didn't say anything about Gabe because I wasn't really sure if he had told his father or not.

The sun was starting to get low and I knew I'd have to get Reno on his way to the fire pit soon so we could take it real slow getting there. I wanted to find Tommy and Gabe to let them know. I hoped to find Luz, too, so I could tell her good-bye.

George Hess was still pouring beers when I got back to the livery. I apologized to Reno for putting that saddle and halter back on him, but I kept him without a bit, like I always did, and then I led him out into the street. Every time Art Benavidez saw me riding like that he would scowl, sometimes calling me an Indian, but I never saw the sense in putting a metal bar in a horse's mouth. At least, not one like Reno.

"Nice try, number seven," Chase Rutledge called out from the front of the store. He was smoking a cigarette with Jack Crutchfield. Nobody liked Jack except for Chase. He was one of those useless, overfed, and spoiled kids who got everything he wanted and just seemed to make Chase more powerful and more difficult when he stood behind him.

I didn't say anything, just pretended like I didn't hear him at all.

I found Tommy and Gabe over by the truck. The engine was already running, so I knew Tom was anxious to leave.

"We're going to get the horses and we'll meet you out there," Tom said. "If you want, I could switch to the stock trailer for Reno, too."

"That's okay. If you bring it tonight, though, we could all ride out together tomorrow. We'll be walking it slow. I'll see you there," I said. I knew he wanted me to leave with him right now. I looked around, scanning the crowd by the beer kegs. "Where's your sister, Gabe?"

"She went over there to get a soda," he said, pointing to the big lawn outside the community center.

"Uh-oh," Tommy said and then got in behind the wheel.

"I'll see you guys there, then."

They drove off, me wondering what they'd be talking about right now, looking across at Luz sitting in the cool grass there, drinking a canned soda. I walked over to her and let go of Reno's reins. He took a couple big chomps out of the grass, and I hoped nobody was watching.

"Mind if number seven sits down with you for a second?"

She just smiled and patted the grass beside her. I sat real close. Our knees and feet touched.

"We're all camping out at the fire pit tonight," I said. "I know you can't get away, but maybe you could ride out that way in the morning."

"Don't tell me you boys are going to cook breakfast."

"I was actually hoping you'd bring it."

I put my hand on top of hers there in the grass. I couldn't see her parents anywhere.

"Maybe for five hundred dollars."

"It's a date then," I said. I set my sweaty hat down in the grass beside me and plucked at a few blades, letting them fall onto the brim. "Luz, I just wanted to tell you that you've . . . that this past year has been . . ." And then I stopped and inhaled a deep breath and pulled my one knee up to my chest.

"I love you, Luz."

I felt her squeeze my hand. I looked at her and it looked like she was going to cry.

"I love you so much, Troy Stotts. Rider number seven."

And I know we would have kissed then, in spite of everyone being there, but we both heard her father calling out, "Luz! Luz!" from across the street. And I couldn't say anything else.

FIFTEEN

Reno and I walked slowly along the south shore of the lake toward our fire pit, that red bandana tied like a flag around the knob of his saddle horn, the wrinkled number seven pinned with four brass safety pins to my chest; me staring straight ahead and not really seeing anything that was there, just taking it all in, and imagining myself sitting on that cool grass next to Luz Benavidez, feeling the touch of her hand on my body.

The last bit of sun was just going down. Bats zipped and flitted between the trees, clicking, sometimes coming right down in front of my face.

Out on the still and smooth lake, turning black at the edges and lighter than the sky in the middle, little circles popped up where fish broke the surface. The evening smelled like horse and pine and dry summer dust as we moved along; me swinging back and forth with that comfortable and confident gait of

Reno's. A baby hawk screeched from somewhere high in the trees.

Isn't this about the most beautiful place in the world, Troy?

It was.

I rode past the big rocks where we would swim the next morning, cutting in along a narrow trail beside the shore. I took my hat off and brushed my hair back and then put it back on, tilted back a little so I could see the sky, the first stars beginning to shine, and the pale piece of moon climbing up behind the black trees on the other side of the water.

I could see a spiraling wisp of smoke rising from the trees in front of me, a glow casting yellow light between the trunks at the bottom. I could hear Tommy and Gabe laughing. They had already begun the ritual, the telling of stories, the jokes, the laughter, the routine we had followed so regularly for so many years that came and went and came and went.

They didn't notice when I stopped Reno back in the shadows of the trees and sat there, watching them, Tommy sitting on that old saddle in the dirt, facing the fire with his boots up on the ring of rocks that contained it, drinking from a tall red plastic cup. And Gabe, standing on the other side, flailing his arms around in some weird dance like a crippled bird and then falling down, talking loudly about something I couldn't tell, and then them both erupting in laughter.

"What's so funny?" I said and rode Reno into the light.

"It's about time you got here," Tommy said, and then stood up. "Hey, Stottsy, look what I got."

I got down from Reno, led him toward the truck where the

other horses stood, and Tommy turned on the headlights. In the bed there was one of those kegs of beer, sitting in a galvanized tub of melting ice. I unbuckled Reno's saddle and threw it over the side of the truck.

"George Hess just told me to take it and bring it back empty. He was so happy, I think he'd never made so much money off that race before, so he just said for me to take that beer and go."

"Maybe Clayton just didn't shake him down for his cut yet," I said.

I took my hat off and threw it in the window on the passenger side. "And I bet you didn't argue with him about that. Is there any left?"

Tommy grabbed one of the cups sitting down in the ice in that tub. "Let me pour you one, number seven."

I looked down at my chest, that number still pinned straight. "I will, then."

He handed me a cup, foaming over white and frothy. I drank it all right away and Tom took it back from me, saying, "Dang!" before filling it a second time.

"Gabey! Gabey! Come on over. You said you'd have one, too, when Stotts got here!" Tommy said, cheeks reddening. "Come on, Gabey!"

"Well, okay."

Gabe walked around to the gate of the truck and took the cup from Tommy.

"Drink, my son, straight from the altar of the temple of F one-fifty," Tom said, and made a cross in the air with a cup, teasing Gabriel.

Gabe took a gulp, like he had seen me do, but I could tell he nearly gagged on it.

"This stuff is nasty," he said, frowning.

"It grows on you," I said.

We carried our beers, walking through the white of the headlights, and took our places around the fire.

"Stoke! Stoke!" Tom said to me.

I grabbed two thick branches from the pile beside me and crossed them on top of the flames, then added two more across those and the fire kicked up so it was taller than any of us. Tommy sat, leaning back on that old worn saddle, and Gabe and I sat to either side of him, right on the ground, backs propped against rocks that we had placed just perfectly, so our knees would be bent with our feet up on the fire ring. Tommy pulled a can of tobacco from his back pocket, snapped it down three times, then took out a small wad and without saying anything or even looking at me, launched the can like a flying saucer to land right on my lap. I took some, too, and tossed the can back.

Gabe was still frowning from the taste of the beer.

"I wasn't sure you'd make it, Gabey," I said.

"Well, I had to promise my dad I'd be home in the morning for church."

"You could've promised to grow wings and fly there, too," Tommy laughed.

"We were going to go swimming at the rocks," I said.

"It won't be the first time I get in trouble for missing church," Gabe said.

"We'll baptize you in the lake," Tommy said. "It's just as good."

"You know what my dad said, Troy?"

"What?"

"Don't get mad or nothing, but he said the only person he knows who needs to go to church more than me is *Troy Stotts.*"

"I guess I might as well be sitting here drinking beer with Satan himself as much as you two, then," Tommy said, and we laughed. "In fact, I think I'll have another."

"Bring one back for the devil, too." I handed him my empty cup.

"Good man, Stottsy." He dragged his feet and almost tripped going back to the truck.

"Why do you think he'd say that?" I said.

"I know," Tommy called from behind me as he poured those beers. I could hear him walking back toward the fire now. "I know. It's 'cause of Luz. That girl wants you, Stotts. I can see it."

Gabe smiled and looked at me like he was expecting me to say something. Well, I wasn't going to say it, anyway. He took another sip and grimaced.

"I've seen Mr. Benavidez geld a horse," I said, instead, "and he wouldn't think twice about doing that to me, too."

Tommy handed me down my beer and went back to the saddle.

"You know, Stottsy, that was the other bet George Hess was taking money on. Whether you'd still have your balls when you turn seventeen or if they'd be in a jar on display somewhere in Art Benavidez's office."

Gabriel laughed loud, spitting a spray of beer.

"What's the money favoring so far?" I said.

"Doesn't look good for your boys."

Gabe said, smirking, "And he's got someone's in there. In that office. I seen 'em."

"Those would be yours, Gabey," Tommy said and then spit and we all laughed.

I drank my beer down. It tasted real good. Even Gabe finished his and said, "I'm hungry. Let's break out the food."

"You bring stuff to eat, Tom?" I asked.

"I always do."

Gabe stood up and I reached out my hand to him. "Help me up and let's get it."

Gabe pulled and I almost toppled forward right into him.

"You're drunk, Stotts," Tommy observed, still reclining back on that saddle.

"I know. You want another?"

He handed up his cup, and I took Gabe's from him. "You're having another, too, Gabey."

Gabriel and I went to the truck. I poured out three beers and Gabe opened up the leather saddlebags draped over Arrow's saddle. He pulled out a bag of chips, some peanuts, and a package of jerky.

"Looks like Tommy brought health food," I said.

"It's all they eat at the Bullers'."

We went back to our places by the fire and sat and drank and ate for a while, staring into those flames. I was feeling a little rubbery, and I saw Gabe working hard on that second beer of his, but soon he started to get that reddening color in his face, too, and I knew he was getting drunk.

"I want Stotts to tell us a story," Tom said.

"How about Gabey doing it this time?" I asked.

"I'll do it," Gabe said.

"Well, okay then," said Tom.

I put some more branches on top of the fire.

"This happened a long time ago, before you and your dad came here, Tom," Gabe began. "But I think it's a kind of good story about me and Troy. I don't remember exactly how old I was, but I was either just in kindergarten or first grade, probly, and Troy would have been about eight or nine."

Gabe took a sip and leaned back against his rock. "We decided to build a fort in front of our house one day."

"I remember that," I said.

"Good. But I'm still telling the story, so shut up. Our moms were inside doing something and they pretty much forgot all about us since we weren't bugging 'em. I don't know where Luz was then, but it was just me and Troy and we started digging this big hole for our fort right out under the willow tree in our front yard."

I remembered the day, our mothers sitting and drinking coffee together. It was kind of strange hearing Gabriel talk about my mother. It made me feel a bit sad at first, but it also felt good to know that he had a picture of her in his head, too.

Gabe went on. "We used big shovels from out of the barn and plywood and stuff. It seemed like we were out there for hours digging on that thing because it was pretty big."

"Or we were pretty small." And I remember thinking as we sat by our fire and Gabe told his story that I supposed that all boys dug forts and played on roofs.

"Yeah, well, we were both covered with dirt by the time my dad came home and when he saw what we had done to the yard he looked like he could've killed us. First he went in the house and got mad at my mom 'cause she didn't know what we were doing and then he came out to get us and his eyes looked like a demon's."

"How would you know? You were hiding."

"Well, I did hide under the plywood roof, thinking my dad wouldn't find me. You remember what he called us, Troy?"

"Dirty little goats."

"Yep. He said, 'I don't work this hard around here to have some dirty little goats tear up my property.' And I was so scared I practically peed my pants."

"You did, I think."

"Shut up." We both took another drink of beer, and Gabe went on, "But then Troy says to him, 'It was my idea, Mr. Benavidez. I'm sorry, I'll fix it back. Gabe didn't have anything to do with it.' And I still don't know why he said that."

"'Cause I thought he would really kill you, and I knew he wouldn't hurt me 'cause he and my dad were friends."

"So then, he takes us both in the house to our moms, and we're both covered with dirt and making a mess all over, which made my mom mad, but I think my dad wanted us to get dirt all over the place. And then he says to Troy's mom, 'I'd never hit another man's son, but your Troy owes me a bit of work.' And Troy's mom tells him to go ahead and hit Troy if he wants to."

"Yeah, and that's when I almost peed in *my* pants."

"And so then my dad grabs Troy by the shirt and walks him out to the stable and makes him rake out a row of stalls."

"Well, it wasn't just that," I said. "'Cause I'd never been that close to horses before and I was so scared of 'em. And he took me out to the stables where he had some giant horses in there and he hands me a rake and says, 'Clean 'em all up.' And he made me get in the first stall with the biggest horse I ever saw and I was so terrified that it would kill me. He looked so big that I could stand up and walk under his belly without messing up my hair and I was crying I was so scared of him, but I didn't make a sound, and I remember the tears just dripping off my face as I worked. And Gabe's dad just says, 'Don't just stand there, you've got a lot of cleaning up to do so you better get to it. Ignore the horse. He doesn't care about you.'

"So I started raking and crying at the same time. And while I did, Mr. Benavidez sat down on a crate and smoked a cigar and read aloud to me these weird scary stories that were like poems. I still remember them, by Octavio Paz, he said. And I don't know why, but I thought *that* was really scary, too."

"He read those to me all the time," Gabe interrupted. "I remember the creepy one about the guy who took people's eyeballs."

I looked at Gabe, knowing the story, and continued, "Then Luz came out there and she kissed her dad and then she laughed at me, but she said I was doing a real good job and one day maybe her daddy would hire me to work there.

"I raked out seven stalls and then he said I could stop. When I came out of that last stall, he bent down and put his face right to the top of my head and he grabbed me and put his big thumbs right on my face and wiped at my tears and I heard him take a deep breath in and he said, 'There. Now you smell like a horse. Do you like it?' And I was so scared I just said yes. And then he said I should go home and let my dad smell me, too. And then when he was taking me back to the house he said, 'Troy, I saw those two shovels out there by the hole you boys were digging.' And I didn't know what he meant by that for a real long time." I looked at Gabe, his eyes glassy and calm, and I could tell he was remembering that day when we were so small. Then I took a drink. I had almost forgotten about his father wiping my tears with his calloused hands. "Now, you got a story, Tommy?"

"Not without another beer first."

"Well, okay then. But now we're all pretty drunk, I'd say."

"I'd say it, too, if I was smart as you, Stotts."

Tommy half stumbled back to the keg in the bed of the truck.

"Put some more wood on, Gabey, 'cause I gotta pee," I said.

We all found our places back by the fire, me and Tommy drinking our beers and Gabriel half-asleep. I was lying flat on my back, watching the smoke and sparks twist their paths up into the starry black.

"I know you guys probly won't believe this when I tell you, but I'm swearing to you this is the truth," Tommy said. "And I've been waiting for the right time to say it. I saw a ghost. It happened the night after we killed that mountain lion, too, which made it even weirder. 'Cause you remember how we all painted our faces and Stotts called it 'Ghost Medicine.'"

"Like his horse," Gabe stirred.

"But it's 'cause of what he said it would do, too."

Tommy spit and took another drink of beer. Gabe's eyes were wider now, attentive to the possibility of a real good scary story.

"That night after we buried that lion," Tommy went on, "I woke up in the middle of the night 'cause I thought I heard something. Well, it was real dark and real quiet except for the sound of the wind, just rustling stuff outside like scratching. There was a boy standing in the middle of my room, just standing there looking at me. He was lighter than the dark in the room and I could almost see through him. I was sure it was a ghost, and it was real."

"What did he do?" Gabe asked.

"Nothing. He just stood there looking at me. He never moved, his face never changed, never did nothing. I just looked at him for the longest time, too. I got so scared I put a pillow over my head."

"My dad told me one time that your house had ghosts in it," Gabe said to Tom.

"You're making that up," I said.

"I swear he said it, Troy."

"Well, what did he look like, then?" I asked.

"He had light-colored hair. He was small, probly only about ten or eleven years old. I couldn't really make out what he was wearing. But the scary part was hiding my head under the pillow, 'cause I kept making it out scarier and scarier so that I was almost *shivering* I was so afraid. No. I *was* shivering. I think I stayed there for hours, sweating, keeping my face hid, wondering if I could get up enough guts to look at him again, to see if he was still there. And then I told myself, I know I'm not dreaming now, so if I look and he's not there, then maybe it was a bad dream was all. So I looked again." He swallowed and paused. "And he was still there."

Gabe looked around at the edge of darkness surrounding our fire. "That's really weird, Tom."

"What happened then?"

"I covered my head back up again, and then I guess I fell asleep because the next thing I knew it was light out, and of course the boy was gone. But that morning, I thought it might have been brought on by that ghost medicine, so I took the truck and went out to that lion's grave all by myself. And there was nothing changed there, but it was real spooky. I found that little circle of stones from the creek we'd put on top of the grave just where it was under that tree."

"The angel is sleeping in the woods," I said.

Tom threw a little stick at me. "See what I mean about this guy, Gabey?" Tom said, and then, "You're crazy, Stotts. Well anyway, it was real creepy being there alone. I had my gun, but it was real quiet that day and I felt like I was being followed the whole way, or watched, by that boy."

"Did you ever see him again?" Gabe asked.

"No. But after that I wouldn't sleep in my room. Always out on the couch, and CB keeps asking me if I'm sick or something."

"Well, maybe it *was* just a dream," I said.

"That's what I keep telling myself. Still," Tommy said. "But there's always a part of me that really knows I was awake the whole time."

We all became quiet, overcome by the beer, the fire, the events of the day.

I love you so much, Troy Stotts. Rider number seven.

I could hear that over and over, staring up at the sky, smelling the fire, feeling the earth in my hair.

And I lay there, with my hand on my chest, flattening out that number seven and feeling the bumps of those four little pins that held it there; and all of us fell off to sleep like that, right there in the dirt.

+ + +

We all three woke when we heard the church bells from Three Points. Eight o'clock. The sun was already drying up the cool that had been the morning.

"Oh darn! I missed church," Gabe said, sarcastically.

"I need some water," Tom said.

"So bad," I added.

We got up, shakily. I took off my shirt and brushed the dirt out of my hair with it, then threw it on top of my saddle. Tom scooped two cups of what had been ice out of the galvanized tub and handed one to me. We just stood there and drank two full glasses each.

"How you feeling?" Tommy asked.

"Not perfect," I said. "Feels like my head's swollen."

"Rose would make a dinner table out of mine."

It hurt when I smiled.

"What are you guys talking about?" Gabe said.

"Nothing," I said.

Tommy took off his shirt and poured a cup of ice water over his head, and then on mine.

"Let's drive over to the rocks and jump in the lake," he said.

We got into the truck, leaving Gabe standing there back by the smoking fire pit. Tommy turned the key in the ignition. *Click.* The battery was dead.

He slapped the steering wheel, frustrated. "I left the lights on," Tom said. "We're stuck."

"Let's take the horses, then. After we cool off we'll ride back to your place and get Carl to come out and jump us."

"Let's go!" Gabe said.

+   +   +

We didn't think anything of the time that morning; it almost seemed like the sun wasn't moving at all. But when Luz rode out to catch her brother missing church, she laughed at the three of us, fog-headed, swimming in nothing but our boxers, and I realized that the morning had drifted away.

And then Chase just came out of nowhere, laughing as he stole our clothes and waved my shirt over his head like a flag, riding his horse out through the clearing to the dirt road leading east to Holmes. Tom bolted from the lake, stepping lightly with his stiff knee over the twigs and stones toward the horses.

I said, "Take Reno. He can catch 'em!" Tom was the better rider, but my horse was the fastest.

"That just stinks!" Gabriel said and slapped the water. Luz was still laughing at us. She turned and rode off after Tom and Chase.

I jumped off the rock, exhaled, and sank down, disappearing into the murk nearer the bottom of the lake.

And that was how Gabriel and I ended up that hot afternoon, wet and dusty, out on the trail without our clothes, chasing down Tom Buller and my horse.

SIXTEEN

Gabey, can I have your hat? I'm burning up."

"Sure. It's dirty."

"I know."

And when Gabriel asked about it, as we swatted away the flies and, practically naked, took those horses so slowly along the trail, I told him what happened to me up on that mountain, and how his sister had found me there. And how it felt. Like she brought me back to life.

"Did you make love to her?"

I think Gabriel was just curious, that maybe he wanted to know something hidden about his sister, about me. And at first, I found myself automatically forming the truth, no, with my mouth. Then I thought to lie for some reason and tell him yes. Then I kind of got mad at Gabriel.

"How could you even say something like that about your sister?" I sighed. "That's between me and her, anyway."

"Well, *I'd* tell *you*."

"I don't think I'll live that long, Gabey."

"You know, that's a shame, too. And I was just about to offer my best friend Troy Stotts that he could ride my horse and me take on that old cripple Arrow."

I smiled, knowing that Gabriel was just teasing.

"Am I the only person you told about your going away like that?" Gabe asked.

"Yep."

Gabriel pulled back on Dusty, who turned in the path, stopping both horses and riders. He swung his leg over the top of the saddle and got down onto the trail, wiping away the sweat on the insides of his bare legs with his palms.

"Here, Troy. I'll switch you."

Gabriel held the reins on Arrow as I got down. "Are you sure?"

"No, but you can ride him anyway." And then Gabe was up on Arrow, whose protesting backpedaling signaled that he had already eased into the thought of going riderless. "And besides, Dusty's about the only horse around that I haven't seen you fall off yet so I'm thinking today's going to be his big chance."

I was thankful for the cooling shade of the big trees here, and for the more comfortable gait and disposition of the buckskin. I could see the spot where the trees cleared away, far ahead, the bright sunlight reflecting from the yellow and dry grasses, where the old Butterfield stage marker stood, and the small trail linked onto the dirt road heading east.

"You know she's in love with you, Troy." He said it kind of like it was a question.

"Man, can you stop talking about your sister and me?"

I was embarrassed that Gabe was so straight with me, and

at the same time I guess I felt a kind of pride that he knew, and felt, too, that someday we would be bound together by something more than just our friendship.

"Well, it's true, in case you didn't know. Or in case you were wondering." Gabe rubbed his nose with the back of his hand. "Anyway, it's okay with me."

"Oh. That's a relief," I said, and I tried to change the subject, but I knew he would bring it back again. "You remember what you told us about your dad giving me the horse? How do you know about that?"

I held Dusty back and Gabe prodded Arrow up next to us.

"He didn't tell me it or nothing, but my dad's like a horse witch or something, like my grandfather was. But you know, Troy, because sometimes there are certain horses that can talk to you, and some people can talk to just about any horse. Like my dad can. And you. That's why I said that about him giving you Reno. I just made it up 'cause I was just trying to tease you about Luz."

"Oh." I looked out down the trail.

"You don't need to tell me. I mean, if you love her. Because I already know. That's what brought you back here when you left; otherwise Reno would've made you go away."

you disappear

Gabriel stretched his arms out and yawned. Arrow lowered his head into the grass to the side of the trail. "One day, will you take me up there?"

"To that cabin?"

I looked at Gabriel.

"Sometimes I feel like I need to go back there, almost like it's calling me to prove that it wasn't just a weird dream or something. But if you just want to go up there and fish, we could go anytime. And Gabe, you won't say anything, will you?"

"About where you went?"

"No. About her."

Gabe held out a fist and I punched his knuckles.

"Gabe?"

"What?"

"Why do you act like you're scared of her?"

Gabriel smiled. "She can beat me up, Troy."

"I think you let her."

"Okay," he said. "But she never lets up on me, either. I think it's 'cause I'm the boy, and that's what our dad always wanted. So she always had to prove she was tougher and smarter. Then I guess he ended up realizing that she really was."

"She's just trying to fool you, Gabe," I said. " 'Cause she knows how good you really are. And she thinks that one day your dad's gonna see you're good enough to run that ranch. She told me."

"She did?"

"I swear it."

Gabriel yawned again, pretending not to think about what I just said. "Was it tough coming home?" By the time he said it, Arrow was already back to stumbling his front right foot on the ground, feigning a trip every few steps, which would inevitably lead to a more stubborn protest to come.

"Not at all."

"He's not going to move, Troy." Gabriel exhaled in frustration above the stubborn Arrow's lowered, pretending-to-eat head. "I think we're going to have to walk 'em again for a while."

"We've been gone for an hour now and we haven't even gotten to the dirt road yet. Tom's likely already home and dressed by now."

"You should've never offered up Reno for him. That Tom Buller owes you more than he'll ever be able to pay back."

"What do you mean by that?" I asked. Arrow flinched at Gabe's prodding.

"Well," Gabriel said, "you saved his life when he got bit. And you'd do anything for him, and stick up for him and his dad. You're such a good friend to him."

"And he would do anything for me," I said, then let out a sigh watching Arrow win the silent argument with Gabriel. "I never understood how someone who can ride like Tommy would settle for a horse like that Arrow. If you want yours back, I'll take him."

"It's okay. Walking's walking anyway. And I guess old Arrow thinks its kind of funny about us being stuck out here in our underwear, too." Gabriel paused. "Remind me next summer if we all spend the night out after '49ers Day that we need to bring some extra clothes."

"Yeah. And you remind me not to let Tom Buller talk us into drinking beer, too."

"I could do that."

We walked along slowly, Gabriel taking an occasional swig from his canteen. The stage marker was just ahead, and alongside it, the wider, level dirt road leading east into Three Points and Holmes beyond. On the right of the trail, a circle of light cut through an opening created in the space between a sapling and a taller, drooping pine tree. In that circle, the stone marker rose, reflecting the sunlight of the open roadway.

"Hey Troy, look at this." And Gabriel bent down and grabbed an apricot-sized stone off the ground. "Gabriel Benavidez paints the outside corner of the plate with a vicious side-arm curve."

Gabriel fired his arm from below his waist, sending the rock up and then down, then cutting sharply in to the left to sail cleanly through the opening and *whack!* into the left edge of the marker, splintering shards of flagstone off into the sunlight.

"Bet you can't get one in there."

"I might as well just pay you up front as soon as take that bet." But I picked up a rock anyway. "Why don't you play ball in the league in Holmes?"

"I don't like it enough, I guess." Then he yawned. "Why don't *you* go to church?"

"I guess there are a few people around who'd ask the same thing about you."

"I go enough."

"For what?"

And I hurled my rock, but couldn't get it past the little sapling. "Okay. I guess that's five more dollars. Between you and Tom, you guys are going to take all my pay."

"Yeah. Well, you could dot the 'i' in Butterfield with that bolt action of yours."

And I admired my friend for his willingness to overlook my shortcomings.

✦   ✦   ✦

We had miles to go, the two of us walking alongside those two tall horses. We were out of the woods and back in the sunlight that spilled onto the tree-lined road. A dark stripe of sweat soaked through the band of Gabe's hat. I took it from my head and wiped my hair back, thinking of Luz, remembering how she combed my hair with her fingers when I fell from my horse, and how much I wished she was there with me right at that moment. I waved the hat in front of me.

"Sorry, Gabe."

"For what?"

"Your hat," I said apologetically, showing him the sweat stain.

"It's character."

"Want it back?"

"Uh, I don't think so, Troy. You know the sun doesn't bother me too much. You're pretty red, though."

Gabe was always brown-skinned, even in winter. In summer, he just got darker while his hair got lighter. He never seemed to sweat too much, either.

"I shouldn't've left my hat in that truck."

"Yeah, and if we didn't leave the lights on, we'd be trailering this lazy horse out of here."

"Let's get up on 'em again."

"Why don't we just tie Arrow here and both ride Dusty?"

"Gabe," I said, and I know I was smiling, "just think of how ridiculous *that* would look if anyone saw us."

Gabriel laughed out loud. "I must be delirious."

We heard the boom of thunder atop the mountains across the lake. Gabe looked up at the sky, over his shoulder, that little gold chain glinting for a moment as though it could have been the lightning bolt that made the sound.

"It poured on me one night when I was up in that cabin. I never seen it rain so hard in summer."

"Were you scared?"

"Lots of times. But not 'cause of the rain."

Gabe looked back up toward those two granite fingers, the thick gray clouds swelling and inflating above them, crucifix dangling backward between his shoulder blades like some kind of protective charm against the sound of thunder.

"I had a lot of weird dreams up there, I think, because I got so tired and stayed up so many days in a row. I got scared at nights, being awake. Thinking that something was out there, following me. But I got most scared during the day sometimes because it was so quiet and a lot of times I thought I'd see things that weren't there."

"Like what?"

"You know. You just think you see a person, or an animal or something moving through the trees out of the corner of your eye. But it turns out to be nothing."

"I couldn't've stayed up there that long by myself. That's really scary."

"But I kept telling myself, it's not anything real that's scaring me. The real stuff I could handle, no problem. It was just working myself up about thinking things. Or dreaming them."

We had talked about dreams plenty of times around the fire. I remembered how it was Tom Buller who'd said that he never had dreams; that he just slept and then woke up. And I envied him for that, too, and knew that it must have been the snake medicine in him; that beginning every day like he was breaking out of some dead cast-off shell of himself, forgetting about it, born again; alive and not afraid.

I wished I could be like that.

How about a scary story, boys?

The fire was dying down to writhing orange worms.

What's the scariest dream you've ever had?

No one was ready to answer that. I was getting sleepy, staring at the coals.

I had this dream. I was in the woods, alone. I saw Gabe, sleeping under a tree, glowing white, curled up like a baby. I walk up to him, quietly, and he turns onto his back and sits up. His eyes are all white like the eyes on a marble statue. He looks at me, and he's asking me why did I kill him. And I said, because I wanted to be the only son. But I'm also thinking — you know, with the not-dreaming part of my brain — that it's like the story from this book I read about this guy whose kids get murdered by another child of his from a different woman. And then I'm looking up the trunk of this huge tree — a redwood, and it turns into these pointy, tall doors on a cathedral.

Man, Stotts, you're weird.

The doors fall open, and then they slam shut, and they're the lid of my mother's coffin, and then the belly of a big white plane, upside down. I'm sitting on Reno, looking up. I know Gabey's gone, even though I'm not looking down at where he was. Reno starts to back away and he steps into a squirrel hole. Remember when he did that, and we thought he'd break his leg? Then the hole gives way and we both fall underground. It's like a dark dirty cave and I can see the roots of the tree like they're dripping down from the ceiling. Then I got too scared and it woke me up.

About the scariest dreams I have are going to church or school in my underwear.

You guys are both messed up.

Okay, then what about you, Tommy?

I don't have dreams.

Running out of chewing tobacco.

And he sleeps standing up.

✦ ✦ ✦

There was another clap of thunder.

"You know when we went out after that big cat?"

"I won't forget that."

"Well, I'm sorry about what I did, Troy. But I wasn't scared. I don't think I was."

"You still holding on to that?" I asked. "I don't mind saying it scared the hell out of me."

Dusty nudged my shoulder with a sticky nose.

"And Gabe?"

"Yeah?"

"I felt horrible about that. I still do. About what I said to you."

"It's okay, Troy."

"Can't get mad at Gabe Benavidez for being Gabe Benavidez."

"Sure you can. My dad does all the time. I know he'd like me more if I was like you. Or Tom."

"I don't think so, Gabe. Your dad loves you, he's just a tough guy who wants you to be tough, too," I said. But I knew that Gabriel would never be the kind of man his father pictured running the ranch, and felt sorry, too, that Mr. Benavidez couldn't see what I did in his son.

I cleared my throat. "When we get up a little closer by Three Points, let's try to ride the horses around through the woods south so we don't have to go past anyone. Then we can cut up to the Foreman's house and borrow some clothes from Tommy."

"I bet he only owns one pair of pants. And they're gonna be dirty," Gabe said.

"Then they're mine. Sorry," I said, and Gabriel smiled.

I tilted his hat back on my head. The sun was dropping behind us now, our shadows stretching in front of us. The thunder over the mountains had died out, and clouds dotted across the sky, high up, like splatters off an oversoaked paintbrush.

"Troy," he said, "I've been thinking about something that's kind of funny. You know how you're always walking like that with your head up, looking straight ahead. Well, I've been noticing something and I think we should consider it."

"What?"

"Well, it just struck me that we didn't ride here yesterday 'cause me and Tom trailered Arrow and Dusty to the fire pit. But I'm seeing these three sets of hoofprints heading west, going the other way. See 'em?"

I looked down. I should have noticed them, but it was one of those things that's just invisible until someone rubs your face in it.

"And I think these ones here are Doats 'cause he's got that prancy foot up front. See?"

We stopped moving and looked at the dust covering the old dirt road. I turned back to face west. I had just assumed, believed, that Chase would have gone back east — toward Three Points — and I felt so stupid now that I realized they'd come out on the road ahead of where we were, but had gone the other way, toward the bluffs at the shallow end of the lake.

"Chase went this way and Luz and Tommy must have followed him."

Gabe looked at me like he had already figured that out.

"So. We should just keep going anyway," Gabe said. "It won't take too much longer to get around to Tommy's and get some clothes. Then we can get after them if Tom and Luz aren't back by then."

"I can't stand that guy."

I looked back down the road from where we had come, trying to imagine where the three of them could have gone; towards that west end of the lake where the rocky bluffs rose up. I exhaled a disappointed sigh. "Let's follow 'em."

"Aw hell!"

But that was all he said before we turned around and headed west.

SEVENTEEN

Maybe they're going back to the truck," Gabe said.

"Well, they're going this way. That's for sure," I said. "How's that Arrow doing?"

"He's doing good," Gabe said. "I hate to say it, but I guess I weigh less than you."

"He just doesn't like me," I said. "Dusty's a good horse." And I patted his neck and scratched his black-tipped ears. "You should run him harder and jump him."

"I have a hard time letting him go like that with me on him," Gabe said.

"Tom could show you. You know what he said to me? He said, 'Just stay on the saddle. The saddle will stay on your horse.'"

"That sounds like what he told you when we took that kayak over the falls."

"But, oh Gabey, we both got really messed up that first day

we tried to catch those wild horses out there. That was one of the funnest days ever."

"Then how'd you catch 'em?"

"We just kept trying and we got better at it. We caught my black mare first. But then it took us four more tries to get that big red stallion of Tom's and he almost killed us once, too."

"And you already got 'em gentled?"

"Mine's on a halter and I can lead her. I sacked her out good, too. But she's gonna foal any time now."

"Why do you help her out — that woman?"

"I like her. A lot. And I'm afraid those horses are going to starve, especially now we put them back on her land after that fire. One day, I'm going to get 'em all."

"And then what'll you do?"

At this part of the south lakeshore, the woods got denser and taller, which is why we liked to camp here. The turnoff to the fire pit was just ahead now and I could almost smell the embers of that big campfire we had the night before. I pulled Dusty right up alongside the other horse and told Gabe to stop. I reached down into Tom's bag.

"I ate 'em all," Gabe said.

"I'm getting some tobacco," I said.

"Sick."

"Want some?"

Gabe didn't say anything. We had come to the turnoff to our fire pit, two ruts cut in the underbrush by the regular coming and going of the truck and trailer, of us and our horses. We could see the track of the other horses still going on west down that dirt road, but without saying anything about it, we both moved on to that turnoff and rode to our campsite.

The truck was still there, parked right where the trees gave way to the sloping rocky ground that spread to the shoreline. I got down from Dusty.

"I'm trying it again."

Gabe stayed on Arrow. I knew it was useless to try starting the truck, but it's just one of those things you do, hoping somehow that things just heal themselves when you know they can't. So it wasn't so much of a surprise when I turned the key and heard nothing but that dull and distant click. I opened the glove compartment, remembering that missing five thousand dollars that nearly cost the Bullers their jobs and home, that had now become one of those things that we just didn't mention and couldn't explain. But I knew what happened.

You don't have to tell me that Benavidez doesn't really care about the money and stuff, 'cause I figured it would be like that.

There were some cigarettes in there and another can of Tommy's tobacco; so I knew Tom didn't come back this way.

But there was my flat-brimmed black Stetson on the passenger seat, just where I'd left it. I took off Gabe's hat and pushed my sweaty hair back straight over the top of my head. I thought of Luz, could see her if I closed my eyes. I put my old hat on and it felt cool, like dipping my head in water.

I went back over to the horses and gave Gabe that dirty hat of his, which he put on. "I didn't know you wanted your hat back. I'm sorry, Gabey, you want your horse back now?"

"Naw, I didn't want my hat, either. It's just easier to wear it than to do anything else with it. It's okay about Dusty. You can ride him. Let's get going. I bet we can catch 'em now and get home."

So we rode back out to the road and turned west again. The horses were moving comfortably now, maybe smelling the closeness of other horses. *Maybe*, I thought.

"Hey Troy!" Gabe said, pointing down in front of us. "Look at that. It's footprints. Bare feet. Tommy got off Reno."

Of course Tommy had left his hat and boots under the trees back by where we had been swimming — he took off so fast after Chase.

"Well, I guess so," I said, "'cause he's standing right up there."

And up the road a little ways, walking barefoot away from us, a little crooked and stiff on that bad knee of his, wearing only his boxers, was Tom Buller.

"My heroes!" Tommy said when we rode up to him. "Salvation is here. Even if I never asked for it."

"What happened to you?" Gabe said.

"What happened to my horse?" I asked, then tossed him down a can of tobacco.

"Well, you know," Tom began after dipping a wad of black tobacco into his lip, grinning that coyote squint-eyed grin of his, so I knew he wouldn't spare us the dramatics. "I gotta tell you boys that riding a horse as big and fast as Reno wearing only your boxers is not the most comfortable experience, if you know what I mean. Anyways, after that punk Rutledge cut back this way, I had to stop for a minute. 'Cause I figured that this way was a dead end anyways, unless he knows some way around those bluffs that I never saw. So I got down and took a pee, and then along comes Luz and Doats just as fast as I ever seen her ride, so I kind of turned away in the bushes and then Reno takes off after 'em like he thinks it's a race or something.

Next thing you know, I'm walking. Just following the prints. That was about a half an hour ago, I guess."

"What's she thinking?" Gabe asked.

"I don't know, but she shouldn't be riding after Chase," I said.

"So which one of you two is going to walk?" Tom said.

I got down from Dusty, bent onto one knee, and laced each shoe up tightly.

"I'll run. You two ride. I bet those horses'll have a hard time keeping up with me anyhow." And I took my hat off again and gave it to Tom, who put it on and then looked questioningly at Gabe, who didn't react at all, so Tom went ahead and got up onto Dusty.

I started running.

I noticed a long time ago that when I run, with each step it seemed like I got smaller and smaller. Not physically, I mean, but after a minute or two it was like the *me* part of me didn't exist anymore and as the sweat would break and the breathing would pulse in rhythm with the crunch of the footfalls, it always becomes breath and sweat and feet hitting the ground and side-blurred vision of the world flowing evenly past like a stream of warm water.

I imagine that's what it's like to be a horse; you run, you breathe, sweat, your feet dig in and you stare straight ahead and watch all those things flow and flow. And you keep running because it just feels good.

✦   ✦   ✦

I was ahead of the horses, but they were moving along now, even Arrow. I hadn't been through this part of the shoreline in years, and I was surprised to see that the fire had burned so far north, this close to the lake.

"Dang, it's all burned up," I heard Gabe say.

Here, the trees alongside the dirt road were black and dry; they still gave off the reek of a wildfire. Most of them were burned to a shiny, thick black all the way up their trunks, then branching out with withered, curled arms holding black porcupine quill needles. Some weren't completely burned, and had a green branch or green treetop high above where the height of the flames had come through. Everything that could be blackened was, even rocks. Just the dirt of the road seemed to retain its regular color, peppered with ash, and so added to the surreal appearance of what had once been forest.

I stopped. The sweat running down my back felt like racing spiders. I waited for Gabe and Tom to catch up.

"Any more water in that canteen?" I asked Gabe.

"Here." He handed it down to me.

I drank and brushed my hair back over my head. Then I passed the canteen up to Tommy.

"We must be getting close," Tommy said.

"Luz! Luz!" Gabe screamed. But there was no answer, just the sound of the wind blowing through the dead trees.

Tom handed the canteen back to me and I took one more gulp. I wiped my mouth with the back of my forearm and gave the canteen to Gabe. The water was good. I was ready to run again.

Once we had gotten past the charred strip of land where the fire had burned almost to the lake, I felt better. The trees were green here and somehow made the afternoon air cooler. Gabe and Tommy were well behind me; Arrow had gone back to walking. The horses had moved a lot in the past two days and I felt sorry for them, even though that stubborn-headed Arrow was more used to working than Gabe's buckskin.

I stopped in the middle of the road, sweating hard. My hair was plastered down to my neck and the side of my head. The waistband of my boxers was soaked dark with sweat, white salt at the edges where the heat had evaporated it.

Then I saw Reno up ahead, standing in the road and looking back at me.

His ears shot up when I whistled at him, and he gave that chuckle of his and started trotting to me. I could swear he was smiling, looking at me with those soft and forgiving eyes, still wearing the red bandana Tommy had given me yesterday morning tied around his saddle horn.

My horse got right up to me and pressed his nose into my chest, smelling me, and then even trying to lick the salty sweat from my skin, which tickled and made me laugh.

"I know I can't be smelling too good right now, bud." And I patted his shoulder and hugged him around his neck, feeling his slick warm hide against my body. "And you're not smelling so good, either, pal."

Gabriel and Tom had caught up to me.

"Thanks for ditching me," Tommy said to my horse.

"They gotta be somewhere right around here," Gabe said.

"We'll get that guy now," I said, and then called out, "Luz! Luz!"

+ + +

We all grew up the day that Tom Buller, Gabriel Benavidez, and I left our clothes on the shore and went swimming off

227

those tall rocks in the lake. Me, Tommy, Gabe, and Luz. But we didn't ask for it, even though it's a common thing to want to be grown-up when you're a kid. And maybe I knew better than my friends that it wasn't something that would happen in your sleep, like a dream, but it was event after event, piling up, bricking a wall between me now and that boy I had been, sitting on my mother's lap, looking out that churchlike window, past the dog-eared fence. And each brick, once laid in place, would never be moved: the good-byes, death, secrets, falling in love, loving your friends more than yourself.

It seemed like a year since I took off on that race the morning before; and now here we all were, riding along that dirt road heading west, wearing nothing but our boxers, the bluffs rising up ahead of us so I knew the road would cut south soon, along past Rose's property and ultimately to the paved highway and off Benavidez land entirely.

"You want your horse back?" Tommy asked Gabe.

"You ride him till we catch up to our clothes, then I'll take him home 'cause I don't know if Arrow's got it in him anyway," Gabriel said. "But I kind of like this big mean horse of yours."

"You two planning on just leaving me out here then?" Tom asked.

"I'd walk him in," I said. "You could take Reno and go get Carl. And if I do, you better bring me something to eat."

"How 'bout some beer?" Tommy asked.

"No thanks."

Gabe said, "How 'bout some turkey?"

I just gave him a mean look and pulled my hat down low across my eyebrows.

"Look at that," I said to Tommy, pointing down at the dirt of the road. A thick, curving snake track cut across the road from our left to right, disappearing into some mustard weed.

"That's a big one," Tommsy said. "He's probably just laying in that shade right there watching us."

"I don't think they can see too good."

"They don't need to see if you just set on 'em," Gabe said.

✦   ✦   ✦

We were at the place we called the end of the road. Not that the road ended, although years ago it had; but here it took a sharp turn left, to the south, and would ultimately connect to that easement road to Rose's place and then, farther on, to the main highway.

"You can see the tire tracks where CB and Ramiro hauled that hay out for the horses yesterday," Tommy said.

"I noticed that."

"Hey!" Gabe said. "There's her horse!"

About two hundred yards ahead, where the trees opened up on a big flat meadow, I saw both horses, Doats and that leopard Appaloosa of Chase's, riderless, grazing in the grass off the side of the road. Our clothes were slung over the front of Chase's saddle, and some had fallen into the dirt. I nudged Reno into a run.

EIGHTEEN

*L*uz!"

And then I heard her scream, but the scream was cut off and I could tell she was in trouble.

"Haw, Reno!"

I saw my pants on the back of Chase Rutledge's horse as I rode past, my shirt with the number seven still pinned to it lying in the dirt. I saw Chase Rutledge in that meadow, where he had chased Luz Benavidez.

And I saw Luz, facedown in the grass with her knees curled up under her. Chase had her hair twisted in his left hand and was pinning it to the ground as she tried to claw at his arm with both hands.

He was trying to rape her. It makes me sick to say it even now.

His pants were pulled open, down around his knees, and he was on top of her, biting at the back of her neck, reaching around to the front of her waist with his right hand, trying to unbuckle her jeans, tugging at her shirt.

I leapt down from Reno and smashed my right foot up into the side of Chase's sweating red face, sending him rolling over, still pulling Luz's hair with him. Luz broke free, gasping and crying, and moved behind me.

Chase shook his head and squinted up at me. He looked ridiculous sitting there in the meadow grass, naked down to his knees. A deep cut had opened up under his left eye and thick blood ran down his face.

"What the hell do you think you're doing?" I said, my fist held back slightly, ready to hit him again.

Chase struggled to get his footing, hastily trying to pull up his pants as he did, but I took a swing at him before he could straighten himself. He ducked under my right fist and came back with an uppercut just below my sternum, doubling me forward onto my knees.

He was going to hit me again, too, but just then I heard a gunshot and Chase fell down right in front of me.

I couldn't breathe. I was still reeling from his counterpunch. I looked back toward the road. Luz was standing there with her back to me, shaking, next to Tommy. Gabey stood in front of them, holding the .40 caliber that had been inside Arrow's saddlebag.

Gabe just stood there, pointing the gun straight down at the ground beside his foot. Tommy, barefoot, half limped, half skipped through the grass to me. Luz followed him. She knelt and put her arm around me, resting her face on my bare shoulder. I could feel her tears, warm and slick on my skin.

"Are you hurt bad?" Tommy asked me. He turned away and I heard him start laughing wildly. "Gabey!" he said. "You shot him right in his big white butt!"

Then I realized I heard Chase moaning in the grass in front of me.

"Clean across the ass cheek!" Tommy said, still laughing, "You gotta see this! Man, I don't know if you're the worst shot or the best shot ever."

Chase whimpered.

Tom spit on him. "Shut up, punk! He hardly even nicked you."

I still couldn't breathe. Gabriel stepped up beside Tommy, looking down.

"Well, I tried to get him on the other cheek," he said.

"You shot me! I'm gonna kill you," Chase cried at Gabe. "I'm gonna kill you!"

Tom just spit on him again. "You're not going to do nothing. Except have to face your daddy with a bullet hole in your ass for what you tried to do to this boy's sister."

I felt Luz's hair, her face on my shoulder. She was still shaking a little. I put my lips to her ear, smelling her hair, whispering, "It's okay now. I love you, Luz. It's okay."

She kissed the side of my neck and held me tighter. And I thought how strange things were, me standing there in my boxers, holding her close, her body against my skin. I combed her hair with my hand.

"Oh my God, Troy, if you hadn't found me, he would have . . ."

"It was Gabe who saw the tracks and turned us around. Otherwise . . ." But I didn't want to think about the otherwise. "But you're okay. Did he hurt you?"

"No. Just knocked me around a little. He got mad 'cause I

laughed at him when he fell off his horse and I got down to pick up your shirt and then he was after me."

I kissed her again. I didn't care if Tommy and Gabe were watching or not. Then I walked over to Gabe and held out my hand.

"Give me that gun," I said.

"You don't want to do that," Tom said.

"Give it!"

Gabe handed the gun to me, its hammer cocked back, ready to shoot.

I stood over Chase, who was facedown in the grass, that dirty baseball cap flipped over above his head, the cut left side where I had kicked him turned up, his pants still half-down, bleeding all over himself. The wound was nothing more than a big ugly gash across the left side of Chase's butt, about three inches long, and tearing through the skin.

"Pull your pants up and roll over," I said.

He tried to pull his pants over that graze wound and I could tell he was in agony. I grabbed the top of his pants tight in my left hand and jerked them up to his waist, smearing blood onto my hand and up his pale back as I did. A bloom of blood began oozing through the seat of his jeans.

"Turn over," I said.

Chase turned over and attempted to zip and button his pants. I stepped my right foot down on his chest and he moaned, then I bent forward and pressed the muzzle of Tommy's gun right up into his nose. He started breathing hard. Snot bubbled from the other nostril.

"Troy, don't!" Gabe said.

"Ease up, Stottsy."

"I wonder what you and your dad will say about this?" I said. I put the gun right over his head and fired a round into the ground. A casing ejected onto Chase's belly.

Chase whimpered.

"You don't deserve to be shot in the head," I said, and then I pressed the gun with force right up between his legs. I know that hurt him. He gulped hard, and stopped breathing.

"Cool it, Stotts!" There was an edge in Tommy's voice.

"Tell them you took that money out of Carl's truck."

Chase didn't say anything. I moved the gun and shot down into the dirt right between his legs. The smell of urine rose up from him and a big circle of wetness expanded from his groin. Then I jammed the barrel back up into his balls.

"I took that money," Chase half whispered.

I pushed the gun up hard again, then I jerked it back and shot twice more into the ground at his crotch. Chase screamed. The slide on the gun locked back. There were no more bullets. Chase began crying.

Tommy breathed heavily, relieved, and I handed him the gun.

"I'm glad you thought I might really do it," I said, turning my back on Chase.

"I would've if she was my girl."

"Good thing it ran out, Tom. 'Cause I don't know what I was thinking. Let's go get our clothes."

We went and picked up our clothes in the road, leaving the whimpering Chase lying in the meadow. I shook off the shirt with the number seven on it and pulled it on. It felt hot and itchy.

I took my pants from Chase's saddle and pulled them on. Luz stood away, not saying anything, not watching us.

I brushed off my feet and slipped them back into my shoes. "Sorry about your boots, Tom."

Tommy was still barefoot.

"At least I got my pants back."

He opened up his can of tobacco, knowing well enough not to offer any to me in front of Luz, and put it with his gun back in Arrow's bag.

Tom said, "I guess we should go back and see if he's dead yet."

"You stay here," I said to Luz.

Chase Rutledge was on his knees when we got back to him, cupping a hand tightly over his left back pocket, damp with blood. His left eye was closed from the knot underneath where I had kicked him.

"You don't look so good, Chase," Tommy said.

He turned his head, exaggeratedly, so he could see the three of us with his right eye. "I'm coming for you first, Benavidez. You'll be seeing me."

Tommy spit a brown blob at Chase, and Chase twisted to get out of its way. "I guess if you can't get his sister, you'll settle for scrawny little Gabe."

"You just remember if you ever come after any one of us that you're damn lucky to be alive right now," I said.

"Let's take his pants and make him ride home without 'em," Gabe said.

"I can't ride! I can't even walk!" Chase cried.

"Leave 'em his pants," Tommy said. "I wouldn't want to touch 'em, all soaked with piss and blood."

"You're on your own, Chase. You'll make it back. And if you don't, I'll just tell your daddy to look for the buzzards," I said. "And when you do get back, I guess you're gonna have to come up with a story about how you got shot in the ass but there's no bullet holes in your pants or underwear. That should be a good one. So have a real comfortable ride home. I'd recommend going sidesaddle."

"You can't just leave me here!" Chase cried out as we walked through the meadow.

"Besides not stealing your horse and leaving your pants on, that's probably about the nicest thing we'll ever do for you, Rutledge," Tommy said.

I heard him back there, crying like a little kid when we got the horses together and mounted up. And then I said, "I'm gonna stay back with Tommy if Arrow gives out on him. Even if it takes us all night to get back home."

"Well, I'm not leaving, either," Gabe said. "Hell, you know I'm just going to end up getting in trouble anyway."

Luz didn't have to say anything. I knew she'd stay with me.

We walked the horses slowly east down that dirt road, our shadows stretching longer in front of us. I was sure that Chase wouldn't be in any kind of hurry to catch up to us, and found myself feeling kind of ashamed because things could have turned out much worse for him, and then where would we be? But then I was also angry still because if we hadn't turned back this way, I'd hate to imagine what Chase would have done to Luz.

And then I wondered, too, where Gabriel was aiming.

"Gabey, what would you've done if you'd've killed him?"

"Stole his horse for Tommy to ride," he said. "I was trying to miss, I just wanted to scare him so he wouldn't hit you again."

"Thanks."

"Were you really trying to miss?" Tommy asked.

"No."

* * *

It was an awkward ride back. I could tell we all wanted to say something, but none of us let the words come. And with each step, I found myself wanting more and more to go back and kill Chase Rutledge.

Every once in a while, I stole a look over at Luz, but she didn't say anything; never acknowledged the looks each of us timidly gave her.

* * *

We were almost back to the fire pit when Tommy said, "Well, if no one else is going to say it, I guess I will. What're we going to do about this when we get back?"

"It's trouble. He's probably going to arrest us," I said.

"Then he'll have to arrest Chase, too," Luz said.

It took us a while to register that she had finally talked.

"I've already been through that with Clayton," I said. "You watch, nothing'll happen to Chase again, but me and Gabe and Tommy are gonna get taken in."

"We should call the county sheriff," Gabe said.

"Like your dad did when Clayton broke my nose? Maybe we should just shut up and see what Chase does," I said.

"It's not going to be good, either way," Tom said. "You know it's not going to be good. But whatever happens, we're in this together."

✦　✦　✦

We stopped off to get Tommy's boots. It was dark by the time we made it back to the Foreman's house.

"Can I just stay here tonight?" I asked Tom. "I'll call my dad."

"Sure, Stotts. We'll go out for the truck with CB in the morning."

"I'm scared to go home," Gabe said.

"You can stay here, too," Tom said.

"He's gonna need to come home or it will just make him madder," Luz said.

Gabe sighed. He was real scared, but not about his father. I could tell.

"I'll put Reno and Arrow up, Tom."

I walked the horses back around to the stalls. They were happy to be back, to smell the alfalfa in the feeders, to be free of those saddles. Luz came with me. I put my hat on top of Reno's saddle on the hitching post and brushed the hay off my arms when the horses were in. She didn't say anything, just leaned against the hitch and watched me work there in the dark. I still had that number seven on my chest. I could hear Tommy and Gabe talking to Carl inside the house. I wondered what they were saying.

"I'm glad this '49ers weekend is over," I said. "It seemed like forever."

"I was scared, Troy."

"So was I. We just have to make sure things work out right. That means we'll have to tell what happened, 'cause no one should get in trouble over this except for him. I'll tell 'em I shot him."

"You can't lie, Troy."

"I didn't think I could shoot someone, either, but if that gun didn't run out I would've. I know it."

Luz turned to me and we embraced. I put my hand in her hair and she grabbed my head. We fell onto the grass below the hitching post and I lay on top of her, holding her. She said, "I wish we could run away."

"We can. If we were alone now, I'd . . ."

I heard the screen door open and I got up, then pulled Luz up by both hands. I put my hat back on. We looked at each other and I smiled at her with my straight mouth. I held her hand as we walked around to the front of the Foreman's house.

Luz and Gabriel went home, and Tommy and I were inside his house. I had called my father and told him I'd be staying and that we had a lot of work to do in the morning with getting the truck and baling the field. Carl looked grim, said there was something he needed to talk to us about, so we all sat down out there in the great room where I'd be sleeping, while Carl drank a beer, which made my stomach sour a bit.

"Me and Ramiro dropped some bales out for those horses yesterday," he began. "We brung out some box community feeders, too, to keep it in better shape and spread them out so those horses should all be fine for a while now. And we found that woman, too, boys." He took a long drink. "She was dead in her car out on the side of that easement road, just sitting there like she was asleep, but she'd been dead for a while."

I felt like I'd been punched in the stomach again. I looked

over at Tom and I could tell he was shocked, too; and neither of us said anything, we just stared at Carl.

"I guess it was her heart or something," Carl said. "The fire wasn't close at all to where we found her. The county coroner came out in the afternoon and took her away."

"She had a cat with her," Tom said.

"There wasn't any cat there yesterday," Carl said. "Just that woman."

"What'll happen to those horses? And her place?" I said.

"Well, I guess the coroner's gonna look for her next of kin," Carl said. "They usually do that."

"She had a lawyer in Holmes," I said. "But I don't know who he is. He handles her money and stuff."

I put my head down in my hands.

"We could try to look him up tomorrow," Carl said. "I'm sorry, boys, I didn't realize you all had become such friends."

NINETEEN

I couldn't sleep. I just lay there on the couch under the blankets, sweating and staring out at the dark room. Then I got scared, thinking about what happened with Chase, thinking about that ghost story Tommy told. I got up and went into Tommy's room. He was in his bed, with his face turned to the door. I couldn't tell if his eyes were open or not. I heard him gasp when he saw me standing there.

"You thought I was that ghost, huh?"

Tommy sat up. "Maybe."

I sat on the small couch against the wall. "I'm sorry, 'cause I can't sleep anyway."

He threw a pillow at me. "Neither can I. You can camp out here if you want."

"I got scared just now, Tommy," I said. "Sometimes I get so scared thinking that everyone around me is gonna die."

"Well, they are, Stotts."

"I know."

"I guess that is pretty scary," Tommy said.

I put my head on the pillow and lay down, staring up at the darkness of the ceiling, knees bent because the couch was so short.

"I feel sorry for Rose," I said. I wiped my hand across my eyes. "And sorry for those horses and her place."

And Tommy said, "Don't cry about it anymore, Stotts."

"Okay."

"Maybe there's something we can do. But we'll have to get out of here quick in the morning before that deputy comes looking for us."

"I don't think he wakes up too early."

"Well, he will if his boy comes home bleeding all over the place and crying about how we shot him."

"He would've already been here, then."

◆　◆　◆

Somehow I went to sleep, but woke when Tommy shook my shoulder. I could smell coffee cooking in the kitchen. The sun wasn't all the way up yet. Tommy gave me a clean T-shirt and I got dressed and carried my hat out into the kitchen, where Carl was sitting at the table, smoking a cigarette, cup of coffee and phone directory in front of him. Tommy poured two cups and I sat down next to his dad.

"Looks like there's only one lawyer listed in Holmes," Carl said. "So I don't know if it's the right one. I circled the name: Clifford Wickham. Sounds like a lawyer, don't he?"

I took a sip of coffee. It tasted good. "What time is it?"

"Five-forty," Tom said.

"Probably not exactly lawyer hours, I guess," I said.

"Wake him up," Carl said to me. Then, turning to his son, "We gotta get that truck."

While Carl and Tom walked to the stables to get another truck, I called Mr. Wickham and woke him up, like Carl said, and found out that he was the lawyer that Rose had hired. He already knew about Rose dying, but he was most interested in me for some reason, he seemed to have expected my call. And then he said that Rose had named me and Tommy Buller as beneficiaries to her holdings because she didn't have any surviving family members and that the paperwork had been notarized weeks ago. Then he asked if he could come see us later that day and I gave him directions to the Foreman's house. Before I hung up, I said, "But we might be in jail in Holmes later today, too, so I'll write your number on my hand."

I was pouring another cup of coffee when they got back, and carried it out with me so we could get on our way. They had Gabe with them in that other truck, too, so I knew he didn't sleep good, either; he never woke up early on his own, and he looked pale and sick. I got up into the bed of the truck, careful with that hot coffee, and I could hear Carl say, "Okay with me" from inside and then the door opened, wafting out a puff of cigarette smoke, and Tommy and Gabe got out and sat down in back with me. Tommy pulled out his can of tobacco and the truck started to roll away down that bumpy road toward the lake.

I grabbed Gabe by his shoulder and pulled him toward me.

"Did you see her this morning?"

"Yeah."

"Tell me if she's not okay, Gabey."

"She's okay, Troy. She told me to tell you that."

"She did?"

"Yeah."

"Did she say anything else?"

Gabriel looked over at Tommy once, and then back at me and said, "No. She just told me to tell you she's okay."

But his look told me something more.

+   +   +

The morning was still and cool. The sun was just coming up as we sat with our backs to the cab, watching as a curling tail of dust kicked up behind the truck. I gulped the last of my coffee, hit the grounds at the bottom, and poured the sludge out over the side.

"That Wickham was her lawyer, Tom," I said. "And you won't believe this. He told me she willed it all to me and you."

"What?"

"Her land, horses, everything she had. She didn't have any family so she left it all to us. What do you think about that? He says he's coming out to see us this afternoon over at your house."

"What'd you say?"

"We might be in jail."

I held out my hand so he could see the black marker scrawl on it. "So I wrote down his number."

"Luz said she won't tell Dad," Gabe said. "Unless she has to. She said she wants to forget about it."

"Well, that won't be easy for Chase Rutledge to do, I bet," I said. "In some ways I'd like to see Luz tell everyone what happened. In some ways, I wish we would've killed him."

No one said anything to that. But I looked at Gabe and

244

Tommy and could tell they were trying not to look back at me.

Then Tommy shifted himself and asked Gabe, "What did your dad do to you? For missing church and everything?"

"Nothing yet. I snuck out this morning. He doesn't know I'm here."

"You see what happens when you get a couple beers into an altar boy?" I asked Tommy. Gabe kicked me and tried to smile, but he was scared. We all knew he was thinking about Chase's promise to get even with him. I felt sick, like I was drunk and couldn't shake it out of my head.

Tommy was smiling, looking back at the road winding away behind us. "Damn! We got our own horse ranch, Stotts!"

"It's half-burned land and a burned-out steel house with about fifty horses that might starve this winter and a few goats we need to get rid of," I said. "We got a lot of work to do, Tom."

After we jump-started the truck and lamely tried to excuse and explain that keg of beer still sitting in its bed, Carl let the three of us go out to see those two horses we had left by the fence line, as long as Tom and I promised to meet him at the stables for our regular work before noon. Carl drove away, swearing, "If you boys get drunk and kill that battery this time, you might as well hitch yourselves to the bumper and tow it back yourselves 'cause I'm not coming out here again."

We all piled into the cab and Tommy swung the pickup around and headed down the road toward Rose's place. Tommy pulled out his tobacco and passed the can to me, so I took some, too.

"If I'm going to jail, I might as well take some of that stuff, too," Gabe said and Tom started to laugh.

"Damn, Gabey. Shooting a sheriff's kid really turned you into a hardened criminal," Tom said, and I handed the can over to Gabriel.

Even Tommy had to watch, despite attempting to drive, as Gabe fumbled with that can and its potent contents. Of course, Gabe spilled some on his lap when he opened it because he didn't pack it down by whipping his wrist, and he spilled some more when he scooped up a clump between his thumb and index finger. He held it up in front of him, looking at it like it was some kind of insect.

"You just put this in back of your lip?" he said.

I nodded.

"And then what?" he asked, still holding it up.

"Just do the first part first and you'll figure it out," Tommy instructed.

Gabe shut his eyes, pulled his lower lip out with his left hand, and packed the tobacco down, frowning and puckering.

"It's okay," he said, but there was a tear almost breaking from his eye. Tommy and I laughed. Tom spit out the window, and then I spit in the cup.

"Just spit, don't swallow," I said.

"It's hard not to swallow what's in your mouth," Gabe said, talking like there was a clothespin on his tongue. A trickle of brown drool leaked from his lower lip. He put his head out the window and spit.

"Crud," he said, "I spit all over the truck."

"Poor truck," Tommy said. "Watch where you aim, Gabey. You wouldn't want to wash any of the horse crap off it."

"I feel really weird," Gabe said. He held his hands out, bracing himself on the dashboard.

246

"Hell, if it wasn't so early, I'd offer you a beer," Tom said.

"If it wasn't warm as piss, I'd probly drink it, too," I said.

Gabe laughed, and some of the tobacco plopped out of his mouth, and then we all laughed. And then I looked out the windshield and realized that Tommy had just made that turn at the place we called the end of the road. Gabe and Tommy realized it, also, because it suddenly seemed real quiet inside that rattling truck. Tommy stopped the truck at the meadow where we found Luz's horse.

"You wanna see if he's laying there dead?" Tommy said.

"It was just a scrape, Tom. There's no way he's dead unless he had a heart attack or something," I said. "But we could look and see if we can pick up all the spent casings."

"We already did that when you were playing kiss-the-hero with my sister," Gabe slurred, trying to hold in his spit. Then he opened the door and spit down on the dirt.

We all slid out of the truck and walked, like we were under some kind of spell. When we got to the spot where Gabe had shot Chase, it was almost as though we were expecting to be greeted by something more than just an open meadow with green grass and white flowers. We stood, looking down like we were at some graveside ceremony.

"There's a little blood there," Gabe said, pointing down.

"What kind of medicine is that, chief?" Tommy said.

"It's not. It's poison."

I looked at the back of my hand, remembering I had smeared Chase's blood on it yesterday. Less than a day ago. Gabe took the tobacco out of his mouth and threw it down there, and then spit.

"Let's get out of here," he said.

Farther south, we drove through more burned-out forest and fields before getting to the south pasture where Tommy and I were keeping his stallion and my mare. The stallion was trotting back and forth, agitated, head bobbing up and down. My mare had foaled, probably some time the day before, because she and the little one were both up and moving around. Tommy pulled the truck up alongside the corral and we all got out and went right to my horse's pen.

"It's a little colt," I said, "like Carl said it would be."

We just stood there, me with my foot up on the corral's railing, staring at that little foal and Ghost, his mother. And he'd look at us, and then run and kick behind her. Tommy spit, turning away from the corral. I saw him looking out past the fence at all that land Rose had given to us.

"It was your tobacco," I said.

"What?"

"Why she gave it to us. You gave her that whole can of tobacco that first day, remember?"

"And I wasn't even nice to her," he said.

"Yes you were, eventually," I said. "I know she liked you, and you liked her."

"But it was you," he said. "You were the one she really liked. She wouldn't've cared if I never came back again with you. As long as you'd carry the chew." He looked back out at that land. "She got us drunk that time."

"We almost killed ourselves. That's why."

Tom smiled.

"What're you gonna name him?" Gabe asked.

"I'm naming him after you, Gabey," I said. "I'm calling him Gunner."

"Shoot," Gabe said, and swatted at me with his dirty hat.

I climbed between the pipes of the corral. Ghost looked nervous, keeping her ears back and putting herself between me and her foal. Tom and Gabe stayed out and kept quiet as I walked slowly and silently toward the mare, holding my head low and my hand out to the horse. She was scared and tense, but after she ran around me twice she let me touch her, and as I stroked her nose I'd sneak a half a foot closer until my body was right up to her shoulder and I could see over her, right at that nursing colt's silvery-rusty back.

"Let's bring 'em home, Tom," I said.

"To your place?"

"I've got four stalls off my barn. I need to take better care of 'em now, I can't just leave 'em here."

"What about that big one?" Gabe asked.

"I think we should try to get him, too," I said.

"Let's let 'em go," Tommy said. "I'll catch him again."

I looked over at Tommy in disbelief, and he repeated, "Let's let 'em go, Stotts. So he can run around on Rose's land again."

I said, "You could catch him again. I know."

And Tom Buller looked sad and proud at the same time when we opened the gate on the stallion's side of the pen and stood back as that horse took off, scattering the smoke of black ashes and dust away from his hooves. Tommy didn't say anything else about it, he just quietly watched that horse galloping away. It seemed to me that Tom Buller was setting a piece of himself free, too. Tommy walked to the truck, looking away from me, and backed the trailer through the gate on the mare's side of the pen while Gabe tied a little rope halter for the colt.

"I don't know if you can get it on him, but if you do this should work," Gabe said, slinging the halter over the top rail of the corral. "You might just have to pick him up and carry him in and hope he doesn't bang around too much."

Tom parked the truck and I opened the gate to the trailer as he came around into the corral. Gabe stood behind the big trailer gate so he could shut it, and I grabbed the mare's halter and lead rope.

"If I can't lead her in, we'll flag her in with our hats," I said.

"That'll do," Tom said.

I worked that black mare on a long lead rope, so I could use it like a longe line. I had it attached to the bottom of her rope halter, with the lead coiled up beside it in my left hand. She saw the rope when I started moving toward her and she walked away, escorting her foal with her. I had to walk around, leaning this way and that for a good ten minutes before she would stand still and let me get up close enough to her. I got her to turn her head toward my chest and I stroked her neck and talked softly to her, telling her she was good. I got the rope over her neck and she moved a little, but she knew that rope meant stand still. And she saw the halter coming up below her face and started to move her head just a little, but I brought it up and then reached around her neck with my right arm to tie it off. Then she started to run away, but I just gave her some slack and followed her at her shoulder, keeping that lead loose in my left and waving at her hips with my right until she calmed down and turned her head back toward me. All the while, the colt trotted along with her, making a squeaking kind of whinny.

"I'm gonna try and lead her on first, Tom," I said.

"Maybe the little one'll follow," he said.

She hesitated and froze up right by the door of the trailer, but Tom got behind her and waved his hat at her and she went right in. The colt wanted to follow her, but Tommy stopped him up so I could halter him. The colt didn't like that halter at all, and struggled against it. It was amazing how strong he was and how fast he could move those gawky legs, but I managed to tie it on so at least I could hitch him next to his mom at the front of the trailer. When they were both inside, the mare clattering her hooves back and forth, from side to side, and him just trying to hide his face in her belly, Gabe shut the door.

Tommy punched fists with us.

"Good job," I said.

"Thanks, Gabey," Tom said. "Let's get 'em over to Stotts' place so we can get back before noon."

Well, my dad was quite surprised about my new additions to our barnyard, but he didn't mind because he knew I was the one who'd take care of them. We got the trailer backed up to the open breezeway door and I went in the barn and opened up a stall for the horses. Gabe manned the trailer door again. My dad stood by the gap in the breezeway.

"I don't think you should watch us get them off, Dad," I said. "It's pretty scary."

"We might need him," Tom said. "If you just block that gap between the trailer and the barn, she won't run at you."

"What if she does?" my dad said.

"Don't fall down."

Getting that mare off the trailer was a lot more work than putting her on. She just refused to pass over the tail end. I pulled from the front, Gabe held the door, Tommy spun a lead rope at her butt from the back, and she lifted up, pulled back, spun around, and even kicked at Tom. When she finally came down, I just let go of the lead and let her run down the breezeway. Since the one stall was the only open doorway at the end, she charged right in and the little one followed right behind.

"Oh my God!" my dad said. I knew it would take at least a year to get him on a horse after seeing that.

Tommy went in the stall and took off the halters and leads and Gabriel closed the trailer back.

"We'll make it back to the ranch in time, I guess," Gabe said.

"Do me a favor," I said. "Please get them some food and water so I can get about five minutes to go in and shower off and get some clean clothes on. I've had these on for three days."

"I know," Tommy said. "Believe me, I know, Stotts. Okay, five minutes."

We made it through the main gates of the Benavidez ranch well before noon, so I knew Carl wouldn't be mad at us for taking too long. We drove right past the Foreman's house and up the drive toward the big stable, Tommy chewing tobacco and spitting out the window as we passed Reno and Arrow in their stalls out back. As we came to the top of the hill, all three of us gasped simultaneously, and I could feel Gabe and Tom turn icy alongside me.

"Shoulda never given you the chance to take that shower," Tom said. "I bet you changed out of those lucky boxers of yours."

Deputy Rutledge's black-and-white Bronco was parked at the stables, and he was standing there, watching us.

TWENTY

I *'ve seen ghosts, too, Tommy. Only the ones I seen follow*
me everywhere.

$\bullet \quad \bullet \quad \bullet$

"Stop the truck!" Gabe said.

"It's too late," Tommy said. "He's looking right at us."

Gabe slumped, putting his face in his hands, elbows on his knees.

"Just don't say anything, Gabey," I said. "Don't tell him any-thing."

"It'll be okay," Tom said. "We're the tribe, remember?"

He held out his right hand and we all grasped and shook, not one of us taking our eyes from that black-and-white and the deputy standing beside it. Tom pulled the trailer up in front of the stable and parked the truck, facing Rutledge's car. The deputy was hatless in the shade of the stable's façade, his receding hairline thinly topping a broad, sweating forehead. With that belly spilling over his belt buckle, he always looked hot and uncomfortable. Standing beside him was a thin, small man with collar-length stringy black hair, parted in the middle, wearing black wire-framed glasses, dressed in a white shirt, unbuttoned on top with rolled up sleeves, tucked into black jeans. He looked almost Asian, pale, with nearly gray lips.

"I guess this is it," Tom said. "I hope they feed us in jail, 'cause I'm hungry."

He opened the door and spit on the ground.

"You gonna open your door?" I asked Gabe.

Gabe, holding his hat by the brim with both hands like he could hide behind it, sighed and got out. I slid out after him. Rutledge looked at me, then at Gabe.

"You Tommy Buller?" the deputy asked Gabe.

"I am," Tom said, his voice real steady like we were about to be in a shootout.

"You're not Art Benavidez' boy, Gabriel, are you?"

"Yes."

"Damn. You don't look Mexican."

"My mother's from Italy," Gabe said.

"I thought she was a Mexican, too!" Rutledge said, shaking his head. "Damn! I bet she can cook good."

"Questioning like this'll make you confess to just about anything, I guess," I whispered to Tommy.

"What'd you say, boy?"

I didn't think he heard me, but I wasn't close enough for him to take a swing, either, this time. "Nothing."

Tom spit.

Carl came out of the stable doorway and leaned against the truck, lighting a cigarette.

He sucked in a long drag. "I put a list on the whiteboard in there," he said. "You better get on it as soon as you're through here 'cause it's a good two days of work there."

He exhaled a cloud of smoke up above his head and looked at the deputy.

Rutledge scratched his neck and said, "This fella stopped by my office a bit ago. I told him I'd take him out here. He's a lawyer for that woman with them goats."

"I'm Cliff Wickham," he said, holding out his hand to me.

"I'm Troy Stotts," I said, and looked at the showered-off smudge of black on my hand where I had written his phone number, "and this is Tom Buller."

Tom shook his hand.

"Well, like I told you this morning, Troy, not two weeks ago Rose came in to see me and had me draw up a will in which she left all of her property and savings to you boys. She's got a bit of money in savings, probably enough to pay for her burial, but the property and livestock is substantial, almost thirty acres with a house and several outbuildings. You probably know that, I guess," Wickham said. He seemed real calm and sincere.

Carl puffed another drag. "That's quite a bit."

"We been to her place," Tommy said.

"She gave us those horses," I said.

"She really liked you boys. She talked about you every time I'd see her," he said. I noticed he was looking at my shoes.

"Yeah. My shoes."

"Her only husband died over fifty years ago. She didn't have any family," he said. "It's a simple matter of filing the paperwork and changing the title. It should be all cleared in a couple months tops. Here, let me give you boys my card." And he handed me and Tommy his business card.

"Can I have one of those?" Rutledge asked, holding out his hand.

Wickham looked embarrassed. "I only had two."

Tom and I put the cards in our pockets.

"And I didn't think that woman even had any friends," the deputy said. "You'd never see her around."

"We helped her do stuff. We brought her things," I said to Wickham. "She was real nice to us. We went and got her out of there the day of the fire, but I guess it was too much for her. Anyway, the place burned real bad."

"We'll fix it up, though," Tom said.

"Well, if you need to draw up some kind of partnership agreement . . ."

"We already did that," I said.

"Oh." He cleared his throat.

Gabe was just standing there, looking pale.

"Mr. Wickham," I said.

"Cliff."

"Well, uh, about the funeral and all. If you'll make the arrangements I'll see to it that it gets paid for if there wasn't enough money in her accounts. And I'll pay you, too, for whatever you need to get done on this," I said. "I could give you five hundred dollars right now."

My dad was still holding on to my winnings from the biathlon.

"Really?" he said. "Well, I'll let you know, Troy. And thank you."

"Thanks, Cliff," Tommy said, then turned and spit.

Wickham turned to open the passenger door on the Bronco.

"Hey!" Rutledge said. "That reminds me. About that race . . ."

I looked at the deputy. And I thought, *This is it*, as I felt the blood draining from every part of my body.

"Any of you boys seen Chase around? I haven't seen him since Saturday night."

I glanced at Tommy, both of us with our mouths part open, both of us wondering which would tell the lie, and relieved, too, that Chase hadn't shown up around Three Points yet.

"We haven't seen him," Gabe said. His voice was as steady and calm as if he were in church. "And we've all been together for the last three days, ever since the race."

"Well, I figured," Clayton said. "Now that he's eighteen I hardly ever see him. And put money in his pocket like that and he's as good as gone till it runs out. Well, let's head on back, Mr. Wickham. My belly's tellin' me it's getting on to lunchtime."

They got in the sheriff's car and slammed the doors.

"His belt should be telling his belly to shut the hell up," Tommy said.

"Thanks again, Cliff," I said, and waved as they pulled away.

When the car had hit the top of the hill and began to sink down out of sight, I collapsed onto my back in the dirt. Carl just stood there, looking at us curiously, smoking. Gabriel smiled as Tommy slapped him on the back and said, "Damn, Gabey!"

"What's that all about?" Carl said.

Tommy looked at me and Gabe and shook his head.

"I think we better get to work," said Tom. "Come on, get up, Stottsy."

And he kicked me once, then held out his hand and yanked me up to my feet.

"You boys can start by cleaning out that trailer, so I can take it up and unhook it. Hurry up now, 'cause I'm wanting to go get my lunch, too," Carl said.

"You could take that keg back to George. And bring us something back," Tommy said. "We haven't eaten anything yet today."

"Maybe."

Carl lit another cigarette while Tom and I set to sweeping out that trailer. Gabe stayed to help us, too.

"You're gonna have to go back home eventually," I said.

"I know." Gabe pulled a hose into the trailer through the front side door. "Maybe if I beg 'em enough, I can talk 'em into letting me stay at your house for a couple nights. I know they wouldn't let me stay at Tommy's."

"My dad would be okay with that."

We finished the trailer and Carl drove it off. Then we went inside the big barn to see what jobs he had listed for us on the whiteboard; that was where all the ranch hands got their assignments.

We started with the stalls inside. Gabe took a rake, too; all of us with our shirts off, sweating like it was a sauna, swatting and waving at flies like we were horses with hands. We talked across to the other stalls while each of us worked.

"It says 'hooves' up there, too," Tommy said, pointing at the work board. "That means me."

"I saw that," I said.

"This one here's hooves are all squashed out," Gabe called across the breezeway.

"Thanks, Gabey," Tom said. "And I hope you both know that just because we got lucky right now doesn't mean it's not all gonna fall apart."

"Well, at least I didn't kill him," Gabe said.

"I wish you did. Are you done on that side yet?"

"My dad doesn't pay *me*. He pays you guys," Gabe said. "So I'm quitting."

"Time for those hooves, I guess," Tom said. "'Cause I'm done here."

"You boys want some food?"

It was Luz, standing at the open slider doors, calling to us.

I opened the stall gate and walked out into the breezeway, looking down to those big open doors where I could see her silhouette standing there with a basket in her hands, the sunlight glinting off her hair.

*   *   *

We all ate together, and we talked about the land and horses Rose had left for us. Luz wanted to know what we would do with it, and both Tom and I were kind of surprised because there was never any question or debate in our minds what we would do with it all. When we finished, Luz and I walked out to the back of the barn and stood in the shade and the cool breeze, drying the sweat on my skin. And me, leaning against the wood slats of one of the small corrals so that the top rail pushed against the brim of my hat, trying to look like I was watching the yearling stud colt inside, when I was really looking at her.

"Thanks for lunch," I said.

"Well, I saw Carl and he said he was going to pick you up something, so I told him not to bother."

"Your mom and dad mad at Gabey?"

"He'll get it at dinner."

"Maybe I could tell them about the truck breaking down, and with Tom's horse being lame and all," I offered.

"That might work."

"At least it's not a lie, exactly." I looked right at her. "How are you today?"

"I'm okay. Really," she said. "I thought about what happened a lot last night 'cause I couldn't sleep. I wanted to talk to you so bad, Troy."

"I couldn't sleep last night, either," I said. "But I'm worried about Chase. He's going to try and do something real bad now, I think. He's like that."

"I think he's scared of you."

"He's scared of Tom. I gotta watch out for Gabey." I pushed my hat back with the top rail and looked at her. "I wanna see if your folks'll let him come stay at my house with me for a couple days. It's farther away from town, and Gabe'd be less likely to run into Chase all of a sudden."

The colt came to the railing and sniffed my hand.

"Troy, last night you said that if we were alone you'd — and then Tommy came out. You'd what?"

I looked down. It felt like there was a hard-boiled egg, shell and all, in my throat.

"Nothing," I said. I looked away. "I'm an idiot."

She reached through the rails and grabbed my hand. The colt backed away.

"I don't think that," she said. "I wish sometimes we could be up at that cabin again, Troy. That we could have that night back."

260

Then she kissed me real soft next to my ear and turned back toward the barn.

"I better let you two get back to work," she said. "But stop by the house before you go home, Troy, and talk to my dad about Gabey. It'll make things better."

Then she whirled into the darkness of the barn and left me there, staring at that frustrated colt.

+   +   +

I was surprised when Mrs. Benavidez forgave Gabriel so quickly for missing church and breaking the arrangement he had made with his parents, and especially when she told me, "I don't know what you boys have been doing, Troy, but as long as your father is there, it would be fine if Gabriel spent a few days with you."

"He'll come to work with me and Tom every day, anyway. And I'll make him brush his teeth." I tried to smile.

And Gabe nudged me and said, "Shut up."

"His father's always been trying to get him to work here, so if you boys can do it, he would be very happy," she said with that frowning, scowling mouth. "I trust you, Troy. But you both better leave before his father comes home."

It was late afternoon. Gabe and I rode north around the lake to my house. Going home, finally, after what seemed like such a long time.

"Thanks for helping me out, Troy."

"Well, I hope they don't blame me if you come back skinnier, 'cause we'll have to cook for ourselves at my house. My dad doesn't do it anymore 'cause I'm gone so much."

"Do you know how to cook?" Gabe asked.

"Nope. But I know how to not starve to death."

"I don't know. Some people say you're doing that right now."

"Do you know how to cook?" I said.

"I can pour milk on cereal without spilling it."

"We'll survive these next few days, then," I said. "You can sleep on the couch in my room that makes out into a bed. You wouldn't want to sleep in the living room 'cause some nights my dad stays up until dawn. Ever since my mom died, at least."

Gabe didn't say anything. The horses walked lazily. They liked each other, but I knew Reno would be jealous and act up when we came home and he found those other horses in his barn. I was thinking I'd just keep him and Dusty in the outside corral tonight till he got used to the smell and the company.

I had my shirt with that number seven pinned to it draped over Reno's flank. It was so grimy and dirty now, I'd probably never wash it, just hang it up on the wall in the barn just like that. And that red bandana of Tommy's was still twisted around the horn of my saddle.

We were almost at that little bridge now — the place we had met the day we went out after that lion; the place where Clayton Rutledge stopped me that night. Gabe had his hat way back on his head.

"You really gonna name that little colt Gunner?"

"Yep."

"After me?"

"Gunner's for you, Gabey."

"That's embarrassing."

"Only you and me and Tommy know. It's our joke. It's a good name."

"I guess I like it. It suits that little colt." He paused. "When you wanna get ropes on him, let me know. I'd work on 'em. I know how to do that, I grew up with it."

"I'd like that. You could help with all of 'em. We got a few of 'em, now, that's for sure."

◆　◆　◆

It took a while for it to sink into my dad that Rose had left all that land and those horses to us, and he got pretty excited. I gave him Wickham's card and told him to call if he wanted to ask him anything.

Mr. Benavidez had called to say it was okay for Gabe to stay with us for a couple days. And he wanted to see me in the morning. I felt a little scared and nervous about that; it sounded kind of ominous.

"And you boys are going to have to make your own dinner tonight, because I've already eaten," my father said.

"I was just telling Gabe that right before we got here," I said. "Okay, Dad. Come on, Gabe, let's go put the horses out and feed 'em all."

We put Reno and Dusty out in the outer corral, fed them, and brushed them down. I could tell Reno could smell the other horses nearby, the way he was curling his lips and pacing around the corral with the unconcerned buckskin. I yawned; I was worn out and sleepy. We went to the barn to check on the new horses and feed them.

"That little guy sure is pretty," Gabe said.

"He looks like a zebra with that brush mane of his."

"He's gonna be mean. You can tell."

"You think so?" I said. "Well, mean's okay as long as he's not stupid."

"I'd take mean over stupid in a horse any day, too."

"You want him?" I asked.

"To keep?" Gabe said, looking at me.

"You can have him," I said. "I got a lot of 'em now. If you want him."

"Thanks, Troy!" Gabe patted me on the shoulder.

"Only you can't change his name."

"Gunner," Gabe said. "Can I go touch him?"

"You could try."

"Thanks, Troy. Thanks."

"Go get him."

And Gabe went into the stall and the little colt wasn't afraid at all, but he had to turn that big mare around because she was looking ready to take a kick at him. Gabe touched the colt and it stood there for a second and then, twitching, jerked away.

"If she kicks you, your dad'll kill me," I said. "Let's go get something to eat."

I turned off the light in the barn and we went back to the house, Gabe saying "thanks" about a dozen more times before we even opened the door.

TWENTY-ONE

Gabe thanked me again for the foal in the morning when we went out to feed the horses after a breakfast of toast and coffee. We rode out in the dark, so we'd be back at the ranch by six o'clock.

I knew Mr. Benavidez would be waiting, so our first stop was at the door of the main house.

"You're coming in with me," I told Gabe as I knocked, kind of softly, almost hoping nobody inside would hear.

Mr. Benavidez opened the door. He smiled and shook my hand.

"Good morning, Troy."

Then he kissed Gabriel on the top of the head. "Have you boys had breakfast?"

"We ate at Troy's house," Gabe said.

Mr. Benavidez stepped out onto the front walk. "Well, I won't keep you from your work, Troy. I wanted to tell you that Carl and Mrs. Benavidez and I will be driving out to New

Mexico this afternoon to pick up some horses. We might be gone for a week. I wanted to know if you would like to come with us, of course, if your father permits it. It would be good experience for you."

I didn't know what to say. "I'd like to, Mr. Benavidez, but my horse just foaled, and I kind of need to stay around here." It was a terrifying prospect going anywhere *alone* with Luz's father like that 'cause I knew he'd want to talk.

He just stared at me. He looked disappointed. I could tell he was running through a discussion in his head, maybe the one he wasn't going to get a chance to have with me.

"Well, I'll have Carl leave you and Tom a list of work to do while we're gone, then. Luz and Gabriel will be coming, too."

Gabe spoke up. "Troy gave that little colt to me, Dad. Can't I just stay with him and you all just go?"

"It's okay with my dad," I said.

He looked down, thinking. "Are you sure you don't want to come along?" he asked Gabe.

"I really want to stay," Gabe said. "I already have my clothes and stuff over at Troy's, anyway."

Mr. Benavidez exhaled. "Go tell your mother."

Gabe squeezed between us and rushed through the door, running.

"Luz won't want to go, either," he said.

And he just stared at me, unblinking.

So I stared back, scared.

"I'll tell her you said good-bye."

"Maybe I'll get a chance to before you all leave today," I said. I gulped. "If you don't mind, please."

I did get to say good-bye to Luz. She came out to the barn

at lunchtime, her father and mother and Carl all waiting in the big diesel truck, engine running, with a stock trailer hitched up to it. She had been crying. I knew she didn't want to go. Everyone knew that. And we couldn't even touch each other because they were all watching us from that truck. I just kept looking over her shoulder at them.

"It's not such a long time," I said. "You'll have fun. I'll still be here when you get back."

She touched the back of my hand, softly, brushing past it with those cool fingers.

"I love you, Troy."

I looked down and she was gone, disappearing behind the door of the truck. I waved as they pulled away.

✦ ✦ ✦

With Carl away, Tom and I were assigned the jobs that he usually did, which were better and more fun than our regular chores. So when the afternoon began turning toward evening, we were out in the open pasture pulling a trailer load of alfalfa bales with a tractor to drop into the feeders, which were spaced along an entire length of fence line. And all those beautiful Benavidez quarter horses out there knew the sound of the tractor and the time of day, so they'd come clustered in small herds with their heads and ears up, following us with their eyes as we dropped flakes into one after another of the J-feeders along the fence. Tommy was driving and I was riding back on the flat trailer, cutting the baling line and throwing the feed.

At the last feeder, Tommy turned around in his seat and put his foot up on the big back tire. He spit.

"You know, Stotts, I don't really want to stay in that haunted house by myself," he said. "Why don't you and Gabey move in while they're all gone? It'd be fun."

"Fun," I said, stoically. "A haunted house. A regular vacation."

Tommy was shaking his can of tobacco. I took some, too.

I said, "If you haul us back to my place so we can get our clothes and stuff, and then in the mornings to feed the horses, I guess it would be okay."

"I bet you can't stand up on that flatbed all the way back to the barn without me shaking you off."

"I could try. For money."

So Tommy lurched that tractor forward, me standing on the trailer like I was riding a huge surfboard over that pasture field and whooping, and every so often one of the Benavidez horses would pull its nose out of a feeder and look at us like we were insane, and then go back to eating. But I never fell off and when we got back, Tom admitted he'd owe me five.

We got back to my house in the early evening and Gabe and I gathered up our clothes. My dad was one of those people who liked being left alone sometimes, so he seemed happy to get rid of all of us for a week, even though we'd be back every day to tend to the horses.

And I already knew he was just waiting to get the chance to talk to me away from my friends, that he was going to say that he wasn't going to let Rose's land and those horses keep me from going to school, so I kept Tommy and Gabe right beside me as I grabbed the things I'd need just so he wouldn't start the conversation I knew we were going to have one day.

My dad said he'd talked to Wickham and that he seemed like a real nice man who was going to work everything out for me and Tom. Rose's funeral would be at the Three Points church the next Monday, and of course we'd all be there for her. We left and drove out to Papa's store to pick up some groceries and then, just as it was getting dark, we all went back to the Foreman's house.

We played horseshoes until it was too dark to see where we were pitching, and Gabe beat us both with that arm of his. Tommy said he'd make dinner the first night, so we ate macaroni and cheese and a box of Hostess donuts. We were all sitting around the big kitchen table, finishing the donuts. Tom and Gabe drank milk, but I had a glass of water. Tommy said he had to show us something and he ran to his room.

Then the phone rang, something that rarely happened at the Bullers', and Tommy called out, "Hey, get that, Stotts, it's probly CB checking up on me."

I picked up the phone. "Hello?"

"Just so you know, Buller. That kid you work for is dead. And then you're next." *Click.*

I didn't recognize the voice. I was certain it wasn't Chase Rutledge's, though. I hung up. Gabriel was drinking milk, not even looking at me.

I'd heard Chase say that kind of stuff before, too, and never took it seriously. But threatening Gabriel Benavidez was something more ominous than hollow, because everyone who knew Gabe also knew his innocence and goodness. I just resigned myself to keep a better eye on him until his family came back; or until things worked out.

Tommy came back into the kitchen, a tablet of paper in his hands. "Who was that?"

"No one," I said. "There was no one on the other end."

Tommy just shrugged. "I want to show you what I drew up," he said.

He placed the pad down on the table in front of me, sweeping aside crumbs. I could tell right away what it was; Tommy was an excellent artist. It was Rose's house, viewed from above, with plenty of additions around it.

"We'll put a road going down this way, along that creekbed," he traced with his finger, "and on this side, we'll have a big pasture. Over here will be a smaller enclosed field, maybe for yearlings we're working with. We'll run water lines off that well here and behind the house we'll put the working pens and a big round pen. This'll be a big covered shelter here for a riding arena, and we'll put these shelters out here and here for the winter and to keep the hay. Then the big barn'll be right off the house with ten stalls and a breezeway tall enough to drive a big stock hauler through."

"That looks awesome, Tommy," Gabe said.

"We'd have to start small, Tom. Fixing up the house and laying the water lines and putting up the fences on the fields and maybe a few of those stalls and the round pen," I said. "I like it. It's what I always wanted."

"Me, too, Stotts. Let's do it."

I punched his fist. "Deal."

"Can we start on it this week, you think?"

I suddenly felt so sad for Rose, and I wasn't sure if I even wanted to get back there right away. But there was something always kind of healing and forgiving in Tommy Buller's energy, a renewal of sorts that I just couldn't deny. I envied him so much for that.

"Let's," I said, and I looked at Gabriel. "As long as Gabey's in on it with us."

"I'm there," Gabe said, and wiped a line of milk from his

mouth. "And if we were at the fire pit right now, I'd ask you to tell Tommy that story about where you went. About what you did."

"Aw, Stotts. This sounds like a good one. Sounds like we're gonna be staying up tonight for this."

We stayed up late and I told Tommy the whole story about what happened to me up on the mountain, Gabe listening intently, because this time I put in more details about that trip than when we were chasing after our clothes just two days before. When I had finished, Tommy looked kind of disappointed.

"How come you never told me that?"

"I never told no one till a couple days ago," I said. "I guess I was kind of embarrassed, running away from home like some little kid. And then I was going to go back up there when I wanted to quit working at the ranch, but I just couldn't, and I felt real stupid and depressed, especially after getting hit like that by Clayton. And then it didn't matter anymore. But for the longest time I guess I been scared about everything."

"Damn, Stotts. I don't know whether you're the luckiest guy I know, or just cursed," Tommy said.

"I never felt lucky."

" 'Cause you don't need it."

" 'Cause things just happen anyway. There's no luck to it."

"Well, I want to see it," Tom said. "Let's all go up there before they get back from New Mexico."

◆　　◆　　◆

Tom was making coffee in the kitchen when I woke up. It was still dark and Gabe was asleep on the bed he'd made on the living room floor. It was 3:30 and Tommy was already dressed and had his boots on. I got up off the couch and limped into the kitchen, yawning, and sat down at the table.

"You wanna go up there today," I said.

"We'll need to get a lot of stuff packed up on the horses." He poured two cups of black coffee. "Then I'll need to set up Ramiro about covering us for a couple days or so."

I called out to Gabriel. "Gabey, wake up! This crazy fool wants us to get on it right now."

Gabe just moaned from under a pile of blankets.

We got Tom's gear packed up on Arrow and then drove back to my house to load up Reno and Dusty. The house was dark when we got there so I knew my dad was asleep. Tommy parked the truck and trailer beside our barn. First we went into the house and packed up our clothes. I grabbed my toothbrush and mess kit, my fishing gear and rifle. I got two sleeping bags, one for Gabe. My dad woke up when we were rustling around in there; we were excited and happy, and I guess noisy, too.

I explained we were going on a campout and would be back in a few days. And I begged him to feed my new horse while I was away, and he said he would as long as he didn't have to get in there with her. I could hear Reno snorting and chuckling from his corral, and figured he knew I was home and was picking up on our excitement.

We brought Arrow out from the trailer and packed up our supplies on Reno and Dusty. Then we went into the barn to feed Ghost. Gabe and I grabbed some hay from the hayshed and walked through the breezeway, tossing some down for the goats, and then crossing the way to see my mare and Gabe's colt.

The mare was standing still, head down, sniffing and prodding her front foot at her foal. The foal was lying on his side. I could see the shaft of a hunter's arrow jutting from his ribs, another in his neck, and a third buried up to its feathers in his belly. There was blackened, glossy blood all over the stall gate and floor.

I dropped the hay right on top of my feet and fumbled with the latch on the gate. Gabe just stood there, pale, dumbstruck.

"Tommy! Tommy!" I called out.

I swung the gate open and left it there. Gabe held on to it and put his chin on the top rail.

"Oh God. He killed him." Gabe's voice sounded soft and high, like a little boy's. He put his head on his arm and started to cry.

I dropped to my knees beside the little horse. Tom came into the stall behind me. The mare lowered her ears and turned around, as though to kick at me, but Tommy shooed her out and closed the gate behind her, trapping her in the outer part of the pen. He turned around, looked over at Gabe, and then down at me and the colt.

I rubbed the colt's ribs, cold and hard.

"I'm sorry, Gabey," I said. "Poor little guy."

Outside, the mare cried. It was a terrible sound, repetitive, panicked, lost, and defeated. I could tell she knew that the little one was dead, but, like all mothers, she wasn't going to stop trying to call him back.

Gabriel said nothing, face in his folded arm, covered with that dirty white Stetson.

Tommy spit. "It ain't right, Stotts. It just ain't right."

I heard the clanking of the mare's nose pushing at the outer stall gate.

"I better get my dad out here."

I walked numbly from the stall, stopping by Gabriel. I put my arm around his shoulder and pushed my face down under the brim of his hat.

"I'm sorry, man," I whispered. "It'll be okay. We'll fix things."

I heard him say, "We can't."

I walked away. Gabe went inside the stall and knelt down beside the colt, wiping his nose along the back of his arm.

+   +   +

My dad insisted on calling Clayton Rutledge, even though each of us pleaded with him not to, and the deputy showed up later that morning just after the vet's truck had come and hauled off the dead foal.

Those arrows were barbed, and I couldn't bring myself to pull them out. The one in his belly had gone all the way through him, and I just pushed it clean through and pulled it out the other side. There was a sickening sucking sound and an awful smell as it passed from his body. I don't know why I wanted to keep that arrow, as if it would offer any testimony as to who shot it. My hands were sticky with blood. The arrow was entirely a foul black, feathers clotted with the colt's blood.

Tommy, Gabe, and I didn't need to say anything; we knew who'd killed the horse.

"We should leave," Gabe said when the sheriff's Bronco pulled up to the house.

From beside the barn, we could all see there were two people in that black-and-white. Chase Rutledge, wearing that permanent baseball cap, sat in the passenger seat up front. I looked at Tommy and Gabe. It was as though we were all looking at a ghost.

"I still want to go," Tommy said.

"Hell," Gabe said. "Let's leave."

The horses were ready.

"Let's go then," I said.

And we quietly got onto our horses and headed out past the barn toward our apple orchard. I never looked back, afraid that I'd see them all there watching us go.

"He's gonna be pissed," Tommy said.

"The deputy or my dad?"

"All of 'em, probly," Gabe said, and wiped across his nose with the back of his hand.

And we rode through the apple orchard, all of us sitting higher than the treetops, sitting on those big, good horses. The tree branches were getting heavier with green fruit, bending them down like willows. In minutes we had passed through the cuts in our fence and were heading up into the cover of the taller trees on those steeply rising mountains with the two granite fingers pointing up into a cloudless and hot blue sky.

We rode up into those mountains, me and Reno in the lead, along the course of the rushing river, fuller, angrier, whiter than it had been in June.

Just past noon we made it to the spot where I'd set up camp that first night, near the waterfall and amid a stand of redwoods. We rested the horses and had a lunch of beef jerky and canned pudding.

+ + +

Three arrows. I didn't want to say it, didn't need to. I knew they were thinking the same thing. Three arrows. Three of us. And me, wishing I didn't always see signs in things. I carried that blackened arrow up there with me, hopeful that it would offer us something, or, better, break what had fallen on top of us.

"This sure is a pretty spot," Gabe said.

"I slept right here under this tree," I said. "Slung my food bag up over there, 'cause of bears."

I pointed to a branch, perpendicular to its massive redwood trunk.

"If we stay here long, we better sling Gabey up there," Tom said. "He's got chocolate pudding all over his face."

"Shut up. I bet bears would eat tobacco if they could," Gabe said. "There's a picture of one on your can."

There was an edge in Gabriel's voice. He was still hurting, and Tom looked apologetically at us both.

I got up and went to the edge of the river, lying flat on my belly on the warm white granite rocks to put my face down and drink. I wiped my mouth dry with the front of my T-shirt.

"We could make it all the way up there by dark if you think the horses'll hold up," I said.

Tom came over and took a drink, too, then pulled a can of tobacco from his back pocket.

"I think we should keep going," Tom said. "We'll take it easy and if it gets dark before we get there, we can just set up camp for the night. Here."

He tossed me the can of tobacco. I took some.

We both looked at Gabe, who was licking the inside of his pudding container.

"It's okay with me," he said, standing up to join us at the river's edge.

We got back onto our horses and continued up the mountain, following the sound of the rushing water. Eventually we came to the meadow where I had fallen asleep and then fell from Reno, busting my head open on a rock. I swore I found that exact rock and pointed it out to Tom and Gabe.

"Yeah," Tom said, "that rock does pretty much match the dent in the back of your head, Stotts."

I spit.

"Why do you think he came this morning?" Gabe said. "Chase, I mean."

"He probly wanted to see what we looked like. After finding Gunner," I said. "Just to see our faces, I bet."

"I woulda kind of liked to see his face," Tommy said. "'Cause I bet he's got a good black eye where you kicked him, Stotts."

"I hope he had to sit on a pillow to get in his dad's Bronco," Gabe said.

"Anyone who'd do that to a little horse," I said. "I don't think he's done yet."

"Neither do I," said Tom.

I heard Gabriel sigh. Then he started to whistle.

He was scared.

∗　∗　∗

There was still an hour or so of light left when we arrived at that clear cold pond up where the tree line ended, and there was still plenty of snow, turning pink with the dusk, left on the rocky peaks above, and those two pale fingers poking up, one looking a little more crooked, as though it could topple at any time.

The pond looked bigger, calmer. I could see the dark stand of trees around on the north side where I had found that cabin.

"It's over there," I said. "Let's hope nobody's home."

I looked at Gabe. He looked a little nervous, and shifted in his saddle.

"I could go check it out first," I said. "I know the place pretty good."

"I'm coming with you," Tommy said.

"I'm not scared," Gabe lied.

So we rode around the shore of the pond, me pointing out the place up on the peak where I had found the plane and telling my friends how easy it was to get the fish here. There was no sign that anyone had been up here, no evidence that even Luz or myself were here at one time. The cabin looked exactly as I had left it.

"Dang," Tom said, "you wouldn't even notice it if you didn't know it was here. It's like part of the mountain."

"Let's go in."

We left the horses on the side of the cabin by that old steel trough and walked slowly to the open doorway. Everything was still there: the table by the window with the plate and the forks exactly where I had left them, the wooden Coke crate on the wall, the two books resting atop it, the plank bed where Luz had slept as I held her hand, the old stove, and even the coffee grounds from the coffee she had made were clumped and dry, like old tobacco, in its belly.

"This place is great!" Tom said.

"Let's bring our stuff in and get some wood for a fire," I said.

When we were all settled into the cabin, my sleeping bag on that plank bed and the others spread on the floor, we got a fire going in the belly of the stove. It was dark, and we were all hungry and sat where we could to eat potato chips and the sandwiches Tom had made that morning.

"Man, I could live in a place like this," Tom said.

"You do," I said.

"Hey Stotts, you remember that turkey you had to butcher?"

"Yeah?"

"Well, I brought another to butcher up here." And Tommy went to his knapsack and pulled out a gleaming bottle of Wild Turkey whiskey.

"You're out of your mind, Tom."

"Not yet, Stottsy. Not yet."

"Count me out," Gabe said. "I'm not getting drunk with you guys again."

Tommy twisted away at the top of the bottle, then waved it under his nose, sniffing. The look on his face convinced me he had never tasted whiskey before, but I could smell it, too, across the cabin. Then Tommy looked at me with that wry coyote smile of his, squinting his eyes so they sparkled in the little light thrown out from the open stove, and he put that bottle to his mouth and tipped back his head. When he brought the bottle down he bent forward at the waist and blew out his mouth, shaking his head. Then he coughed like he had been punched in the stomach.

"That doesn't exactly look fun, Tom," I said.

"You tell me," and he stretched his arm out to me, head down, offering the bottle.

"One time," I said. "That's it."

I held my breath so I wouldn't smell the whiskey as I brought the bottle up to my mouth. It was like jumping from a bridge, you didn't want to stay at the edge thinking about things; so I just put the mouth of the bottle inside my lips and tipped back, filling my mouth full and willing myself to swallow that entire dose in one gulp. My stomach contracted and churned, and I had to fight the urge to throw up. I bent my head forward, shaking it as Tom had, feeling that burn like molten metal tracing its path down my throat toward my belly.

I couldn't talk. Tears were pooling in my eyes. I looked over at Gabe.

"No way," he said.

I gave the bottle back to Tommy, who took a couple quick breaths like a swimmer about to go under, and then he took another long swig. This time it didn't appear to hit him so hard. He held the bottle back, admiring its label, as if to make sure it was the same stuff he had just drank a moment ago. He gave the bottle back to me.

"The second one's real smooth," he said.

I took another gulp, bigger than the first. And he was right. This time, my stomach did not rebel against the whiskey. It didn't taste so bad. I looked at the bottle. It was nearly half gone in those four swigs of ours. I was starting to feel hot and lightheaded.

"That's enough," I said, handing the bottle back to Tom.

"Maybe for now," he said.

I wiped at my mouth. "This stuff makes me feel like punching something just to see if it'll hurt."

Tommy smiled at me. "You smell like whiskey," he said.

I leaned to my left and smelled Gabe. "Even Gabey smells like whiskey right now."

Tommy laid back on his sleeping bag, feet toward the stove, open hands pillowing his black hair.

"You and Luz slept here?" he said.

"Yes."

"Did you —"

"I didn't even think about it, Tom. Not then."

"I bet she did," he said.

"I'm *sure* she did," Gabe said.

Then they both laughed, and Tommy punched Gabe's arm like they had some kind of secret joke.

I pushed Gabe's shoulder hard and made him topple over onto his left side. He lay back on his sleeping bag and kicked Tom's leg, laughing again.

"That's your big sister," I said. "She's the one who goes to church."

"Yeah," Gabe said, grinning wickedly, "and maybe she needs it more than you and me put together."

I got up and walked to the door in my socks, making it an obvious point to kick both of them hard as I passed. I stood in the doorway, looking out at the stars wriggling in the pond.

I wished she were here.

"What're you looking at?" Tom said.

"Nothing."

"Can we fish tomorrow?" Gabe asked.

"That or starve," I said.

"How long we gonna stay here?"

"We could rest the horses a day or two. Then we can get back before your folks. Before the funeral."

"I like it up here, Stotts."

"So do I," Gabe said.

"I like that whiskey," I said. "At least right now I do."

We drank again. And then Tom Buller started singing, "You're wanted by the police, and my wife thinks you're dead." It was an old Junior Brown song, and me and Gabe laughed so hard and Tommy just kept singing and singing until we both caught on to the words and sang it, too.

TWENTY-TWO

Of course we didn't know it then, but the next morning Chase Rutledge set out through our apple orchard, following our trail.

We slept late. The sun was already up and the day was warming fast when I got out of bed. Tommy and Gabe were still asleep as I dug through my bag and pulled out the coffeepot and some coffee.

I saw that blood-blackened arrow in there, too.

I started a fire with the coals in the stove and filled the pot from the drip pipe outside. I sat down on the bed and waited for the sound of the boil. I opened up that Dawson folder of mine and chipped away at a log in the back wall. By the time the first trace of steam started from the spout, I had carved a neat TS into the wall of the cabin.

The coffee was boiling. I kicked Gabe on the shoulder and Tom on the back. Tommy moaned. Gabe turtled his head down into his sleeping bag.

"Those fish aren't gonna walk out of that pond and just jump on the stove for you," I said.

"Just pour that coffee on my head," Tom said.

"I might have to. I only brought one cup."

"I got one," he said, and got up and crawled to his pack.

"I want some, too," Gabe said, muffled from inside his sleeping bag. "Tommy, get a cup from my bag, will you?"

Slowly, Gabriel emerged from the sleeping bag, hair wild and electrified. We all sat on the edge of that plank bed, holding our coffee with both hands to warm them.

"I heard you doing that," Tommy said, nodding toward my initials in the wall.

Gabe saw my knife sitting there on the bed and picked it up. "I want up there, too," he said as he opened the blade. Tommy flinched away in exaggerated terror as if he thought Gabe would accidentally cut him.

"Shut up," Gabe said.

"Didn't say nothing."

When the coffeepot was emptied, they were all three up there in a straight line: TS GB TB.

"That makes it as much ours as if we peed on it," Tommy said.

"That reminds me," Gabe said, and slipped his shoes on and went outside, followed by me and Tommy.

+ + +

I only had one fishing pole and some smelly cheese bait, so we all took turns using it. Gabe had seven trout well before lunchtime and left them tied on a line at the shore with the others that Tom and I caught, to keep them for dinner. We still had some jerky and candy bars, which we ate for lunch, and all three of us spent some time stacking wood for the stove and grooming our horses. After lunch, Tommy said, "Well, are you gonna take us up to see that wrecked plane?"

"I don't know."

"What do you mean?" Gabe asked. "We wanna see it."

I looked at them both, so they could see I was serious.

"Look, it was a really weird time. I thought I was crazy or something." I sighed. "Mostly I kept thinking it was all a dream, or maybe I didn't see it at all."

"I know how to find out," Tommy said, then spit.

We rode north, past the pond on that rock-strewn gap in the peaks where the trees grew sparser and sparser, under the guard of those towering granite fingers. Gabe was drinking from his canteen, Tommy looking intently forward and up to where that plane would be, still obstructed by a stand of low, twisted trees and a mound of rock shards.

And I felt less and less easy as we went along.

"That's it!" Gabe said.

I wasn't even looking. Gabe was pointing up at a $\vee$ between the peak of the fingers and a lower peak to the west, a slash of white snow, peppered with the dark rocks that rolled by themselves with each freezing and melting, and there we saw that plane. It was much cooler here, we could feel the chill on the breeze as the air brushed over that ice and barren rock.

"Well, it's real, Stotts," Tommy said. "It's a pretty big one."

The fuselage was torn open on the top, a big black slash cutting across it, and the one wing we could see from our side was bent back, nearly shorn completely free of the rest of the wreckage. It looked like death, like a big, sad, dead animal left to decay slowly.

"Someone had to've died there," Gabe said. "You can see a propeller down the slope from it, in the snow. See?"

I followed Gabe's finger down that swath of peppered white and saw, starring out like a flower, three blades of a propeller, black and straight.

"Is that a propeller, or a body?" Tommy said.

"It's been there for years. No way it's a body," I said.

I hadn't been to my mother's grave yet, not even once; had never seen the headstone, never left flowers.

Tell me about Will, Mom.

She always remembered things, carried them with her. One time, when I was brushing Reno, she was standing behind me, watching, and she said, "You brought Reno home a year ago today."

And I didn't know that. She loved Reno, but never rode him, told me he would never want anyone but me to ride him, she could see it in the way he carried his head when I was on him.

I knew it was Will's birthday. I saw her holding his photograph against her lap, rubbing the edge of the yellowing glossy paper with her thumb, how she touched her finger to her lips and, then, placed it softly down on the picture. And she never blinked.

I sat beside her, on the couch in our front room. My father was still at school.

I held her hand that folded carefully on the picture's border.

He loved to draw, Troy.

I know. I seen the pictures you keep.

And he loved to sing.

I can't remember that, Mom.

I can still hear it in my head.

Was he a good boy?

He never did anything mean to anyone.

Did he like me?

You were his best friend.

I can't remember it, Mom.

"We should go up there," Tommy said. "I bet there's dead guys in it."

"We can't," I said. "It'd take too long. And the horses wouldn't make it anyway. I showed it to you, now I kind of want to go back."

"I'm hungry," Gabe said. "Let's go eat those fish."

"We'll come back, then," Tommy said.

"Good." I turned Reno around to head back down to the cabin.

"Hey, Stotts?"

I held Reno up and turned back. Tommy held his fist out and I punched it.

"We'll come back sometime," he said, holding out his tobacco. "Want some?"

"Sure."

Tommy threw the can across to me and said, "You don't have to say nothing."

＊　＊　＊

It was a fine dinner. We cooked more fish than we could eat, and heated beans right in the cans sitting on the stovetop. Afterwards, Gabriel said he wanted to put a line in the water before sundown for some fish for breakfast, so we all sat out at the pond's edge as the sky darkened through all its colors before night. This time, he wasn't so intent on keeping the fish, though, and he let the small ones go, keeping only the largest three on his string. We all had our shoes and socks off, cooling our pale feet in the icy water.

"I brought that arrow with me, you know?" I said.

"Go get it. I want to see it," Gabe said.

I hobbled over the rocks and dirt and brush back to the cabin and brought out the arrow, the grooved triangular head scabbed over with that little colt's blood. I also found the bottle of whiskey Tommy had brought, half-drained.

A full moon was rising behind us.

"Here," I said, and handed the arrow, point up, to Gabe. Then I opened the bottle and took a swallow of whiskey and it just about knocked the wind and my fish dinner out of me. "And here," I gasped and handed the bottle to Tom.

"Damn, Stotts," Tom said. "I better stand up for this."

288

I pulled Tommy to his feet and watched him tip that bottle up and arch his shoulders back as he took a long swallow.

Then we saw Gabriel Benavidez do something I never would have thought he could do. He held that arrow tight in his left hand, like he was holding a pencil, and he jabbed the point of it right into his right wrist, not deep enough to really injure, but plenty deep enough to draw his blood. And we watched, amazed, as he held his right forearm up in front of his face and a bead of blood painted a thick slow line toward his elbow.

"Tell me about horse medicine, Troy," he said.

I took the bottle from Tommy; didn't hesitate. This time I drank from it twice before handing it back.

"I'll be damned, Gabey," Tommy said.

"Give me that," I said, and held out my wrist in front of Gabriel.

Gabriel watched me, his pale eyes looking right into mine, without any expression on his face. And then he put the point of the arrow down onto the soft flesh of my wrist. I clenched my fist. He pushed.

I felt the pain as the point broke through me, watched the blood pool in the recess at the wound. Blood ran off my wrist and spilled down on Gabe's knee.

"You're tough, Gabey," I said. "You stuck me better than you stuck yourself."

Tommy took two big gulps of whiskey. The bottle was nearly empty. We both looked at him, knew what he'd do. He held his wrist out in front of Gabriel.

"Do it, Gabey."

He winced as the arrowhead cut down on his wrist, making

a popping sound before Gabe pulled it away to reveal a separation of the flesh and the bright red blood that ran across Tommy's arm, dripping from both sides of it.

"Tell me, too," Tommy said.

I sat down next to Gabriel and grabbed his right arm. Then I took my own and pressed our bloodied wrists together. And then I held my arm out for Tom and it stung as he pressed his own blood into mine, and then he made it final by matching his arm with Gabe's.

Tom sat and we finished that bottle.

"There's nothing I can tell you about horse medicine that you don't already know. And especially you, Tommy. Horse is endurance; it is never giving up. It's will over the physical, 'cause a horse can run until he runs himself to death if he's running for a good reason. And everything you ask a horse, the answer is yes. Horse is forgiving. And 'cause every day is a new start to him, and he'll forget every horrible mistake you've made even if you keep dragging the past along with you. People think horses are stupid because of that, but you know the horse is asking, 'Who's the stupid one?'"

Gabe rubbed the blood from his wrist between two fingers, then smelled it, and licked at it. "I don't think they're stupid."

"Better not. It's in you now," Tommy said.

"I like the way you talk, Troy," Gabe said. "No wonder she's fallen for you."

"That black mare, or your sister?"

Gabe didn't answer. I said, "Let me have that arrow, bud."

Gabe handed it over and I launched it like a javelin into the pond. It was dark now, and as our eyes followed the course of

the arrow into the blackness of night meeting water, we saw, beyond the opposite shore, set back within the tall trees of the
forest, the orange glow of a campfire.

We all saw it at the same time; we all tensed. Then Gabriel
whispered, "Who do you think that is?"

"Fishermen, maybe," Tommy said.

"Maybe," I said. "But they'd be up closer to the water then."

I shook out my socks and pulled on my shoes.

"What're you gonna do, Stotts?"

"I don't think we should wait for morning to see who's out
there or what they want. There's enough moonlight, so I say we
sneak around and see who it is."

Gabe's eyes in the moonlight were wide and unblinking.
Tommy pulled on his boots.

"I'll be right back," he whispered and then went off toward
the cabin. I knew what he was getting. Gabe put on his socks.

"I guess we got no choice."

"It's probly nothing to worry about, but if it is, we want to
know now."

Tommy was coming back from the cabin. I heard him stum-
ble and fall, then laugh. He got up and spit. "Aw hell!"

"Okay, Surefoot. Just don't do that on the other side."

We started following the shore around to the south, toward that spot in the trees lit up by a fire. The moon was so
bright it cast our shadows down, blacker than anything, on the
ground before us. Tommy led the way, and I guessed that fire
was about a mile away, so we didn't have to worry too much
about keeping quiet yet; but still we whispered when we
talked. Neither Tom nor I could walk a decent straight line af-

ter that whiskey. I grabbed Gabe by the shoulder and leaned down on him. I could smell my own whiskey breath, hot and sour, as I talked.

"Gabey, you're in charge, okay?" I said. "Don't let me and Tom do anything stupid."

"Too late for that," Gabe said. "We're going toward that fire. That's pretty damn stupid right there."

Tom spun around on his heels. "And how are *you* gonna stop *me* from being stupid?" Then he fell over backward and his feet ended up straight at the sky, and Gabe and I laughed, struggling not to be loud.

Then Gabe pounced on Tommy's chest and pinned his arms down with his knees.

"Let's throw him in the water!"

I scooped up both of Tom's kicking feet while Gabe fought against his trying to turn him over and pin him. Gabe rolled around and got Tom under the armpits and we had him up off the ground. Three steps over to my right, and we tossed Tommy out into the icy pond.

Tommy came right up, huffing and shaking the water from his hair.

"Like that, that's how," Gabe said.

Tommy sloshed his way out of the water and picked his hat up where it had fallen, then put it on his dripping head. He held out a fist and he and Gabe punched knuckles.

"That was good, Gabey. That was good. But you're gonna get wet."

And then Tommy just scooped up Gabe like he didn't weigh anything at all and he easily threw him a good seven feet out into the water. And Tommy started laughing and I couldn't help myself because it was so funny seeing Gabe flying like that. I threw off my hat and sat down and began taking off my shoes and socks.

"What are you doing?" Tommy said.

"Not giving you and Gabe a chance."

And then I jumped into the pond, too, clothes and all. It was so cold I couldn't inhale at first, but it was what I needed to straighten out my head. As I wiped my eyes and started walking back to shore, I saw Gabe and Tommy throwing my shoes and socks in after me.

"Thanks a lot."

"You deserve it, Stottsy, for putting this guy in charge. Now we'll probly all get killed."

"Or pneumonia," I said.

I managed to get my shoes and socks back on, but not straight, and we all set out, dripping and shivering a little, but smiling at each other, in the direction of that mysterious campfire.

When we got to the southern shore of the pond, we entered the woods. We were silent now, almost close enough by this time to hear, or be heard, by whoever was at that fire, which grew brighter as we approached.

"Make sure and keep enough trees between us and that fire," Tom whispered.

We crept along behind Gabe, watching the ground so as not to trip and, at the same time, looking over toward the fire. Soon we could see the glowing shape of a little dome tent and the white-hot blast of a propane lantern. A shadow moved across the lantern.

"There's at least one there," Gabe whispered.

We followed him up closer, behind another redwood.

"There's two of 'em," I said.

One of the two was big and thick, with a belly on him, overfed. The other emerged from the tent, thinner and tall. Then we saw the thin one put on that unmistakable baseball cap, moving with a stiff walk around the fire. It was Chase Rutledge and the bigger one was his friend, Jack Crutchfield.

TWENTY-THREE

When we got back to the cabin we all changed into dry clothes and began gathering up our belongings to leave. Even though none of us wanted to ride at night, we all agreed that the best way to avoid any more trouble would be to get out before the sun rose.

Tommy pulled his gun out from the wad of his wet clothes and dried it off with his T-shirt. He ejected the magazine and wiped off each of the bullets, then reloaded it.

"I want you guys to know it's full this time," he said.

"Let's not shoot anybody," Gabe said.

I chambered a bullet in my rifle.

We got the horses loaded up and cleaned out the cabin. The stove was cold, which was good because I knew Jack and Chase would be here tomorrow and I wanted it to seem like we hadn't been here. I was hoping they'd follow our tracks up to the plane; I knew we'd be back home by then. We walked the horses slowly, the full moon giving us plenty of light to ride confidently.

"They came for *me*, didn't they?" Gabe said, whispering.

"They came for *us*," I said, hearing that phone call in my head. We all knew who they wanted most.

And Gabriel had that same look as when he panicked that morning we went out after the lion, and I didn't like that. Maybe he'd bought in to all the doubt his father had in him, I don't know, but there was always something about Gabriel that made me feel like I needed to protect him.

"Well, they'll have to take us all on, then," Tommy said. "So we might as well turn it around on 'em, 'cause we can't just run away forever."

"Give me some tobacco," I said. "I was thinking the same thing."

"Are we gonna kill 'em?" Gabe asked, his eyes squinting, biting at the inside of his lip.

Tom and I didn't have an answer for that.

We knew we couldn't go back down the way we came. Chase and Jack were camped right at the end of the trail we'd followed to the cabin, and I knew their horses would hear ours if we tried to make it past them in the dark.

So we took the horses right along the water's edge and then cut off to the west, which brought us higher in elevation, but we had to steer well clear of that campsite as we tried to find a wide path back around to the river that would lead us down.

"What day is it?" Gabe asked.

"It's gonna be Friday."

Gabe yawned and slumped forward in his saddle.

"You'll wake up when the shooting starts," Tommy said. Then he turned to me. "The moon's going down."

"I know."

It was getting harder to see the ground in front of us. I had no idea where we were; where we were going. I intended to cut around the woods where Chase and Jack were, then double back and look for the river to lead us back down. But now the moon was dropping below the ridge, and the trees around us were getting taller and denser, so all I could do was guess which direction I was leading my friends.

A big owl sat up on a branch over us, calling out to another, somewhere in the dark woods. We rode in single file, me in the front, Tommy in the back; and as we went I could just see the ten or so feet in front of me. Where we were going and where we had come from were swallowed in black. The moon was gone. I could feel Reno's hooves sinking into the soft bark-mulch ground and I turned us all south after I figured we had gone far enough. South, I judged, would mean downhill and with such soft ground it also meant the horses' legs would be straining, so every so often I'd have to look back and make sure Tommy and Arrow were still with us.

Gabe, exhausted, sleeping, started to fall from his saddle, but caught himself on the seat, tugging the reins across as he did. Dusty pulled hard to the left and started to rear up, which I'd never seen that horse do before. Gabe calmed him, but not before the buckskin had spun around and taken a couple steps back into Reno's hindquarters, which made Reno flinch like he was getting ready to kick.

The horses were nervous. Gabe was mad.

"That's it. I'm getting off here and taking a nap!" he said. "You can both go on if you want. I don't care what you do."

"It's okay, Gabey," I said. "We could rest now. I think we went far enough." I sighed. "But I don't know."

"I must be tired, too, 'cause I didn't even laugh at you, goof-ball," Tom said.

We hitched the horses and each of us sat with knees up and backs to tree trunks, hats over our heads. Tommy kept his gun next to his hip, and my .22 rested beside me. Gabe went right to sleep, and I looked out from beneath the brim of my hat while Tommy shifted uncomfortably. Maybe we had gone far enough, I thought. This would be okay, and we were all so tired. We formed a triangle of bent-up, tired riders under those tall trees; the sky showing no sign of any morning in the little patches visible beyond their tops.

sleeping in the woods.

See you at the bottom of the falls, then it's Gabey's turn.

Blackness. Then little beads of light, like stars; the light shining on the row of morphine vials on the table by my mother's bed.

These will help her when the time comes.

The doctor showed me how to break off the tips and squeeze out the contents under her tongue.

This will help her die more easily. More comfortably. You'll both know when the time comes.

And my father, then, in the room on that terrible night. That long night. My mother staring straight up at the ceiling, unblinking, the breaths coming in gargled gasps, only once in a while. Exhales were raspy moans. And him breaking open that first vial.

Don't do that, Dad.

She needs it now, Troy.

You can't help her die. She doesn't need that.

She's not coming back.

No!

And I grabbed him from behind and pulled his arm away. When he spun around, I swatted the vial out of his hand. I pulled my hand back, a fist, to hit him again, in the face, and he picked me up with both hands, tight around the neck of my T-shirt and slammed me back against the wall. Pulling the shirt so tight it began to cut into my skin. I could feel myself passing out and then he slammed me into the wall again and dropped me there.

I ran out of the room. Into the woods.

And I found someone in the woods, a man, I think, but I couldn't see his face because he just looked like a shadow, like I could see through him. Like a ghost. But I heard the voice from that mouthless form.

I can tell you've been in a fight of some kind. You have bruises on your neck. Someone tried to hurt you?

And Clayton Rutledge reached out his stubby hand to touch my neck, and I saw those fingers, the first one bitten off by a horse. I was looking at Ramiro and he touched me with that incomplete hand and the fingers were cool and smooth.

Luz's hand, reaching up inside my shirt, her smooth marble fingers on my chest, pinning that number seven to me, and then her hand trailing down, stroking my belly.

Those fingers. Those granite fingers towering above me. Calling me like voices from a minaret, like someone on top was watching me.

+ + +

"Wake up, Stotts. Wake up. He's gone." Tommy was shaking my shoulder. "Gabey's gone!"

I put my hand up to my forehead, pushing back my hat. It was daytime, maybe even afternoon. I was lying on my side, in the dirt under the tree. I sat up.

"What?"

"Gabe took off on us!"

I looked at Tommy; he was staring intently, desperately, right into my eyes. I looked at the horses; Dusty was gone; turned my sticky eyes to where Gabriel had sat down to rest after his near-fall. Gabriel was gone.

I stood up, and spun around and kicked the trunk of the tree, hard enough to nearly break my foot.

"Damn it!" I said. "I knew he was in a mood to do something stupid like that! How long were we asleep?"

"A long time, I think," Tommy said. "I think it's afternoon. And at least he didn't take our guns."

"He probly should've. Did you just wake up?"

"I walked out a ways, following his track, to see if I could see him or hear him, but he's gone. He's way gone, Stotts. He's heading back toward the river, but when he starts crossing some of those big rocks, we're gonna lose 'em."

"We better get on after him, then."

I heard a loud rumble of thunder off over the high peaks from where we had come.

"That's all we need," I said.

I drank from my canteen, then handed it up to Tommy, who was already on Arrow. I got up on Reno and we set off in the direction of the single set of hoofprints heading west, I thought, in the direction of the river that we had followed up here.

We lost his trail when we came out of the woods and crossed a big, smooth, curving floor of granite. We both believed we were heading the way Gabriel would have gone, and we both kept hearing the phantom sound of swift rushing water, but as we plodded on we became less and less confident in our path.

"Remind me not to drink whiskey anymore," Tommy said, and spit.

"Deal."

"I keep hearing that river," I said.

"I keep hearing horses behind us."

"So do I."

* * *

By late afternoon we came to the meadow where I had fallen from Reno in my sleep, so I felt better about our finding our way down, but there was still nothing to show us that Gabriel had ridden through. Of course, he very well could have, and maybe just a few feet to our right or left, but in our whiskey-fogged state neither Tom nor I would have noticed anyway.

"I gotta get down off this horse soon, Tom. I'm tired and sore and I need to pee. So when we get to those upper falls down there, let's rest 'em for a bit, okay? Then we'll just follow that river down. He'll be down there."

"I won't argue about taking a break, Stotts."

"He's probly at my house right now talking my dad into feeding him."

"I hope so."

I didn't like the way Tommy said that.

We both knew something was wrong. Something bad was going to happen.

But this one — he's always the happy one, isn't he? You want to always have friends like that, so if you're ever starving to death or freezing in the cold, you know he's gonna just say, "It ain't that bad."

I pulled a jacket out from my bag, and when Tommy saw me, he did the same. I could smell the rain coming, hear the occasional drumming of thunder behind us, and as we passed under the first stand of trees at the edge of the meadow the sky opened up, coughing thick, round, stinging drops of summer rain. Within a minute it had become as dark as twilight and we were both soaked to the skin. I kept my head down and watched the faucet-flow of water pour from my brim and run down Reno's shoulders.

"I never seen it rain so hard," Tom half mumbled. The sky

flashed white with lightning that seemed to strike just behind us, the clap of its thunder coming so sudden and loud it nearly created a wind that took away all air.

The horses were slick and dark with the rain, fur spiked and steamy, but they moved forward, however reluctantly, knowing or hoping that at least Tom and I had some purpose in our direction. We stopped under the thick tall trees by that upper run of water. Here we were protected from most of the rainfall, but Tommy and I were already as wet as we'd be if we had climbed right out of that raging river.

It was a relief to get down from the horses, to try to shake some of that miserable water out of my clothes, heavy and stuck to my skin like paint. I took off my jacket and wrung what seemed like a gallon from it. The falls, pouring through the crease of granite and down between huge boulders to the flatter place where I had camped, where the three of us had lunch on the way up, were howling with volume from all the water coming down on top of the mountain. A small tree, broken and twisted, floated past me, then lodged against a boulder above the falls before launching up and over like the broken arm of a catapult.

Tommy leaned against the tree trunk next to me. "We might need to wait a while or look for a way down that's not so steep. Arrow's gonna start slipping on those front shoes and I'm afraid he'll pull his knees."

"We could sit it out. It'll break soon. Sun's going down, I think." I sighed. "I'm sorry, Tom."

"What for? You pee on this tree right here where I'm leaning?"

I smiled. "No. I don't know. I just feel like I gotta say it. You got anything to eat?"

I thought about telling him about the phone call to his house the other night. It didn't matter now. I was sure it had been Jack Crutchfield, though.

"There's some wet jerky, probly."

The rain came harder, louder. Tommy rummaged through his bags for food and produced the jerky and a bag of chips with the top wadded shut. We ate. It wasn't cold, really, but my hands were icy and the food was good.

"I got some tobacco," Tom said.

"Any whiskey?"

"You drank it all, rummy." Tom packed a dip of tobacco behind his lip and handed the can to me.

I sat down against the tree and spit, pulling my knees up to my chest. "I'm cold."

"So am I. And I don't have anything dry after last night."

"Neither do I. You remember that?"

"I wasn't that drunk."

Tom sat down beside me.

"Not enough to sing again."

"Never."

I took my hat off and brushed my wet hair back. I thought about Luz, wondered where she was; if they were on their way back yet. We sat there, not saying anything, staring out at the river, the head of the falls, listening to the roar of the river competing with the roar of the storm.

"Like a horse pissing on a flat rock," Tommy said, disgusted.

"Like every horse in the state."

"The world."

The storm lasted for another hour, then finally broke and cleared to a hot and muggy evening. You could feel the steam rising from the forest floor, evaporating from the big slick rocks along the river. We were stiff and cold, huddled under that tree. Tommy was the first to rise, and made an attempt to brush away the mud on the seat of his jeans. I stood. My pants, stiff and heavy, rubbed and ached against my skin.

"Riding's gonna hurt," I said.

"I was thinking that," Tom said. "I wanna see you get up on that big horse of yours."

I spit. Reno was soaked, the saddle seat was wet and cold. I hauled myself up from the left stirrup and slung my right leg over my horse. I tried to settle in as gently as I could, but it did hurt, and I winced and Tommy grinned that coyote grin, his eyes gleaming and squinting under his rain-soaked hat brim.

I threw my canteen to him. "Here. Fill this up."

"With water, right?"

"Good one, Tom."

Tommy limped over to the edge of the river, balancing on a rounded baby's-head boulder at the top of the falls, dangling my canteen beside him. Reno turned and watched him go. And that was when Chase Rutledge, dark and wet, stepped out of the trees holding a little black pistol in his right hand, which he raised and pointed level to Tommy's head and then he fired.

Tommy spun around, legs twisting across one another, and landed hard and wet and heavy on his back, on the slick granite, making a dull and hollow thud, sending my canteen clattering away down the rock face of the falls.

TWENTY-FOUR

Everything was blurry and whirling like a dream. Like a bad dream. I started to move and Jack Crutchfield came up and grabbed me by the back of my pants and pulled me down right over Reno's hind. My head hit the ground hard. I started to black out. My hat tumbled away and I knew I was bleeding. I tried to push myself up onto my elbows and Reno startled and backed up, stepping solidly above my right knee, then bracing and pushing off.

I screamed and twisted under that weight. I felt something snap in my leg with an audible crack and Reno bolted forward. I think he knew he'd hurt me. I tried to sit up, and the pain was sickening, intense, washing over me in pulsing waves.

I could see Tommy's legs, bent at the knees, and moving like he was trying to push himself on his back, trying to slide away somehow. I could, even above the roar of the water, hear him moaning, soft and distant; saw his arm move up and across his body, then flop down like he was trying to cover himself, writhing.

I tried to get to my feet, but my right leg was broken and I couldn't will it to do anything. Jack stood behind me. He had a gun, too, pointed right at the top of my head. I knew we were going to die here, together. I couldn't watch Tommy die. I looked up toward the sun, sinking down behind the trees across the river. I tried to close my eyes, but they wouldn't stay.

Blood ran, warm and thick, through my hair and down my neck, feeling like clotting egg yolks, spreading out like a pink mold in the wetness of my T-shirt.

Chase walked over to Tom, still holding that little black wheel gun straight out in front of him; the same gun I had thrown into the trees across from the church — how long ago?

He stood there, I could see his face clearly, eyes fixed on Tom, looking down.

"You don't look so good, Buller," he said. Then I saw him spit on Tommy.

Tommy's legs twitched.

"You better watch this, Stotts," Chase yelled over to me. "'Cause you know where I'm putting this gun right before I shoot you."

Then Chase bent slightly and put the gun right up to Tom's forehead.

And from somewhere in the trees behind me I saw a plum-sized rock whirring and spinning in the air, arcing a curve and then striking Chase Rutledge in the temple. The gun fluttered from his hand, bouncing off into the water, and Chase clutched his head, already spurting purple blood. He tripped across Tommy's bent knees and toppled, trying to stop his fall with his hands against the slickness of the rocks, headfirst into that rushing white water.

"Jack! Jack!" Chase screamed from the water. I just saw one arm flail up and then he was gone.

Jack Crutchfield ran after him, tucking his gun into his pants. He stopped for a second over Tommy, glancing down at him with a grim and hateful sneer, then looked into the river.

"Jack!"

Jack stepped down through the rocks at the edge, his head lowering from my view like he was descending a staircase until I couldn't see him anymore.

I heard Tommy say a kind of "huh?" — soft and low, like he was trying not to wake someone up. I pushed myself around and tried to get my left leg up under me. It hurt so bad. Then I saw Gabe moving quietly between the trees. He looked at me. I was so relieved to see my friend, so thankful for that arm of his, that for a minute I forgot about how hurt I was.

He went to Arrow and took Tommy's gun out. He pulled the slide back, ejecting a round. There already was one in the chamber. He walked by me and brushed my hair with his hand, picked up my hat, holding the gun toward the water. My blood painted his upturned fingers. He rubbed it between them.

"God, Troy."

"Go see Tom. Please, Gabey. Go see to him."

Gabriel, every bit as wet as we were from that afternoon storm, walked silently toward Tommy, like he was standing on ice, holding the gun with both hands, pointing to where Jack had gone down to the water.

"Gabey. Gabey," Tommy said faintly. Gabriel looked down at him quickly, but kept his eyes fixed on the river. He walked over to the edge, standing up straight, and I could see him very clearly, looking down the rushing course of the water.

"They're gone," he said, and turned back to me. "They're both gone."

I tried to pull myself toward the river.

"Tom! Tommy!"

He wasn't moving.

I scooted along the wet ground, dragging my right leg, digging in with my fingernails and kicking myself forward with my left foot. Gabriel knelt down beside Tommy, looked over to see me crawling, set the gun down carefully at his side. He touched Tommy's hand, resting on his belly.

"Tommy?" he said.

I could hardly see, the tears were pooling in my eyes. I felt snot running from my nose, the blood warm and slippery on my neck, and the pain in my leg so intense I could vomit. I made it to Tommy's side. His leg straightened out on the ground. I propped myself up so I could see his face. I was crying, sure I was seeing my friend shot to death.

He opened his eyes. The bullet had passed clean through his shoulder, just above his collarbone. I forgot about my leg and grabbed his head with both of my hands.

"Oh my God, Tom. I thought he shot you in the head."

I brushed his hair back from his brow, amazed there was no bullet hole there.

"Did I get shot?" he said weakly.

"Clean through," Gabe said. "That's better, I think." Gabe pressed down on Tommy's shoulder, wadding up his shirt as he did. "You're bleeding bad, Tom. We should sit you up." He started to pull Tommy up, then let him lay back when he yelled with the hurt. Gabriel exhaled a deep breath and looked nervously downriver again. "Jesus, he was going to kill you. Kill you both."

"Gabey saved you," I said. "You shoulda seen that rock he threw. I never seen anyone get hit so hard in the head. It sounded like a balloon popping. I could kiss you, Gabey."

And Gabe just looked at us both and said, "How am I gonna get you down?"

I leaned away from them and threw up.

"It feels like my leg's caved in." I put my head down on my outstretched arm. I felt sleepy, but knew I should try to keep my eyes open. I saw the brim of my hat lying on the ground where it had fallen as I crawled across that slick granite, and I could see it was soaked through with blood from the inside.

"Did I get shot?" Tommy said again.

"You'll be okay, Tom. You'll be okay," Gabe said. "I'd just like to know how the hell I'm going to get you two down from here."

"What happened to them?" I said.

"They went in the water," Gabe said. "I don't know. They're just gone."

"You keep that gun, Gabey," I said.

"You keep it, Troy. Just in case," he said. "Their horses are tied back over there." He nodded in the direction he had thrown that rock from. "I'm gonna see if they got anything there that can help with Tommy's bleeding. Keep the gun here. I'll be right back."

Gabe picked up the gun and set it down on the ground near my left hip and ran off into the woods, leaving us both lying there, bleeding and breathing heavily, by the side of that roaring water.

"Stotts, I think I need to sit up. I can't feel my arm." Tommy tried to push himself up to a sitting position with his left hand. I pushed his back, and as he sat up I saw all that blood, covering his back and pooled up where he had been lying. His face was white.

I pulled myself up next to him.

"That's not good, Tom."

He rolled his eyes to me, keeping his neck rigid. "You got blood all over. Turn your head."

I could barely move it, it felt like I opened it up when I did.

"You got a cut back there at least four inches," he said. "Deep, too."

"That's not good, either." I touched his shoulder lightly and said, "Does that hurt much?"

"I'm on fire. I feel it in my arm and my back and under my ribs. It's hard to breathe."

"I'm gonna press on it back here. It's bleeding pretty good."

I reached around his shoulder with my right hand and pressed my palm down over the spot where the small hole showed in the back of his T-shirt. I put my fingers over the top to squeeze the other side and Tommy jolted and took a couple short painful breaths.

"I'm sorry."

"How many times you gonna say that today, Stotts? I'm sorry, too. What happened to you there?" He was looking at my legs. My right foot twisted in, looking disconnected.

"Reno broke my leg."

"I swear to God I always knew he was trying to kill you." Tommy pulled his knees up to his chest, but it hurt and he stretched his legs back out in front of him again. He sighed. "What a mess. We're all messed up, bud."

"You'll be okay, Tom. You have to be okay." I wiped my face on the back of my left hand.

Gabriel emerged from the woods, a leather saddlebag slung over his shoulder.

"I let those horses go. Just in case they . . ." He stopped. "I got some good stuff."

Tom half whispered, "Fix us up, Doctor Gabey."

Gabe sat down eagerly in front of us and opened the bag.

"First things first." He produced a half-full bottle of Jack Daniel's. He unscrewed the top and gave it to Tommy. Tommy took the bottle in his left hand, head still bent forward in pain, unable to lift his chin.

"I'm supposed to remind you about that," I said.

"Please let me have some. I promise not to sing." He tipped the bottle, chin down, so the whiskey spilled a bit down into his lap. He winced as he swallowed, but he took three big gulps, then lowered his head and passed the bottle to me. He turned it over and looked at the black-and-white label. "It's even got your number on it."

I love you so much, Troy Stotts. Rider number seven.

"They didn't have anything for first aid or nothing," Gabe said.

"They had this." I drank and gave the bottle back to Tom.

"Give me that knife of yours."

"It's in my back pocket," I said and shifted so Gabe could unclip it.

Gabriel unfolded the knife and began to cut away at Tom's shirt around the wound. I pulled my hand back with the bit of shirt sticking to my palm from the glue of his blood. The holes were small and angry-looking, still oozing blood, with the flesh around them appearing yellow and dead.

"It looks like that was a twenty-two, maybe," I said. "It's small."

Tom took another swallow and turned his chin down, trying to see the hole in the front of his shoulder. "It doesn't feel small to me."

He was feeling better now, so was I. I took the bottle from him and drank some more whiskey.

"Give me that," Gabe said, and I swear I saw Tommy look up with shock in his eyes when Gabriel took the bottle from me. And I realized Gabriel wasn't going to drink it, but when he saw us both look at him like that, I think he changed his mind. He held his breath and tipped the bottle up.

And he didn't even wince or make any sound, either. He wiped his mouth and then turned the bottle over and poured some whiskey on Tom's shoulder. Tommy just about jumped out of his clothes, too, when that alcohol hit the wounds.

"Sorry," Gabe said. He pulled some socks and a T-shirt out of the bag. "Sorry about using my socks, but they're clean." He wadded up the socks, putting one on each side of Tom's shoulder, and I held them there while Gabe tore at the T-shirt and tied it around Tommy's neck and looped under his armpit tightly.

"You're next," he said to me, and he got up and walked around behind me. I heard him pour whiskey on a piece of shirt cloth and I braced myself.

"That needs stitches. I don't think there's anything we can do about that cut."

Then he pressed the whiskey-soaked cloth against the back of my head. I jerked forward from the stinging, and it hurt most when he wiped away the blood that had clotted in my hair. I could feel tears leaking from my eyes.

"That's bad," he said.

"It'll be worse if you used up all the whiskey."

"Sorry, Troy. We don't have anything else that's clean." Gabriel pulled his T-shirt off and capped the collar over my bloody hair, then tied it back behind my head. I must have looked like some bloodied hermit, lost and wandering down from these mountains. I stared at him, a bare-chested blur while he worked over me, watching that little gold cross of his dance like a puppet from his neck. The shirt smelled like him; it made me feel better; and I felt the whiskey and the *thrum thrum thrum* of my heart and the waves of pain and nausea flushing over me. I listened to the churning hum of the water rushing by, the wind whooshing through the trees. And that cross swinging and twinkling in between me and the river and the sky, like a hypnotist's bauble.

He handed the bottle around to me. "You better wear your hat, Troy. It might keep it together till we get some help." He placed the hat back on my head after wiping it out with his bare hand, tilted back with the front of the brim angled up.

Gabe looked down at his open palms, creases lined black with our blood. His mouth hung open; his stare fixed. He jerked his hands down slightly as if to shake them clean. He closed his eyes tightly.

I drank and gave the bottle to Tommy. I could feel the rush of the water through the granite ground, the sound vibrating through my body.

"Do you think I could splint that leg?"

"I think you could cut it off right about now if you wanted to."

"I feel good now. Thanks, Gabey," Tom said. "I think I could help you if you need me."

Tom set the bottle down between us.

"Let's get a splint on him and then we'll make a sling for your arm, cause that ride's gonna hurt you pretty bad. But we need to get down."

Gabriel turned and walked back into the trees, looking for straight branches, I guessed. It only took him a minute and then he returned with two sticks he was measuring against his own leg. I took another drink, and somehow I almost felt like laughing. I looked down at Tommy's gun, still resting beside me.

"Here, Gabey." I handed him the gun. "Put this away."

Gabriel ejected the magazine, then the chambered round. He reloaded it and tucked it into his side pocket. That was pretty smart, I thought.

"One reason you should wear a belt, Troy." Gabe unbuckled his belt and slipped it out of the loops on his pants. "I'm taking yours, too, Tommy. Sorry. Now we're gonna both be like this guy, always pulling up our pants," And Gabriel took Tom's belt off of him, then laid them down, and slid them under my leg. I gasped a little as he fed the ends under my broken leg. After he laid the branches on either side of my knee, he looped the belts through.

"It's gonna hurt, Troy. I gotta pull 'em tight."

He opened the Dawson knife and held it in his mouth. Then he pulled the first belt tight. I threw my head back and bit my bottom lip so I wouldn't scream. Tom took a drink, then handed the bottle back to me.

"You both could probly stop drinking that stuff now. You don't want to end up worse off."

Gabe punched a hole in the belt with the knife so it would stay tight, then he did the same thing below my knee.

"I don't know how good that is, or if it's even good at all, 'cause I don't even know if we'll be able to get you up on a horse."

"If you have to, just leave me here. But leave the rest of the whiskey. Tommy needs help worse than me."

"Shut up. No one's leaving you. You both need doctors." He opened the saddlebag again. "Just shut up." Then he hammered his fist down on top of the bag.

He looked at me for an instant, but I couldn't really tell what it was I saw in his eyes.

"It's okay, Gabey."

He pulled out his T-shirt, still wet from his being thrown in the pond the night before, and cut the bottom half of it off.

He took a deep breath. "This one's dirty. Probly smells bad, too."

"It'll keep me awake."

"I'm gonna put this under your wrist, then you grab your own shirt like this." Gabe clenched his fist over his heart, showing Tom how he wanted him to steady his arm. "Then I'll slip the other end over your neck. It's gonna hurt, but it'll feel better if you don't move that arm."

"Okay."

After Gabe put the sling on Tom, he cut the shirt behind Tommy's neck, then tightened it with a knot to hold his arm level. I was amazed seeing Gabriel move like he was, without being afraid, without confusion. He was someone else now.

I felt sick again, my head swimming like it had been pulled from my body; my legs somewhere else, too.

"I'm gonna bring the horses over."

"We'll wait here," I said, straight-mouthed and drained.

Reno had a guiltless look on his face like horses always do, even after they've done something terrible. Gabriel looked determined, like he was ready to go, even though I really didn't believe I'd get up on a horse. But I wasn't going to argue with him, either.

"I'm going to ride Reno," Gabe said. "We'll try to get you on Dusty first." Dusty was almost two hands shorter than Reno, so it made sense to me, even if he might as well be a giraffe as far as I was concerned at that moment.

Gabe held his left hand out to Tommy. "Are you ready to try? 'Cause I'm gonna need your help."

Tommy took a gulp of whiskey and passed the last of it to me. He grabbed on to Gabe's hand and it took him two tries and a couple painful grunts to get up onto his feet. He wobbled a little and Gabe caught him by the arm.

"Just let me stand here for a while."

"Tell me when," Gabe said and he stood there, holding on to Tom.

Tom nodded and I drained the last of the bottle. I didn't think I'd feel my leg now, but I was wrong about that. Tommy grabbed me under my armpit and Gabe pulled on my left arm. I got my left foot under me and pushed. Then I felt pain like a hot sword cutting through my leg right into my spine. I screamed and they just kept pulling me up. I saw darkness closing in around my vision and they pulled and pulled and then I was up on my left leg, dizzy. I would have fallen forward, but Gabe hugged me around my chest as Tommy wavered and paled beside me.

"You'll have to get up on his right, then sit sideways and try to swing your good leg over the top."

"If I kick him and he bolts, you might as well shoot me."

"I'll hold him. You'll do it. You have to."

The sun was gone. It would be dark soon. Tom and Gabe held me up so, dangling between them, I could get my left foot into the right stirrup and push myself up to sit on Dusty. I almost fell over backwards, but Gabe caught me by the pants as he held the reins to steady his horse. With Gabe pushing my left foot up and Tommy holding Dusty, I managed to get seated in the saddle, already wondering if I'd be able to get off.

Tommy hugged Dusty's neck and leaned into him.

"I don't know," he said. "I don't know if . . ."

The bandage Gabe had tied onto his shoulder was already seeping blood.

"Get up on your horse, Tom," Gabe said coldly. "We got to go now."

Tommy shook his head like he was trying to wake up, and Gabe put his arm around him. "Come on, Tom."

"It hurts." I saw tears on Tommy's face. It was one of the worst things I've ever seen. I looked away.

"I bet it does. I bet it does." Gabe walked Tommy over to Arrow and lifted his foot up into the stirrup. "I'll push you up. Come on."

Tom clenched his jaw and boosted himself as Gabe pushed him up by his seat. When he was in the saddle, I saw his shoulders heave a little. He was crying silently, his head down, face hidden under the brim of his hat, squeezing his eyes with his left hand. He nudged Arrow and they started off, following the path we had taken up here just days ago, ahead of us, toward home. Dusty followed, while Reno gave a nervous chuckle, wondering why I was leaving; and finally Gabe got up on Reno and caught up to us.

"I'm not going to make it," Tommy said. "I need to stop. I need to stop now."

"I'll carry you in. One way or another. You can't stop, Tom," Gabe said.

Tom kept his head down. It was getting dark, darker still under those tall trees covering the lower slopes coming down into the foothills.

"I want you both to know when we get back, we're gonna have to tell 'em what happened," Gabe said.

"What did happen?" Tom said.

"I fired my rifle by accident when Reno stumbled on me," I said. "That's what happened, Gabe. It was an accident."

"Why do we have to lie, Troy?" Gabe said.

"'Cause if we say what happened, then we'll have to tell about what Chase tried to do to Luz." I winced, squeezed shut my eyes. "We don't need to say that, do we?"

"Well, what about Chase and Jack then?"

"We never saw 'em."

"I never," Tom said quietly. His head was down, chin turned away from the side where he'd been shot.

I ached. I felt so bad for Tommy, wondering how he would make it back, wondering what my father would say when he saw us. Gabe was silent for a while, then said, "Then I never saw 'em neither."

And Gabriel Benavidez grew that day in sizes and directions that I wouldn't have believed if I hadn't seen it with my own eyes.

When we got through the fence to the apple orchard, I was wondering if Tommy was still alive; he hadn't said anything at all for the longest time. Gabriel rode on ahead to the house to get my father and call for help, while Tom and I took our horses at a slow walk toward the barn.

I was trembling and I couldn't control it. My leg felt like it was dragging along the ground beneath the trampling horses, and I was more scared than I'd ever been in my life, not from what I'd seen happen up on the mountain, but from what I was watching happen before me as we made our way through the dark orchard. I wanted to scream at Tommy and wake him up, make him look at me so I could see his eyes, but he just kept his head down as his hunched shoulders shook and heaved.

And I told him, *Tommy, you're crying.* And he wiped at his face and said softly that he was sorry and he was real cold, and I said, *I'm sorry, too.* I was so sorry. Because I'd never seen Tom Buller like that and I was scared I'd never see him like himself, either, smiling that coyote grin and being so wild. So I tried to joke that after he got back from the doctor's if he could bring me something to eat and something to pee in because I didn't think I'd ever be able to get down off that horse. But he didn't say anything, didn't move. He just kept his head down and let the horse go along with mine toward the barn.

I bet I'm gonna walk like you, now. Maybe I should get a tattoo of a horse.

He jerk-nodded his head. I couldn't tell if he was sobbing, trying not to laugh, or just agreeing.

I remember seeing all the lights coming on around my house. I saw Tommy's back, soaked with blood, blackening in the thickest spots where it was drying. I knew he was almost dead when I saw that, and I could hardly swallow. I remember hearing the footsteps, quickening out to see where we were, the soft, small footfalls of Gabriel, almost floating, and the heavier, panicked ones of my father.

I swear I'm gonna get that tattoo. After this. You take me there, bud.

Things happen for a reason. It's all put in motion before we're set down on this world. It's cruel and unfair and I don't bother asking why more than once, because I never got an answer yet. Tom Buller knew that about me, but I never knew what Tom Buller believed in, even though I wanted to ask him about it plenty of times.

And I swear I saw Rose and my mother and the same little boy Tommy saw in his house, and now I knew who he was, standing out in the faintness of the dark, looking at our pitiful and pain-wracked bodies atop those tired, frothing horses, their nostrils flaring at the smells of feed and home. And I thought I was saying to those ghosts I was home now, and, please, could they help me; could they help me stop hurting, could they help Tommy come back and make everything else go away, because I could let them go now, but they'd have to let go of me first, and I was ready for that. And I could hear the horses breathing that same *thrum thrum thrum* of the blood pulsing through my ears, the river churning, the hooves scraping along the ground. And in that orchard of ghosts I saw dozens of other people standing behind them, most of them bent and ugly, frightening; and I thought the horses can't see them and I don't know if Tommy's even got his eyes open. And I thought, as a dark cat moved from tree to tree, following us, *Those are just trees, right?*

And I'm gonna get it right here under my heart. And then we're gonna catch that horse we set free, Tom

I know I don't know anything about love that I can rightly express in words. I know I loved Luz and I wanted her, and wanted to see her so bad then and it was a terrible thing to reckon with as my head swam in the flowing pain of my body. And I know I loved Gabriel and I loved Tommy and it was a desperate and awful thing for me to look at him, slumped over and bloody, and me wanting so bad to take his hurt away and see him grin that coyote grin and those squinting, gleaming black eyes; instead, to see that life fading from him with each shallow, stuttered breath, the brim of his hat moving so slightly up, then down, up, then down. And I said, *Tommy, Tommy,* and the hat brim just dipped and rose, up then down, slowly and slower, *I know you can hear me and I can see the house, Tom, and I can hear 'em coming for us, bud.* Up and down, the front of his hat wearily pointed at the horse's neck. Up and then down. Fading.

Tommy Buller was dying and there was nothing I could do about it.

And I think I said to him, *Tommy, you got that charm you made from the snake rattle and the bullet? You're not dying, Tommy. You're not dying.* And I thought, Snake medicine is change. It must feel so good to break out of the old skin and come out whole and new and fresh again and feel everything for the first time all over. *You're not dying, Tommy.*

And then, looking at him as those tired horses dragged us through the old orchard, I thought I could see through him, could see stars and trees and shadows where he was and I knew he was fading away, but like all those ghosts, I just kept trying to tell myself, *It's the whiskey, I hit my head too hard, it's my leg, it's the whiskey, it's the whiskey.* And Tommy was crying and so I said, *Man, we drank too much whiskey back there so now suck it up, Tom, it's almost over, how you doing?*

I saw Reno in the light of the barn and I thought, *What's he doing there?* Like I was in a dream, but I knew I wasn't. And then I looked down and saw the buckskin I was riding, the tree branches cinched with my friends' belts around a leg I couldn't believe was ever part of me.

We made it, Tom.

My father ran toward us, carrying a telephone in his hand. I thought, *I need to say a lot of things to you that I never said since that night, since I left; and I keep postponing them or letting the chance get away; next time, next time.* But things always happen for a reason, and I swear that's the one thing I do know.

And that's all I remember about that ride down from the mountain with Tom Buller.

My dad's coming. We made it.

TWENTY-FIVE

Tom Buller died that night.

* * *

I don't think we ever got over what happened to us on that mountain. I still think about it every day; and probly every few minutes, I see myself looking out at the sunlight glinting off the leaves on the other side of the river and Chase Rutledge raising that gun, the *crack!* of the firing, the flash of sparks and white smoke like a circus cannon, and then Tommy spinning and twisting down to the ground.

Boys like Tommy Buller should never die, even if it seems like they always do somehow. He never came back from that mountain, not even in my dreams, and such a big part of me died with him that I felt like I was hollowed out for the longest time.

I can still feel the emptiness now, a constant ache; a feeling that I can't catch my breath because I've been held under ice water for so long I can't loosen up to take the smallest swallow of air.

And maybe Luz was right about me not telling my friends how I really feel, sometimes. But sometimes the words just want to stay put.

She came to see me when I was in the hospital. I was so busted up the doctors needed to put metal pins and a bar inside my leg. It felt so good to see that door open and watch her peek her face in and smile. I raised my head up from the bed and she just floated in and brushed my hair back and kissed me on the mouth and then again on my forehead.

"Troy."

"I'm wearing a dress."

She slid a chair beside my bed and put her hand on mine.

"Luz, will you kiss me again?"

She smiled. "Are you hooked up to a heart monitor?"

"No. Just something to pee in."

She pressed her face down next to me on the pillow and kissed me again.

"I'd slide over for you, but I can't move."

She looked down at the shining metal rods that passed right through the wrappings on my leg and into the bones.

"Does it hurt?"

"It feels better right now."

She held her hand up over my leg. I swear I could feel something coming out of her skin.

"You can touch it. Everyone else here does, and I don't even know 'em."

She touched my leg, just so lightly: the weight of a snowflake. She rested her hand on my chest.

"I came and sat with you last week. You were sleeping, though."

"You should've woke me up."

The angel is sleeping in the woods.

"I held your hand. I kissed your face. You looked so beautiful sleeping, Troy. I think I stayed here for two hours and then they came and told me I had to go. And then I cried."

"I been here for more than a week?"

"A week yesterday."

"I never had a dream. All that time."

"You were really sick."

"I guess." I put my hand over hers and pressed it to me. "And Gabey?"

"He's here. I made him wait outside in the hall."

I smiled. "I bet you made 'im."

"Troy. I want you to know this," she said, and I looked, unblinking, into her clear eyes. I would believe anything she would ever tell me, even if it were impossible. "There will never be anyone else. Not for me."

I whispered. "I love you, Luz."

"Tommy loved you, too, Troy. He was good. He was a good boy."

"I know." I could hardly say it. I looked away.

And she kissed me again and said, "I better go get him."

And I was scared to see him again; afraid that we could never go back to being those boys who had talked so loud around that fire; that those boys had somehow disappeared. And when he came in, shuffling his feet on the cold, slick floor, he just filed up to the side of my bed like a mourner at a wake, looking at me like I was so fragile, and I know I was looking at him the same way. And neither of us would put into words the thing that was so horrible and thick between us. It was as if there was some stinking carcass, bleeding, just hanging down from the ceiling; and we were all too caught up in just being nice and pretending not to see it.

Gabe didn't say anything for the longest time, and then he looked down at the bars and screws jutting from my leg and said, "Damn. Frankenstotts."

"Yeah. They hurt." I breathed. "I can't stand it here, Gabey." I looked at the window. "They might let my dad take me home tomorrow. But I'm gonna miss school for a while when it starts."

I looked him in the eyes, those eyes cool and pale like his sister's. I needed to tell him something, but I couldn't. I needed to get up out of that bed and shake him, make him tell me to shut up, or punch me, but I knew it wouldn't happen.

I cried when they left. And then I slept.

✦   ✦   ✦

They found those boys' bodies a few days later. It was a horrible thing, from what I'd heard. They found Jack Crutchfield's first, floating in the lake. Then they found Chase Rutledge's, snagged in some trees by the flats above the bridge where the water had gotten lower.

It was driving me crazy. For the months that I spent at home, supposedly recovering, doing nothing but schoolwork, Luz visited often; I knew she had to sneak out of the house to do it because Mr. Benavidez was trying to hold on to her so tight, even though she was slipping away from him. But every time I tried to call her brother he wasn't home, or he would make up some obvious excuse to get off the phone. She told me that her father didn't want them coming to see me; that he said that I needed this time to be with my father and heal, but it was more than that, and I believed Mr. Benavidez was afraid that if Gabe and Luz came near me bad things would happen to them, like they did to me and Tom. He didn't come right out and say it, I knew he never would. But just thinking about Gabey, and wondering — was he mad at me or just scared? — was making me crazy.

Gabriel never told Luz the whole story about what happened to us because he thought it was all his fault and that he did something horrible. He told her about everything except how he threw the rock that hit Chase and made him fall into that water; he just said that Chase tripped over Tommy's legs just when he was about to shoot him again, so Luz thought it was all some kind of miracle. But I did sit down with Carl months afterwards, just before my seventeenth birthday. We drank beers and I told him the whole story, even about the day that Chase stole our clothes and Gabriel shot him. But I never told anyone else the whole story, not even my own father, even though I started to at least a half-dozen times and then just let it go. And Carl smoked about two packs of cigarettes listening to me and finally said it was probably just as well that I didn't tell anyone else, because it didn't matter now anyway.

TWENTY-SIX

It was almost winter before I was fit to go back to work at the ranch. And when I did, Mr. Benavidez called me in to see him right away. I thought he was going to fire me, but he didn't. I guess I thought the whole world was mad at me, and maybe I was expecting to be punished. I don't know.

I walked even more crooked than Tommy did from that snakebite, and the worst part about that was that it hurt me to run, which I tried to do the same day they took that cast off of me. But I didn't care about the pain, I would run anyway.

And I didn't blame Reno, either.

So maybe that horse medicine we all had that night at the edge of the pond worked at putting forgiveness in me, but I never saw myself as holding a grudge anyway. Especially against a horse.

"It's nice to see you up and looking like your old self. Come in, Troy," Mr. Benavidez said at the door to his office. He shook my hand, almost carefully, as I thought about what my old self must have looked like.

I was a little nervous, but I didn't care anymore if he wanted to fire me, or even if he told me that I could never see Luz again, because I already knew what I was going to do; no matter what. I held my hat in front of me and limped over to the leather chair in front of his desk.

"I don't want you to worry about anything, Troy. You seem nervous. I've talked with Gabriel and Luz. And, well, Gabriel thinks the world of you. I'm sure you know, he thinks of you as his brother."

I looked down at my hands.

"I'm ready to work."

"Then you should go."

I stopped at the door, my back turned to Mr. Benavidez as he lit a cigar. "Your son saved my life. That's all. We would've both died without him."

I heard him puff that cigar. Without turning around, I left, closing the door behind me. And I thought, *That old fool probably thinks his son did something wrong again. He doesn't even know his own son. Or his daughter.*

I hadn't seen Luz in weeks, and I felt like it was making me sick. I hadn't slept, and every time I thought about her my mouth would dry up and I'd get that lump in my throat. So I'd call her, but hearing her voice would even make me feel crazier about getting out, just so I could see her again.

And she was waiting for me just outside the front door of that big house. It was windy and clear and cold. The willows had lost nearly all of their leaves, scattered like yellow scales and feathers below them. I had buttoned up my coat and was straightening my hat when I saw her there.

"You look good," she said.

"You look better," I said. "It hurts sometimes. Like today." I looked right at her. Her hair was down, the color of those willow leaves, spilling over the upturned collar of her coat. Her eyes were shining, smiling at me. "I miss you, Luz. I miss you so much. Being here with you. I hope everything's gonna be okay now."

She grabbed my hand. "Can I walk with you over to the barns?"

"I bet your dad's watching."

"I know he is," she said. "I told him I'm going to see you. That's all."

We walked out the little gate, past the willows where Gabriel and I had dug that fort, holding hands. I could almost smell the cigar, feel his eyes on my back. And at that moment I almost wished the barns were a hundred miles away, just so we could walk like that, with him watching, wondering about me, wondering about what had happened; so I held on tight to his daughter's hand and resisted the urge I had to glance back over my shoulder to the window where I knew he'd be.

"I'm coming back to school next week, Luz."

"There go my grades."

We were out of sight of the house now. "Can I kiss you?"

She grabbed my collar with both of her hands and pulled herself into me, combing her fingers through my hair, over the spot where I had all those stitches.

"It's all healed," I said. "But look, my hair's shorter there. And it's brown." I took my hat off and turned around, and felt her fingers working through my hair, parting it to see the scar. She raised up on her toes and kissed me there.

"I need to talk to Gabey," I said.

We started on toward the stables. "I want you to, Troy. He's not doing good."

"I knew it. I know. I'll take him out on a ride. Maybe tomorrow after work. Will you tell him for me? Tell him to be ready, okay? Make him go."

"He needs that."

"So do I. I haven't even been up on a horse . . ." I didn't finish. Didn't need to.

✦ ✦ ✦

I took the truck and drove to Holmes that night.

After all, I did remember making that promise to Tom when we rode through that orchard of ghosts the night we came down from the mountain.

In his things, I'd found a picture of a horse he had drawn. It looked like that stallion he had taken from Rose. I could tell Tommy put a lot of work into it, and although I was scared about the tattooing, Tom's drawing was beautiful. All in black, running, with his head down and his hooves all splayed out and stretching for the ground, like he was moving fast, his mane and tail spraying back behind him. It looked exactly like how that horse ran when we set him free.

They put that horse on my left rib cage, right below my heart, and it took almost two hours to finish. All the while, I felt Tommy sitting over me, grinning, as I stretched shirtless out on the table, watching the artist work with that vibrating bee-stinger needle, hearing Tom asking *Does it hurt* about a dozen times and spitting tobacco. I stared right up at the ceiling, counting the black marks on the rotting foam tiles there, and silently said *no, no,* because it didn't hurt like my broken leg, like seeing Tommy dying, but it hurt pretty bad and the pain was worse the closer it got to being finished.

The artist taped clear plastic wrap over it when he was finished, and blood seeped from its edges. I looked at it in the mirror, dizzy and numb from that pain, like scraping the flesh away to my bones. I liked that horse even more than when I had seen it on the paper where Tommy had drawn it.

I paid and left. I'd stowed some cold beers in the truck and I drank two before starting back for home on that dark stretch of empty dirt road.

The angel is sleeping in the woods.

I left my shirt off so I wouldn't get blood on it; and so I could admire that horse from time to time.

I had spent four months trying to figure out the sense in what had happened, but I never got close to knowing. I pulled the truck over in the dark, looked down at the horse inked into my body, and opened a can of tobacco.

Maybe some things you're just not supposed to know. And you try to figure them out and you just get frustrated when you should just forget them and move on. 'Cause you'll never figure out why you have to see the people you love go away and disappear. I spit out the window, the icy night air raising bumps on my naked skin.

I tried to forget. I tried so hard not to ask why again.

Maybe sometimes a boy'll throw a rock in the water, and the ripples that it makes will rock a boatful of fishermen on the other side of the world, and they'll all look at each other and say, "What was that?"

And maybe every one of them will have a different explanation, but they'll all be wrong. And who would know?

It was cold. I rolled the window up again.

✦ ✦ ✦

One day, I told myself, I would tell my father the whole truth about me and Tommy and Gabe and Luz. But, months later, when he asked about it, about what happened to us all that day, I just said, "Nothing."

TWENTY-SEVEN

Gabriel was tightening Dusty's saddle when I walked Reno into the big barn behind the Benavidez house. I could just see his silhouette cutting black against the bright light at the opposite end of the breezeway. He straightened up when he heard Reno and I could feel myself just about light up when I saw him. I hadn't seen him since I was in the hospital, months before.

And all that time I wondered why Gabe didn't want to see me, what he was scared of now, because he didn't look scared on the mountain. So I told myself that maybe it was just Gabe's way of trying to get rid of his own ghosts.

I grabbed him by the shoulders and hugged him hard, and he squeezed back, only not so tight.

"Gabey, where you been?"

"At home. Mostly."

"I missed you. I missed you so much, Gabey. You okay?"

"I thought I'd get us in more trouble. I thought you were mad."

I took my hat off and held it in my hanging right hand. "Why? 'Cause you got taller than me?" I reached over and touched the top of his head. It looked like he grew at least four inches in those months.

"Well. You need to eat more."

He had a new hat, hooked on the horn of his saddle. A gray, flat-brimmed Stetson. I picked it up. "This is a nice one," turning it around in my hands. It was just how I liked them.

"I liked my old one better. But it got too . . . I don't know. There was blood on it. This one's too stiff. It makes me feel like a clothes store dummy." He took it from me and pressed it down on his head.

"We'll get it broke in. And dirty." I put mine on, too. "I guess that's something about black ones, 'cause you know mine was dripping with blood from this thing. But I kept it anyway." And I touched the back of my head.

"Well, how are you now?"

"I'm good," I said. "But this is the first time I rode Reno . . ." and I stopped myself from finishing, because he knew. "You ready to ride?"

"That's why I'm here. And she told me to, anyway. Where do you want to go?"

"I don't know," I said. "It's getting late. How about we ride out to the bridge over the flats and back?"

We got up onto our horses and trotted them out of the barn and past the house, heading for the big redwood gate and to the dirt road leading into town.

It felt good to be back up on Reno. We didn't say anything at all until we had passed that big wooden gate with their name carved on the crossbeam, and I didn't mind; Gabe just followed along, determined and steady as the sun began turning every-thing orange and colder on that early December afternoon.

"And anyway, I asked you first and you still didn't answer," I said.

"Asked what?"

"I asked if you were okay."

Gabriel slowed Dusty to a walk. "I don't know. My dad said he's tired of me. He said when am I gonna grow up and stop moping around and stop counting on Troy Stotts to always protect me?"

I could tell that hurt him to say. "He doesn't know . . . well, he didn't mean it like that, Gabey."

"It felt like he did."

"I talked to him yesterday," I said. "And I told him. Told him how you saved my life. And that's all he needs to know, so he can stop wondering. 'Cause that's what happened and that's what I said to him."

"Thanks, then."

I never could figure out why Mr. Benavidez never thought Gabe was good enough.

I held Reno up, and Gabe stopped alongside. "I forgot to show you what I did." I pulled my jacket open and lifted up my shirt, so he could see that black horse on my ribs. He leaned close and looked at the lines, still gapped from the needlework.

"I bet that hurt."

"So bad," I said.

"You *are* crazy, Troy."

"Tommy drew him." I put my shirt down and Gabriel cocked his head away, looking at the clouds turning colors over the treetops in the west.

"He was crazy, too." And Gabriel sighed. He nudged Dusty's ribs and the horse started walking forward. "I could never do that, you know. I could never be like you or Tommy."

"I'm no Tom Buller. And who'd like you if you were?"

I kicked Reno into a trot and Gabe kept Dusty up along with us.

"Race to that tree?" I pointed. "You say go."

And Gabe said go and jabbed his heels into Dusty's ribs and the buckskin just about jumped out of his hooves. I had never seen Gabriel ride so loose and free on that horse, his one hand trailing behind him, relaxed, his fingers just tickling at Dusty's side. And I had never seen Gabriel from behind him in a race, either.

Reno snorted and huffed when we came to our stop, and Dusty just circled around in place, his head held back and his back feet shuffling, eyes wild and showing white like he was ready to do it again. I held my fist out to Gabe and he punched me.

"You better not've let me won," he said, challenging.

I exhaled through my nose. I just looked at him. "Gabey." I didn't need to say anything else. We could hear the river behind the trees. The sun was down now, the sky fading peach to blue to gray above us. The bridge was just up ahead.

I heard a car go by, driving over it. We walked the horses, still breathing hard, into the cover of the trees that opened up to the highway and that long, high bridge. We went out to the middle and stopped there, looking out over the calm flats just past where the falls, now at their lowest point, spilled into them.

"I know what's bugging you, Gabriel."

338

He got down from Dusty and stood at the rail, looking down, watching the water.

"What?"

I lowered down from Reno, my leg aching a little from working the past two days, and stood right beside him.

"Do you want me to say it?"

"Okay with me. Tell me."

"Well, okay then, I will." I looked out at the water, reflecting like obsidian in the fading light. "You think you killed those boys. That it was all your fault."

"Shut up, Troy."

"You said it was okay if I said it, Gabe. So I'm telling you." I took my hat off and brushed my hair back. I held my hat over the edge of the rail, spinning it in my fingers. "It's time I got a new one of these, I guess." I looked at Gabe and could see in the fading light that his eyes were filling with tears and I felt so bad for him. I breathed out of my mouth and went on, looking down at the black water moving underneath us. "Well, it wasn't your fault and you didn't kill 'em. It just happened, that's all. What you *did* saved me. I wouldn't be here if it wasn't for you."

Gabriel started crying. He lowered his head, staring down from the bridge into the blackness of the flats.

"I can't stop thinking about it," he said. "It hurts so bad. I'm so sorry."

"I'm sorry, too," I said. "I'm so sorry it makes me sick, Gabe, and there's nothing we can do about it. But it's not our fault what happened, and Tom knew that. I miss him so much. Why didn't you come see me ever?"

"'Cause I didn't want to think about Tommy."

We stood there in silence for the longest time. Gabe snuffled and wiped his nose across the back of his forearm. The horses stamped their forelegs nervously.

"They found Chase right over there." Gabriel wiped at his cheek and pointed across the water. "He was all messed up. They had the funerals together. My dad made me go. He said we had to do it for Clayton. And I saw all those people and the mothers and family there crying like that and I wished I was dead. I wanted to tell 'em I killed 'em. I killed 'em. That I murdered those boys. It feels like everyone knows it anyway."

I grabbed his right hand in both of my hands. "Gabriel, I owe you my life. You're my brother and I could never pay you back for that. You have to know that."

He exhaled heavily. He wiped his eyes with his palm, smearing wet all over his face.

"Gabey, you'd've done it again. I know you would. You didn't have a choice. Chase Rutledge *made* it happen that way."

He started sobbing and put his face in his hands, elbows on the railing of that high bridge. I put my arm on his shoulder and said, "Come on, man. You'll be okay." I thought about Tom Buller fading away in that orchard of the ghosts, crying, his hat just barely moving, just barely showing he was alive on that long ride down in the dark. And I remembered Gabriel in the dim gray drizzle on that distant morning, pushing my gun away from that lion.

He rubbed at his eyes and squeezed the bridge of his nose. "You remember how bad it rained that day? I hated that. It was the worst I ever seen. And it scared me, 'cause I was all alone and I was sure they were following me. I was so wet I thought I could've drowned on horseback."

"So were we."

"I got lost and I circled around. It was raining so hard I couldn't see where I was heading. I could barely keep my eyes open long enough to look if I was going into a tree. Then I found their horses and so I hid Dusty and followed them. I almost walked right into 'em. I thought for sure they'd seen me, but they didn't. I could hear 'em talking and Chase was saying how he was going to shoot me and Tommy first and make you watch 'em do it. I got so scared I didn't know what to do. But I followed 'em and I just stood there and watched when he walked up and shot Tommy. I couldn't believe what I was seeing. I just watched it happening. It was my fault what happened to Tommy. And I got mad and I picked up that rock. And when I saw him standing over Tommy like that I just thought his head was a catcher's mitt and I threw it so hard it hurt my arm."

"I heard it flying, Gabey. I knew it was you right away."

"I saw him go in the water. He tried to get up once but he slipped right under. 'Cause he was hurting before he even fell down, I hit him so hard. And I saw Crutchfield go after him and he got his hand on him once where it was deep and then he slipped, too, right into the fastest part. I knew they wouldn't make it out then."

I spit from the bridge, watched the blob tumble and spin until it was swallowed in the darkness.

"I never asked you," I said. "Why did you leave that morning when we were sleeping?"

Gabriel swallowed. "I knew they were after me. He said it that day, he was gonna get me for shooting him. I didn't want them to find you and Tom, so I left, thinking I'd make it down okay. I thought they'd follow me, not you and Tom. And I knew you guys would take care of yourselves. I never thought they'd do anything to you, I swear. I swear."

It was dark now. A car was coming down the highway, its headlights blinding us; so Gabe turned his head down to shade his eyes with his hat and I held mine up before me, a big black circle between me and the light, as we held on to our horses' reins. The red taillights disappeared off the bridge in the darkness at the other side.

"Well, I know what you did, Gabey, so put it out of your head. You saved my life." I looked at my hat. "I need a new one of these, too." And I let the hat go from the bridge and it floated down and became the blackness.

"Troy," he said, and looked back across the dark water. "I thought about killing myself even. I took a rope and rode out to that big mushroom oak by where we went shooting and I just sat under that tree all day and looked up at the cross on that hill and cried. Pretty stupid, huh? Then I just left that dumb rope coiled up there under that tree and came back home."

"Everyone's thought about killing themselves, I guess," I said. "But, Gabey, you gotta give yourself a break on this. 'Cause I already lost a brother and I don't think I can do it again. You can do this, Gabey. You have to. For me and Luz."

And then I looked at him and said, "Please."

He rubbed his eyes.

"We're gonna ride out and get that rope in the morning, Gabey," I said. "And you have to swear to me if you ever feel that bad again . . . that you're not *going* to feel that bad again, Gabey."

Gabe didn't say anything, just nodded his head a little. Just like Tommy nodding his head, so barely, on that dark ride down.

"Look," I said, pulling back the sleeve of my jacket. "Remember this?" I showed him the little scar on my right wrist. "The horse medicine? We're all brothers, right? If one of us dies, the other two die a little bit, too. No, a lot. I know it, and you do, too. That's why you did what you did up at the river, too. You as much saved yourself as you did me, only you weren't thinking that then."

"I have bad dreams now," he said. "It's hard to stop thinking about it."

"I gave up trying. 'Cause I don't think you ever *do* stop thinking about it. It's just, after a while, those ghosts just don't seem as scary. But they never really go away." I put my hand on the back of his neck and rubbed. I felt so horrible for what Gabriel had suffered; what we all had suffered, even Chase. Reno pushed at my shoulder with his nose, tired of standing on the asphalt of the bridge for so long. "Come on. You ready to ride back home now?"

"I don't want to. But, yeah."

We got onto our horses and rode, in that dark, cold night, off the bridge in the direction from which we had come.

It hadn't really rained much or snowed at all yet this year. It would be a dry winter. Working would be easier, at least. We rode slowly. Something huge and heavy and dark was hanging over my friend Gabriel Benavidez and I hoped he knew that all he needed was to be with someone who had been there, to let him know what he did was right. And I realized that Gabriel, the boy I remembered running around in diapers and nothing else, who dug that fort with me and got me in trouble, who dropped the gun and almost killed us that day Tommy got snakebit, had lost more than blood that night on the mountain.

I was riding next to a different boy than the one I had taken up to that cabin.

"Does that tattoo still hurt?"

"It feels like I got scraped really bad."

"I don't think I could ever do that. Get a tattoo," Gabriel said. "If you play up the hurting, you know, I bet Luz'll kiss you there."

"I'd punch you but I bet you're big enough to take me now."

Gabriel smiled.

TWENTY-EIGHT

W e didn't say anything to each other on the ride out to that oak tree, just patted the horses nervously and avoided each other's eyes, like we were going to a doctor's appointment or something. I felt a little sick, and silently cussed myself for having drunk too much coffee, but I also knew that wasn't really what made my stomach feel so wrung out.

I could tell that Gabe knew what this was about. I could tell that he was sure I would let it be said aloud when the time was right; that it would be something we would talk about on one of those nights while we watched the fire we contained behind stones.

Maybe, I thought.

I saw the cross on the hill. The grass was brown and bent over, wet and heavy with a thick morning fog that glowed gray-white evenly all around, making the universe end fifty feet away. The blackish-green silhouette of the mushroom-shaped oak stood alone like a hunchbacked giant trying to hide something precious beneath its cloak.

And in this spot here, between the cross and the tree, I felt something I didn't like.

"What are you thinking about?" Gabe asked.

Nothing, I was going to say; but I couldn't.

"I wished we were home, Gabey."

I couldn't look at him.

"Sorry. You shouldn't've come."

I tried to breathe. "Neither should you."

And then I thought, how strange it was that Gabriel seemed so emotionless and plain, while I was so horrified and angry and ready to bawl like a baby about being there. I felt like I did when I saw Tommy Buller disappearing on that dark ride down from the mountain. And I remembered watching my mother lying in the bed, eyes open and fixed up at the ceiling, just breathing and nothing else. Just breathing and nothing else.

I brushed my hair back from my eyes. It was wet with the heavy cold fog. I rubbed at the scar, trying to wake myself up somehow; and I caught myself wondering, Where's my hat?

I realized I had been sitting still there. Gabriel had taken Dusty down the slope of that hill toward my right, toward the cover of the tree, fading slightly as the gray fog dimmed the light and color between us.

"C'mon, Reno."

Gabriel was down from his horse, just standing there under that big tree, watching me; or looking past me up to the top of that little hill. I left Reno there and waded through the wet brown grass.

346

The toe of Gabriel's boot just touched that thick coil of rope, one end trailing off through the decaying scatterings from the oak just like that big snake I chased the day Tommy got bit. Looped over the top was a pretty neatly tied noose, its open mouth pulled wide like it was ready to receive an offering. Gabe was looking right at me as I stared down at that monstrous rope.

"I told you," he said.

"I believed you."

I didn't want to touch it. I bent down, my hair dripped water as I did, and scooped the rope up, dragging that loose end toward me from beyond where Gabriel was standing. It felt cold and reptilian, moist, like shaking the minister's hand at my mother's funeral. I felt sick and dizzy, and my hands didn't seem to work right as I fumbled with untying that noose. I couldn't take it home looking like that; but the end stayed twisted and corkscrewed in the damp memory of what it was supposed to do, and I tramped back out across that soggy field and tossed it over Reno's saddle.

Gabe just leaned back against that calloused trunk and watched me as I left and returned. I knew what he was thinking, that he was really going to do it, but I didn't want to say it; still don't want to say it even now.

I felt a tear coming out of my right eye, but I just looked down at Gabriel's boots, thinking dumbly that maybe it was too dark, and, anyway, my face was wet already so maybe he wouldn't see; and I was so mad I just wanted to howl up into those branches and shake that tree, but I did nothing.

I sat down in that spot where the rope had been and stared off at Reno, at that cross, digging my hands numbly and unconsciously into the leaves and dirt, waiting for him to say something that would make it okay, so we could leave, so maybe the day would get on and the fog would burn away and it would get warm.

"You want to know why I didn't do it?"

I stared out at the hill. This must have been the same spot where he had sat.

"'Cause I'm afraid I'll go to hell. That's why."

"Gabe."

"Stupid, huh?"

I put my face down into my hands and closed my eyes, pushing my wet hair back between my fingers. I didn't want him to see me crying.

"You want to wear my hat?"

"No."

I wiped my face and stood up, turning away from that hill. I looked at him then; he was calm and relaxed against that tree.

"Here, Gabey," I said. "You keep this in your pocket. That way, if I tag along, I know you'll be ready to stick up for me, too."

And I pressed a little stone into his hand.

He turned it over and looked at it.

"That's not funny, Troy."

"I know it's not."

"Well, I'll keep it then." And he put the rock into his pocket.

"I bet it's gonna snow tonight," I said, looking away.

Gabriel stooped down and picked up a striped feather tangled in the weeds.

"A hawk," he said. "Messenger medicine. You said it. Remember?"

I did. "Yeah. It means somebody's trying to tell you something, so you need to listen."

"I heard it."

"Well, I don't know about the other, though, 'cause some ghosts just never go away. And they never die, either. Some of 'em."

Gabe wedged the feather's quill into a fissure in the bark of the tree.

"And, Gabey? Your dad was wrong about me always having to come around to protect you. Just 'cause he can't see why we're friends like we are."

"You wanna get on our horses, Troy?"

"We could just walk 'em back on their leads."

"I'd like that."

And so, wet up to our knees, we walked out from that tree and across that damp gray field, lazily leading our horses behind us, probably leaving them to wonder why we were so crazy we would be walking, and them all saddled up and ready to go.

And Gabriel Benavidez never said anything else about that rope we burned in the fire pit that evening, either, but it smoked and stunk something awful.

TWENTY-NINE

I got a new hat when I turned seventeen; another black one, and it came straight the way I liked it, but stiff and hard to get used to until I'd worked a couple good sweats into it. I still wouldn't wear boots, though, and didn't like to wear belts, either, but I know I had grown, because I'd eaten more regularly, and was stronger because I'd been working so hard in all my free time at what everyone just naturally started calling "Troy's place."

I thought I'd stop dreaming after a year had passed, but I never did, the dreams just evolved into ones less troubling; and I came to the point where I almost wished those ghosts would just go on and leave me alone, no longer to feel that frustration at their vanishing that always came with my waking.

Maybe I want to disappear.

Spring ended as quickly as it came in that dry year when so little rain and snow fell; the lake was lower, the rivers slower and narrower. It was already sweltering in May and I was out driving the old truck I had bought, loaded down with treated four-by-fours to replace the barbed-wire fence posts that had burned in the fire of the past summer, or rotted down over the years.

I don't really know why I felt the need to fix that fence, maybe it was just a way to assure myself of what was mine; and maybe it was a way to keep things out.

I had all but moved away from my father's house now that it was warm; I slept most of my nights at the steel house or outside by the fire pit where Gabey and I had been spending more nights than we had in any year since we'd built it.

The things we'd talked about around the fire in the past had vanished behind the heavy cast of the things we talked about now.

Gabriel still missed church occasionally, and still paid the price for it, too. Almost sixteen now, he had grown into quite the opposite of that skittish, backwards-glancing boy I had grown up with. The events of the previous summer continued to haunt him, but he spoke of this haunting freely when we'd talk at the fire pit; and I still worried sometimes about his getting over it. We knew that no one, save for the few of us, would ever know what happened and how those boys died up there.

Both those times I went up in the mountains I left something behind; and that morning when we walked back in the fog after fetching Gabriel's rope from under that tree he asked me, *Troy, do you want to go back up there some time?* and I guess I thought about it without saying anything for at least ten minutes as we waded through that wet dead winter grass, and then finally said, *Only if you do, Gabey, only if you do.*

Evenings, at times, I'd ride Reno out and talk to him, and we'd quietly watch the horses that roamed the land Rose left for me. I'd see Tom's stallion there, and he'd look at me like he was grinning and saying, *Are you going to try to catch me again, boy?* But I never tried. Watching that horse running free was like getting a chance to see Tom Buller one more time, to feel his wildness, to know, somehow, everything was going to be healed.

+ + +

I didn't press my father about keeping his promise to ride with me that summer up the mountain to the old cabin where Gabriel Benavidez, Tom Buller, and I had carved our initials in the wall; and he never brought it up, either. The truth is that I just kind of hoped he forgot about it, like fathers do sometimes just to make things easier. And so my father and I became friends that year I turned seventeen, and I understood then that the things unspoken between men are sometimes more binding than the loudest promises sworn before witnesses.

The mare I'd named Ghost Medicine was pregnant, anyway, and I had intended him to ride her, but she would be foaling by September and wouldn't take a rider. I promised the foal to Gabriel, and he was happy about that, but made me swear I'd let him name it this time. I said that he couldn't name it after me, either, and Gabriel just smiled and said, *Oh shoot*, because he wanted to name it Lucky.

But I felt those mountains pulling at me, always. The pond, the wreck on the mountain, those huge stone fingers, the river;

waiting, wanting to tug me under into a keeper hole I might never get out of again.

+ + +

The line of fencing I was working on was out on the far south boundary of Rose's land, atop low rolling foothills, well past where the easement road cut out through Benavidez ranch for the highway. I was wearing a thin ribbed undershirt, soaked through with sweat and smeared with dirt and rust from the barbed wire, pumping a post hole digger into the ground to sink another four-by-four, when I saw Luz Benavidez riding up the hill on her paint. School was nearly finished for the year; next year would be our last. I struggled with the decision about what to do next; I had already begun making money from those horses, and I found myself more and more comfortable in naming myself a horseman, and less at ease in imagining myself away at university. I couldn't imagine leaving here, leaving her.

Isn't this about the most beautiful place in the world, Troy?

I wouldn't pick anywhere else over it.

And seeing her ride up that sunlit hill, looking toward me, where I was leaning on that two-handled shovel, her hair spilling loose on her shoulders as her horse trotted and bounced, I couldn't help but break my straight mouth into a smile. I raised a hand up so she'd see me there in the shade of those old oaks.

She said she brought a picnic for me, and that Gabey had

pointed out to her the direction in which I'd be stringing that fence. I was already tired and hungry, anyway, and so I was happy for the break, happier still to have her there with me. She spread a blanket out on the ryegrass in the shade and poured two cups of iced tea from a cooler jug.

"I can see that tattoo through your shirt," she said. "Gabey told me you did that."

Gabe was the only one who had seen it. Even my father didn't know about it yet. I was embarrassed; I pulled my shirt away from my skin so the sweat wouldn't show it through.

I drank my glass of tea. She poured me another. We sat on the blanket and she unfolded a pack of sandwiches and strawberries.

"Can I see it?" she asked.

I took my sweaty hat off and put it down on the grass. I pulled my hair back over my head with my palm and lifted the wet shirt up and took it off, laying it down in a ball by my hat. I lay flat on my back and put my arms up in the grass so my ribs stuck out and the horse stretched. Luz leaned close, examining the details of the tattoo.

"Tommy drew it," I said.

She was so close I could feel her breath cooling the sweat on my body. Then she touched the tattoo and swirled her fingers along its outline. I felt her lips and tongue on my ribs there, and her hand stroking past my belly, touching the waist of my pants, following the path of my leg. She sat up and untied my shoes and pulled them off my feet, then my socks, rubbing my feet with both her hands. She held her face next to mine, her breath, warm, smelling like tea and strawberries.

"Rider number seven, your heart is beating so hard," she said.

"I know."

But I could hardly get the words past the thickness in my throat. Nervously, shakily, I unbuttoned her blouse, and pulled her to me.

Luz always drew me back. She brought me down from the mountain that time I tried to escape, and she kept my head and heart held in a safe place where all my ghosts, disarmed, fell silent.

✦   ✦   ✦

And I never worried about her father again because I knew there was nothing in this world that would ever pull me away from her.

✦   ✦   ✦

I told Gabriel that ghost medicine was everything we could ever want; that it was more powerful than we knew, more than we could reckon with. And in the end, I guess it did make us disappear. But it wasn't like a cheap illusion in a magic show, because we didn't realize that it took us in pieces, not all at once; and others could see those bits vanish away and I, we, could only feel them in ourselves, thinking all the time, *This is what I want, this is what I want,* until those lost pieces revisit us in dreams and make us thrash and grab for them only to swish our sweaty, empty hands in the air.

But it never made the other ghosts leave us alone, at least not mine. Not Gabriel's.

✦   ✦   ✦

There are things outside of my life that push in. Some of them are second chances. I know that now. Outside the window in

355

the dark, the madness on the other side, pressing toward me. And me, seeing only the signs, the foggy respirations against the glass, but not the faces.

I always wished I could be Tommy Buller; to smile and squint those black eyes and walk all loose and comfortable like him, and never be bothered by the ugliest things. Of the three of us, he held onto himself the best, because he was stronger than the ghost medicine. But he never needed it anyway because he could drive his own ghosts away anytime he'd just squint and smile or shrug and spit. That was what I could feel, hanging on to his clothes like the smell of a horse on a hot day; that day he'd dressed me up in those overalls and boots of his. And I just wanted to feel like that forever, but I forgot about it, too, soon enough. How it felt.

But then I realized, too, how it was just like Mr. Benavidez said; and that when the end of the day comes, it was me, driven, helpless, counting up all the things we had lost while Tommy Buller could smile that coyote smile and embrace all the things he, we, held on to. *I want to be like that more than anything and just let those things vanish away. This is what I want.*

Giving myself to Luz, our giving, took the biggest part away. Gave the most away. *This is what I want.* I said that to myself, I know she did, too. *This is what I want.* Gabriel and Tom saw it, too.

         ✦   ✦   ✦

Angels sleep all around us, but up there on that mountain, that was their graveyard. It was marked by that fallen plane, a cemetery cross that says, *This is where you come,* sitting in the shadow of a stone hand that keeps coming back to me in my dreams, that I see every day, looking over my shoulder like I remember seeing Gabe look back, hearing thunder; those gray fingers pointing upward, saying, *This is where you go, this is where you go.*

Three boys rode up there.

Not one of them came back.

Maybe all boys die like that.

◆   ◆   ◆

Sometimes I see myself lying in the dirt, on my back on a warm, starry night, with my feet up on those rocks that contain a swirling and noisy fire, listening, laughing, seeing the sparks spinning above me into the blackness like dying stars, disappearing, becoming something else.

I know you will believe that such a place, and such people, and such events could not be in this world, and that's okay with me because I don't need anyone to come looking for anything around here. There's too much stuff that I haven't found yet.

But I told the truth here.

I told them all I would.